The EAGLE and the STAR

The EAGLE and the STAR

Valorie Quesenberry

Copyright © 2024 by Valorie Quesenberry
ISBN: 978-1-948362-85-6
Published by Whispering Pines Publishers

All rights reserved. No portion of this book may be reproduced, stored in a retrieval system, or transmitted in any form or by any means electronic, mechanical, photocopy, recording, scanning, or other except for brief quotations in critical reviews or articles, without the prior written permission of the author.

Except where noted otherwise, Scripture quotations are from The Holy Bible, King James Version, public domain.

The New Testament in Modern English by J. B. Phillips copyright © 1960, 1972 J. B. Phillips. Administered by The Archbishops' Council of the Church of England. Used by Permission.

Printed by Country Pines Printing Shoals, Indiana 47581
www.countrypinesprinting.com

Cover design by Kevin Miles Moser
Author photograph taken by Sarah Wolf Fry

Cover images:
Woman in white dress: iStock.com/Klubovy
Officer inset: iStock.com/ximacx
Burning Building: iStock.com/Marseas
Texture: iStock.com/FREDERICA ABAN
Waffen-SS Soldiers: Wikimedia Commons (Public Domain according to Narodowe Archiwum Cyfrowe), https://creativecommons.org/licenses/by-sa/4.0/

Editorial Note: This is a work of fiction that contains historical reconstruction. The appearances of certain historical figures are included as part of the work, and effort has been made to portray them accurately in accordance with known facts concerning their person and contribution to history. All other characters are products of the author's imagination, and any resemblance to actual persons, living or dead, is purely coincidental. Actual historical events, establishments, organizations, and locales are used fictitiously in a narrative drawn from the author's imagination.

For my father
who passed on to me
the love of heritage, history, and a good story,
and the knowledge that the best tale is yet to come.

ACKNOWLEDGMENTS

A work of fiction doesn't come into being on its own. I've been supported and encouraged in wonderful ways.

As always, I owe much to my family who listened to me, supported me, prayed for me, and even researched with me. You have humored me, put up with me, and believed in me. Duane, Ashley, Autumn, Caleb, Stewart, Kaley, and little Elsie – you are my comfort and joy in life . . . I want us to live out the best Story of all, for now and eternity.

I cannot repay my parents who have nurtured my love of reading and books for as long as I can remember. They were the first ones to tell me about The Living Word and how He changes our personal stories. I am blessed by their unending love and unflagging encouragement.

I am warmed to remember my childhood days filled with books and libraries and dramatized stories and those who shared these things with me. Thank you to my brothers, Jim and Danny, and to my cousin, Joy, for being fellow word adventurers.

I am indebted to Janet Albertson for proofreading and copyediting. She has been a friend indeed in many ways.

I am thankful for Kevin Moser's excellent artistic eye and love of history in the creation of the book cover.

I am grateful for the team at Country Pines Printing. You are more than printers and publishers; you are my friends.

I am glad for many who have encouraged this story along its journey. You know who you are. You made a difference.

I am blessed to be the recipient of the redeeming love of my Savior. Because of the truth I read in His Word, I dare to believe that any life can be salvaged and made beautiful. None of us is past the point of grace. None of us is refused forgiveness when we ask.

Prologue

July, 1943
The Kursk Salient, near Prokhorvka, Russia

> *A victory at Kursk would shine like a beacon to the world!*
> Adolf Hitler to his generals

SS Hauptsturmfuhrer Eryk Steiner felt the concussion of the blast as the *Panzer* to his right exploded. He blinked and refocused his eyes, straining to see through the smoke. Had that been Gessen on his flank? If so, another German wife had just become a widow.

"Sir, do we keep to the present course?"

The words from his driver were terse, the transmission crackly with static from battlefield sounds. He could not see the man from his position, but he knew the red-head in the bowels of the hull had steady hands on the wheel, fully engaged in his task. Of all his crew, Hummel possessed the skill to keep their vehicle moving forward while facing enemy fire from all directions. Eryk would trust him anywhere.

Eryk raised his head to the horizontal slits in his cupola and scanned his field of vision. "Veer to the right, Hummel, and take a course ten degrees south of our present position."

"Yes, sir."

"Krugel, keep the gun at the ready."

"At the ready, sir." Willie Krugel, the gunner, with his head pressed against his sighting instrument, was tensing his jaw muscle, his hands resting on the controls.

Eryk flexed his shoulders and shifted his feet, looking from one vision slit to the next. His orders were to aid in penetrating the Red Army's first defensive belt. His unit, the 2nd *SS Panzergrenadier Division Das Reich*, was one of three involved in an attack across a seven and a half mile front. To the right was the *Tottenkopf* division and to his left was the division *Leibstandarte Adolf Hitler*.

Das Reich, the elite *SS* armored division of which he was part, was the middle power, mowing down any resistance, man or machine that stood in the way as they advanced toward the village of Prokhorova. Its significance was its position as a railway station on a main rail line connecting to Moscow. Eryk hoped they could take it swiftly. The interminable fighting in these Russian wastes was wearing on his men. But what fighting man was not exhausted by the landscape? While many were by now hardened and stalwart fighters, the empty expanse of this muddy land was a psychological foe.

At least, it was summer. Seasons did matter in war, *especially* in this war. The Russian winter cared not if a man were young or old, seasoned or fresh; it killed everyone in the same way. Eryk had listened to many veterans of the Stalingrad campaign tell stories of horrific fighting and dying. He had seen the pinned-up pant legs and scarred faces. He had watched their eyes glaze as they spoke of frosty eyelashes and numb feet and men freezing where they'd fallen in a matter of minutes. Those men were heroes, no doubt, and they proudly wore the medals to prove it, but they were the lucky ones. Many did not return to tell the tale.

Nazi Germany preferred to fight battles quickly, with fast and overwhelming action. She had coined a term for her new mode of conquering – *Blitzkreig*, the lightning war. Only unfortunately, the lightning wasn't striking hard and fast enough on the Eastern front. Yet, the High Command was betting a lot on this action, *Operation*

Citadel, as they had named it. If it proved successful, they would gain significant ground toward a victory over the Bolsheviks.

It was a few hours past dawn and the operation was already well in hand. Eryk had been awake since 3:00 a.m., preparing himself for the day. He had a ritual for days of battle. He preferred to be alone in the dark of the morning, with his thoughts and a cup of Ersatz Kaffee, the only thing available with the current rationing. He'd walk around his vehicle, running his hand over the muzzle of her guns and then stand for a moment by her side, facing outward, imagining what they would encounter together in the coming day. But he would not enter the turret and take his seat until the time for actual departure. He had few fears and gave little credence to superstition, but the commander's seat was for battle, and he would not give himself the pleasure of an adrenalin rush until the time came to use it.

Even now, slogging through the muddy ruts of this Russian wasteland, Eryk could sense the agitation just below the surface of his control. He was most calm when sighting targets and issuing orders, leading his men and engaging the enemy. One of his instructors had remarked that he was a man designated by fate for the battlefield. Oddly enough, he didn't feel fierce enough for that kind of praise though it had pleased him to hear it. Battles were moments that called for responsibility and duty; the glory was not in the blood, but in the victory.

Craning his head to the right, he saw a glimpse of gray metal. He whipped around to the last viewing slit on that side of his cupola and saw an enemy tank advancing on his position.

"Hausser!"

The loader jerked his head to the vision slit on his side of the turret which gave him a better view than the one Eryk had for that side. Hausser's fingers moved so quickly that Eryk heard the impact of the machine gun fire just as he realized the Russian tank was on their immediate right flank. They were on the defensive now. The 7.92 mm gun Hausser was operating wouldn't keep the enemy vehicle at bay, but the advantage of the heavy armor of their *Tiger I Panzerkampfwagen* would give them precious minutes to reposition and fire.

"Krugel, release the turret latch and prepare to sight the target at right!" Eryk spoke in clipped tones to the gunner seated just below him who depressed the plunger to allow the turret to traverse.

Eryk gripped the hand-wheel on his left and turned it in short, rapid motions, powering the turret into firing position. Krugel's right hand was expertly turning the elevating hand-wheel of the main gun, closing in on the Russian *T-34* in his sights, his left foot rocking the footplate to activate the hydraulic system. The *Tiger* purred as she raised her 88 mm gun, dooming the enemy crew even at this distance.

"Target sighted, sir." Krugel's hand rested on the firing bar.

"Fire!"

The *Tiger's* massive gun belched and recoiled as it spewed forth the deathblow. The sheet metal guard beside Eryk's commander's seat grew warm as it absorbed the magnificent power of the gun.

The *T-34* exploded, the turret shearing off and the hull engulfing in flames. Watching the action, Eryk saw a headless body roll off to one side, perhaps the hapless enemy commander, though without seeing the cap or insignia, it was hard to tell. He pumped his fist into the air as high as possible, partially for Hausser's benefit, since the loader wore no headset and would appreciate visual confirmation of the kill. The kid didn't say a word, but the corners of his mouth turned upward. Krugel turned to scratch another mark on his tally on the turret's left wall.

Eryk spoke through his mic. "Great work, men! Hausser, reload; high explosive round."

Since they had blasted through the enemy's armor with the first round, it would be best to use ammunition designed for softer-skinned targets should they need further use of the main gun.

The youth's biceps bulged as he swiveled to lift one of the 23 pound projectiles from the rack below him and to the right. Eryk wouldn't have wanted to be on the wrong side of a fight with Hausser. His papers showed he had worked in his father's blacksmith shop before the war, and he had the bulk to prove it. Hausser slammed shut the door of the breech, his movements fluid and practiced.

"Driver, advance on present course." Eryk had to keep his focus on the ensuing battle. They were far from done with this conflict.

The *Tiger* jerked and began to roll forward, gaining momentum on the open ground. Eryk drummed his fingers on the metal wall of the turret, the sound not even audible above the *Tiger's* mechanical noise. Their division was making progress, but there was much ground to be covered to reach the objective.

Suddenly he was thrown forward against cold metal as the vehicle pitched into a trench. The Russians had dug hundreds of those miserable ditches. He reached up to set his cap right. It was time to get a better view of what lay ahead.

"Opening." he spoke into his intercom as he slowly did a 360 survey, observing the landscape through every vision slit before releasing the hatch. Then he squatted on the lower seat and slowly raised the cupola lid, inching his head out into the open.

A hasty commander is a dead commander. "Sepp" Dietrich's words always rang in his ears when he "opened up."

He climbed up to put his feet on the upper seat position so he could stand in the opening with his head and shoulders out of the hatch. He glanced around quickly, assessing their situation.

He and his men were in a group of *Tiger I* tanks cutting across rough terrain toward the Russian frontline. Far off to his left, he saw several *panzers* in combat and to his right, a few fellow *Tiger* tanks joined the march. Ahead lay miles of Russian steppes, a muddy morass bulging with water from the week's rain. He was grateful that he saw no river in their path at present. The time required to prepare for fording was not only an inconvenience, but risky in enemy territory. The *Tiger* tanks were so ponderous that they could not easily cross deep water.

Eryk spoke into his intercom mic. "Full speed, straight ahead."

He felt the rush of wind as Hummel pushed the accelerator to its top speed. The countryside began to move by more swiftly. Eryk took a deep breath, inhaling the scent of battle along with the smell of farmland. He rested his hands on the sides of the cupola and leaned back against the metal frame. He preferred to be out here, leading in the open, despite the risk.

Make sure your risks are the right ones, Eryk. The words floated into his consciousness, long-forgotten words. It was uncanny how every now and then some remnant of his past collided with the present. He wondered where she was now, his childhood governess, and what his commanding officer would think of her warning. Risk was part of being *SS*; an officer was called to risk, everyday, in many ways. He hadn't questioned a risky decision in years, certainly not since earning his honor ring. He glanced at it now, felt again the stirring in his soul as he remembered the day it had been presented to him. There was no room for questions in the *Reich*; only action.

As another tank fell into rank beside him, he raised his hand in friendly salute to Zetterson, a fellow *Tiger* commander as well as a comrade from days in officers' training. In spite of the melancholy drizzle of the day, many of the commanders were in good spirits. The advance was going well and so far there had been no mechanical failures in his particular unit, a very good day indeed for a company of *Tigers*.

"Think the rain will hold off?" Zetterson shouted above the clink of the tank tracks.

"No, I doubt it will."

"You're too realistic, you know that, Steiner?"

"Ah, one of the traits of a good officer, my friend, is anticipating future complications." Eryk smiled.

"Yes, but don't forget the spirit of optimism that builds morale in the men."

"I'll have a talk with my crew straight away, for your sake."

Zetterson reached for his field glasses and scanned the horizon. "Looks like an unusual number of ditches just ahead."

Eryk looked through his own binoculars. "Yes, our welcome mat from the local citizens." He grinned. "Shall I lead or will you?"

Zetterson waved his hand. "Onward, my realistic friend."

Eryk spoke to his crew again, warning them of the potential hazard as they rumbled nearer the anti tank trenches. Hummel would know what to do, but the driving would be challenging.

Eryk's *Tiger*, turret number 368, moved into the lead position, slowing a bit as they approached the maze of ditches. They made slow progress from then on. The Soviets had certainly fouled up the terrain. It was almost as if they were aware of the Achilles heel of the mighty *Tiger*. The mud was deep, pulling at the tank's interlocking wheel system and oozing into every corner of tracking. It didn't help matters that the rain changed from drizzle to downpour, adding inches of water to the goo.

In the commander's seat once again, Eryk chafed about the delay, but it couldn't be helped. Hummel inched the *Tiger* forward, almost coaxing her as she lurched along.

His headset crackled. "Sir, the progress is slow all along the front. No one has penetrated the enemy lines more than a couple miles." The radioman, Eben, had to speak very loudly since the noise of the *Tiger* engine droned all around them. Eryk leaned back against his seat rest and resigned himself to a long trek; at least they were moving.

The sun was straight overhead when the men in the vehicle heard the sound that filled the nightmares of every tank crew – a whirring, whining sound that meant the wheels were sliding and going nowhere, the tracks gummed up in the mud. Eryk could hear Hummel cursing as he shifted to neutral, reversed, then tried forward motion again, but to no avail. The heavy Russian gumbo held them fast.

"Hummel, let her sit where she is, and we'll dig her out. All crew, open and out."

Eryk raised his commander's hatch and motioned the tank behind him around their stalled position. Zetterson's vehicle crawled by cautiously, stopping a few yards past them to let others progress on the route. According to their combat pattern, he would stay close by as long as possible to ensure they were not left stranded.

Hatches opened as Eryk's crew exited to begin to dig out their vehicle. Eryk grimaced as he watched their boots sink into knee-high mud. The interior would be caked with it when they went back inside, but there were more important things to think about. Besides, anyone who had been on the Eastern front for a few weeks soon grew to accept the sludge and grime. Russians grew mud better than anything else.

While his crew worked to free the *Tiger*, Eryk stood guard with his field glasses, looking one way while Zetterson scanned the opposite direction. He was thankful for this pocket of relative calm; they must still be a considerable distance from the frontlines. That was actually not a comfort in the purest respect, though. The farther to the battle line, the longer the enemy had to fortify his position.

It took almost an hour for the men to clean the tracks and clear the wheels, but finally, they were ready to close up and roll. The men wiped perspiration and precipitation from their faces and banged their boots against the tracking to loosen the Russian grime, then climbed up to their respective hatches and entered – Hummel and Ebengrosser in the hull front, and Hausser and Krugel in the turret. Eryk dropped into his own cupola hatch and motioned to Zetterson to move out.

The other vehicle roared to life and began to move forward. Eryk understood the other commander's impatience. He put on his headset and took his upright position in the cupola, head and shoulders out, as the *Tiger* began to move once more. It was difficult to tell the time of day by the sky since the weather was wet with gray clouds, but his wristwatch showed late afternoon, the day dwindling toward dusk, a very bad time indeed to be separated from the company.

They came to a hill and began to move upward, the ponderous machine slowly lurching forward as its tracks dug into the mud. Eryk decided it was time for a look around, outside of the *Tiger*.

"Halt, *jetzt!*"

The machine stopped, a bit reluctantly it seemed to Eryk; Hummel was always eager to advance. Grabbing his field glasses, Eryk hoisted himself up once again through the turret and climbed over the side. Waving his hand at Zetterson, he walked up the side of the nearest hill, dropping down behind a mound of earth with a couple scraggly bushes sprouting up beside it. He surveyed the landscape, east to west, looking for signs of enemy entrenchment. The Russians were partial to land mines and nests of anti-tank guns. He scanned the scene again, trying to determine the best way to proceed. He'd need to have Ebengrosser contact the division to determine exactly how far they needed to go to rejoin the unit. Satisfied that they could proceed, Eryk was rising from his crouched position when he heard a drone of engines overhead. Pulling his glasses back to his eyes, he stared in horror as a formation of Soviet *Il-2* planes came out of nowhere and screamed downward.

Eryk jumped up, waving his arms, hoping to catch his driver's attention. Though it would be close, they might be able to fire the main gun in time to save their lives. He wanted to run; to warn them, but his training kept him back. He dropped back down to the ground. He saw the turret of his tank begin to turn and knew that Krugel was trying his best to sight the invaders. But at such close range, out in the open, the two *Tigers* were doomed. The gunner didn't even have time to fire; the *Il-2*'s were already sending a barrage into the thick skin of the tanks.

Eryk watched in disbelief as his tank exploded in a mighty fireball, ripping apart the metal sheeting and sending the heavy bolts spewing into the air. Instinctively, he covered his head with his arms as metal flew in all directions. The stone behind which he crouched protected him from the objects, but he felt the heat as the men he'd respected and trained were incinerated. The fuel in the *Tiger* ignited, sending black and nauseatingly pungent smoke toward the sky. Flames of red and orange sucked in the wild grasses and raged onward for more. The proud *Tigers* were billowing blobs of smoke, and the Russian planes became specks in the sky as they gained altitude and continued on their hunt.

Eryk rose, using the rock beside him for leverage as he got to his feet. The fire roared in his ears as he walked forward. His mind refused to accept what he was seeing. The machine that he'd helped assemble was obliterated; his crew was gone. He'd led Zetterson, his friend and colleague, to his death as well.

He strained his ears to catch any human sound, any call for help. But, of course, there was none. The men would have been killed instantly, and any remains would now be charred beyond recognition. As he approached the burning *Tigers*, he forgot to keep his eyes open for debris and suddenly stumbled. Looking down, Eryk saw a black sleeve lying on the ground with a palm attached at the end, the firing bar clutched in fingers which were swollen and dark. He turned as vomit filled his mouth. Dropping to his knees, he retched, holding his stomach. When the bout of sickness passed, he sat back and ran his fingers through his hair.

Russians. Curse of the earth. May God have mercy on any one of them who got in his way. Eryk swung his fist at the ground. Why had they chosen that moment to attack? He'd only been gone a few minutes.

A lifetime is barely a minute to Him. Unbidden, her words were there, even in this surreal moment. Wearily, he stood. He had to start walking, couldn't sit here between two steaming heaps of rubble. The ground was uneven, torn up even more by the strafing of the Russian planes. He felt unsteady as he moved forward. Maybe that was the reason he wasn't watching the ground too closely. Maybe it was his punishment. Maybe it was just a day of terrible luck. But when the mortar exploded at his feet, he noticed the earth rising up to meet him as his ears absorbed a terrific blast and his eyes closed against the heat and flash of fire. Then there was only blackness.

24 years earlier...

Winter 1919
Berlin, Germany

> *If I were a German, I think I should never sign it.*
> Woodrow Wilson, President, United States, on
> the Treaty of Versailles (1919)

The subzero temperature kept back the smell of rotting flesh.

Snowflakes drifted over the line of people outside the church. Shivering together in bedraggled little groups, they were a pitiful sight. A few yards away, children played with horse bones; the meat had been picked clean long ago, and the skeleton was one of many littering the streets of Berlin.

No one could possibly imagine that this was proud Germania - land of greatness, home of the cultured and courageous Prussian people. Her citizens were now reduced to beggars, her soldiers ragged caricatures of previous glory. This was the legacy of the Great War.

Stomping his feet to keep out the December chill, a man in the remnants of a military uniform felt a coldness inside that even a warm coat could not have relieved had he been wearing one. He was not. But though his body was cold, his soul was nearly frozen.

His eyes had seen the devastation which caused this miserable queue for food. The trenches and forests of the Argonne had been his home, a home heavy with clouds of mustard gas and swamps of blood. On desperate nights, surrounded by corpses, listening to the sobs of the dying, one thought had gotten him through – his Magda, with rounded cheeks and smiling lips, sitting in the lamplight, waiting for his return. The spirit of her faithful heart had kept his own beating and hoping through the long and futile campaign.

It was only on his weary return that he discovered she was hardly better off than he. Her sunken cheeks and scrawny limbs testified to the bitterness of the Allied blockade. The absence of pine cones and nettles was a stark tribute to the main source of food for those who fought for their lives at home. The strong face he presented to his battalion had crumbled; he'd cried in the fragile arms of his wife.

Now, he stood in a soup line, defeated like his country. If it weren't for the coming little one and Magda's health, he'd sooner starve. The Germany he knew was not filled with waifs and tramps, but with strong, hale citizens who worked the land and passed on their heritage, but that Germany was cold and lifeless, a casualty of a war so horrific that his dreams were still invaded by its icy fingers. And now, in the days following Christmastide, where the Fatherland used to shine with light and celebration, there was a pall of death and humiliation.

Condemned for the *Kaiser's* alliances, blamed for the horrors of war, and assigned to pay staggering damages back to the Allies, Germany was on a death march. The rattle of its struggle tapped in Helmut's ears as he shuffled behind the old man in front of him. The Treaty signed by the German delegation had sealed the fate of their future. He and his neighbors, his loved ones and friends, everyone who claimed the Prussian homeland were to be witnesses to the execution. The injustice of it turned his stomach. If there was guilt to be found, it was not among these wretched souls who stood hollow-eyed, eager for watery soup. No, the real blame rested elsewhere with others who controlled the wealth and caused political unrest. Someday, the truth would be known.

When it was his turn, he lifted his pail to receive the ladle of turnip soup. It would keep Magda alive and give her strength to nourish the child within her. And as he pulled the gray scarf tight around his neck and turned toward his home, he made a promise to his unborn child. He would do everything in his power to restore the glory of Germany. There was no price too high.

PART ONE
Berlin to Terezin

1

1929
Berlin, Germany

> *We're fighting for Hitler, for freedom and bread.*
> *May Germans awaken! and Jews soon be — dead!*
> Brown Ballads, Hitler's Hymns of Hate

Eryk pushed his tanks into a straight line on the library rug. The third one was his favorite; it was the one with the hooked cross painted on the side. It was the same cross that his father wore on the armband of his brown uniform.

"What does it mean, Father, this twisted cross?" He had voiced the question at dinner one night.

"It isn't twisted, Eryk, it's reshaped. It stands for good luck and pure people. It means that Germany is a great country, and that all Germans should come together to put the past behind us and to move forward to what is right."

Eryk remembered how his father had touched the cross and then reached out to put his hand on his son's. "It's the symbol of a great future, son. Do you know what a symbol is?"

He hadn't really understood what his father was talking about, but didn't want him to think he was dumb so he nodded anyway.

His father had looked pleased. "Good boy. You will be a good German soldier someday, Eryk."

And now as Eryk arranged his soldiers for battle, he felt proud of his daddy. *Herr* Steiner was an important military man, and he thought Eryk would be a good soldier. It was all Eryk dreamed of doing, wearing a uniform like his father and commanding others, winning battles. It was his favorite theme when he was allowed play time. He would plot strategy, study his military maps, and plan how to be victorious. In fact, he was in the middle of a conference about the battle, with all his play generals standing together, when a solid little black shoe upturned the first tank. He slapped the floor.

"Don't do that, Nadya. Can't you see I'm in a meeting with my generals?"

A pout appeared on little pink lips, hands rested on tiny hips. "But I want to go outside and look for birds' nests and flowers. *Tante* says we may go now that your lessons are done."

He scoffed. "Birds and flowers are pretty, but I'd rather play war."

"I don't like war." The dark eyes looked so very big and sad.

"Why not?"

"It's loud and scary." She tossed her head.

"Not for a brave German."

"How do you know?"

"My father says so, and he is a hero. He even has a medal." Eryk straightened his posture and puffed out his chest a little.

She turned away, and he saw a hand lifted furtively to brush at her eyes. He stood up and walked around to face her.

"Why are you crying? Is it because you do not like my father?"

"No. *Tante* says your father is a good man. It isn't that."

"Well, then what?" He scuffed the toe of his shoe against the polished floor.

"I told you. I don't like war. It makes me sad. So, I'll just go outside and look by myself."

"No, Nadya, stop! Wait a minute. Tell me why. Please?" Eryk didn't know why anyone could be that bothered about war. Battle was adventure and excitement with grand uniforms and lots of guns. That anyone would feel differently had never entered his mind. But then, Nadya was a girl, and that must explain it.

The little girl was silent. Her mouth puckered a little and her eyes started to look watery. And that made him feel bad. A German man was not unkind to women. That was what he had been taught. Though he was only ten, he knew that he must behave properly. He must make her feel better.

Eryk reached out a sweaty palm and put it on her shoulder. "I'm sorry I made you cry. Won't you please tell me why war makes you sad?" He looked into her eyes and thought they seemed soft like the brown teddy bear he used to play with when he was little.

"It is because war made my mommy and daddy go away." She said it with a little catch in her voice.

Eryk was horrified. How could something as splendid as war be the cause of his playmate's loss? Surely, she was mistaken. "Why did they have to go away?"

"I . . . can't tell you."

"Well, then I'll ask my *Hauslehrerin*."

"*Tante* won't tell you either. It's a secret."

"If you tell me, I will get you a treat. I know where cook has put the *strudel*!"

"No, I can't tell you. Maybe someday."

Eryk was curious. He had to find out more. Maybe Father knew the answer. Yes, that's what he'd do; he'd ask Father. For now, he'd give in to Nadya; her funny little ways made him happy, and he didn't mind a few birds and flowers once in a while.

"All right, I will finish my battle later. Which tree shall we look in?"

Dinner that evening

As soon as the meat was carved and Louisa, the serving girl, had left the room, Eryk asked his question.

"Father, do you know why the war made Nadya's mother and father go away?" Stuffing a forkful of tender pork into his mouth, he chewed and waited for his father's answer.

Helmut Steiner was an impressive man, even at dinner, or maybe especially at dinner. The flicker of the candles glittered on the medals on his chest and gave his wheat-colored hair a silvery cast. Even if the family dined alone, the sight of his uniform reminded them all that he was a man of importance, rising with the new power.

The officer paused at his son's words, his goblet halfway back to the table. "What do you mean?" *Herr* Steiner glanced at his wife.

Magda Steiner's face was unreadable, empty of emotion. She was glad to have husband and children around her table, but her personal demons left her little time for celebration, even in happy moments. Her eyes lifted blankly to his in answer. *So?* Eryk had always been a precocious child. Any information he came across brought about a torrent of new questions. It was common enough.

Eryk wiped his mouth with a napkin. "Today, *Hauslehrerin* brought her niece again for playtime. When I asked her why she didn't want to play war, she said it made her sad. And then she said that it was the reason her mother and father went away."

Helmut polished his knife before carving his next bite. "Perhaps her father was a soldier and her mother became ill while he was away. It's possible they both died."

Eryk scrunched his eyebrows together and thought. *Maybe that's it. She lives with my* Hauslehrerin *so she must not have any other family. I don't blame her for being sad.*

"Why didn't you ask her to tell you, Eryk?" His father looked straight at him.

"I did, and she said it was a secret." Eryk pushed his cabbage around on his plate. He was getting full, but he must finish his dinner or there would be no strudel.

"I see." Helmut wiped his hands on the napkin in his lap, pushed his plate slightly away and looked thoughtful. "I'm sure it was nothing important, son. She will tell you sometime."

Reaching out for the serving bell, he looked fondly at the faces of his family – Magda, his son Eryk, little Frederica and baby Annaliese. They were happy, healthy and faring well even in the recent economic setbacks caused by the financial collapse in the United States. The *National Socialist German Workers' Party* was rising, and Germany would one day be whole again. Surely the evil days were over, and he would do everything in his power to keep it that way. His son's question triggered that little place of doubt that sometimes bothered him, but he had become very good at pushing it back down again. The thing to do was look to the future and to the new leader, Adolf Hitler.

He smiled and rang the bell. "Louisa? We are ready for the strudel!"

2

April 1933, Berlin
Berliner Philharmonie Concert Hall

To continue giving concerts would be quite impossible without [the Jews] –
*to remove them would be an operation which would
result in the death of the patient.*
Wilhelm Furtwangler, Conductor, Berlin Philharmonic

The music streamed over her and filled the gigantic hall with a beauty Nadya could almost touch. Nothing quite compared to the wonder of the *Berlin Philharmonic* and seeing *Tante* Zelda in the string section always brought a proud smile to her face, though no one could see it with the house lights down.

Tante, always happy about whatever music was being played, was especially eager tonight. A guest pianist from Prague had the concert hall delirious with joy over a magnificent rendition of one of Chopin's concertos. Berliners were passionate about music, even more so since the Führer was a great aficionado of the symphony. It was said that he could listen for hours to the phonograph, and that he was personal friends with the family of the great Wagner.

Tante Zelda didn't care much for Wagner's music; she preferred the rhythmic rise and fall of the Baroque masters over the brass fanfare that so enraptured Mr. Hitler. "It is the ebb and flow of the strings and horns and woodwinds that gives real music its heart, not the blast of trumpets that sets feet to marching." That is what she believed.

But, secretly, Nadya thought that marching music was exciting. Sitting in the velvet seat with her eyes closed, she remembered the recent parade in honor of Chancellor Hitler's election victory.

There had been columns of officers and infantrymen walking in step, their uniforms crisp, their boots mirror-shiny. A few high-ranking officials rode in the horse-drawn coach with the *Führer* who stood with military stiffness, his eyes shining as though he was proud to be the leader of such a generous people. Though she thought his eyes were beady and mean, she did understand why he liked the marching music. It stirred something in the soul and made one feel part of the rising of the German nation.

Yet, Nadya had been experiencing things in school and on the city streets that made her wonder about what was rising in the hearts of the people she used to call her friends. There had always been "feelings" against the Jews, according to *Tante* Zelda, long before Nadya had been born and stretching back even to the ancient times. Surely, *Tante* admonished, Nadya remembered the stories of the slavery in Egypt and how the people of Israel were made to work for the Pharaoh, building his monuments and perpetuating his dynasty. Throughout history, there had been prejudice and pogroms against the Jews. It was just part of being the chosen people.

Tante Zelda reminded her often that, though she was only half-Jewish, she was still a member of God's people, first through blood and then through choice. Nadya had been raised in a home where Christ was honored as the Messiah. Her father and his sister, Zelda, were converts to the Lutheran church as were their parents before them. This legacy of Christianity had been in their family long before Nadya was born. She had known nothing else. So, the taunts at school were sometimes confusing to her. They were the same ugly words thrown at the rabbis with their prayer locks. Still, their family did recognize Jewish holidays and also observed some of the traditional rituals. But she had always considered herself to be just like her fully Gentile classmates, a Berliner, a German.

Still, as she listened to the soaring of the music below her, she remembered that being Berliners had not saved her parents; her mother's Polish blood had been a curse after all. That was why she and *Tante* Zelda had made their pact. They wouldn't talk about Poland to anyone. Perhaps the officials weren't as good at keeping records as they claimed. It was best to concentrate on all things German.

But, at ten years old, Nadya could figure some things out for herself. The situation was not getting better for people with Jewish ancestry; it was getting worse. Why, only this month, there had been a boycott of Jewish shops. Her friend, Greta, lived above the millinery shop run by her father and mother. They made the most beautiful hats in Berlin, and many stylish ladies came to shop there. Yet, before the boycott was called off after three awful days, Greta had told Nadya how silent and empty the shop was, her father kept restocking shelves and her mother kept dusting and sweeping in the back rooms.

Nadya hadn't been sure why merchants being Jewish contaminated the goods they sold, but that seemed to be the opinion of the new government rising under Chancellor Hitler. He appeared as stiff and coarse as the bristle of a mustache he wore above his lip. Surely, he must be terribly confused to mistake good German craftsmen for criminals. But, she was noticing that some of the students in her school were acting a little differently too. But, it was more because of the way *Fraulein* Metzgar had looked at her than anything else.

Nadya had always done well in school; some even accused her of being "teacher's pet." But yesterday, *Fraulein* Metzgar, who had always encouraged her to write down her thoughts and who had suffered her through long division, gazed at her as though she were scraps on a dinner plate, like garbage to be tossed aside. Nadya wondered if that was what it felt like to be forsaken, as had been their ancient ancestors that *Tante* Zelda talked about.

Tonight, Nadya felt a chill as she watched *Tante* Zelda make her magical music. What would happen when Chancellor Hitler decided that Jews were no longer good enough for the *Berlin Philharmonic*? She had a terrible feeling in the pit of her stomach.

3

May 10, 1933, Berlin
Opernplatz Public Square

> *In the presence of this blood banner which represents our Führer,*
> *I swear to devote all my energies and my strength to the savior of our*
> *country, Adolf Hitler. I am willing and ready to give up*
> *my life for him, so help me God.*
> Jungvolk Oath
> (taken by ten-year-old boys on first entering the Hitler Youth)

Eryk straightened his neckerchief one more time, adjusting the woggle to hold the folds securely as he stood with his unit of *Hitler Jungvolk*. It was a clear spring night and dusk was falling now on the great public square in the heart of Berlin. Eryk could hear the chimes from the tower of St. Hedwig's Cathedral behind him, though they were nearly drowned out by the flurry of activity taking place before his eyes.

An enormous pyre had been constructed in the middle of the square, and University students and uniformed *SA* men were dumping boxes of books onto it. Eryk tried to see some of the titles as the procession continued. There were books of every size and color, and as they were tossed onto the pile, their pages fluttered in the evening breeze. He imagined the rustling of so many pages would have been quite loud had the boots of the soldiers and the shouts of the students not been so noisy.

He was lucky enough to be on the end of the formation and was closer to the action than others in his group. He strained his eyes to make out the words on the books and was leaning slightly forward in the process when suddenly something hard landed on his foot.

It didn't hurt much, coming through his solid marching boots, but he reached down to pick it up anyway. It had fallen from a box carried by a young student who had just passed him. Eryk could see the precarious stack that remained in the box. It was as though the students couldn't wait to carry reasonable loads; they wanted to get rid of those books as soon as possible.

He turned the volume over and noticed English words. *The Story of My Life* by Helen Keller.

Glancing around, he cautiously put one finger into the book and tried to look down to see the page without moving his head too much. Their leader was very particular about posture and formation.

> It is with a kind of fear that I begin to write the history of my life. I have, as it were, a superstitious hesitation in lifting the veil. . .

The book was yanked from his hands. *Herr* Bauer stood in front of him, glowering. "This book is subversive literature, Eryk. It is to be burned, not read."

Eyes straight ahead, face impassive, Eryk stiffened in response. "Yes, sir." He shouldn't have said more, but he did. "I only wanted to see why it should be burned."

His leader looked directly into his eyes. "You are a Hitler Youth. You are being trained to lead Germany into a new era. You must learn to take orders without understanding why. Soldiers do not question; they obey. You know this, *yah*?"

Eryk nodded. "Yes, sir."

"Then you must follow what you have been taught. It is the way to victory for Germany, and that is what is most important." *Herr* Bauer put a hand on his shoulder and held out the book with the other. "Now, to demonstrate your obedience to the *Reich*, you take this book to the pyre."

Eryk saluted, snatched the book and marched forward. Just then, someone put the first torch to the great pile of books. With a whoosh, the fuel-soaked pages caught fire. The flames leaped skyward. Eryk instinctively jerked his head back, although he was still several feet from the fire.

As he continued to walk carefully forward, he could feel the heat rolling out of the inferno. The blaze was gathering force as it gorged on the thousands of pages lying in its bosom. Eryk raised his arm and heaved the little book into the fire. It disappeared into a bluish chasm. Turning smartly, he marched back to his troop, raising one hand to slick back a lock of blond hair that fell below his cap.

The crowd around the gathering was a grand mixture of university students, *SA* men, Hitler Youth groups and Nazi officials who all had some kind of interest in the event that night. Of course, there were also many common citizens of Berlin who had come to watch the action and see what exciting things might happen. Fires always draw crowds. It was something Eryk was just learning and something that he would never forget.

As the flames leaped higher still, the crowd applauded, and there seemed no end to the enthusiasm as the young people and officers continued to approach the fire and hurl books.

Then, the Propaganda Minister, Dr. Joseph Goebbels, walked toward a small podium draped with the swastika. He stood for a moment, observing the action, and then began to speak.

> *My fellow students, German men and women . . . the era of exaggerated Jewish intellectualism is now at an end. The triumph of the German revolution has cleared a path for the German way, and the future German man will not just be a man of books, but also of character, and it is to this end we want to educate you. To have at an early age the courage to peer directly into the pitiless eyes of life; to repudiate the fear of death in order to gain again the respect for death. That is the mission of the young, and therefore you do well at this late hour to entrust to the flames the intellectual garbage of the past. It is a strong, great and symbolic undertaking, an undertaking which shall prove to all the world that the intellectual basis for the November Republic is here overturned, but that from its ruins will arise the lord of a new spirit.*[1]

Eryk listened to the small man and his strident, ringing voice. He was dressed immaculately as always; Eryk could tell that even from a distance. His dark hair was brushed straight back on his head, and his eyes were alive and bright. The message he gave reminded Eryk of so many he had heard since becoming part of the *Hitler Jungvolk*. It was one of which he and his comrades never tired.

It was a chant of hope, a promise of bright tomorrows when young men would conquer their enemies and live strong lives with pretty wives and bouncing children. It was a reminder that, at heart, the German *Volk* were a people of the land, proud caretakers of the mountains and fields, masters of the *Deutschland*. It was a message that gave them purpose, yet it was also a warning against the decadence of western culture, that immoral greed which would violate their souls and crush their Aryan heritage.

As he stood ramrod straight and listened to the Propaganda Minister, Eryk marveled that he should be so fortunate as to be born at a time when these great truths had been discovered. And even more fortunate that he would soon be of age to join the fight for the cause. His birthday was in a few months, and he would be moving into the *Hitler Jugend*, the next step toward manhood and a life devoted to Germany.

Yet, he couldn't help but wonder how the small book he had held for a few short seconds could be so terrible that it would subvert an entire people. Was the author, this Helen Keller, so powerful that her words could demoralize millions of people? What kind of words would have that strength?

Even as he thought about it, he remembered other words. They had been spoken not long ago by his governess, his *Hauslehrerin*, about the black book she always carried in her teaching satchel.

"*These are God's Words, Eryk. They are more powerful than a sword, And they are living.*"

"*Truly alive,* Hauslehrerin?"

"*Yes,* Liebchen. *They are living because they are His truth, and it never dies. It is always the same, for every people, for every time.*"

As Dr. Goebbels finished his speech, the masses began to sing. All around him were strong young voices lifted triumphantly and rows of straight young bodies whose souls were already devoted to the nation who bid them toss books into a fire. Eryk started singing too.

Dr. Goebbels walked down the aisle of people, shaking the hands of those closest to his path. Instinctively, Eryk put out his hand and felt it grasped by the propaganda minister. He looked up into the craggy face of the misshapen little man and felt the heaviness of his gaze. Then he was gone, and Eryk almost shivered in spite of the flames that hissed merrily as they ate thousands of books.

4

June 30, 1934
Berlin, Germany

> *Struggle is the father of all things.*
> *It is not by the principles of humanity that man lives or is*
> *able to preserve himself above the animal world, but solely*
> *by means of the most brutal struggle.*
> Adolf Hitler

Nadya tried to concentrate on the music in front of her. She'd much rather be outside in the beautiful evening with her friend. The summer holiday was going by too quickly and she and Greta had so much yet to do. With the warm sun shining on Berlin streets, with the parks and gardens abloom with colors, there was much for two young girls to enjoy. Matinees at the theater and cones of frozen custard from the sidewalk stand, catching butterflies for next year's nature project and dreaming about a beautiful future – these activities occupied most of their time.

But, *Tante* Zelda required daily practice. She would not indulge her niece's fancy for unrestricted freedoms just because school classes did not keep in the summer. If one would learn to make beautiful music, one must practice the discipline of daily rehearsal.

"I promised your mother that you would play the violin." *Tante* would say in her sweet, but firm voice.

But *Tante* Zelda is an accomplished musician, Nadya thought as she rosined her bow. It was easy for her to forget that scales and etudes could be foreboding for a student whose skills were still emerging. Even as she played, she could hear the difference in her tone and that of her aunt's. *Tante* Zelda's music was magic, a mix of velvety lows and silken highs that intoxicated the listener. Trying to mimic it was excruciating for a student who would rather look at a magazine with her best friend and giggle about boys.

"Nadya? Are you all right?" *Tante's* voice behind her made Nadya jump.

She almost dropped her instrument. "Just struggling with my scales, *Tante*." She sighed. "When will I ever play like you?"

Tante's eyes twinkled. "When you've mastered your scales."

"But, they sound wretched when I play them."

"That's because they are not music to you, only sounds." She picked up her own violin laying nearby in its open case. "Hear, let me explain." Her bow glided across the strings as her fingers hopped from one position to the next. The scale was not a mere exercise after all. In her hands, the scale became a lovely melody, a cadence befitting the great hall where she often played.

Nadya's shoulders slumped as she listened. She would never be that good.

Tante stopped, her right arm still. "*Liebchen*, you will play it even better someday."

"Oh no, *Tante*, I don't think so."

"Well, you leave the thinking to me because I know what I'm talking about. You have music in your blood. It is your heritage. Your grandfather was the finest violinist I have ever known. And your father. . .." She stopped and turned to the side, laying down her instrument. "He would have been concertmaster in the symphony."

"Was he so very good, *Tante*?"

"Good? My child, the moon and stars shined brighter when he played. His music could bring the gruffest of men to tears. Never have I heard a man interpret the masters like he did." *Tante* shook her head sadly. "The world will not hear him again, but it will hear you, his daughter."

"I hope so."

"It will." *Tante* put her hands on Nadya's shoulders. "I have this feeling, and I have prayed for you. I have an impression that God will do great things with you in the future." She kissed her niece on the cheek and walked out, pulling the door gently shut behind her.

Nadya wanted to live up to her aunt's wishes, but she still felt wooden when she played. Though she had taken lessons since she was five, she could not glimpse the fire of soul that *Tante* spoke of so often. But, perhaps that would come in time. For now, the quickest way to get outside and see Greta was to finish up her allotted time. Determined to see it through, she raised her bow again.

Nadya was awakened by screams. In the dark, she sat bolt upright, looking around her room. Nothing was disturbed. The curtains were drawn; books remained on the shelves and her dresser looked undisturbed. The blouse and skirt she had worn to the party last night with Greta still lay where she had tossed them. She grabbed the clock from her nightstand and pulled it close to her eyes, trying to catch the faint glare of the moon through the window. It was 3:00 a.m.

Thinking she must have dreamed the sounds, she rearranged her pillow and pulled up the coverlet to go back to sleep. But then the pounding started. Someone was beating fists on their front door.

She was beginning to be frightened. Under her door, she could see the glow of a light switched on and padded footsteps sounded in the hall. *Tante* was going to the door.

Nadya had to see what was going on. Flinging back her blankets, she grabbed her robe and opened her door. She blinked as her eyes adjusted to the light and then she could see her aunt opening the apartment door just a crack.

"Yes?"

"Zelda, oh, Zelda!"

It was their neighbor, *Frau* Reinhardt. She lived one floor down with her husband, a military officer, and their two teenage children. Nadya had often been sent to their door with a plate of pastries or complimentary tickets for the symphony. The woman had always seemed very composed and practical. The sight of her now was disturbing. Her hair was disheveled and frowzy, flying free from its customary coronet braids. Her dressing gown was buttoned incorrectly and she was barefoot. Her face was contorted in agony.

Tante Zelda threw open the door. "Maria, what is it? Come in."

The woman took a step across the threshold and wobbled, almost collapsing on the floor. *Tante* caught her and hooked her arms under the other woman's. Seeing Nadya staring at them, she ordered, "Nadya, quickly, help me." Together, they half-supported, half-carried the woman to the sofa where she slumped against the cushions, sobbing.

Nadya and her aunt stood together in front of her, not quite sure if they should ask again or not. After a moment, the woman lifted her head. Her voice was croaky. "They've taken my Frantz. He is dead." She let out a howl like an animal.

Tante sank down beside their neighbor and clasped her hand, her face serious. "How do you know this? Are you sure?"

Frau Reinhardt nodded. "They came for him just after midnight."

"Who?"

"The *SS*."

"But your husband is a member of the *Storm Troopers*!"

"But he has disagreed with the opinions of the new Chancellor. He has even spoken to his superior about it."

"And for that he was taken?" *Tante's* voice was a mix of incredulity and sadness.

"For that, he was killed!" *Frau* Reinhardt beat her fists on the sofa cushion. "O God, have mercy, they've killed my husband!"

Tante placed her hands on the woman's arms. "You know this?"

"Yes, one of his men came to tell me. He and others are hiding now, but they saw the *SS* officers take them to the old *schulegebraude* outside the city. Then there were shots, many of them, and they are shooting still, he said."

Tears were running down *Tante's* face. "Oh, Maria, I'm so sorry."

"My Frantz is dead, oh, my Frantz." *Frau* Reinhardt's shoulders shook as she wailed.

Tante reached out to the woman and embraced her. Rocking gently back and forth, she murmured to her as one would a child.

Nadya stood very still. She barely breathed. Surely *Frau* Reinhardt was mistaken. The Reinhardts were fine people; they attended the same Lutheran church as she and *Tante*. They had well-mannered children, and they were kind to many. Officer Reinhardt had once protected Nadya herself from a pair of bullies who threw vegetables at her and called her a vile name. Why should he be killed because he didn't agree with the chancellor? Was that a terrible crime?

Tante began to pray then, asking the great Father in heaven to surround and comfort them, to watch over Germany and to give strength to them all. Suddenly chilled, Nadya inched closer to her aunt and squeezed her eyes shut too. If there was a God like she had been taught, she hoped He would look down on her with protection.

5

September 1936
Nuremberg, Germany

> *I begin with the young. We older ones are used up. We are rotten to the marrow. We are cowardly and sentimental. We are bearing the burden of a humiliating past, and have in our blood the dull recollection of serfdom and servility. But my magnificent youngsters! Are there any finer ones in the world? Look at these young men and boys! What material! With them, I can make a new world. This is the heroic stage of youth.*
> *Out of it will come the creative man, the man-god.*
> Adolf Hitler, *Hitler's Letters and Notes*

As he marched down the streets flanked by medieval style buildings, Eryk snaked a glance at his comrades. There were thousands of them, their feet thudding on the pavement. Along the route were *NSDAP* party banners, crisp and brilliant even in the early hours of this Sunday morning. Ancient statues and courtyards with fountains decorated the city. A profusion of flowers bloomed in window boxes, in city parks and indeed almost anywhere one looked. Fresh green wreaths adorned with Nazi symbols hung on walls that faced the street. Towering above the marchers were church spires, witness to this glorious celebration of Germany's power. Even the pigeons flew out of their nests in the belfries as if they knew the importance of the day. Like every other part of Germany when the Führer visited, Nuremberg had put on its best dress.

Proud mothers and fathers leaned out of windows as the thunderous sound of young feet in rhythm passed by. Some waved; others saluted. Cars stood still to let them pass. Every roadway today was filled with marching young feet.

Eryk felt almost numb with the pride of it all. The rigor of months of training that preceded this moment hardly seemed worth comparing to the exhilaration of being part of such a grand assembly. He let his mind wander back to those first days when he entered the ranks of the *Hitler Jugend*. Like the other newcomers, he had been intimidated by the strict regimen, the shouts of the instructors and above all, the toughness of the bullies. But, like everyone else, he soon learned to navigate in this new military-type world. The secret was to be tougher than fear, tougher than pain, and tougher than the challenge. Daily, the *HJ* leaders drove them to exceed their limits, physically and mentally. Everything undertaken was a duty for *the Führer*. There was no honor in failure or in humiliation. Victorious, unbroken soldiers were the magnificence of Germany.

Without exception, each of Eryk's classmates dreamed of the day when he could enter *SS* training. All of the boys knew that they were being groomed to man the *panzers* and fly the planes and defend the *Fatherland*. The *Führer's* dream was becoming their own. The glory of battle was what they now desired.

Parading now in perfect step with *HJ* fellows from all over Germany, many of whom he had never seen before, Eryk could sense the glory his leaders had extolled in their lectures. It was so real he felt as if he might reach out and grasp it.

As they made the last turn onto the rally grounds, Eryk felt an overwhelming presence rush out to meet them. It pulled them forward, adding energy to their already brisk steps. As the pavilion came into view, his heart somersaulted inside. Though he had been here before, the sight swept over him with fresh thrill. There was majesty here, majesty, beauty and might; surely Germany was being blessed of God.

The *Lupolditerena* was filling with column after column of young men as *Hitler Jugend* and *Jungvolk* groups from all over Germany came for this grand celebration. Coming out into the pavilion area was like being welcomed into the vastness of heaven. The canopy of blue sky above looked down on the enormous grandstands and fluttering flags and the youth of Germany, by the thousands, sitting and standing on the parade ground as far as the eye could see. The main grandstand was at the opposite end of the *Hall of Honor*. Eryk let his eyes drink in the massive golden eagles posted on each end and the trio of swastika banners rising above the platform from which the Führer would speak. Choirs and music groups clustered close to the platform in readiness for their performance.

Glancing around, he felt a swelling in his chest at the mighty throng of boys and girls who filled the stadium this morning: everyone alike in dress and in mind. Thousands of girls from the *League of German Girls* were here as well. A sea of khaki brown and black filled the boys section and white and navy decked the girls. The soul of every young person in the stadium was fixed on the glory of Germany and his or her part to play in bringing it to pass. Eryk tugged furtively on his tie; it had gotten slightly skewed in the march.

The Führer was due at 10:00 a.m. As the last group of young people marched in and took their places, a hush fell over them all. No one dared breathe too loudly. Mothers hushed small children. The flapping of flags sounded loud in Eryk's ears. He waited, feeling the anticipation grow almost unbearable.

A command thundered out and thousands of legs and bodies stiffened in response. Then through the entrance, just a tiny figure from his vantage point, Eryk glimpsed the man whom all Germany gathered to see. Adolf Hitler strode purposefully onto the granite paving, followed by a small group of men in uniform.

A deafening sound filled the stadium as *Heil* leaped from 50,000 young throats and from other mature ones. Youthful arms were ramrod straight in salute. The Führer's hand cocked back in return. Eryk strained his eyes for a good look at the *Führer*, but the arena was so massive that he couldn't distinguish any of the details of his face. Adolf Hitler turned to say something to the man beside him, and Eryk wondered if he was pleased. He knew from the portraits he'd seen that the man possessed a steely gaze and a clipped mustache. Even from this distance, he could see the Führer slide his hand through the lock of black hair falling onto his forehead.

The crowds did not relent in their appreciation as Hitler mounted the steps of the main grandstand. Only when the *Reich Youth Leader*, Baldur von Schirach, stepped forward and signaled for silence did they reluctantly relax their hands and lungs. The emotion was invigorating, enough to feed the hunger of a proud nation.

The *Youth Leader* paused and then spoke forcefully into the microphone. "Youth of Germany . . . the supreme commander of the *Third Reich* - Adolf Hitler!"

Eryk licked his lips, his heart wild with excitement.

The Führer scanned the crowd for a moment. "*Heil*, my youth!"

Then all the pent-up energy of the preceding days was released in a chorus of return greeting as the adolescent citizens of the *Fatherland* saluted their leader. Out of the corner of his eye, Eryk saw a couple of *German League* girls fall to the ground in a faint. The glory of the Führer's adoration was overwhelming. He himself felt a little wobbly in the knees.

But he did his best to stand very straight as the ceremony unfolded – a trumpet fanfare, and then songs and the presentations of the flags which had been carried throughout all of Germany on their way to the assembly. After a short speech by von Schirach, the moment they had long anticipated arrived.

The Führer came forward once again. He stroked his fingers through the lock of hair on his brow, shifted his stance and began to speak.

His voice compelled Eryk to listen; it slid smoothly past his ears and descended to his heart, warming him through. The moderate rise and fall of his voice wove a spell on the young people as Hitler spoke of the greatness of German heritage and the superiority of the Aryan people. The diminutive leader learned forward at the podium and praised the youth gathered that day; he spoke softly about the way they warmed his heart for the promise of future Germany. Because of their dedication and discipline, he said, the Hitler youth, his youth, would lead the way in battle and in victory. On them rested the hopes and dreams of a nation. In them dwelled the spirit of heroism. They were his cherished youth; they would win, no matter the odds. They were the glory of Germany. Hitler became more animated, his voice no longer petting them, but commanding them, inspiring them, invigorating them.

Eryk wanted to rise up off the pavement and fly. At that moment, he would have jumped off a grandstand tower or lay in the pathway of *panzers* if the *Führer* wished. To have his esteem was payment enough for one's service and even death, if need be.

The world was open before him. Eryk could feel it. He and his comrades would meet the challenge. It was their hour. Past generations had laid the way for this time. Nothing would hold them back. No empire would restrain the German people from their rightful place. He could sense it everywhere - in the brilliance of the morning sun and in the throaty *Heil* of the crowds and in the splendor of the Nazi eagle watching over the stadium. This moment of glory would be theirs, always.

6

November 9, 1938
Berlin, Germany

> *Literature is an act of rebellion.*
> Gunter Grass

A loud pounding made him jump. It took a minute for Eryk to realize that it was coming from his bedroom door. He pushed back the quilts, struggling to untangle his feet and get out of bed. The person outside didn't wait, but threw open the door. Bright light from the hallway streamed in. Eryk shaded his eyes and squinted at the face. It was his father's.

"Get ready. Quickly. You are needed."

"Why? What's happened?"

"There is violence in the streets, buildings on fire. All men in uniform are asked to report to their divisions." *Hauptmann* Steiner grabbed Eryk's boots and tossed them toward his son. "There is no time to waste. I am leaving now to see what I must do."

"But how did this happen, sir? What is the cause?"

His father paused in the doorway, turning back to look at his son for a full, calm moment. "I don't know, Eryk, but whatever it is, you may be sure there is evil in it. I will tell you more when I know."

"Yes, sir." Eryk was already pulling on his trousers and shoving his feet into his boots.

His father strode into the hall, hurrying toward the stairs, but Eryk heard him say. "God go with you, son."

Eryk shrugged a bit at the words. He would be in good company tonight; the Führer was at the helm. What need did he have of God? Yet, perhaps it was a father's way of giving farewell. Sentiment was often the preferred language of parents, though he had to admit, not often in the case of his father. Though Eryk had seen him occasionally embrace his mother or stroke his sisters' braids, *Hauptmann* Steiner was not usually a man of affection.

Running a hand through his hair, Eryk grabbed his cap and raced into the hallway. His mother caught him just before he reached the stairs. Her eyes were wild, though that was not unusual. Nights were her worst times, and they had been even worse since *Hauslehrerin* had left them. Now, Magda Steiner grabbed her son, her fingernails clawing into the flesh of his arm.

"Don't leave me! Not you too!"

"Mother, I must go. I have been called by my unit. Please. You will be all right here with Frederica and Annaliese. The servants will come if you need them."

His mother stared at him with frantic eyes. "They told me you would be different, but they lied."

Eryk looked at the woman who had given him birth and wondered what had happened. How had the vibrant young girl in the family album become the disheveled woman whose constant companions were fears and anxieties? How could his father continue to keep his equilibrium when his wife couldn't cope with daily life? More importantly, how could he get away from her right now?

Eryk tried something he had seen his father do. He put his arms around his mother and hugged her tightly for a long moment. He felt her relax at the comfort of human touch. "There, now, *Mutter*. You know I will be alright. I have duties. But I will come back to you."

She lifted her head from his shoulder and looked at him as if she were the child and he the parent. "Do you promise?"

"Yes, *Mutter*, I promise you. Now, let's get you back into your bed."

He led her to her room; she was clutching his arm and stumbling a bit. When she had climbed in and pulled up her eiderdown, he patted her shoulder gently and quietly walked out, closing the door behind him.

It took him only a few minutes to run lightly down the stairs, get his bicycle and head toward the city center. He was sure his unit would meet at their usual spot on the *Bergenstrasse*. It took only five minutes to get there.

But, as Eryk peddled furiously toward the heart of Berlin, he saw that the streets were brighter than normal tonight. In front of him, he saw flames reaching skyward. He had heard nothing about a public demonstration for the *Reich*. Perhaps it was a fire in an official building and his unit was being called to help put it out as community service. After all, military recruits were supposed to serve the citizens of the *Fatherland* in every possible way.

At that moment, his bicycle tires crunched on something on the sidewalk. Eryk looked down and saw a thousand glimmers shining up at him. The sidewalk was covered in glass, broken glass.

His tires crackled and winced on top of it. Looking around, Eryk noticed that the shop windows beside him were gone. Gaping holes were opened to the night, as though a huge predator had forced a massive fist through the window. The shards on the sidewalk were all that remained of the storefronts. Signs above the shops dangled precariously from their chains, as though holding onto life with a last gasp. As he passed under one of them, he noted the name of a Jewish merchant he had once visited with his *Hauslehrerin* – a baker whose sweet rolls had given him such pleasure on those long-ago outings. On the side of the broken window there was an epithet scrawled in rude lettering. For a moment, Eryk was stunned. That old man? He was the farthest thing from that description. It was still a little difficult for him to put the label on these people that his military training encouraged him to do. The attitudes and principles he had been taught so long ago were hard to forget.

In a few more minutes, he had reached his destination and found himself among a group of rowdy teenage boys and men. Some had clubs, others had pickaxes or shovels. None of them were in uniform. Eryk scanned the faces and found someone he knew from his troop.

"Johann! Wait."

The young man turned toward him. "Eryk! There you are. But, what are you doing in uniform, *dummkopf*?"

"Why not?"

"Because this is not official. We are only to help as fellow citizens, not as military agents. Come on, get out of that!"

"But I have nothing else to wear!"

The youth grabbed at the pack on his back. "Here, I always keep extra clothing in my knapsack. Go in that building there and change. Quickly!" He shoved the pack into Eryk's hands and motioned toward a doorway.

Eryk hesitated only a minute before doing what his friend said. It seemed a little odd, but Johann had always been correct in his information, so Eryk assumed he knew what he was talking about.

He ducked into the doorway and tried the first knob he came to. It swung open with a squeak, and Eryk could see that it was another vacated shop. He needn't have come through the door; the plate glass in front was missing, and the night wind riffled through the clothing on the racks around him. It was eerie. He stood for a moment, and then darted toward the back, pulling off his shirt as he went. In the shadows, he changed quickly and stuffed his uniform in the knapsack, pulling it on his back as he hurried toward the front of the store. He decided to go out through the door again to avoid cutting his legs on the broken glass front and was just turning the knob when the door jerked back on him, slamming him backward onto the floor into a thousand slivers of glass.

He yelped, and scrambled to his feet. But he was almost trampled by the bodies that came rushing into the shop. Eryk managed to get out of the way as people poured past him and started yanking merchandise off the racks. The light from the fires on the street and the torches held by the men outside illuminated a scene of chaos as townspeople snatched costly clothing from the shelves and played tug-of-war with their neighbors over the best items.

His hands and arms were cut. Eryk could feel the warm liquid dripping from them, and he tried to hold them against his shirt, or rather against Johann's shirt, to absorb the bleeding. But even as he knew that he must get some first aid, he was mesmerized by the drama in front of him. It was sheer madness. Not at all what he was used to seeing in refined Berliners. He backed out of the shop and walked as swiftly as he could back to his group.

Many of his unit were gone now. Johann was swiftly walking away too when Eryk reached out to grab his arm.

"Hey! I need help."

"What happened to you?" Johann eyed Eryk's bloody arms.

"I fell into the glass in that shop. Or rather, I was pushed into the glass. It is crazy in there!"

Johann grinned. "*Yah*, it is. Come on, we need to join our group."

"But I can't work like this!" Eryk tried to wipe his arms against his chest, but the blood kept dripping.

"Who said anything about work? Besides, I'll swing the club for you! It will give me more points."

"Points? What do you mean?" Eryk's arms were really starting to burn now from the lacerations.

"This is about how many lessons we can give to the *Juden*. Come on, Eryk. Do I have to spell everything out for you?"

Johann looked around and snatched up a big piece of fabric lying on the street. "Here, this hasn't been burned yet. Wrap it around your arms and stop whining. Let's go."

Eryk took the fabric and started to wrap it around his bleeding arms. It was plush fabric, warm and soft. There seemed to be tassels of some kind on the edges too. But he didn't have time to worry about it. He was going to be left if he didn't hurry.

Holding his wrapped arms against his chest, he followed his friend down the street. They walked a few blocks and stopped where others were gathering. The building in front of them was ablaze. Eryk didn't need anyone to tell him what kind of building it was. He could see the star. It was a Jewish synagogue. Tentacles of fire reached out through broken windows and enveloped the ornate carvings in smoke. On the street was a pile of books, caps, *Kiddush* cups and *Torah* scrolls. Eryk knew what they were because his *Hauslehrerin* had once taken him inside a synagogue. An *SA* man Eryk recognized as a friend of his father's poured kerosene from a can onto the pile, then struck a match and threw it toward the items which erupted into flames as well. The crowd broke into applause, some of them dancing around the inferno.

Eryk couldn't very well do anything with his arms and hands in their injured condition, and he was almost glad of it. He had understood the purpose of his presence tonight was to help prevent mischief and vandalism; instead, he was party to spreading it. Around him were familiar faces; in fact, many of them had been his comrades in the *Hitler Jugend*. He recognized other adult members of the *SA*. But none of them were upset about what was going on and no one was trying to bring order. Some were actively participating in the melee and others were calmly watching, but all appeared to be perfectly at ease about it.

Out of the corner of his eye, Eryk glimpsed a couple shadowy figures flattened against the building next to the burning synagogue. Saying nothing, he watched them out of the corner of his eye while they began moving, creeping away from the fire. At first, he thought they were fellow party members just tired of the ruckus. But, in another instant, he noticed that one of them wore a robe, and immediately he knew who they were.

So did the others.

With a whoop, a couple *SA* men dashed toward the two figures. In the blazing light of the flames around him, Eryk could see the struggle that ensued as the fugitives resisted. One of them almost succeeded in getting away. But, in the end, the storm troopers held onto their prize and pulled the two figures into the center of the gathering where they shoved them onto the pavement.

Eryk could now see that both of them were quite old, a man and a woman. The man appeared to be a rabbi. He wore a robe dirty with ashes, and he had long chin whiskers and side locks and wore a *yarmulke* on the crown of his head. He was stooped and pulled himself slowly and jerkily to his feet. Eryk was so close that he could see the rabbi's eyes and was startled by the way they glittered like stars in the wrinkled old face.

Even in his inexperience, Eryk could detect fear in the man's gaze, but something else as well. Pride? Determination? Strength? The man reached down a gnarled hand to assist the woman whose feet were tangled in her skirts. She had trouble getting free and standing up but finally did so, and the crowd laughed and jeered as someone standing near pushed her back down.

Eryk's eyes were drawn to another *SA* man who was inching toward the rabbi, taking exaggerated steps as one would in playing a game with children. The *HJ* teens standing around began counting his steps. *Eins! Zwei! Drei! Vier!*

The storm trooper stopped in front of the old man, and stood staring at him. Then he spit in his face. Eryk watched the saliva slide down the weathered cheek in a glistening trail. The old man did nothing; he just stared back at his tormentor. The *SA* man smiled in a condescending way and, in a motion quick and violent, grabbed a handful of the rabbi's beard and tore it from his face.

The old man gave a guttural cry and stumbled backward against the woman who had once again gotten to her feet. But she could not hold his weight and both of them crumpled to the ground. They were close to the burning pile of synagogue items, and Eryk saw the man flinch and draw back even as he held a hand to his mangled chin.

But the onlookers had no sympathy. As the couple tried to stand to their feet, the men again pushed them onto the pavement. Then, one of the *HJ* cadets raised his club and struck the old man on the head. Another clubbed the old woman. Others joined in. The couple tried to cover their heads, rolling onto their sides and curling to protect themselves as much as possible. But this only infuriated their captors and they hit them harder.

Eryk was a mix of emotion. Because of his messed-up hands, he couldn't join in the free-for-all, and he still wasn't sure he wanted to.

Though he had no great love for these old Jews, he did have respect for a civilized way of handling obstinate people groups, especially those who were elderly. In spite of himself, he could not forget how he had been raised. He was reluctant to participate in such violence. He could chant against the Jews at rallies and avoid doing business with them and wish them to be gone from his homeland, but as yet, he had not been able to raise his own hand against them. Tonight's persecution was way beyond any pogrom of which he had been a part. How did this help the German cause or give the *Volk* the living space to which the Führer endlessly referred? No, the battle must be won on the fields of war, not in the streets as hoodlums.

Eryk turned his back.

'Where are you going?" An *SA* man grabbed his shoulder and stared into his face. "You need to stay here and witness the indignation of the German people against the Jewish pigs."

Eryk stood ramrod straight and glared up at the man. "Sir, I have been injured tonight in the activities, and I cannot do anything." He held up his arms, which were beginning to seep blood through the fabric.

The man glanced down. "So, I see. Injured yourself on the glass, did you? Well, I wish all our youth were as passionate as you for the cause." He patted Eryk on the back. "Go home. There will be another day for you to fight."

Eryk didn't need any more encouragement. He looked for his bicycle, but it was gone. It would have been difficult for him to ride anyway with his injuries. As he turned and walked away, he saw the group of men and boys moving on further down the street, carrying their torches and insults to other victims.

Near the smoldering rubbish that once was his place of glory, the old rabbi lay broken, moaning as he writhed in his own blood. The woman no longer moved at all. Her head was bashed in on one side, its contents spilling onto the street. Eryk looked for a moment and then broke into a run. Down the streets of Berlin he raced, ignoring the fires and broken glass and screams and chants. He didn't stop until he reached the gate of his own house. It was only then, as he stood in a puddle of moonlight that he saw his arms were wrapped in the soft folds of a synagogue tapestry, its fringes soaked with his blood.

7

September 1939, Poland
Leibstandarte SS Adolf Hitler

> *Accordingly, I have placed my death-head formation in readiness – for the present only in the East – with orders to them to send to death mercilessly and without compassion, men, women, and children of Polish derivation and language. Only thus shall we gain the living space (Lebensraum) which we need.*
> Adolf Hitler, August 22, 1939

The September heat was taking its toll, and Eryk lifted a grimy hand to swipe at his forehead. With a full pack on his back, he was sweating terribly. The days since the invasion had been ones of marching, always moving forward. His regiment was advancing swiftly through the Polish countryside, on to Warsaw, the capital. So far, they had been victorious. The pitiful attempts by the Polish Army had not been strong enough to stop them. There hadn't even been enough resistance to keep the same battle front longer than a few hours.

First, there had been the air attack, wave after wave of bombers descending on the Polish countryside and cities. Hermann Goering bragged about the superiority of the German *Luftwaffe,* and to Eryk's way of thinking, he was right. He remembered chatting with his cousin, Gunter, who flew a *Junkers 87*, or as it was known in the ranks, the *Stuka*. Gunter had been confident of success when they talked about future battles. Grinning, he assured Eryk that his little dive-bomber with the wailing sirens would be a formidable weapon for the German forces.

"If you hear a wail, just look up and give me a wave; I'll be protecting your tail from the sky."

Eryk smiled to himself now as he thought of his devil-may-care cousin who wore his cap at a jaunty angle and whistled all the time. If all the pilots were that cocksure, they would certainly make a good showing, whatever the outcome.

But as the days had progressed, Eryk was even surer that victory was inevitable. In many villages, they had been greeted by cheering Polish citizens; some held out flowers or waved swastikas. There were even a few peasant girls who offered kisses to the conquerors, and a few men who took advantage of this on the sly. But, for the most part, the German men ignored such tempting obeisance. After being in this country for a few days, Eryk understood why.

Never had he seen such a primitive and filthy people. The huts in which they lived were hardly more than hovels with dirt yards in which goats and chickens clustered. The people were dressed in ugly clothing, often of mismatching patterns. The women wore clunky shoes and dingy head scarves. And the children! The little ones were barefoot and grimy, with runny noses and limp hair. The babies wore only ratty diapers and most likely smelled since it was common knowledge that the Poles rarely bathed. Not that Eryk had been that close to any babies lately. It was a vile way of life so far as he could see. He had heard that there was more culture and sophistication in the cities where there was an abundance of vehicles, flower boxes, grand architecture and fashionable cafes. But he wondered if there would be any of that left to see after Gunter and his friends had their way from the skies.

They were approaching another village now. In front of his regiment was a *Panzer* brigade, their heavy tracks kicking up the dust from the ruts the Poles called roads. Eryk felt a rush of pride at the mechanized force of the German military. Following the *Luftwaffe*, the *Panzers* had literally rolled open the way for thousands of soldiers on foot. Together, they were moving like lightning onto enemy territory.

The village was small, like many others he had seen. It didn't take long to go through. As he passed the last building, movement in the forest beyond caught his eye. Curious, he watched as a group of people huddled together beside a grove of trees. The men wore tall hats and even from a distance, he could see the dangling side curls that identified them as Jews. Women clutched babies, and toddlers hung behind their skirts. He was far enough away that he couldn't see everything going on, but he could distinguish a few *SS* men kneeling in front of the little group of people. Not quite sure what he was witnessing, Eryk's eyes widened as there was a burst of gunfire, and the huddled group toppled together in a heap. He heard no cries; there was only a puff of smoke rising to show what had taken place.

Eryk swallowed and turned his head back to face forward. It was one thing to conquer the people; it was another matter to kill them, at close range and with no dignity. Of course, the victims had been Jews, as well as Poles. That was a double strike against them. Still, was that, in itself, justification enough to mow them down?

Surely, if there was one good Jew, there could be others. But how could one be sure? By what scale could a Jew be measured? The Nazi doctrine taught that they were greedy and unscrupulous, with strange religious practices and a feeling of superiority over others. Their attitude corrupted the populace and insulted the working man. They had to be removed from society before all of Europe was infected. Young Jews would grow to become adult Jews and perpetuate the race. It was a matter of ethics; the job must be done.

He turned his attention back to the rows of mechanical machines in front of him. Watching the *Panzers* in their glory these past days had brought to the front a dream he had cherished since his boyhood exploits with toy soldiers. He wanted to command a *Panzer*, to sit at the controls of one of those marvelous machines, to play his part in the strategy of battle.

When his twelve months of qualifying were complete, Eryk had decided he would enlist in officers' training at *Bad Tolz*. He would be done with the marching and the dirty work of war if he could pass the training for *panzers*. From a commander's cupola, he would be above all of that. Yes, that was the answer. There was always a way out if one thought long enough about it. Unbidden, words from the shadows of his memory trooped to the front of his thinking.

"There is a way that seemeth right unto a man, but the ends thereof are the ways of death."

Eryk pondered why he should remember that verse and why it made him feel uneasy. She had been a Jew, after all, his *Hauslehrerin*. That's what he had learned on the day when she had been dismissed from the family service. True, she had been a converted Jew, according to the information his father had been given. But that made no difference to his mother. While his father had been willing to look the other way, Magda Steiner would have none of it. No Jew would continue to teach her Eryk, a loyal son of the *Fatherland* and a Hitler Youth to boot. So Zelda Goldman had gone, and he had been taught to hate her kind, to loathe the people whom the Führer blamed for the problems Germany faced.

But, in spite of all he had heard and regardless of the policies and laws and indoctrination, Eryk remembered the woman who had saved him from his mother's nightmares and whose words had been his earliest instruction. Even now, her words shouted to him as he marched further away from home and conscience.

8

November 9, 1939
The *Feldehernehalle*

> *The best political weapon is the weapon of terror.*
> *Cruelty commands respect.*
> *Men may hate us.*
> *But, we don't ask for their love; only for their fear.*
> Heinrich Himmler

It was midnight. Eryk's fingers felt icy even in gloves as he stood in rigid form before the sacred Nazi monument. Hundreds of men in uniform were all around him. They filled the *Odeonsplatz*, their dark clothing blending in with the night and their armbands glinting in the light of the memorial torches.

They stood in exacting formation, no man further from his comrade than the prescribed distance. In front of them, dominating the scene was the overpowering image of the *Feldehernehalle*, the architectural memorial to the tradition of the Bavarian Army, commissioned by King Ludwig I. Eryk knew this because of the history he had studied as a child. But its use as the night's venue was not because of historical honor, but out of sentiment. For this was now considered one of the most revered sites in Germany, the scene of the failed *Beer Hall Putsch* in 1923. Here, the SS continually provided an honor guard for the sixteen pillars topped with flames and etched with the names of the men who gave their lives in the early Nazi cause.

Every November 9, this tremendous ceremony was held for the swearing in of new recruits. Eryk could feel the energy of his comrades standing all around him. It seemed they were all imbued with a special sense of power and purpose. This was the moment for which they had waited.

Reichsfuhrer Himmler's voice rose and fell, weaving around the young men who stood eager to serve. He praised their initiative. He commended their racial purity. He urged them to loyalty and unwavering service. In hoarse tones, he called upon the spirits of their Viking ancestors to fill their hearts with courage and determination. In spite of the warmth of his uniform, Eryk felt a chill shake his shoulders as the man appeared to speak not to them, but to some unseen force.

The "blood flag" was hoisted, its stains an unforgettable testament to the martyred sixteen. Then hundreds of arms shot straight into the night sky and male voices rang out, gaining momentum as they uttered the powerful phrases:

"I vow to you, Adolf Hitler, as Führer and chancellor of the German Reich, loyalty and bravery. I vow to you and to the leaders that you set for me, absolute allegiance until death. So help me God".

[2]Under the arches of the commemorative loggia, the massive stone lions cast shadows on Eryk and the men with him who no longer owned themselves, neither body nor soul.

9

December 1940, Baker Street, London
Special Operations Executive

"Set Europe ablaze!"
Winston Churchill to Hugh Dalton, civilian of the *SOE*

"You've passed every test, Miss Brighton. Your instructors have given their approval. Your conduct has been exemplary."

The old man looked after her for quite a few minutes. He had the feeling that he had just sent a lamb to the wolves. But, of course, there was no other choice. War was a nasty business, and a woman could be used often where a man could not. Still, he would have preferred to send one more hardened, less shining and new, though her instructors claimed she had a battlefield persona that was tested and ready. He would never have agreed to her assignment if there had been doubts.

He picked up her dossier and stared at her picture. She was a beautiful girl with a certain bearing that reminded him of the German women he'd seen in his travels. She'd fit in well. He didn't worry about her performance; he worried about her. *You're getting soft, Archie.*

When did you last worry about your people this way? She has a job to do; she needs your support, not your sympathy.

Still, he hoped he'd made the right decision. He felt accountable to his old friend, her uncle. But by the time relatives found out about her work, the war would be over and she would either be safely home or tucked away in some unmarked grave where no one would ever know the details.

Yes, the war had to be won; this conflict that was set on destroying civilization just as surely as the Thames flowed through London. If they didn't win, there'd be no more decency on the earth.

So, the man opened a desk drawer and filed the sheaf of papers, turning the lock when he was done. Emma Brighton was buried; another woman had taken her place.

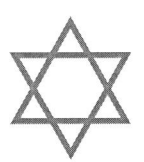

10

January 1941, Bad Tolz, Germany
SS Junkerschule

"My honor is loyalty."
Waffen-SS Motto

Eryk sat in a classroom of thirty young men and waited. There was not a sound in the room. Every man sat with feet flat on the floor, back erect and eyes straight ahead, a notebook opened on the desk in front of him. The upperclassmen told them it was a game the instructors played with the cadets. They waited outside the door, making the students remain seated and motionless for as long a time as they could, daring them to make a sound, trying to find a reason to flunk them.

As silly as it sounded for grown men, Eryk and his fellow cadets were up for the challenge. They would die in their seats rather than be the first to move. It was a matter of willpower and endurance. Both were nonnegotiable for a *Waffen-SS* officer.

That's what Eryk had set his heart on becoming – an officer in the *Waffen-SS*. He was determined to rise to the challenge, to get that gleaming eagle, to find his wings.

He felt that his father would have understood that desire. They hadn't talked about the future as much as Eryk would have liked. It was understood, of course, that Eryk would follow the family tradition and serve in the German military. He had done so. But they had never gotten beyond that beginning, had never had the chance to discuss what career might await the younger Steiner. All those future talks were stolen from him on that night of broken glass in Berlin. He had come home with his wounded arms to find his mother in hysterics and the household in an uproar, a household of which he was now the master. His father's commanding officer delivered the official word: *Hauptmann* Steiner had been killed in the line of duty. He would be honored always as a protector of the *Third Reich*, etc, etc.

To Eryk's ears at the time, the words had sounded stilted and formal. He only knew that he had new responsibilities, and that he had lost the only parent with whom he could talk. His mother hadn't been able to share his life for years.

So, he had valiantly shouldered the duties of his family as best a teenage boy could do. Of course, with the family's heritage and money, he hadn't worried much about providing for their food and shelter. No, it was more the daily load of being the man in the house for his sisters and mother. Gratefully, neither of his sisters had inherited their mother's fragile emotional condition, but with both of them in the throes of adolescence, they were still difficult to understand at times. Even now, he remembered the defiance that bubbled up in them after Father's death and the way they would march off to their *BDM* groups as though that were their true families.

Now, as he sat in a cold, stone classroom and waited for the footstep of the professor, he hoped the sisters were all right, back in Berlin, with him away and their mother in such a sad condition at the state hospital. She scarcely left her room anymore, never combed her hair and could usually be found by the window, engaged in a nonsensical dialogue with an unseen person. Even he was at a loss for how to deal with her when he visited, and Fredericka and Annaliese had never felt comfortable with her in those strange moods.

The only one who had really been able to calm *Frau* Steiner was his *Hauslehrerin,* and she wasn't coming back.

The door flying open snatched Eryk from his daydream. The tall, blond officer who walked in was known for his harsh words and uncompromising manner of grading. He had gained a nickname too. The "Perfect Monster." He did nothing wrong, every word and movement by the book, yet he was extremely unpleasant. An afternoon in his presence had a negative effect on even the most conscientious student.

Today, he was the instructor in *Racial Policies and Practices for the Waffen-SS Officer.* Eryk opened his textbook and gripped his pen as the lecture began.

It was good to be outside. Eryk had always loved the outdoors, felt one with it. And the many outdoor activities and especially the sports were the things he heartily enjoyed in this training program.

It was winter, and there were piles of snow for the cadets to tromp through as they accomplished their three-hour wilderness hike in the wooded areas of *Bad Tolz.* The air was still quite cold, but it was an invigorating kind of chill that made Eryk march faster and breathe deeper. The brisk whip of the fir tree branches and the scattering of the hares in the undergrowth made him remember boyhood days with his father and uncle, when they hunted and told stories by the fire. Those good memories stirred within him the desire to fulfill his destiny, to become the man that those stalwart heroes before him had thought he could be. He wanted to carry on the Steiner name in honor, and he would do that in the *Waffen-SS*.

As they marched, the cadets chanted and sang. Germany had always been a nation of song, and they were used to easing their labors and invigorating their spirits with throaty tunes. Old marching songs had been passed down through the generations, and Eryk remembered a couple of them his father had taught him. But the tune the group was now singing was newer, its words a call to action.

> *Onward, brothers, to the barricades!*
> *The Führer calls, follow him now!*
> *Reaction has betrayed him*
> *But the Third Reich comes nevertheless.*[3]

Strong male voices lifted passionately echoed among the rocks and through the forests. It was an invigorating, inspiring sound. Eryk was glad to be part of such a chorus, the future of Germany. As they passed once again through the arched main gate of the *Junkerschule,* he felt satisfaction that he was still among those worthy to be a cadet.

He was often pressed to the full of his endurance. The demands were rigorous, but so far, he had maintained a nice edge in field games and combat training, and he excelled in tactics, as well as in map and terrain reading. This was due, no doubt, to hours of listening to his father talk military strategy with his uncle and to the hours of imaginary battles on the carpets of his childhood home. Of course, his governess had never failed to issue a gentle warning, "Remember, Eryk, *Liebchen*, that a good soldier only fights righteous battles."

As he dropped his field pack to the stone floor beside his bunk and collapsed onto it, he wondered fleetingly if anyone could tell which battles were righteous. The Führer said that to fight for him was to fight for the *Fatherland* and that was supremely honorable. Death was the supreme stroke of honor for any man of the *SS*.

But, Eryk knew his old governess wouldn't agree. She would see the passionate oratory of Adolf Hitler differently, he thought. Even the cadets here, filled with youthful tolerance, could see the undisguised hatred. They chose to ignore it for the sake of their country, their families and yes, for the sake of their own pride. Hitler might be Germany's last chance, and they, the young men of the *Fatherland*, would take it, whatever the cost.

On these troublesome thoughts, Eryk closed his eyes for a few minutes' rest, but was jostled awake. His friend, Horst, was standing above him, nudging his shoulder.

"You missed mail call, Steiner. Here's something for you." Horst tossed an envelope onto Eryk's chest.

Eryk grabbed it and sat up, swinging his feet to a sitting position so he could read the thing better. It was addressed to him from the *State Sanatorium and Mental Hospital* in Bernburg, the center where his mother was receiving treatment.

He hoped there wasn't a problem with her care. She had been there only a short time, having been transported there a few days after Christmas. Surely, it was too soon for the doctors to tell if the treatment would improve her condition.

He opened the envelope and unfolded the first sheet of paper.

To the Family of Frau Magda Steiner,

    Thank you for placing your loved one in our care. We at the *Bernburg Sanatorium* consider it an honor to give service to our citizens in emotional distress. However, it is with regret that we inform you that your mother has passed away. We did all we could to insure her good health and improve her condition, but she refused to eat and finally fell ill of pneumonia. The end was peaceful.

With the stresses of wartime upon us all, we understand the limitations of many families and so have taken it upon ourselves to have your loved one's remains cremated at no expense to you. If you would like to have these remains shipped to you, please contact us at the address given below for further instruction.

We express our deepest regret and heartfelt sympathy for your loss. May you find comfort in knowing that your loved one was given the best of care in her final hours.

Sincerely,
Dr. Schneider
Head Physician, Bernburg

The next sheet of paper was a death certificate.

Eryk stared at it. His mother was dead. Really, physically dead, not just the emotional death she had been living for these many years. She no longer breathed, and her body was already ashes.

He knew he should mourn, but he wasn't sure how to go about it. How did one grieve a mother who could not embrace her son or give him the slightest bit of comfort in his childish woes? How did one mourn a mother who did not cook or clean or read stories or make sauerbraten or pastries? Indeed, how did one feel any kind of remorse for a woman who had tried to kill her child?

He couldn't.

He was sorry she had suffered. As an adult, he had recognized that her illness had prompted her behavior, and that she was a victim. The youthful beauty his father had married bore little resemblance to the haggard woman she had become in the last few years. The sparkling temperament of which others had spoken had flown away entirely. His mother hadn't meant to harm him, he was sure. But because he had always seen her as pitiful, wretched and frightening, he had never been able to bond with her. No, another had kissed his skinned knees and heard his nightly prayers and given him crackers and milk on rainy afternoons. And she was as good as dead to him now as well.

Eryk realized he was now motherless as well as fatherless. But the family nest was far from empty. There were two young girls who were still his responsibility. He would have to take leave to tell them what had happened and make plans for their future.

He got up from his bed and walked to the window. The sun was giving a last farewell to the mountains, bathing the grounds of *Bad Tolz* in amber light. He wondered if his mother had ever gazed in silence at the beauty of a sunset and then, in the same moment, remembered the woman who had never let him pass one by. His life had been marked irrevocably by two women. Now, all that remained of one of them was ashes.

11

September 1941
somewhere over Germany

> *We were all young, we were all different,*
> *but we all had the feeling in the beginning that we were*
> *going to be helpful. That was why we went into it.*
> Odette, Samsom, *SOE* Operative

The thrum of the Whitley's propeller matched the speed of her thoughts as agent Emma Brighton waited for the green light. No, make that Hanne Lager. Once she fell from the belly of this friendly plane, Emma was no more.

Hanne would fall 600 feet in the night sky; Hanne would drop correctly and land without breaking any bones; Hanne would retrieve the equipment canister; and Hanne would creep off into the countryside to forget she was British and remember her Prussian blood on her father's side. Her life depended on that remembering. More than that, her country depended on it; in fact, the world was involved in this operation.

As a member of the newly formed *Special Operations Executive*, Emma had volunteered for a mission like this, a dangerous one that would put her in the very cauldron of the *Third Reich*. Just getting her there was a risk for the pilot and drop-master. The plane was camouflaged, and they were flying low to avoid radar detection, but once in enemy airspace, they were on their own. London could do nothing to aid them.

Emma glanced at the canisters waiting beside her, filled with supplies she would need, mostly of the explosive type. Hours of training in the use of arms would serve her well in the days to come. Absently, she patted the holster under her shoulder to feel the reassuring bulge of her hand weapon. Cold steel was her best friend now.

Many agents had a radio operator either dropped in with them or already waiting in the zone. But she had none. Her use of radio would be infrequent; there was too much danger from the German radio detection squad. She would have to be extremely cautious when sending information back to *HQ*.

Emma found herself staring at the red light above, knowing that any second she would find herself at the open door. All those practice jumps through the old fuselage at the training ground now seemed inadequate preparation. She gritted her teeth and turned away from the light.

"Nearing the drop zone." The pilot's voice droned in her ear from the loudspeaker above. Flight sergeant pilot George Harry Pickard, aka "Picky," was red-haired and loud and one of the best pilots in *Squadron 138*, a special group assigned to drop and extract agents behind enemy lines. Even in the few short hours that she had known him, Emma had come to rely on his confident spirit and skill. She hated to leave him, her new friend, for the cold world below.

But contemplation time was over. She stood, stretched and clipped her chute cord onto the static line above. The door of the plane opened noiselessly and the jumpmaster stood like a phantom, hand raised.

Emma looked once over her shoulder at the safety of the plane and then turned her face to the biting wind. The jump light changed to neon green. The jumpmaster yelled and patted her back, and Emma Brighton walked out into the black air and died as she hurtled toward the ground. Hanne Lager took her place.

12

June 1942
Berlin, Germany

Formerly our friends, they now begrudged us the very air we breathed.
Pearl Benisch

The day the notice came began like any other. It was June in Berlin; streets were lined with lush green trees, the sidewalk cafes wafted out their fragrances, and everywhere there were flowers, bunches of flowers.

Nadya loved this time of year, summer when everything was alive and blooming. She and *Tante* Zelda shared a love for growing things. Together, they would walk to the market where farmers from the countryside around the city would bring their vegetables to sell in the brightly painted booths.

They would ooh and aah over the vibrant tomatoes and the bulging squash and the plump strawberries. *Tante* would bring a basket and they would fill it to the brim, taking care not to crush the delicate produce. It had been their weekly tradition during the summer months for all the years of Nadya's childhood. As she had gotten older, Nadya would sometimes go to market alone if *Tante* was busy rehearsing or had some other obligation with the symphony. But they still enjoyed going together whenever possible.

But now things were different. Jews were given reduced rations and even restricted from certain shopping areas and certain items. The market was one of the places they could no longer go. Nadya missed the sunny place and the friendly farmers they used to know. The last time they had been allowed to shop there, the bushy-haired men and aproned women hadn't seemed as glad to sell to them. The merchants were now frequently glancing around to see if there was a *Gestapo* agent watching their transactions. Well, that wasn't just merchants; most of the citizens of Berlin were wary and watchful. The *SS* and *Gestapo* had eyes and ears on every street corner and in every gathering.

At least, Jews could still grow flowers in pots outside their tiny apartment. *Tante* was even trying to grow potatoes and beans in garden pots; she loved the sight and taste of vegetables almost as much as she loved growing flowers. Before being forced out of their home, they had taken care to dig up *Tante's* prized rose bushes and also to bring their dahlia seeds from last year's blooms and tulip bulbs. The tulips wouldn't be planted until fall, but they had been coaxing along the dahlias and the rose bushes. Nadya loved the full-bodied, gorgeously colored dahlias. They were bursting with vibrant life and beauty, a contrast to the world that seemed to shrink all around them. *Tante* had a theory about flowers and life.

In the spring, as she pruned her roses, she would point to the clipped, barren stalk. "Life is in there, *Liebchen*. You can't see it, but it is there, waiting to burst forth when God calls the earth back to bloom. No one can hold it back. It will happen because it is the principle that He set to function in our world. The life in a seed or in a bush or tree will come out in His time." She would rock back on her heels and smile then. "We are like that too, if we believe in the Lord Jesus for salvation. His death works life in us and no matter how things change for us, no one can take away the life in us. It will spring forth too when He calls."

But Nadya struggled with the changes that were happening to them. Even *Tante's* position in the *Berlin Philharmonic* had not kept them from being moved out of their grand old neighborhood and into a special section of the city only for Jews. On the street entrance beside the nameplate there was a sign, a black star on white paper, which marked the apartment building as *Judenhauser* – a house for Jews. Though the place was filled with many people they knew, it was a sad atmosphere inside. There was something about being put in this section of the city and then put into special buildings that made one feel like an animal being penned up and reserved for something terrible. This part of the city was old, its walls crumbling and its streets filled with gaping holes. Its drainage system was inefficient, and its water pipes often leaked. Nadya had heard that the city officials were refusing to fix any of the problems which the inhabitants regularly reported. No one wanted to help Jews. They were on their own.

Of course, *Tante* had a philosophy about the ghetto, too.

"Remember, *Liebchen*, that our ancestors were put into a ghetto in Egypt, the land of Goshen, and there, God performed wonderful miracles for them. They were spared from the plagues that came on the Egyptians and the deliverer, Moses, came to them. We must be on the lookout for God's unusual works here."

Nadya liked the sound of that. If they were truly God's chosen people, then the idea that He would fight for them and rescue them and lead them to the Promised Land was thrilling and comforting. The problem was that God seemed to have changed His mind about all that since the days of old. She hadn't seen any sign that He was defending or rescuing them. Instead, they were labeled and mistreated and deported. She couldn't tell *Tante* so to her face but inwardly, Nadya wondered if God had forgotten them.

When the yellow star became mandatory in the fall of 1941, (was that only a few months ago?), Nadya had been horrified along with most of the Jewish population of Berlin. How could their home country, the nation of which their parents and grandparents had been citizens and even war veterans, require such an insulting practice? The humiliation of being tagged like cattle was unspeakable. But the Nazis made sure that no one tried to hide the star or wear it inconspicuously; there were terrible penalties for doing so. So, Nadya and *Tante* bought the necessary fabrics and made the stars to sew on their clothing. It was heartbreaking to ruin their beautiful clothing with those ugly yellow stars. Even if the time came when they could remove them, the material would be forever ruined with the stitches and the pronged imprint.

There was one exception though. They did not have to put a star on *Tante's* black evening dress and fur coat which she wore to play with the *Philharmonic*; *Herr* Furtwangler had obtained permission for his players to be excluded from this stigma while they were playing for the *Reich*.

Tante Zelda had tried to comfort her while they sewed. She reminded her of the stories from the *Torah* of the Hebrew people in Egypt and how they had been marked for slavery, of the captivities the Jews had suffered under the Babylonians and Persians and Romans, of the pogroms that had been happening for centuries. Still, God's people survived and remained.

"The Nazis may be able to mark us, but they cannot erase us." That was *Tante's* opinion on the matter.

But Nadya wasn't so sure. Every week brought more restrictions. How much more could be taken without the Jews being lost forever?

Jews in Berlin could not use public transportation, public parks or Aryan air raid shelters. They must shop at Jewish-owned businesses only. They were banned from the theater and the opera. They could not make calls on public telephones and they could not be out after 8:00 in the evening. Jews could no longer own radios or typewriters or bicycles or electric stoves. Even hand mirrors were forbidden. Nadya wondered wryly just what "luxury" the city *Gauleiter* would decide must go next. Indeed, the baker down the street from whom they bought their sweet rolls and *Challah* bread laughingly declared that surely the yellow star, being in such demand these days, would be the next item the Nazis required them to surrender. Nadya didn't see much humor in it, but *Tante* laughed when he said it.

But there was no laughter in the notices that arrived daily for families in the *Juden* section of Berlin. They were deportation notices or "evacuation" orders as the Nazis like to call them. People of Jewish race were being resettled in the East. They were allowed to take with them fifty kilograms of luggage per person. They had to report to the train station in Berlin and bring the money to buy their railway tickets after making sure all utility accounts for their present residences were settled. Every week, Nadya saw people she knew from the grocers or school or other places in Berlin walking down the street in a large group, the men often wearing their best suits and hats, the women sporting their finest high-heeled shoes and holding the hands of bright-faced toddlers who clung to dolls or balls or books. Some were Orthodox; you could tell by the side curls, the top hats and the fringes on the prayer shawls on the men. But many were not. Up until a few years ago, Berlin had a large Jewish population who were members of the Lutheran church; Nadya knew many who attended the church where she and *Tante* used to go. Of course, now they were forbidden to do that as well.

The people in the evacuation group never really knew where they were going. To the East was the only location given. Nadya heard from a friend that up to one thousand people at a time were taken. Sometimes, family members still in Berlin received letters from them, saying that they were being well-treated, had enough to eat and were working in the country. The relatives put great stock in these reassurances, and everyone hoped they were true. At least, that hope made life bearable for the present. *Tante* encouraged her to pray for those being transported. But Nadya could not; she was overtaken with fear that they would be next.

Today, it happened. In the mail, there was an official envelope from the *Jewish Cultural Center*.

Berlin, 15 June, 1942

    By official order, we inform you herewith that you are to be evicted from your residence. We ask you to please appear at our office building Oranienberger Strasse 31, third floor, on 17 June 1942, at 11am, with everyone living in your household, including children. People who are in the labor force must obtain leave of absence for this purpose. We must point out that you must appear to avoid more severe measures.

                                    The Jewish Cultural Organization of Berlin

Nadya hadn't wanted to believe it. How could her aunt, a member of the celebrated *Berlin Philharmonic,* be put on the list for evacuation? *Herr* Furtwangler had assured them that all his players were valuable; none of them would be deported.

For a moment, Nadya considered burning the offending piece of mail. Maybe no one would find out. But just as quickly, she realized how futile that was. The *Jewish Council* would have a list of all those who had been issued a letter. They would be treated horribly by the *Gestapo* if they tried to hide.

No, this was not something they could avoid. The black day had come. When *Tante* came home, they would cry together and make their plans. Nadya folded the letter and put it in the envelope on the table. She had to start packing.

August 1942
Quedlinburg, Germany
Quedlinburg Castle

His uniform was sticking to him. The late summer heat was stifling, even at night. Standing at attention, Eryk tried not to move even his eyes as *Reichsfuhrer* Heinrich Himmler strode down the line of men, pinning medals and giving words of commendation.

This place was one of Himmler's favorites, he had heard. Apparently, the castle fit in with Himmler's view of the *SS* as an order of Teutonic knights. The ceremonies took place in the courtyard, the uniformed men flanked by two dark stone columns adorned with the *SS* runes and each holding a brazier in which burned a flame. It was an impressive setting, but by now, Eryk was accustomed to the pageantry which accompanied these rituals. Still, when the *SS* leader finally stood in front of him, he felt a bit overwhelmed despite his familiarity with it all.

"*SS Obersturmfuhrer* Eryk von Steiner, you are hereby promoted to the rank of *Haupsturmfuhrer*. Lead your men in dignity and in victory. You have also earned the right to carry the honor dagger. Wear it with pride in your people and in the noble tradition of your ancestors.

Use it to defend the honor of the *Fatherland* and the Führer. Your loyalty is your honor."

Himmler touched each of Eryk's shoulders with the blade and then extended the dagger toward him. Eryk, in the prescribed manner, reached out and grasped it. Their eyes met. Himmler released his grip and Eryk pulled the weapon to his chest, clicked his heels, gave the Nazi salute and then stiffly put it into the sheath on his belt.

What would his father say if he could see him now?

Would he be proud of the way his son was coming up through the ranks? Would they have this in common, this commitment to national pride and honor?

The *Reichsfuhrer* moved on down the line, uttering noble phrases, granting dignity to these uniformed men who looked to the *Third Reich* for understanding of their own manhood. The flames in the braziers licked at the darkness, illuminating young faces, revealing their eagerness, their fatigue, their determination. It was a small corner of the world, to be sure, but mighty all the same if the consensus of the men assembled counted for anything, with their sparkling new decorations and their spirits demanding new action. Beneath starched jackets, male hearts raced at the thought of the challenges to be brought down. The scent of domination was stronger than the incense thrown into the fires.

Yet, without someone with which to share it, the night's coronation was hollow. A group of *SS* men invited Eryk to pass the night with them, celebrating in the local beer halls. No doubt they would memorialize the evening in the arms of some eager *fraulein*, perhaps adding to the growing number of Führer babies and thus promoting the future of Germany.

For a moment, he considered it, but, just as suddenly, discarded the notion. His father would never have approved of such conduct. Neither, came the unexpected thought, would she.

The image of his childhood governess came floating to him through the humid night, her eyes looking deep into him, her words plunging into the fragment of conscience he still possessed.

God says there must be one man for one woman for life. That is where you will find true love, Eryk.

But there are so many pretty girls, Hauslehrerin.

Yes, Liebchen, *but God knows which pretty one is for you. You won't be truly happy with all the others.*

He wondered if it was true. How could she possibly know that? If it were so, he'd probably already ruined his chances. He was now a living rebel to everything Zelda Goldman had taught him. Her God would never want him to find happiness.

So, as the ceremony finally ended and the men were dismissed, Eryk decided that he would simply go to bed and forget the partying. He was tired anyway.

13

June, 1942
Bouschouwitz, Czechoslovakia

> *"Elegance will now disappear from Berlin along with the Jews."*
> Magda Goebbels, wife of propaganda minister Joseph Goebbels, upon observing many of her favorite Jewish designers disappearing.

The transport train had been better than Nadya expected.

The car in which she and *Tante* Zelda had ridden had been by no means plush, but it had seats and windows. The one thing it did not have, however, was a restroom. Though the trip had taken only the better part of one day, the bucket in the corner was sloshing onto the floor by the time they pulled into their destination. Nadya and *Tante* had simply made a pact not to look at it, and they had taken only small sips from the thermos they brought with them. Surely, better facilities would be provided on their arrival.

The worst part of the trip was the crying of the children and the murmurings of the people all around them. There were artists and chefs and professors in their rail car, as well as a couple fine musicians whom *Tante* knew from performances in the city. None of them really understood where they were being taken. Most tried to be positive, pointing to the fact that they had been made to purchase actual tickets and choosing to believe that their Berlin neighbors would never be part of something sinister. There were hardships, of course; it was wartime. Jews had always been on the lowest rung when society was separated into classes. No nation on earth welcomed them unequivocally. But eventually, history had taught them, if they were patient and cooperative, the tide would turn and they would be able to return to their homes and their lives. It had always been thus.

But, in her own way of thinking, Nadya wanted to bring up other things. Like the fact that she knew for certain that the lovely homes of friends transported earlier were now being occupied by Nazi officers and their families. Like the increasing hostility they had all seen, growing by the week, the day, the minute. Like the way they were all packaged and processed through the rail system like so much cattle, without regard for their professions or past. Like the way the guards ogled the women and pushed the little children and disrespected the men. These things made her very unsure about their predicament.

Tante was thinking the same kinds of things, she was sure. Though outwardly she appeared calm and resolute, Zelda herself had taught her niece to think from all the angles, to be observant, and always to have a plan.

Inwardly, *Tante* must be suffering a great deal. Not only had she lost her coveted position with the *Philharmonic*, but she had been forced to leave behind so much music as well as the heirloom furniture and china. Of course, those things had been lost in the first move they made to the ghetto section. But still, knowing they were now gone for good must hurt. The only luxurious bit of their past life they had brought with them was *Tante's* beloved violin. With this, they had, so far, refused to part.

The trip had taken longer than it should have because they were discovering that transport trains didn't move very fast. A couple times, they'd had to stop on the tracks and wait for other trains to go through first. They'd pushed up all the windows that would open, but still the air was stagnated and hot. Babies fussed and little children with flushed cheeks and wide eyes laid their heads against the seats in pitiful exhaustion. There was no water in the train car; those who hadn't brought any with them looked miserable.

Finally, they'd arrived at their destination. According to the rail signs on the route, they were now in Czechoslovakia. The small station sat forlornly by itself with a post that read *Bouschouwitz*. Everyone was in a hurry to get off the train, to get outside, to go somewhere.

But where were they to go? Where were the living places, the factories, the city?

They had crowded off the train, pushing and shoving to get their luggage and stay together.

"Silence!"

The words came from a loudspeaker. Nadya glimpsed an *SS* officer holding a megaphone, standing a small distance from the platform. He was a tall, handsome young man. He was smiling.

"Silence! Ladies and gentlemen, you have arrived in your new home. For your protection, you will see our Czech policeman assisting you. Please do not be alarmed. The town where you are being resettled is only a short distance, only three kilometers. Stay together in groups; take your hand luggage and your children and follow the road. Exercise is healthy and will prepare you for your new life. For the elderly and sick, there is transportation provided. Any luggage which is marked you may leave here. It will be delivered to you at your new accommodations. When you arrive in the town, you will be taken to your new quarters and given your work assignment. Welcome to the *Führer's* special town for the Jews – *Theresianstadt*. Now, form a column and begin walking. Thank you."

They began to walk up a dirt road, carrying their luggage, Nadya wondered again at the horrific changes that had come about in a matter of a few days. It had been only a week since they had received the evacuation notice. It seemed like years. In spite of every bit of logic she knew she should exercise, she found herself wishing to be back in the decrepit ghetto which they had disliked so much. It had been crumbling and crowded and smelly, but right now she would have run to it gladly.

On either side of them were fields. Electric poles rose here and there. Uniformed Czech policemen walked beside them, silent, watchful. The road was uneven and dusty. A woman behind her gagged as she coughed on dusty air.

Beside her, *Tante* carried a bag in one hand and her violin case with the other. Wherever she was, *Tante* would make music. She had insisted that Nadya bring her instrument as well. They had stuffed a few favorite pieces of music into their luggage. The rest they would have to call up from memory or create.

The early evening air was humid and her clothes felt damp from perspiration. What she wouldn't give for a cool drink and her chair on their balcony in their little home back in Berlin's professional district. How long it seemed since last summer when she had enjoyed such luxury! What would their new dwelling be like? They had heard that many of the upper class among their evacuation group had paid exorbitant fees for a better place than average. Nadya wished that she and *Tante* had done the same. Surely, having a comfortable room would make even a resettlement camp more bearable!

The sun inched farther down the skyline as they trudged along the road. The people from their transport walked in groups, some as families, some as thrown-together friends. The elderly who had opted not to take the cart inched along, often stopping to catch their breath.

The children walked too, many carrying luggage or pails or quilts. There wasn't much talking. It seemed they had used their words on the train. What was there to say now? Whatever was ahead, they had no alternative. They had to keep moving but they didn't have to talk about it.

Now on one side of them was a kind of earthen wall which stretched as far as Nadya could see. It was quite high but above it, she thought she glimpsed chimneys. Lots of them. What sort of place was this? Was the special city behind this wall of earth? Were the chimneys from factories? They had been told that there would be work assignments. What would they be doing?

Suddenly, Nadya felt chilled despite the warm evening air. What if she and *Tante* were separated? How would she survive alone? She stepped closer to the older woman and sneaked a sideways glance at her face. There was fatigue in her expression, but the familiar calmness in her eyes. Nadya felt reassured just seeing it. Whatever this was, they would face it together.

Now, they were approaching the entrance to this strange city. A bricked structure was built into the earthen wall; an arched gate held a small opening. To get to it, they had to cross a bridge which spanned a moat. The bridge was quite wide, but the gate itself was very narrow. Along the bridge, guards were stationed, holding machine guns. They wore the black uniform of the *SS*.

Hardly any of the group was walking fast. The heat and fatigue and perhaps fear had drained their emotional resources. But as they approached the entrance to whatever lay ahead of them, a bit of energy seemed to rouse Nadya. Others must have felt it too for there was a kind of surge toward the gate, as if no one wanted to be last.

The narrow entrance became jammed as families tried to hurry through together. The guards went to work, pulling some out of line, giving orders.

"There is room for all. Do not get out of line. All Jews will have a place in this special city."

When their turn came, Nadya walked through at the same time as *Tante*. They entered an immense courtyard area. Large stone buildings with framed windows and arched entrances surrounded them. A truck of luggage was being unloaded. Bewildered, the new arrivals were talking and gesturing and trying to figure out what to do next.

"*Achtung*!

A man on a raised platform lifted his hand to signal for silence and began to speak into a microphone on a stand.

"Welcome, fellow Jews. Welcome to *Theresienstadt*. I am the elder of the *Jewish Council*; my name is Dr. Jakob Edelstein. Here, we govern ourselves and all the work here is done by Jews. Everyone who is able to work will be expected to contribute to our community. Though this life will be somewhat different from where you have come, you will soon adjust to the way we do things here. There are certain rules which must be obeyed for the good of all. Please cooperate. Those who insist on disregarding the rules will be treated accordingly. The Council will do all we can to assist you in making the transition to your new life. Now, please move to the registration tables to begin processing."

He motioned to several long tables set up to his left behind which sat men in business suits. From where she stood, Nadya could see crates and paperwork on the tables. The people around began to form lines in front of the tables. Then, she saw a man in an *SS* uniform step to the microphone on the platform.

"Jews, you will now surrender your valuables, all money, jewelry, cigarettes and cosmetics; these things are prohibited in *Theresienstadt*. Do not try to hide anything. After you have registered, you will be examined by *Reich* doctors and then deloused. All of this is part of the preparation for your new life. *Raus!*"

Nadya looked up at *Tante* as they took another step closer to the table. *Tante* was holding her violin close. She closed her eyes briefly, then met Nadya's eyes with a grim smile. Nadya wondered if musical instruments were considered valuable and thus forbidden here by the *SS*. If so, how would her aunt be able to cope without her music?

14

January 1943, Berlin, Germany
Gestapo Headquarters
Prince Albrecht Strasse

> *Whoever can conquer the street will one day conquer the state,*
> *for every form of power politics and any dictatorship-run*
> *state has its roots in the street.*
> Joseph Goebbels

Gestapo Sturmbannführer Rolf Beckmann fingered the stripe on his sleeve and smiled. It had been a long time coming. But he was finally where he belonged – a member of the security police in Germany's Nazi state.

He had long dreamed of being stationed in the capital, of working with the men of the High Command. Now, he had arrived. He had an office with arched ceilings, a mahogany desk and a secretary.

Life had not been easy for Rolf Beckmann. But he was determined to make it yield, and slowly, steadily, his luck was changing. He was beginning to feel that the wheels of fate were turning in his direction. In Adolf Hitler, he had early sensed a man who could wield power with extreme cunning. From his own trenches in politics and military service, he had kept an eye on the *Führer's* rise. By ingratiating himself to his superiors along the way, he'd been able to attend enough state dinners and gala affairs to observe the man in various settings.

He was a fascinating study, a mix of toddler temper, artistic eye and dictator attitude. He could charm women at a formal banquet and sway crowds in a huge arena. But he could also scream with fervor when addressing the lawmakers in the *Reichstag* and expect loyalty to the death from the SS, his protection squad. He was colorful and bland; moody but charismatic, terrifying yet pitiful. He was a vegetarian, a music lover, and a painter. He advocated the glories of peasant life and folk dance. Yet, he was a hypnotist, a fanatic, and a despot. He privately urged death and destruction.

Beckmann was under no illusions about the unpredictability of the man. There were risks when harnessing oneself to someone with such variance in nature. But the lure of power carried greater pull than the hint of danger. He had witnessed just the smallest taste of what was possible at the Nuremberg rallies; it had been enough to intoxicate him and drive him to get more.

Of course, it would take a while to get to the place where he could benefit from some of that prestige and power, but he was on his way. He would bide his time. His patience was paying off.

He settled down into his desk chair and picked up a cigar. Life was getting better all the time.

March 1943, Terezin, Czechoslovakia
Theresienstadt Ghetto

Zelda Goldman closed her violin case and snapped the latches. The evening concert had been a success. In all the nights she had spent in plush opera halls with bejeweled and fur-caped audiences, none could compare to the stark beauty of music performed in *Theresienstadt*. Here there was a bleak edge to life that drove the listeners to dive deep into the sounds of Mozart and Beethoven. They sat on hard wooden chairs and wore soiled and faded clothing, yet no audience had ever drunk more fully of the balm that music is to the soul.

The Psalmist had written "How shall we sing the Lord's song in a strange land?" (Psalm 137:4)

Zelda had come up with an answer for herself. She'd play her song because it was His, not hers. He had given the gift of music; she could use it anywhere.

Many of her colleagues played to forget, to lose themselves in the beauty of melody and rhythm, to revel in a world where things were once again balanced and predictable. This was a tempting approach to her work as a musician. But, at the end of the concert, one must always put up the case, fold the music and trudge back to the crowded bunks and stinking rooms. One must go to bed with a still-hungry stomach and with the threat of deportation looming. It was not enough to forget for a few hours. This would never make life bearable. Music as an opiate was a dismal failure in the long term.

Yesterday, a woman who sat beside her in the orchestra voiced what many of the musicians of *Theresienstadt* believed. "We have lost our community, our relationships, all which defined us. We are gone; nothing is left. Life for us is no more. Let us try to forget for a few moments with our music."

Thinking about it now, Zelda smiled in peace and confidence and whispered to the walls.. "Oh no, my dear, we have not lost it all. There is our relationship with our God. It goes on and on. We are never lost."

She constantly reminded herself of the connection to the God above through the medium of music. The notes and timing and rests were all His, all part of His marvelous creation. She had always felt that He came close to the musician who played with this understanding. She had felt Him often at her very elbow, and the music was sweeter than anything she could have done on her own.

Here in Theresienstadt she had done her best to play for Him. Even as she looked out on starving children and hopeless adults, she drew her bow in faith and played the strings with resolve. Not that she was above the anguish that living here brought; far from it. The desolate life of the "paradise" ghetto could chill even the most optimistic heart. But Zelda had learned through many hard years that bleakness cannot separate the soul from its Maker, and while He granted her the opportunity to use her musical gift, she would do it in His honor.

But no one else knew that tonight was her last concert. Maybe forever.

She had received the deportation notice while at rehearsal. Her number was on the list for tomorrow's train. Such an offhand thing for such a life-changing event.

She didn't know the destination. But, wherever it was, it most likely would not be an improvement over her present conditions. As she stood and smoothed her hand over the skirt she tried so hard to keep nice for these events, Zelda looked out over the darkening room and located her niece. Nadya would now be alone in the world, her parents dead, her aunt deported. What would become of her?

She felt the heat of tears in her eyes. *Dear Father in heaven, please watch over her. For now, I cannot. It is out of my hands. I ask You, my Lord, do not forsake her.*

She dabbed the tears with a quick hand and then pushed the music stand out of her way, picked up her instrument case, and started toward the back. She would hide the instrument, and she would leave her precious niece in the hands of the Master.

PART TWO
Kursk to Kassel

15

July, 1943
Field outside the village of Prokhorovka, Russia

> *We have seriously underestimated the Russians,*
> *the extent of their country, and the treachery of their climate.*
> *This is the revenge of reality.*
> Colonel-General Guderian, *November 9, 1941, in a letter to his wife.*

When Eryk awoke, it was dusk. It took him a couple seconds to recall why he was piled in a heap in the mud. But one thing he knew immediately was that his head was pounding and his arm was throbbing and sticky. Then the last memory fragments of the battle kicked in and he closed his eyes as if he could stop the onslaught. Nothing could ever make him forget the sight of his charred *panzer*. They hadn't had a chance, and he would very likely have ended up in the same condition if he hadn't stepped away to reconnoiter.

All at once, he wondered if the prompting to walk to the top of the ridge and investigate had come from some other Source than merely his own instincts. In the past decade Eryk hadn't given much attention to the subject of the Almighty. In fact, the training he had received since his early days in the Hitler Youth had all but convinced him and his classmates that *they* were almighty, the potent force with which the world needed to reckon.

But he knew, deep in his consciousness, that there was more. He couldn't forget the teaching of his boyhood, words spoken with conviction and lived out before him. *She* believed that God had a hand in the living and dying of everyone. She would tell him with no hesitation that God had spared his life. However far he had journeyed away from faith, even Eryk knew there was a greater power at work in the place where he now found himself.

Rolling to a sitting position, he tried his shaky legs. They wobbled a bit as he stood and he pitched forward a little crazily, but he was mobile. His right arm hung at a bizarre angle. Though he felt the throbbing and knew the pain would intensify soon, he couldn't feel it at present. Clumsily, with his left hand, he loosened the buttons on his jacket. Then, slowly, using his teeth and shaking movements, he shrugged his left arm out of the garment and, groaning when he jostled his injured arm, he somehow peeled off the other side. Sitting down again by the rock, he used it and his knee for leverage and tied the sleeves together at the wrists to make a sling. It wouldn't be the best, but maybe he could make it work. He gingerly put it around his right arm and then with his left hand, got it over his head. It pulled his injured arm up high and made him yelp with pain. He tugged at the knot at the neck and loosened it a little. Still hurt. No matter; he had to get going. Maybe, with a good amount of luck, he could make it to the German lines or another tank unit. He had to try.

He wished for a drink of water before he took off, but nothing would be left in the tank even if he had the guts to look inside. And he didn't. Without a backward glance, he started off.

Eryk regained a little of his energy as he walked, watching for planes and tanks and anything moving that bore a red star. He had several miles to cover before he could reach the rest of the *Das Reich* unit and he had only the pistol at his side and a sheathed knife. True, he was dangerous with either of these in his hand, but he did not prefer to defend himself at close range.

The sky was now beginning to streak with shades of purple and gold as dusk set in. He glanced at his watch. Maybe if he kept going, he could rejoin the ranks by dawn. His stomach rumbled, and he tasted ashes in his mouth. His clothing smelled of burning things, and he knew his mind was seared with the horrible images of the last few hours. Nothing in his training had quite prepared him to watch his own crew burst into flames before his eyes. Eryk had seen his share of dead men; the *SS* were well acquainted with death and prided themselves on their indifference to their own, but the responsibility he felt for his men made him almost beside himself with grief over their loss.

A couple hours later, Eryk saw the outline of buildings in the distance. He had no way of knowing if the village had been captured or not. But he knew he had to stop soon to rest. And he needed food. The moon was now faintly shining, its crescent shape reminding him of the moon and sickle symbol of the Red Army.

Curse the Russians! Barbaric Bolsheviks!

Coming nearer the cluster of huts, Eryk walked slower, listening for the sounds of humans and animals, especially dogs.

It was a typical Russian village, its hovels made of boards, some at odd angles, others leaning as if they were tired of the bleak life they endured on the steppes. The buildings were huddled close together with sheds for animals packed between. He saw no signs of life. Creeping up to the nearest house, he backed against the wall and sidled up to a window. A curtain fluttered in the night air; craning his neck to see inside, he glimpsed bowls on a rough table but no fire in the hearth. He heard no voices. Crouching down, he slipped up to the next dwelling. A similar scene greeted him there. He kept walking, searching. The village appeared deserted. Had they left of their own accord?

He decided to take advantage of the food and shelter for the night. He'd look for the unit in the morning. Cautiously, he pulled open a door and stepped inside. Moving to the part that served as a kitchen, he searched for food. A loaf of dark bread lay wrapped in a towel and the beginnings of a stew of some sort was in a pot on a shelf. He grabbed both of them and sat down on the floor, trying to stay out of sight. He bit into the bread; it was tough and grainy, but it was food. He tore off a piece and chewed it hungrily.

Then, he heard a mewing sound, feeble and soft. At first, he thought it must be a cat and kept eating. But he heard it again. This time, it became more of a whimper.

Eryk put down his meal and unsnapped his holster, slowly reaching over his body and pulling out his Luger with his left hand. Keeping it down at his side, he lowered himself to a crawl position and inched toward the door, listening to determine the direction of the sound. It was awkward, trying to squirm along with an injured arm. It was beginning to hurt in earnest.

Opening the door, he stayed in the shadows as he crawled painstakingly from shack to shack, peering intently into every corner. As he rose to stand by the last one, there was a thump to his right, then a low cry. He whipped around, pointing his weapon at the spot.

As his eyes settled on the object, he could make out a huddled form, thrashing and moaning. He took a couple steps nearer and then drew back.

A Russian woman lay in a heap on the dirty floor, her skirt tangled, her hair matted with blood. Beside her lay a tiny body, face down. Her hand patted the baby tenderly; her eyes stared, hollow, vacant. She moaned again and again. Blood was seeping through her dress with every beat of her heart.

A dying Slavic civilian. He had no duty here. Eryk started to turn away, holstering his Luger, his hands fumbling in the task. He was still unsteady on his own feet after his ordeal that day.

Then he heard a hoarse whisper. "*Ushli*."

His Russian wasn't fluent, but he knew a bit of the language. All officers had to. The word she spoke meant *gone*. Was she speaking of her family, the villagers, everyone? Of perhaps the hated *SS*? Had this been the path of his own unit?

Whoever she spoke of, whoever had done this, was not coming back. Not in time either to help her or to finish her off. There was no way she'd make it. What did it matter? She wasn't a German woman, and he had to find his division. Soon.

He turned back to the shadows, and as he did, his eye caught a glint of something in the rising moonlight.

It was a silver Jewish star on a chain, clutched in her hand. The fingers of her right hand were wrapped tightly around it. And a trickle of red was running down her arm onto it.

Suddenly, Eryk was seeing the exact same star, held in the hand of a woman who embraced a sobbing little boy on her lap.

"*Don't cry,* Liebchen. Your Mutte *will be alright.* "

"But she was crying when they took her away."

"Yes, I know, Eryk. But they are going to help her. You will see. All will be well."

The boy touched the woman's hand with his chubby one and was surprised to feel something in her grasp that was pointed and cool. He lifted it with his fingers.

'What is this?"

"It's the Star of David. It represents my people and my God."
"Are your people good?"
"Not always, *Liebchen*. But my God is. He is faithful and merciful."
"Like you, ..."
"I hope so, Eryk. And also like the man you will become someday."

"*Vody.*" The guttural voice of the present whipped Eryk from the scenes of the past. He understood that word too. It was the one whispered in every language by the dying. *Water.*

He would give her water, though he knew he shouldn't. He was wasting time here. But he opened his flask and held it to her lips, though his injury made it impossible for him to help her raise her limp head. She tried to drink through cracked lips, but only gurgled, the water spilling out of the corners of her mouth and running down her neck. But her eyes looked at him gratefully.

"*Spasibo.*"

He found it ironic that she was thanking a member of the *SS* when no doubt his unit or one like it had decimated her village and inflicted her suffering. The other residents of this unfortunate village were probably lying in a mass grave nearby. While the *Panzer* units focused on fighting units, infantry often destroyed the villages in their path.

The woman suddenly gasped and gurgled and gripped his arm with her free hand. Then she went totally limp as the air *whhhhksed* from her lungs. Eryk loosened her hand from his sleeve, and it fell back onto the filthy mud floor. There wasn't time to bury her or her infant even if he had two good arms to do so. He would have to leave them to whatever or whoever came by next.

But he couldn't leave the star. Making his decision, Eryk pried open her still-warm fingers and took the talisman. It was wet with the woman's blood. He picked up a fold of her skirt and wiped it clean. Then he palmed it and slid it into his trousers' pocket. Maybe the woman would forgive him for stealing her star; he *had* tried to help her, a little.

But standing there in the moonlight, Eryk felt the fingers of shame, the unwelcome emotion that was becoming familiar to him. He turned his back and walked away. The sooner he got out of this village and found his unit, the better.

16

July, 1943
Near Kassel, Germany
Arbeitslager

> *The prisoners [transferred to labor camps] would have been spared a great deal of misery if they had been taken straight into the gas chambers at Auschwitz.*
> Rudolf Höss, Commandant of Auschwitz.

In the new social system created by the Nazis, the camp culture was certainly the lowest form of existence. There, behind the iron gates, men, women and children deemed to belong in its confines were kept in conditions thought to befit their status. Jews, of course, ranked lowest, even under the heading of subhuman races. They were considered no better than an offending piece of dung, a revolting bit of waste to be cleansed from the earth.

There were slits of pink showing through the gray morning as a line of figures shuffled into the massive building. Their lives consisted of work and sleep. They lived for the good of the *Reich,* and by its goodwill too, if being partially fed and partially clothed so that one could work could be called goodwill.

The people of Germany had extended this privilege to some of its enemies. True, many were gassed upon arrival; but many were also selected for work. The many subcamps of Dachau and Buchenwald and others were fed by a stream of human beings coming through the gates to labor that the *Fatherland* might thrive.

There was variety in the work, though not at the choice of the laborers. Some were busy with sewing machines while others assembled mechanical pieces. There was construction to be done, roads to be paved, and aircraft to be built. There were even a few selected to "contribute" to the medical field, though the only thing required of them was that they be breathing when they entered the laboratory; guinea pigs only need to be usable. Still others were chosen for more specialized work, helping the *Reich* in the production of armaments. Men and women in striped clothing worked on airplanes and tanks, outfitting the enemy with the means to rid the land of their friends and neighbors and family.

Zelda Goldman wasn't quite sure how she came to be part of this last group. She wasn't particularly knowledgeable about armored vehicles and wasn't an especially healthy specimen of a worker. Her heart didn't always keep its rhythm and her long-distance eyesight was poor, especially since her eyeglasses had been taken for the coffers of the *Reich*. But she had always been good at bluffing, and perhaps that is what made the difference. She had seen many who hung their heads and demurred, even in the face of uniforms and jackboots. But she could never do that. If she must march to her death, then she would go with a head held high and a posture that bespoke dignity.

As it turned out, she only marched to and from the factory every day, much better than a final descent into the block walls of a gas chamber. She could glimpse a bit of light in the early dawn when her shift began and then catch a breath of cool breeze at night when she plodded to the barracks. She had fared better than most; the meal rations for workers in the armament plants were slightly better than for those who labored in the fields or on the roads. The *Reich* needed their planes and *panzers*. Even a Jewess from Theresienstadt had value when it came to the assembly line at *Henschel and Son Werks*.

Today promised to be like yesterday and tomorrow a repeat of them both – a day filled with noise and sweat and aching eyes and backs. Today, she would sit at her spot on the line and fit together the little metal pieces of the instrument panel for the shining new *panzers*. It was monotonous work, and painful too because she knew the dials and gauges she assembled were destined for the fields where men would use them to maim and kill. She grieved for them, for the destruction taking place in their own souls as they used these new killing machines. She prayed for them. With every piece she placed into its casing, Zelda prayed for the *panzer* crew who would use it. She prayed for their victims and for the return of peace. She prayed for the love of God to follow them relentlessly and rescue them from the filth of battle and the stain of killing.

It wasn't a particularly noble thing to do because many times all she could feel inside was excruciating anguish. Mornings like this one added to the loss, sending emotions surging through her that she felt too broken to handle. She missed starting her day with Nadya, drinking coffee together and discussing the day's plans. In the "golden years" as she liked to think of days long past, before the war, there had been school and lessons and giggling with playmates for Nadya, and tutoring and performing for Zelda.

But when the streets of Berlin became too hostile for Jews and the schools and musical organizations disgorged them from their assemblies, the days had become different, quieter and filled with activities in their own apartment. Still, they had been together, puttering around in the soft, filtered light of morning, deriving strength from each other and leaning on one another for companionship. Zelda missed being able to see her niece working on music or stirring a pot on the stove, working around the home, and becoming a young woman. All the love she had built up for her younger brother had spilled over onto the toddler daughter he left at his untimely death. Through the years, she had clung to the girl, the only family either of them had. Their relationship was sustenance to them both, and when it was taken away, Zelda had grieved as though it were a death. Which for all she knew it could very well be. There were no certainties for either of them. She didn't even know if her niece was still alive. Was she still in the "paradise" ghetto? Or had she too been deported to some camp?

So, she prayed for the German crews, yes. But it was an exercise in spiritual discipline. The Savior's command was to love one's enemies and pray for them who persecute; she knew full well the meaning of those definitions. There were times when it took every bit of her will and all of the grace available to her from the Lord to pray for these men who dealt continually in human blood.

But when it came to Eryk, she had less trouble putting passion into her petitions. She could not hate the boy grown into a man who might one day sit behind one of these machines. She didn't know the particulars of his present life, and she was sure that Satan had not given up the bid for his soul. But he was made for so much more! He could be a powerful channel of life instead of death. So she laid her hands on the controls and asked the Father to rescue him before it was too late.

17

July, 1943, Brandenburg, Germany
Beelitz-Heilstatten Hospital

> *One basic principle must be the absolute rule for the S.S. men. We must be honest, decent, loyal, and comradely to members of our own blood and nobody else.*
> Heinrich Himmler

Even in the fog of his semi-consciousness, Eryk knew the star was gone. It was a mystical kind of knowing before he could rationalize that his uniform was missing and he wore a hospital gown. Instinctively, he was certain it was gone.

He pushed his eyelids open and without moving, glanced around the room noting the stark cleanliness of his surroundings. After weeks in the theater of battle fighting mud, blood and the stench of death, the room with its antiseptic aura was welcome, if lacking in cheer.

He appeared to be bandaged in several places, and he wasn't able to move his right arm. He wiggled his toes, celebrating the fact that they obeyed his wishes. He turned his head slowly from side to side and up and down and tried to go back in his mind, dredging up the events that had landed him here. He could remember the fierce battle, the dark haze hanging over the field, and the explosions all around his *Tiger*. He closed his eyes against the memory of his crew, their faces dancing before him as he had last seen them, intent on their duties, awaiting his orders, loyal to the end. Then, the long trek through the Russian plains, trying to find his unit and when he did, the discovery that his wound was quite serious and becoming infected. He could recall only bits and pieces after that. But obviously, he had made it to a hospital. Where? He looked around for any sign.

It was bright outside, so it was daytime. There were German words on the bottle sitting on the bedside stand. So maybe he wasn't a prisoner after all. But he didn't see any of his personal possessions. That could be a problem.

He raised himself up on his left elbow and scanned the floor, trying to look under the bed. He leaned over as far as possible and then felt himself getting woozy. He sank back against the pillows, irritated with his limitations, refusing to think the worst.

He heard footsteps and looking up, Eryk spied a nurse in the hall, her uniform swishing with her practiced movements. He tried his voice. "*Bitte!*"

The nurse turned, and Eryk saw that she was merely a girl masquerading as a woman. How young did nurses come these days?

She walked to his bed and took his arm to feel his pulse. "You're awake, *Herr Captain*. How are you feeling?"

"My arm hurts."

"You have had surgery, *Hauptsturmführer* Steiner. I will get you something for the pain. But first I must let the doctor know you are awake."

"Have I been unconscious for long?"

"Yes, since the surgery, you have been under sedation. We did not want you to injure your arm while you were recovering from your ordeal."

Steiner looked at the bandaged lump that he could not move. The wrappings were tight; he focused on drawing a breath. "How bad is the injury?"

"I will have the doctor talk to you as soon as he gets here."

He reached out with his good hand and caught hers. She was so very young, about the age of his sister Annaliese, too young for the sights she now saw and for the brisk manner she wore like a mantle. She looked at his hand, then into his eyes. "What is it?"

"Please, I must know, where is my clothing?"

"Your uniform?"

"Yes, I really must have it."

"*Captain*, it was removed when you were transported here from the field hospital. I don't think it was in very good condition."

Steiner clutched her hand. "Did they burn it?"

"Maybe, if it was contaminated. Did you come in contact with any toxic substances in the battle?"

He closed his eyes and remembered the acrid smoke billowing from ruined tanks. "I don't know. Probably not."

"Then it was probably just put into the hospital garbage."

"Is that emptied every day?"

"Usually, but with the shortage of workers these days, sometimes, it doesn't get done every day."

"Would you look for me?" The request must sound pathetic but he had no other option. Whatever aura his rank held was surely lost here in this sea of human flesh who were now barely worthy of the classification as men.

The nurse looked down at him and drew in a breath. "Yes, I will, but I am afraid it might already be gone."

"Thank you." He nodded. "I'm grateful."

He released her hand, noticing the pressure marks where he had gripped her wrist. She rubbed it lightly with her other hand as she walked away from him and out the door.

~~~

Screams in the night woke him. Instantly, he was awake and tried to sit up. It took a minute for the dimly lit room to register in his mind. He was in a hospital. He was wounded. He could do nothing about the screaming. The sounds were drifting from further down the hall. Feet were walking swiftly outside the door, no doubt on the way to stop the noise.

Eryk Steiner had seen much and heard much. The *Waffen-SS* did not coddle its officers; his training had been complete in every respect. He had been trained to handle battle stress with questions. What could be the cause of the screams? Physical pain? Grief? Anger? If he could figure out the reason, he could then file away the image or sound with the cause and refuse to let it enter his conscious mind again. It worked remarkably well. In this situation, since he didn't know the reason for the screams down the hall, he assigned it to pain and blocked it out.

Shifting his weight as well as possible with his unwieldy bandages, he wondered if the nurse he had talked to earlier had found his uniform. He barely remembered the doctor coming into his room before he swallowed the pill that soothed him back into a world apart from battles and questions and missing stars. But now, he wondered what would happen if he didn't find it. Or worse, what would happen if it had already been found by someone else. There was no explanation that would remove the possible consequences.

His legs twitched with anxiety. His mind refused to relax, and in spite of his battle-hardened soul, a desire to weep crawled up within him. Was he falling apart? Was he experiencing battle shock? Were the rigors of war too much for him? If only he could forget the Eastern front, the trenches, the graves, the bodies. In spite of himself, faces rose before him, nameless faces, haunted faces, hungry, sick faces. He turned his head to the wall, willing them away, gritted his teeth and closed his eyes. But they came anyway, bobbing eerily toward him, mouths open in silent wails.

"No!" His own voice startled him. He raised a hand to his sweating forehead as the nurse dashed to his bed.

"*Captain*, are you all right?"

"Yes, *danke*." Eryk hid his hand beneath the sheet. It jerked in rebellion. "Just a little trouble going back to sleep."

"Would you like a sedative?" The nurse pulled the sheets tighter and smoothed them down around his chest.

He shook his head. "No, I'll be alright. I'm sorry I disturbed you."

"That's fine, *Herr Hauptsturmführer*. I will look in on you later."

He listened to her footsteps recede down the hallway, trying to hold onto the image of her young face, to fill his mind with youth instead of death. It must be this place of suffering that was causing the trouble. He was an *SS* officer after all and accustomed to death and dying and being the cause of it. He had seen scores of dead faces since the war began. As a defender of the *Reich* and the Fatherland, he could not avoid these sights. Disturbing images were the price a soldier paid to participate in the struggle, to preserve the honor of his people. It was unusual for him to think about them. He dealt with them as he had been taught, resolutely, impassively, and then tucked them away in a file never to be opened. But tonight, he was upset. That was the reason.

Tomorrow, he had to find the star. No matter what. His life depended on it. He needed it in his hands again.

As he drifted toward sleep, Eryk imagined he could see gentle eyes. His playful hands held a bird's nest, and he looked up at the woman standing beside him with all the rambunctious joy of a small boy.

"Where is the mother?"

"She's gone, Liebchen. Perhaps a hunter found her."

"But why?" The little boy's eyes were getting misty. "Her babies need her. She wasn't hurting anybody."

The eyes grew sad. "Maybe he just liked to kill."

"I hate killing. I will never kill anything."

Kind eyes gazed into his. "I hope you will never have a killer's heart, Eryk. While sometimes it is necessary to kill in order to eat or to protect those you love, it is never right to love to kill." She knelt in front of him. "I pray you will be a protector, not a killer, Liebchen. Oh, God, make it so."

He put his hands on her shoulders and looked into her eyes. "It's all right, Lehrerin. I'll remember. I'll be the answer to your prayers." He lifted a grubby hand and wiped at a tear on her cheek.

She caught his hand and held it to her face. "Of course, you will, Eryk. You have been the answer to my prayers for a long time now." She smiled and got to her feet. "Now shall we go and see if we can feed these little ones with an eye dropper?"

Nodding, he took her hand and they walked through the still forest toward the chateau, holding the nest as one would a cask of treasure.

And as Eryk dropped off to sleep, he thought he could see the green of her sweater as she draped it around the boy's small shoulders.

18

July, 1943, Brandenburg, Germany
Beelitz-Heilstatten Hospital

> *So far you have been treated as an officer and a gentleman, but don't think that this will go on if you don't behave better than you have done. . . .*
> Reinhard Heydrich to captured British agent

"I found your uniform, *Herr Captain*."

Eryk looked up from his breakfast tray as the young nurse walked to his bed with a bundle in her hands. She held it out to him.

He reached for it with his good hand. "Thank you very much. I hope it wasn't much trouble."

She smiled. "It wasn't too hard. My brother works with the Hitler Youth in sanitation services. He found it for me in the hospital's burn bins."

Eryk forked a bite of eggs. "Thank him for me. Or, better yet, have him stop by and I'll thank him myself."

"He'd love that, *Hauptsturmführer* Steiner. Meeting a *panzer* commander will be thrilling for him." She poured some water in his glass and winked. "Of course, it's a thrill for nurses as well."

Eryk kept his gaze down. Better to pretend he hadn't heard her last statement. It bothered him that another pretty German teenager was ready to offer herself to an *SS* man, playing the game so nobly touted by Himmler and the *Reich*. "*Führer* babies" were being born all over Germany. He had friends who were the fathers of these infants. To be honest, he had been tempted a few times himself. Battle fatigue and loneliness attacked a man's code of honor and left him vulnerable. But he hadn't been able to bring himself to take advantage of a girl who could have been one of his own sisters in similar circumstances. While he understood the need for a rising population for the German people, he refused to believe it should happen at the expense of their daughters and sisters and cousins. These girls of the *German League* were idealistic in their own way, full of the rhetoric of the *Reich* and afresh with young passion; it was a toxic mix that Himmler used to advantage in his push for a birthing boom. But so far, the predominant emotion it caused in Eryk Steiner was revulsion.

He put down his fork and touched her hand, looking into her eyes. "You're a very pretty girl, much too pretty for an old Captain like me. Wait for that special young man to come along and marry you and give you a home and children."

She brought her hand to her throat. He had to strain to hear her muffled words. "Don't you know there may not be time for waiting? Who knows what is going to happen in Germany? Better to grab a little happiness today than to be lonely."

Eryk laid down his napkin and shook his head, finding it strange that a man of battle should become a counselor against despair. But then, he should know; he fought its downdraft every day. "You're wrong. Bad choices do not bring happiness. You know that, don't you? We must continue to hold honor both for ourselves and for Germany. It's a battle each of us can fight, wherever we are."

She was looking at him with stricken eyes. "What if one has already made bad choices?"

What indeed? If Eryk knew the answer to that dilemma, he would be the most popular man in the *Reich* just now.

"I suppose we must try to redeem the past with the future." *And hope no one discovers the depth of the past.*

The girl picked up his finished tray and gave him a small smile. "You're quite a philosopher for a *Panzer* commander, you know. Maybe I should bring my whole family to see you, not just my brother!"

Eryk lifted his hand in mock salute. "I'll be glad to see anyone you bring."

"Careful! That dressing on your arm needs to stay in place, especially if you hope to be released this week."

"Do you think it will be that soon?" He hadn't dared to hope it would.

"It's possible." She started away from his bed. "But don't leave until you see Heinrich."

Eryk pulled the bundle she'd brought toward him. Was it possible that it was still there? He felt the fabric, noticing the tears and stains and the acrid smell of it. With his left hand, he fingered every inch of the jacket and trousers, but found nothing.

The star was gone, and he could soon be a dead man. Sighing, Eryk tossed the clothing onto the floor and lay back against the pillows, closing his eyes. A little sleep would be good right now. The day would be busy soon enough.

"Were you looking for something, *Captain*?"

Suddenly wide awake, Eryk looked up to see the young nurse standing by his bed.

"Um, yes. My notes from the battlefield. I thought they might still be in the pocket of my jacket, but I can't find them." He tried out a small smile, as though it were not important.

She came closer. "Heinrich didn't find any notes."

"Oh, then I guess they must have fallen out in the irksome Russian mud." He turned his good palm upward and grimaced.

"But he did find this." She reached into the pocket of her apron. With her other hand, she felt for his good hand under the sheet. Glancing around the ward, she pressed into his palm a sharp, metal object. He fingered it, knowing already that the star had found its way back to him.

Her face held a question that her lips didn't ask. But he could read all the implications in her eyes. She was young, inquisitive, trained to be loyal, and the *Gestapo* lingered in the hospital corridors like so many vultures. The pieces of his demise were all there.

She looked at him and gave a brief nod. "You have a good reason, I'm sure, *Herr Hauptsturmführer*. Heinrich insisted it must be important evidence from the battle. He knew you would want to have it."

He met her eyes and held her gaze. "He is a smart boy. Be sure you wake me when he stops by."

"I'll do that, *Herr Captain*." She straightened the sheets on his bed. "Now, get some rest."

Eryk watched her retreating back and calculated the chances that she wasn't going to report him. Maybe the odds were better than he thought. Or maybe she would smile when they hanged him.

19

July, 1943, Brandenburg, Germany
Beelitz-Heilstatten Hospital

> *One must not be sentimental in these matters.*
> *If we did not fight the Jews, they would destroy us.*
> *It's a life-and-death struggle between the Aryan race and the Jewish bacillus.*
> Joseph Goebbels, diary excerpt from March 27, 1942

Eryk awoke when he felt fingers probing his arm, unwinding the bandage and turning it this way and that. The surgeon stood over him, talking in low tones to his assistant who was making notes on a chart. The sun was shining brightly by this time outside the window, and Eryk could hear the clatter of dishes in the ward. He must have dozed until lunchtime.

Noticing his patient was awake, the doctor sat on the edge of the bed and met Eryk's eyes. "We are going to release you, *Hauptsturmführer* Steiner." His tone said it was not a favor.

"Thank you, Doctor. I'm grateful for your care."

"I believe we should be thanking you, sir, for the service you are doing for the *Reich*. I am aware of the great danger you have seen in recent days." The doctor removed his spectacles and wiped one lens with the sleeve of his white jacket. "It is a pity we can't let you remain here and rest longer."

Eryk looked straight into the man's gaze. "Doctor, I insist on being released at the soonest possible moment. I have responsibilities to attend."

The doctor sighed. "Yes, I know. Unfortunately, you will not be able to function at full capacity for a while."

"What do you mean?"

"The arm will take a while to heal. You were hit with shrapnel which lodged deeply and caused some nerve damage. We won't know how much until you are able to begin using it. You will need to go slowly and take therapy."

Eryk clenched his jaw and swallowed before he spoke. "Are you saying I might not regain full use of my right arm?"

"There is that possibility."

Eryk turned his head to the wall, willing the words away from him. A one-armed *panzer* commander was worthless. Not only would he be unable to function in battle, it would be highly unlikely that he could even climb inside the commander's cupola.

"What are the odds?" This was something he could understand. Numbers were solid, measurable things, unlike the nebulous promise of hope he himself had held out to the young nurse. Fool that he was, he shouldn't have tried to change her mind; probably she was right after all.

"Much of that depends on you. If you assume full battle responsibilities immediately, I can almost promise you that you will never use that arm again in its normal functions. Now, don't look at me like that. There are many duties you can manage until the healing is complete. I will give you a signed statement for your superior detailing what I recommend." The doctor stood. "I also recommend that you give it to him." He took a step back and let out his breath. "If you want to return to your *Panzers*, you'll follow my advice."

Eryk nodded and watched him walk off. It wasn't the news he wanted to hear, but still he should probably be thankful. It could have been so much worse. He had barely felt the wound when the Russian planes had obliterated his *Tiger*. The shock of the blast and the trauma of seeing his crew sent to their deaths must have kept him from feeling the physical pain, the cause of the red rivulets that he now remembered seeing running down the black sleeve of his uniform.

His crew. Hausser, Ebengrosser. Krugel. Hummel. Dead.

They had trained on that *Tiger* together, had coaxed it from assembly line blush to monster status. Now, the laughs they had shared, the battles they had weathered, the victories they had gained were all memories. They would never operate a *Panzer* together again. He would miss them. Grieve them. Revenge their deaths if he got the chance, although that was unlikely anytime soon. He would not get back to the battlefields of the Russian front.

But battlefields were not all that the vast land in the East held tight in its barren bosom. There were other kinds of fields as well, fields where death occurred in a grim choreography until the earth fairly heaved with its sodden victims. Eryk had long ago closed off the memories of that day in Poland when he had glimpsed the execution in a field. But others of his comrades in arms were not as close-mouthed, nor felt the need to be. He hadn't ever invited them to share their experiences, but many of them simply talked about their experiences. In the military community of which he was a part, serving in an execution squad was a type of bragging rights. Those who did it usually talked about it. Though he tried not to think about it, somehow lying on his back, surrounded by antiseptics and cleanliness, his mind pulled him heedlessly back to an earlier conversation in his barracks. He had been a young cadet then, awed at the power wielded by those over him. And he had never forgotten the words he heard as he sat on his bunk and polished his boots.

> *We worked all day, in the rain or sun, didn't matter. The Jews kept coming, by the truckload. We put 30 men from the village to work digging the pits. And we made them work fast. That was the hard part, the digging. It takes a long time for men to get a hole large enough for the rows of bodies. The killing part was easy. The crazy Jews didn't even resist. Not even when they had to undress and take off their jewelry. They held their babies in their arms and calmly stepped up to the pit. But they didn't look down. They just stared straight ahead and then fell over when they got their bullet. Of course, many times, we threw the baby in the pit before we shot the mother; no sense in wasting a bullet. It was a mess in the pit, a squishy muck of blood and waste and gore with all the bodies. Some of the officers had to walk in it when someone hadn't died and was trying to get out; they would shoot them again with a pistol. My captain said it was like walking on china, the bones of the little ones crunched.*

Even now, two years later, Eryk felt incredulous when he remembered those words. Not at the grisly description, for he had heard and seen much, but at the casual tone in which the soldier had reported the event. Death for the killing squads had ceased to be horrible; it was simply routine, as much a part of their lives as slaughtering chickens was for the village butcher. The Jews were the human livestock of which the German people must dispose. It was a job to be done. In the Eastern lands, the Special Action Commandos, the *Einsatzgruppen*, had accomplished the job in fields and pits.

Predictably, his thoughts turned to the one Jew he had known very well and his hand reached for the star hidden in the mattress, his contraband treasure. What had become of her, his childhood governess? Where was she spending the war? In a ghetto? Perhaps in a labor camp like *Matthausen* or *Ravensbruck*? And what did it matter? She was *Juden*, after all. She had been a gentle and caring governess certainly, but that did not bind him to her in any way.

But even as he thought it, he knew it was untrue. His soul was bound to hers more closely than anyone else knew. He owed his life to her. All this, the uniform, the status, the promotions, were his because she had made it possible for him to live to adulthood. Now, with the manhood he had achieved, he had forgotten her, abandoned her. He now used his station in life to promote the regime that condemned others like her.

Could he really have discounted such a great debt? Could youth be that calloused? Could training be that encompassing? While he lived the privileged life of an *SS* officer, was she starving in a rat-infested ghetto? Did she remember the little boy she had raised who no longer remembered her? Did she think about the hands she taught to hold a pencil and even imagine that they now held guns and *Panze*r controls? Did she have warm clothing? Did she still make beautiful music on her violin?

Eryk didn't know the answers. All he did know was that she was a Jewish woman in Germany. All the strikes were against her. He knew that she had no options. To be a Jew in Germany was a death sentence. He knew that very well.

Eryk gripped the star with his good hand. The image of the Russian woman lying in the bloody dirt refused to leave his mind. That could have been Zelda Goldman. As incredible and incongruous as it sounded, he knew he had to find out what had become of her.

20

August, 1943, Berlin, Germany
Reich Main Security Office

> *You ask, what is our aim?*
> *I can answer in one word: It is victory, victory at all costs,*
> *victory in spite of all terror, victory, however long and hard*
> *the road may be; for without victory, there is no survival.*
> Winston Churchill, May 13, 1940,
> Speech in the House of Commons

Hanne put the last folder in the file drawer and closed it with a sigh. Time to go home at last, and she was ready for it. Working in the headquarters of the SS wasn't always physically taxing, but it was mentally exhausting. She supposed she should be glad however. Many women in Germany were working much harder than she, some of them trying to fill the shoes of men who were never coming home. Just being a mother to the large brood the Nazis recommended was bound to be exhausting. At least, she was responsible for only herself.

Hanne reached for her hat and settled it smartly on her head. Someday perhaps she'd have a gaggle of children, but God forbid they should be like the model Aryan tots that were paraded up and down the streets of Berlin. How sickening to see the competition of the women, each of them striving to outdo her neighbor in excellent motherhood. It was all for nothing anyway, because when the children reached ten years of age, they were bound for the *Hitler Youth* or *League of German Girls* where they learned to love the state above everything. Not even parental instruction could compete with the *Reich* for the loyalty of their children. The women were deceived, and they didn't even realize it. They were devoting themselves to bear and raise children, broodmares for the Fatherland which would gobble up those very children.

"Going out tonight, Hanne?" Ilse's voice pulled her away from her thoughts. "*Sturmbannführer* Beckmann is in town, isn't he?"

Hanne smiled, hoping she looked demure and maidenly. "Yes, I'm meeting him for coffee and pastries."

"Always coffee, Hanne, never a moonlight stroll or a romantic evening at the opera. That man is either very slow or you are putting him off. You'd better say yes if he asks! Believe me, he wouldn't need to look far to get someone else." Ilse put her hands on her hips and made a face at Hanne. "I'd even be willing to take him off your hands."

Hanne laughed. "If I decide to turn him down, I'll make sure you know, Ilse."

"You do that. A man as important as the *Sturmbannführer* needs a wife and children, especially children." Ilse smiled saucily and gave Hanne a broad wink.

"Sssh!" Hanne glanced around. "Don't say that so loudly. It isn't a policy that the *Reichsfuhrer* would like to announce to everyone."

Ilse rolled her eyes. "Well, maybe so, but the officers don't mince words about it. You should hear them talk."

"I have." Hanne didn't care for the ribald tidbits she'd overheard here and there. It seemed many younger officers of the *Reich* were delighted with the prospect of fathering many children, especially when the marital status of the mother wasn't an issue.

"Well, no matter. The *Reich* couldn't spare you right now anyway. You're too important to spend nine months in a mother's home. Didn't I hear that you're being reassigned?"

Hanne nodded as they stepped out onto the Berlin sidewalk. "Yes, temporarily. I am to assist an injured *Waffen-SS* captain with some clerical work, dictation, typing reports and such. His last name is Steiner. Ever heard of him?"

"No, but it must be important if the *Reichsfuhrer* can spare you. You know you're one of his favorite secretaries."

Hanne slapped playfully at her friend. "Oh, stop it now."

They had reached the U-Bahn station where they parted ways, Ilse waved as she took the steps to her train. "See you tomorrow."

"Goodbye." The train whooshed and was gone.

Hanne walked slowly to her own train, engrossed in her thoughts. Word traveled fast at headquarters. She had only learned a couple hours earlier that she would be assisting *Waffen-SS Hauptsturmfuhrer* Eryk Steiner and already Ilse knew about it. For all the secrecy of the *SS* in their work for the *Führer,* there were considerable gaps among the personnel on her level.

She put her hand in her pocket for her ticket, but came up empty. Great. She'd have to step to the side and look for it. That would make her late meeting Beckmann. Hanne opened her purse as she walked, trying to avoid a collision while she rummaged. She would have been all right except for the uneven place in the tile in her way. Her heel caught on it and suddenly she pitched forward, her purse dropping to the ground as she flailed very ungracefully, trying to catch herself.

But she fell anyway, or almost did. Her hands caught thick fabric and she gripped it to steady herself. Her feet continued to slide for a moment before she could right herself. When she did, Hanne found herself clutching the arm of an injured man. He wore a *Waffen-SS* uniform with a captain's insignia. His right arm was bandaged and held in a sling. His eyes were steely and unsmiling.

She stepped back, quickly dropping her grip on him and smoothing her skirt. "I beg your pardon, *Hauptsturmführer*."

He stooped to pick up her purse. "There is no harm done. Are you hurt?"

She reached for it, took it from his free hand. It was best not to play demure with the *SS* boys. Often they didn't return the favor. She had only the imagination and stamina to work on one Nazi at a time – Beckmann was it for the present.

"No, *danke*. I was searching in my purse for my ticket and wasn't looking where I was walking. Forgive me . . . for running into you." She'd almost said for running you down, but he didn't look as though he were in danger of that, now that she looked up at him. Even with an injured arm, he looked as fit and vigorous a specimen of German manhood as she had seen. She looked away, wishing that he would just leave.

"Think nothing of it. I'm happy to have kept you from falling." Did she detect a note of laughter in his voice? Was he making fun of her discomfort? Suddenly, all of her fight came back, full force.

"Thank you, *Captain*. I'm grateful. Now if you will excuse me, I must catch my train." She gave a quick sweep of her head, dismissing him. "I must not be late for my appointment."

"Of course not, *Fraulein. Auf veidersehn*." The man gave a short bow and stood back to let her pass him. Out of the corner of her eye, Hanne still thought she saw a little quirk of his lips. Pompous jerk. Why did the country have to be filled with more men than she could take down?

"I was beginning to think you had left me all by myself, Hanne." *Sturmbannführer* Rolf Beckmann toyed with his wine glass, his eyes half-closed. The arrogance of the man!

"I'm so sorry." She soothed with her voice. "I misplaced my ticket and almost missed my train."

"Of course, I forgive you, Hanne. I know you wouldn't abandon me." He lifted his glass for a sip, and then patted his lips with his napkin. He reached across the table to touch her fingers. "And you also know I want to spend every minute possible with you."

She looked away, letting an embarrassed smile play at her lips. "Oh, *Herr Major*. . ."

He tugged at her hand. "Really. I am serious. And I think it's time you called me by my name. After all, I can't have other men thinking you're my secretary or something, can I?"

"I suppose you're right."

"It's settled then. You must call me Rolf. No more of this '*Herr Major*.'" He winked at her.

She nodded.

"Say it then. Now. I want to hear it from your lips."

She said it low, but he heard it. "Ah, hah! I like that, my dear. Now, I have some wonderful news." He leaned forward, taking both her hands. "I received the promotion, Hanne."

Hanne was suddenly extremely interested. She glowed up at him. "Tell me about it."

"I'm leaving soon for the ghetto of Theresienstadt on the Czech border. I will be in command of interrogations at the prison there."

The sour taste in her mouth was accompanied by a feeling of anger. Now he would be involved in more torture and death. She wanted to shudder, but denied herself the pleasure. Hers was an indignation that could only be indulged in continuing the battle. "What an opportunity for your career!"

He didn't even hear her, so intent he was on sharing the grand details. "The *Gestapo* office commands a prison which holds political prisoners from all over the *Reich* – thousands of them. There are interrogations every day. The staff is always busy. This is certainly a step up for me." He squeezed her fingers. "And, who knows? The salary might be enough for me to make other plans." He looked at her meaningfully.

She ducked her face, knowing she needed to be coy and demure, but actually trying not to think about what he was saying. "I don't know what you're talking about."

"Don't you? I thought I had made it plain enough, Hanne. Surely you know how I feel about you."

"I thought perhaps you cared, but I didn't dare hope that it was really true." She was amazed that the words just flowed out so easily. *Oh, Father, how often you punished me for lying and now here I am living the biggest one of all.*

"I won't ask you now, Hanne, but please think about what it could mean for us." He pushed back his chair and stood. "Come, I'm anxious to leave."

Beckmann pulled some bills from his pocket and laid them on the table. He moved to her chair and slid it back for her. He was close enough for Hanne to smell the sickening sweet scent of his cigar. She strengthened her resolve and walked out beside him.

The streets of the city were beautiful during the day, but as night grew closer, they became deserted as Berliners got home as quickly as possible to avoid being out after curfew. It was dusk now and blackout curtains were being pulled. The *Sturmbannführer* hailed a cab and gave the driver her address.

Once inside, he put his arm around her as they rode through streets that were quickly emptying. Hanne had a fleeting thought about the difference in his embrace and the one she had fallen into at the U-Bahn station. Beckmann was a nicely-proportioned man, a prototype of the German agent – self-assured, physically fit and impeccably groomed. But when he held her, she was a captive, overpowered. This afternoon, in the *Captain*'s arms, she'd been protected. Funny, when they both wore the uniform of the enemy, and she should not enjoy the embrace of either.

When they reached her apartment, Beckmann helped her out. He walked with her up the steps and unlocked her door and helped her inside. It wasn't wise to linger outside at night. The moon was already coming up, a bright full orb, a bomber's moon.

He'd never pushed her for anything more than a kiss, but Hanne was anxious each time he brought her home. She'd heard that Himmler wasn't too concerned with the morals of his men so long as there was no public scandal. Everyone knew that Himmler himself had a mistress. Despite her bravado that day long ago in London, she hoped to stay out of such entanglements, though it would no doubt be beneficial to her cause. Still, the teachings of childhood were difficult to forget; wouldn't Father be surprised that some of it had stayed with her!

He pulled her against him roughly, and kissed her. "Think about what I said, Hanne. Don't keep me waiting, all right?"

She nodded, avoiding his eyes. "I will think about it."

"Goodnight then." He opened the door and was gone.

Hanne wiped her lips on her shoulder and locked her door. She needed a hot cup of tea.

21

Berlin, Germany
SS Headquarters
Reich Main Security Office

> *The victor will never be asked if he told the truth.*
> Adolf Hitler, Hitler's Letters and Notes

Eryk rubbed his jaw as he stood in the outer office of the *SS* Command, thinking back over the past two weeks. He had to keep the details clear in his mind; Himmler was expecting a full report from the front. In his hand, he held the document which contained the official record of his mission. He also had several papers from his commanding officer at the front to pass on to the *Reichsfuhrer*.

Eryk walked down the hall and entered the door. Speaking to the secretary first, he took a seat in the anteroom and sat rigidly, willing himself to stay awake. Himmler detested sloppiness of any sort. Absently, he felt his collar and glanced at his dress boots, then looked around at the others in the room, enlisted men and officers waiting like him to see the man who wielded an enormous amount of power, the face of the *SS* to Germany.

Eryk leaned back in the plush chair and briefly closed his eyes. The clack of the teletype was hypnotic; even after a few days of rest, he fought the urge to doze.

The opening of the door to the inner office startled him. He looked up as a young woman stepped through the door. She rustled some papers in her hand. "*Hauptsturmführer* Steiner? The *Reichsfuhrer* will see you now."

She led him into the inner office, knocking softly and announcing him, then stepping aside for him to walk in. He walked to the desk and clicked his heels, saluting. "*Heil*, Hitler."

Himmler returned the greeting. "Please, sit down, *Hauptsturmführer* Steiner."

Eryk walked forward and laid the papers on the massive desk, then sat in one of the chairs facing the man. Behind the desk, an imposing portrait of Adolf Hitler glared down on the room. Great windows flanked the portrait and military memorabilia sat here and there. On Himmler's desk was a bronze *Reichsadler,* the arrogant imperial eagle, with wings extended.

The *Reichsfuhrer* took the papers and looked through them quickly, raising his eyebrows from time to time and occasionally muttering something. Finally, he looked up and took off his spectacles, rubbing his eyes before he replaced them and peered out at Eryk. "You have just returned from the Eastern front, Operation Citadel."

"Yes, *Reichsfuhrer*."

"Tell me of it; I want to hear details. How did the *Waffen-SS* units progress in the battle?"

Eryk relayed his report, making sure he gave specifics including the positions of the different divisions and the casualties that he had witnessed and the level of resistance from the enemy. He told about the loss of his tank and the Soviet planes. He spoke of the mechanical problems with the *Tiger*, its inefficiency in the Russian mud and resulting vulnerability."

"So, it is your opinion, *Captain* Steiner, that you would not have lost your tank had you not stalled in the mud?"

"Yes, *Reichsfuhrer*. We lost precious time digging out of the mud, time that we could have used to catch up to our unit. The Russian planes would not have caught us in the open and alone if we had been able to keep going through the afternoon."

Himmler nodded. "Yes, yes. I am so sorry to hear of the loss of your crew, and that of *Captain* Zetterson. You will attend the ceremonies in their honor, of course."

Eryk swallowed. "Yes."

Himmler swiveled in his chair and turned to stare out the window. "You may know, Steiner, that we are, at this very moment, drawing up revisions for the *Panzerkampwagon IV*."

"I had heard that was a possibility, sir."

"Yes, it is very important, *Captain*. You are no doubt also aware that the Allies are preparing for some sort of invasion. We must have machinery that is reliable to meet that challenge. The *PKW IV* is deadly and relatively safe for the crew, but her mechanical and navigational flaws are of vital concern to me," he looked directly at Eryk, "and to the *Führer*.

We need someone who is intimately acquainted with this machine to help our designers with the modifications. We need someone who has commanded this machine and knows where the problem spots are. We need you, *Hauptsturmführer* Steiner. Because of your battle injury, the lighter duty will be good for your healing as well. You will be assigned to temporary duty here in Berlin while these design plans are settled."

"Yes, thank you, *Reichsfuhrer*." Eryk knew he had no choice, but protocol demanded his gratefulness for the decision of his superior.

Himmler was already shuffling papers on his desk. "I will make all the necessary arrangements. You will have light duties so that you can spend most of your time at the *Henschel* assembly factory in Kassel. You will have travel permits as well as an assistant to help you with your paperwork and whatever else you may need until your arm is healed." The man smiled as he spoke, satisfied with his decision. "You will be doing the Fatherland a great service, *Captain* Steiner."

"I will do my best, sir."

"Then, let me also offer my sincere thanks for your loyalty to your division while in the East. There is no greater honor for a member of the SS than to fulfill his duty, and you are certainly a man of which Germany can be proud."

Eryk bowed his head, accepting the praise. "Thank you, sir."

Himmler stood and walked around the desk to stand squarely in front of Eryk. "I will be watching your work with interest."

"Thank you, sir." Eryk saluted and walked to the door, opening and closing it quietly.

As he walked down the hall, he thought about the turn of events and above all, a chance to rest and face the loss he'd been dealt. Himmler was nobody's fool. He knew that Eryk was running on adrenaline at this point. Losing his entire crew was something he still hadn't dealt with fully. He had pushed it back, waiting to grieve another time. But he didn't know how he could climb into another *Panzer* or accept another crew in his present frame of mind. He just needed a little space to gain his balance. This new assignment would provide that. He would actually feel like he was avenging their deaths by contributing to a better design.

22

Berlin, Germany

> …. People with no moral inhibitions exude a strange odor.
> I can now pick out these people, and many of them really do smell like blood.
> Annette Schücking-Homeyer,
> Red Cross Volunteer on the Eastern Front
> letter home, November 5, 1941

The sky was bleeding, a scarlet color that poured from the clouds like rain. Eryk was sitting in a stalled Panzer. Around him were his comrades, stiff and gray with death. Ahead of him was a great mound of earth. From behind it came sounds, horrible sounds. He put his fingers in his ears to stop the sounds, but they didn't go away. He jumped down from the Panzer; he must get away. But from somewhere came a man with a gun. He pointed it at Eryk and motioned to the hill, "Look!"

Eryk shook his head and tried to dodge out of the way. But the man nudged him with the barrel of his gun and motioned again.

Eryk walked up the hill with the man right behind him. He was almost to the top when he stumbled, falling onto his belly in the loose dirt. He stared below at a ghastly scene. In the ditch were thousands of dolls, large, lifelike dolls with staring eyes and arms and legs that *flopped about. They made no sound as they fell, just piled up in a silent, white heap.*

Eryk wanted to look away but he couldn't. He was powerless to close his eyes. He raised his hand to shield his face from the glare. Something was glinting in the sun. He squinted and leaned forward.

A star.

There in the mud with the dolls was the star. He looked behind him for help, but the man was still holding the gun on him. Eryk reached out, trying to grasp the tip of the star.

Almost there.

His fingers brushed it, and he leaned out just a bit farther. But as his fingers closed around the metal, he lost his balance and toppled forward into the pit.

"HELP!"

Eryk screamed up into the sky, but no one heard. The man with the gun just stood there laughing, throwing back his head so that the skull insignia on his cap shined in the crimson light of the sky. He pointed to the dolls and to Eryk and laughed.

Eryk writhed, trying to crawl away from the dolls and the pit and the laughter. As he plunged his hands into the mud and started to climb, he saw that his fingers were dripping red, like the sky.

Eryk gripped his coffee cup and wished for the sun to shine. He hated rain, on the field and in the city. Rain was a soldier's enemy. It reminded him of the slog on the Eastern front, and much as he was prepared to do his duty, he disliked the terrain of Russia as much as other men who had fought there.

He tipped back his cup for another drink. Maybe it would help him stay awake. He hadn't gotten much sleep last night. The twisted quilts on his bunk were proof of his restlessness. He couldn't hold back a shudder as he thought of the macabre dream. Perhaps it had come because he'd been reading too many reports. Aside from the execution he'd witnessed in Poland, he'd never been to the killing fields, although he had heard about the work of the Special Action groups there. Some of the men who had served in those squads had been ruined forever as men and soldiers. He wasn't sure how any of them remained normal in the face of such extermination sprees, if some of the rumors he'd heard were true.

Tales of blood and brain-spattered uniforms and pits full of heaving corpses were sometimes bantered through the ranks like the one he remembered overhearing in the barracks. He'd even seen a few photos some young bucks took of themselves by their "work." But, he'd hoped that most of them did not enjoy the ghastly deeds.

Still, as an officer, he'd always rationalized the necessity of the "special treatment." Killing others wasn't a task that any civilized soldier wanted, but it was thrust upon him in the defense of his homeland and way of life. Somebody had to do the distasteful jobs. Accepting duty, any duty, was the responsibility of a soldier.

Eryk put down his cup and laid some coins on the table. Reaching for his hat, he got up and waved to the proprietor of the small café as he walked to the door. Old Frederic had been a friend of his father's for as long as he could remember. The pastries in his shop were the best in Berlin.

Now he was on his way to see another of his father's many friends, a colleague from the days of the previous War. Making his way into the building that housed the *Reich Main Security Office*, Eryk made his way down wide halls and up two flights of stairs, his boots clapping against the marble floors. It was an enormous building, its interior crowned with arches and stonework and gigantic windows, never smudged. No matter how many people were in the place, it always felt empty, so vast was its cavernous personality. Still, Eryk was sure that the walls, like the rest of Germany, had eyes and ears. This headquarters of Nazi power made one speak in a lowered voice, even when there was the insignia of command on the uniform, like his own.

Finally reaching the office he sought, Eryk walked up to the young adjutant and inquired. "Is *Major* Hunsdorf in?"

"Yes, *Herr Hauptsturmführer,* he is."

"Please inform him that Eryk Steiner is here at his request."

The man got up quickly and knocked on the door behind him and when beckoned, entered in one swift movement. Through the milky glass of the window in the door, Eryk could see the adjutant go toward the *Major's* desk and then pivot and come back out. "He will see you now."

Eryk acknowledged this with a nod and held his cap in his hands as he entered the office of his father's old friend.

"*Heil*, Hitler!" Eryk raised his right arm in a rigid salute.

Hunsdorf returned his gesture. "*Heil* Hitler, yes . . . come in, Eryk. It's so good to see you, son." The man came around his desk to grip Eryk's hand, his eyes bright and his stance solid despite his age.

"Thank you, sir; it is good to see you as well."

"Please have a seat." The older man motioned to the plush red chairs and sat down in one of them himself. "I want to hear about that incredible battle and about the new piece of metal hanging from your collar." He pointed with his cigar to Eryk's Iron Cross. "Care for a smoke?"

"No, thank you, sir."

"Ah, well, you're the better for it, I suppose. Though I'm not sure how you can be in the *SS* and not smoke something." His eyes twinkled. "Your father would be proud though. He never smoked either, not even so much as a pipe."

"But, sir, you knew about my father's breathing difficulties as a child."

"I did indeed, Eryk. We were boys together, you remember, as well as officers in the same regiment in the Great War. I had hoped that we would be fat old Generals together too." Hunsdorf looked off in the distance and sighed. "But it was not to be."

Eryk was silent. His father had been gone almost four years, but when he was in the presence of his longtime friends, it seemed not that long at all.

"But, I must get back to the purpose of your visit. Tell me about Kursk, my boy. Just what was your experience in this campaign they called Operation Citadel?"

So, for nearly an hour, Eryk recalled positions and orders and scenes for the *Sturmbannführer* who was a most gratifying listener, sometimes sitting forward on the edge of his seat as Eryk told of risk and danger and of course, death. He shook his head at the loss of Eryk's crew. "It's a hard thing to lose one's men, Eryk. Never get accustomed to it; value your crew and treat them like your family on the battlefield." He slapped his leg. "But what am I saying? You were groomed by the best; your father was the finest commander in the *Wehrmacht*, and there's not a man who served under him who would argue." The old man stood and walked to the window, pausing to look down at the busy Berlin street. "Now, I have his son, a decorated hero, in my office, and I'm about to tell him something out of honor for my old friend." He walked to his desk and tapped his cigar on an ashtray and then sank down into his desk chair, pulling open a drawer and laying a file of papers on his desk. "Come here, my boy."

Eryk approached the desk and bent to see the papers to which Hunsdorf was pointing.

"Do you know these names, Eryk?"

Auschwitz-Birkenau.
Belzec.
Chelmno.
Majdanek.
Sobibor.
Treblinka.

"Yes, sir, these are the names of camps in Poland for undesirables – Jews, Poles, Slavs, Gypsies and the like."

"Do you know what they do in these camps, Eryk?"

"The prisoners are made to work and eventually many die as a result of natural selection. And, of course, some are selected for special treatment upon arrival so that the camps may not be overcrowded."

The other man rocked back in his chair and folded his hands. "Yes, that is the official *SS* wording. You know it well, Eryk. I suppose one cannot be too surprised, since you were a model member of the *Hitler Youth* and raised in the hotbed of National Socialism. Still, I wondered if you might feel differently."

Eryk wasn't sure where this dialogue was headed but he was a bit alarmed. He had heard things here and there about the *Major*, whispered suspicions and knowing glances that made him fearful his father's longtime friend was involved in some of the anti-Nazi plots that were always swirling just below the surface here in Berlin. He knew the man to be a loyal German and remembered that his father had considered him one of his closest confidantes, but still he wondered if some of the rumors were true. Eryk shifted his leg as he sat and as he did so, felt the sharp prickle of something sharp in his trouser pocket. As swift as a stab of conscience, he was reminded that his high and mighty criticism should start at home. Who was he to condemn a fellow officer and a superior at that, when he was violating his own oath by cherishing a forbidden icon?

He struggled to answer in a way that was respectful of the older man and yet did not betray his own dilemma. "*Major* Hunsdorf, as you say, my answer does reflect my training and loyalty to the SS. Do I detect that you are unhappy with the sentiments I've expressed?"

The *Sturmbannführer* regarded him with sad eyes. "Let us say that I was making sure, my boy, just making sure. It is a strange world in which we soldiers find ourselves, and a man may be tossed about with many things he's heard and seen and been taught."

Eryk put all his skills into the bluff he was creating. "I do not feel confused, *Herr Major*. On the contrary, I can see the wisdom of the policies under which I serve. Please do not feel concerned for me." He tried to smile reassuringly at the old man.

Hunsdorf shook his head and leaned forward to look into Eryk's eyes. "But I must feel concern, son, out of honor for my dear friend. We made a pledge to one another to look out for each other's sons should the need arise. That is what I am trying to do."

"I'm sure my father would greatly appreciate it, sir. I do thank you for your concern, and I hope your mind can be put at ease about me." That much was true. He didn't need anyone in the High Command developing any interest in his philosophies or allegiance.

The *Sturmbannführer* pulled the cigar from his mouth and looked at it. He was silent for a few moments. "Eryk, have you ever wondered about the death of your father?"

The man now had his absolute attention. "Wondered, sir? I'm not sure I understand."

"About the cause, the time of it."

Eryk hesitated. This was uncharted territory. He was almost afraid to broach it. He answered cautiously. "We received an official notice, of course. He was killed in the Polish campaign, in action. He was awarded a medal posthumously for bravery."

"Yes, I know." Hunsdorf tapped his cigar on the glass ashtray in front of him. "I looked up the records myself."

"I'm not sure what you are implying, sir." Eryk looked around the room and, deciding to take the risk, continued in a softer tone. "Are you suggesting that there was something suspicious in connection with his death?"

The old man leaned toward him, holding his gaze, also speaking softly. "I am not saying anything for sure, Eryk. But I do believe there is more to this story than either of us know."

"Sir, if I were to believe what you are saying, it could lead to . . ." Eryk couldn't say the word aloud. *Treason.*

The old man nodded. "Indeed it would. I would never ask you to put your life at risk for a small matter, son, but your father and I were very good friends, and I must be assured that he was not betrayed." Hunsdorf shook his head sadly. "He loved his country dearly."

"Then surely he would not have been a target for anything shady, sir. He was fighting for his country. The *Führer* protects those who serve him." Or at least that is what Eryk had been taught to believe.

"Yes, that is what I have believed. That is why I supported National Socialism and proudly served its flag. But, I have seen things in the last few months that have made me wonder. Are we truly fighting for something honorable, Eryk?"

"Surely, sir, room for one's people to live and prosper is a good thing, worthy of support."

"But room and wealth that we have forcibly taken from others? Prosperity gained from the deaths of women and children and old men?" The *Sturmbannführer* crushed his cigar into the ashtray. "These are questions I have been asking myself, Eryk. I have not yet found the answer. I have begun to wonder if your father asked them too, before he died."

"I don't know, sir. He didn't discuss anything on this subject with me." How many times Eryk had wished he had been able to get his father's opinion on troubling matters within the *Reich*. Though they had never had a really close relationship, he had known that his father loved him to the best of his ability, and he was certain that he had been a moral and loyal soldier. Those attributes alone made him somewhat of an anomaly in Eryk's mind.

"No, he probably hadn't come to any conclusions, my boy. He was always a man who made sure of his course before he acted. I believe that, had he returned, he would have talked with you about these very things. That's why I am doing it now."

This was news to Eryk. Had his father really intended to mentor his only son in a more purposeful way? "I'm grateful to you, sir, for remembering my father and doing your best to be faithful to his memory. Like you, I have had my share of questions, of wonderings. But I must be loyal to my oath." Eryk raised his hands, palms up. "I have given my word to serve my *Führer*. This choice was already made. I am obligated. To be truthful, sir, I am not certain how to be convinced of what is actually morally wrong anyway. Look at the good the *Führer* has done. See how our families are thriving and our economy is stable."

"Yes, I recognize that the German people are no longer the half-starved and pitiful nation they were just a couple decades ago. But, this prosperity, Eryk, is partially the benefit of plunder, I believe. I am not sure if our people can endure if this war continues much longer. We simply do not have the resources."

"Which is precisely why the *Führer* wanted to advance in the East; Russia is rich in resources." This Eryk knew to be a fact. The richness of the East was coveted by the *Reich*.

"That is true, but look how the Battle of Stalingrad ended. Now, this plunge into the Kursk salient has been called off. In fact, I heard that most of your division is being sent to France to refit and recoup. So much for gaining the resources of the Eastern peoples!"

"Yes, most of my unit is being sent to France, that is true. I am being kept here though on special assignment for *Reichsfuhrer* Himmler."

"I see." Hunsdorf regarded Eryk with shrewd old eyes. "I would consider it a distinct favor then, my son, if you would not mention the misgivings of a grizzled old soldier to the *Reichsfuhrer*. I'm sure he has enough on his mind without worrying about me."

Eryk stood and clicked his heels. "Of course, sir; you are my father's friend. I will keep your confidence." Truthfully, he would not have considered otherwise. There were some things that one conveniently forgot. He was not the *Gestapo*.

Hunsdorf stood as well. "Thank you, Eryk. Perhaps one day we will both have the answers we need. I congratulate you on your battle honors. You may be confident that my wife and I will offer prayers for your safety – both of body and of mind." He gripped Eryk's hand. "Take care, my boy. Remember, life is precious, a gift from God."

Eryk shook the old man's hand, turned and walked out and pulled the door shut behind him. He was more than a little concerned over what he'd heard in the last hour. If men like *Sturmbannführer* Hunsdorf were concerned, the situation was grave indeed, and if such men decided to take action against the *Reich*, they were all doomed. But what bothered Eryk more were the implications the man had planted in his mind about his father's death. Though they had not been close, Eryk believed implicitly in his father's honor and dignity. If he had been conveniently discarded by the *Reich*, Eryk was ready to indulge his doubts just a bit further.

23

Berlin, Germany

We must always take sides. Neutrality helps the oppressor, never the victim. Silence encourages the tormentor, never the tormented.
Eli Wiesel, Holocaust survivor and author

Hanne tugged on her perky hat and slammed the door to her apartment. It was a sunny morning and the walk to her office was usually a pleasant one. Thankfully, this morning there were no steaming piles of rubble in the neighborhoods she passed. The Allies had spared Berlin of more bombing last night.

Thinking of her birth country as the enemy was beginning to feel eerily natural. She was so far underground that she almost forgot now and then that she wasn't part of the master race. There were days when she was so immersed in Berlin culture that it seemed she really had grown up in a staunch Nazi family and attended *BDM* meetings with her girlfriends. Of course, being the daughter of a man who lived in Munich as a boy was a great benefit. How lucky that her father had spoken German in the home and taught the language to his children; their tongues were naturally accustomed to the guttural sounds that so many found difficult to produce. Hanne was sure that Father would not call it luck, but Providence, and she wouldn't argue the point. It was almost impossible for someone who had lived undercover as long as she to deny the fact that there was a God who often looked down in mercy. She herself had been the recipient of it.

She had a feeling that she was going to need more very soon. *Waffen-SS* Captains were not fools. Staying ahead of her new boss would require all her skill as well as a good dose of womanly charm, as her old mentor would be sure to remind her. To do her job as a *Reich* "secretary" efficiently and try to make the captain fall in love with her and also gather the information London required would be a colossal undertaking. She would be glad for any divine help. After all, it wasn't that she didn't believe in God above, she was just rather soured on her prior experience with Him. But she was open to any blessings He would send.

It was a countdown to Monday; zero hundred hours was set to begin then. Yet, even today, on Friday, she had work to do besides what was waiting for her at her desk in the *Reich War Ministry*. At 11:00 this morning, her new assignment, *Hauptsturmführer* Steiner, would be attending the services for his fallen crew. It would be a very military event, filled with *SS* ritual, and she, as his new assistant, would be there as well. Though she wasn't officially working for him yet, she had been given permission to attend. She planned to sit in an unobtrusive spot and watch the man. It was always helpful to observe the target in a natural habitat, and for a *Waffen-SS* officer, there was hardly a more natural habitat than an *SS* event held in Berlin. It was time to do reconnaissance, *SOE* style.

Waffen-SS Hauptsturmfuhrer Eryk Steiner was solemn as he took his place in the honor guard in the great hall of the *Reich Chancellery*.

There were no bodies to view, no caskets to carry. What was left of his crew had been scraped from the charred *Panzer* in the Russian mud and brought today in four small boxes. Today's ceremony was more than mere formality though. The *SS* was a tight brotherhood, bound by honor and loyalty to the *Führer* and to each other. They trained together, lived together, fought together and often died together, and in that death gained the greatest honor of all – sacrifice for the Fatherland.

Eryk was filled with emotion as the "service" began, but he held tightly to his control, not letting his sadness override his resolve as an officer. Krugel and Hausser and Hummel and Ebengrosser had died in a way befitting their character; they had not flinched; they had fought to the end. As their commander, it was his duty to honor them by his presence and his demeanor. Their wives and families needed to see in him a firm commitment and calm spirit. It was the last gift he could give his men.

There was no chaplain today, rather a high-ranking *SS* ceremonial officer was in charge, giving the eulogies and offering up words of commendation. The *SS* had little time for prayers to God or words of Scripture. They turned instead to the promises of their *Führer* and the security of oath and allegiance.

Candles were lit and there was a moment of silence as the "blood flag" was brought forward. Stained with the ebbing life of men who fought in the Munich Putsch, it was considered extremely sacred and used only on rare occasions. Eryk was touched that Himmler had authorized its use in the ceremony for his fallen crew. He winked his eyes to dispel the mist in them as the office intoned his final words.

These brave men that we honor today are part of Germany. They are part of our past as they grew from children to men; they are part of our present as they fought in this great struggle, and they are part of our future as the blood they shed will spur us on to greater sacrifice and to victory. They fell in conflict with our enemy and there is no grave that we may decorate today. But, in our hearts, we salute them and bring them sentiment that never fades or withers. And we know they are at peace. For wherever a German soldier rests in foreign soil, that too is home, that too is Germany.

Today we will lay wreaths in the national cemetery in their honor. Today and always we will hold them close in our hearts. They fought for the Führer and the Reich; they fought for Germany. We will continue the battle in their honor until we have gained the ultimate victory.[4]

As the blood flag was lowered to touch the altar in front where four small boxes sat symbolizing the fallen men, Eryk stood at attention, unable to salute because his arm was in a sling.

His thoughts wandered to the assignment which started tomorrow. In the Führer's name, he would help design a *panzer* that would avenge the deaths of his comrades, a machine to invoke fear and cause destruction. Only then would the blood-stained earth be satisfied. Only then would the German people have land to thrive. But as he lowered himself to his seat, a sharp prick in his inner shirt pocket reminded him of another mission unfulfilled. Time was running out.

Hanne watched *Hauptsturmführer* Steiner with a practiced eye. Like most of the *Waffen-SS*, he was the committed type. Germany had spawned a generation of men who would march into the face of death with hardly the blink of an eye. Indeed, they were taught that it was their duty to die for Germany. She had once visited the training school at *Bad Tolz*; there the air was thick with Nazi sentiment and the recruits were fanatical in their allegiance.

It was her job to use his loyalty against him, to find the crack in his formidable armor. She'd read a top-secret dossier on him. It had taken some doing to gain access to it, but it had been worth it for it contained a wealth of information - father dead, a war hero; mother from old aristocracy, deceased after being a patient at a state-run sanatorium; two sisters in the *BDM*, a bit rebellious. It listed his military record which was impressive, his personal stats, preferences, hobbies, and so much more. But there was nothing quite like eyes on a man to help you know how to approach him.

She had to admit that looking at him was a fairly pleasant task; he was a very good-looking officer. She wished there had been more in his file about his relationships with women. Surely a man with that kind of looks and presence had known more than a few. But the facts were few – never married, some dates with a few women, but nothing serious on the record. Hanne wondered about that. A man his age usually didn't get too busy for female relationships. She had to find out why. Her life and many others depended on it.

24

Berlin, Germany
Reich Security Main Office

Give us the tools, and we will finish the job.
Winston Churchill, radio broadcast, London, February 9, 1941

From the moment he saw her, Eryk knew his "assistant" would be trouble. Well, this was actually the second time he had seen her. He immediately recognized the young woman in his office as the same one he had "rescued" at the *U-Bahn* station. She was as pretty and arrogant as he remembered; both very bad signs. Inwardly, he groaned; outwardly, he gave her a brisk nod and a "Good morning, *Fraulein*."

She gave no sign that she recognized him, though he was quite certain she did. She assessed him coolly, her stance haughty. So much for the gentle spirit of the German woman touted in verse. This girl was the embodiment of the new Aryan femininity; in fact, he had seen a few *Gestapo* men who could take lessons from her manner. And that was saying something!

He tried a genial approach. "I understand, *Fraulein,* that *y*ou have volunteered to be my assistant for the next few weeks on an important military project. I'm grateful for your help. As you can see, I'm rather limited in my usefulness." He lifted his sling and tried a smile, but the chill of her eyes killed it immediately.

"I serve the *Reich, Herr Captain*. I am glad to offer my services while you are incapacitated."

"I see. Your letter of commendation says you are skilled in dictation and typing and that you have a rudimentary knowledge of armaments. These are all very important in the work we will be doing."

"I'm glad I meet the specifications of the task, sir." The green eyes were unwavering, untouched.

"Yes, well now." Eryk leaned back in his seat. "The job we have to do will entail quite a bit of travel and possibly some exhausting hours. We will be leaving tomorrow morning to tour the *Henschel and Son* factory in Kassel. We will leave in the morning at eight o'clock sharp."

The young woman nodded her expression as tight as the bun of reddish-brown hair she wore. "I will be ready."

"Good. Now, have you looked over your space in the office?" He gestured to the desk in the room on the other side of the door. "Do you have the equipment you need?"

"Everything is satisfactory, *Captain* Steiner. Even down to the sharpened pencils."

"Good. The *Führer* is expecting much from us; we must not fail."

Her eyes lifted almost imperceptibly to the portrait of Hitler hanging behind him, facing her. "I will not fail. We will not fail, *Herr Hauptsturmführer*." Her words were strung together with steel thread. There was no hesitation.

"I am glad for your commitment, *Fraulein* . . . " He glanced at the dossier in his hand. "Lager. *Fraulein* Lager, then. You are dismissed. I will see you in the morning."

She stood and saluted him. "Thank you, sir. *Heil Hitler*."

He returned the words and she left the room, her regulation laced-up shoes clicking on the polished floor.

Eryk leaned back in his chair and watched her go. She moved with the efficient grace he had come to associate with the women in the *SS*. No wasted movement, no clumsiness and no charm. The young females who joined the ranks of the *Schutzstaffel Women's Corps* left feminine whims behind. In the competitive atmosphere of the Hitler's elite guard, there was no place for softness. Women were trained for toughness, for rigid duty. It was evident in the crisp uniforms and in the set of their taut, young faces. They were trained automatons of the *Reich*. Still, she had an undeniable beauty and natural grace. It was an interesting combination.

He turned her file over in his good hand and opened it flat on his desk to look at it again. She came highly recommended, had even been considered as a secretary for the *Führer*. Her security clearance was very high. She was said to be extremely intelligent and unquestioningly loyal. She was also very young to be filling such a position. But then, Germany's youth had no limits these days.

He slapped the folder closed and put it in a drawer. As long as she could help him with the paperwork he could put up with her. He would even work with *Frau* Goebbels if it would develop a better *Panzer*. Managing a tiny smile at that thought, he shut the desk drawer and walked to the door. It was time for his second shift, a casual visit to the office of records in the Department of Jewish Affairs.

25

Berlin, Germany
Reich Main Security Office

*Espionage, for the most part, involves finding a person who knows something
or has something that you can induce them secretly to give to you.
That almost always involves a betrayal of trust.*
Aldrich Ames

Hanne Lager had only gotten this far because she was willing to play the part of the indifferent German woman, ambitious and eager to serve, with no sentimental attachment. In truth, she often wondered if she had become the part. She had done the training at the special *Reich* school in Oberenheim that made her fit to be part of the *SS-Helferinnenkorps*. She had endured the indoctrination in Nazi ideology, fitness, "mothering" skills and specialized communications. She had lived tight-lipped and close-vested for months, pretending to be the perfect specimen of German womanhood who was thrilled to be joining the elite *SS*. Sometimes she wondered if it had soaked in more than she realized. Living alone and working alone for so long had not strengthened her social skills, and she was prone to muse if her mental balance was a bit off. She didn't have to pretend as much now. She rather preferred a caustic way of speaking and a grim outlook. This war did not spread sunshine. And like the mole she was, she had become accustomed to the darkness of the underworld; she had embraced the subterfuge that kept her alive.

As she walked out of the *Reich Headquarters,* her thoughts were on the plan for tomorrow. She would get her first glimpse of the *Henschel and Son* factory in Kassel. It was a huge break in her work. The months she had spent working her way into the *SS* might now begin to pay off. It had been a terrific disappointment when she was passed up for a secretary to Hitler. Imagine if she had actually gotten that close to the demented little corporal. What a frolic that would have been! Her tears of disappointment when she was not chosen had not been feigned; she had brooded for a week over it.

Maybe now she had a chance to get back on track. Everyone knew there was an Allied invasion in the works. Not many knew the details, but it was going to happen, she was certain. If she could gain information about the tanks the *Wehrmacht* might use, it could help save a few of Britain's boys, not to mention all the other tidbits of intelligence she might be able to glean from being around the brass with whom Steiner associated.

He was a different kind of bird for sure. She wasn't used to genuine smiles from a Nazi officer. Of course, it might not have been genuine. Perhaps he was disarming her so he could be all the meaner later on. Perhaps he knew about her. No, her cover was impenetrable. She had flawless papers and spoke German like a native. She could fool Adolf himself if she had a chance. But it was best to keep playing the ice princess with Steiner. He was a smart one, and no one was immune to tiny mistakes, the kind which could be disastrous. On the whole, Nazis were razor sharp. She was thinking that Steiner easily fit that category.

He looked as healthy in body as in mind. Of course, she hadn't met one *SS* officer who wasn't. They were stalwart, hale and hearty, the lot of them, exuding masculine confidence and charm when they wanted. It was easy to forget that they were monsters on the inside, trained to kill without remorse, nurtured in hatred and skilled in the sport of violence. He was no different than the rest of them. She had simply been away from honorable men for too long and now even the enemy looked appealing.

She grimaced. Close cropped blond hair, strong jaw and lean frame be hanged; he was a Nazi. She despised him all the more because he was pretty. Kicking at a rock, she shut down her thoughts. She'd kill him if she got a chance just because he had the nerve to make her feel like a woman again. She had a gun after all; of course, it was a *Luger*. Everything she now owned was German issued. The only thing British she still possessed was her soul and sometimes she wondered about that. If it took the liquidation of an *SS Captain* to help her reclaim her self-respect then, so be it. She would do it with relish.

26

Berlin, Germany
Reich Main Security Office
SS Race and Settlement Office

> *Anti-Semitism is exactly the same as delousing. Getting rid of lice is not a question of ideology, it is a matter of cleanliness. In just this same way anti-Semitism for us has not been a question of ideology but a matter of cleanliness.*
> Heinrich Himmler

Eryk looked down at the deportation list in front of him. Nazi record-keeping was orderly and accurate. Accounts of racial heritage were so important that there must be no mistake. He knew that his own file contained a family tree which dated back to 1750, proving he was free of Jewish blood. No SS man could be accepted with less than that. Germans were serious about racial purity.

But finding a particular Jewess amidst the mass of files was a daunting task. Since 1938, all Jewish women with non-Jewish first names had to add the mandated "Sarah" for race identification purposes. But still her first and last name should be the same. Unless she had married since leaving his family's employ. No, he didn't think so.

Of course, this job was more difficult since he had to search covertly. No one was above suspicion in the *Reich* these days. Anyone could topple, could find himself facing prison or a firing squad, and there were many *Gestapo* agents who would gleefully witness his comeuppance. Wouldn't they just love to find a *Hauptsturmführer* in the *Waffen-SS* searching the deportation lists for the name of a Jewish woman? The secret police squad that dogged the steps of nearly everyone in Germany was getting out of control. Their jurisdiction knew no bounds. They had insidious means of interrogation and were notoriously without feeling. It was best to stay out of their line of vision and the easiest way to accomplish that was not to call attention to oneself. So, to follow that rule, he had to conduct this search in secret, to search in the shadows, literally. Under the guise of keeping notes from his recent mission on the Eastern Front, he had been able to gain access to the sacred room where the *Juden* files were kept. Since Heydrich's assassination in 1942, even tighter guard was in place for all things pertaining to Jewish affairs. It wasn't difficult to see that this place was of the utmost importance to the German High Command.

Now, he hurriedly scanned the lists, looking for her name or maybe that of one of her family members he could recall. Had she been deported? If so, to which camp had she been taken? Was she part of the slave labor force? Or had she been gassed upon arrival? Had they discovered her heart condition? If so, she was probably part of an experiment somewhere.

It was hardly possible that she had escaped deportation. Playing in the *Berlin Philharmonic* was no protection; her brother had also been a distinguished member of that group and he had been deported to Poland years ago. Eryk had already found the documentation for that.

Having worked for an Aryan family was no assurance either. His father had not been unkind to her as far as he could remember. But his father had also been a loyal German. If the *Reich* determined her people were a threat to the nation, he would not have felt an obligation to secure the protection of a Jewish woman who had worked as *Hauslehrerin* and tutor for his son. There were some things an officer simply did not question. Or, at least, that's the way it used to be, and his mother certainly wouldn't have helped the situation with her suspicions and hysterics.

Eryk thought back, tracing a mental timeline. He didn't know her birth date, but he did recall that she told him she'd been born in Poland and had moved to Berlin with her parents as just a child. She had seemed ageless to him then, but as he thought about it, he imagined she must have been in her early forties when she took her leave of the Steiner family. Until that time, he'd never thought much about her olive coloring or the star she always kept with her. It had seemed a natural part of the woman who was integral to his earliest memories.

He remembered sitting on her lap while she read fairy stories and trudging with her through the snowy streets on wintry Berlin days. He could picture her tucking him into his bed and saying a prayer, her hand gentle on his head. When screams from the other part of the house woke him during the night, she was there to calm him, whispering reassurances and standing between him and the terror of his mother's illness.

As he grew, she coddled him less and spoke to him more. In those formative years before the *Hitler Youth* became his family, she was the voice of conscience and civility to him. She chipped away at his awkward boyish manners and worked on refining him. She challenged him to chivalry and kindness and honesty and integrity. She taught him that there was a God who can see all and who will judge all. He was sure she prayed for him with fervor and then wept over him when he outgrew her care and walked stubbornly away from her voice.

Eryk swallowed hard as he remembered her face on that last morning.

"I don't need a governess now, sir." He'd addressed his father with all the insolent assurance of youth. "Besides, I'll be gone on marches and campouts on the weekends with the Hitler Youth."

She'd merely nodded and laid a hand on his shoulder. "I will miss you, Liebchen, but I suppose you must grow up now, jah?" Turning to his father, she said, "I will pack my things, sir. Thank you for allowing me to serve your family."

She was gone when he came home that evening. But she had left something for him, under his pillow; her special star with a little note. "Remember God, Eryk. Honor him with your manhood. I give you my star so you will remember my prayers for you."

Horrified, Eryk had flung it into the fireplace in his bedroom. He wanted no further part of it, and he hadn't thought of the star until that night in the hut in Russia. That terrible night after he had watched his crew incinerated in their own *Panzer*.

Eryk rubbed his eyes and sighed. He had to acknowledge defeat in the search for tonight. Her name wasn't on any of the lists he'd seen. But he would find her. There were only so many camps, and he would search the records of them all. He refused to think about the other possibility. A woman with her strength and stamina surely could have survived this long, even if she did have a slight heart condition. So far as he knew it had never been entered on her medical records. He was the only one who knew. He was the only one who had seen the little bottle she kept in her pocket.

He closed his eyes at the thought that prison officials would have taken the bottle. Prisoners were not allowed to keep anything with them in the camps, and knowing her, she might have thrown it out a window herself. But she was alive somewhere. She had to be. He willed her to be. He would find her. It would just take a little more time.

27

Autobahn to Kassel, Germany

> *'Spy' is such a short ugly word. I prefer 'espionage.'*
> *Those extra three syllables really say something.*
> Howard Taylor

"*Fraulein* Lager, I need you to get the papers out of this case for me."

Hauptsturmführer Steiner held up his wrist and indicated the attaché case handcuffed to his good arm. She had noticed it earlier and knew he could never take the files out himself. It was no wonder the *Reich* had insisted upon an assistant. With one arm in a sling and the other chained to a case, the man was practically helpless, that is, if one could call an SS officer helpless. Hanne couldn't recall that she ever had.

The *Schutzstaffel* were their own breed and carried with them a scent that Hanne had come to recognize – a mix of arrogance and power and full-tilt masculinity. They believed in their mission, they believed in their training, and they believed in their skills. Most of all, they believed in their own importance. This potent sense of authority was as distinguishable as a whiff of fish and chips on the wharf back home. She could smell it now as the man leaned toward her in the small space of the staff car. Hanne shifted in her seat, trying not to be overtaken by the raw force he exuded. But he held the case with his good hand and laid it in her lap and held up the key as if to signal that his actions were nonthreatening.

"My apologies, *Fraulein*. I have crowded you. Here is the key." He dropped it into the hand she stretched toward him.

"*Danke*" Hanne fingered the key in her right hand while she steadied the case with her left, then turned the lock and heard it click. The clasp snapped open, and she looked up at him.

They were on their way to the factory in Kassel, Germany, where the colossus of mechanized armaments was manufactured. She was actually going to see how the magnificent *Panzerkampwagon IV*, the *Tiger,* was made. If she could have been any giddier, Hanne couldn't imagine it. Well, maybe a bit giddier if say, Hitler were found run through with a British flag stand or something equally cataclysmic. But for today, getting her very own eyes on the metal beast in production would do. After all, she did have that remarkable memory her instructors at Baker Street had discovered and coached and marshaled into service. What a beautiful opportunity to use it.

"Thank you, *Fraulein*. Now, take out the files and open them to mechanical designs and spread that out for me." His voice was not deep, but even and steady, accustomed to giving orders, no doubt. She knew the type; had seen them often in the days of her training with the *SS*. Many officers could direct a mass killing with that same calm tone. It didn't take a cruel man to be a Nazi, though there were many who were. All that was necessary was a belief that he was superior to certain people groups, a belief that it was his duty to rid the world of life not worth living. She had yet to find out if Captain Steiner had bought into that thinking.

She opened the files, smoothed them out so that he could read them. There it was in black and white, the plans for an even more effective killing machine. Soon, young men in the Allied lines would be facing this monstrous hunk of metal as it came roaring toward them, smashing everything in its path and obliterating obstacles with its mighty gun.

The captain used the index finger of his good hand to trace the design of the hull, his eyes focused on the schematic of steel and nuts and bolts, then leaned his head back against the seat and gazed into the distance for several moments.

Hanne kept her face forward and used the time to study his hands while he was unaware. It was her belief that she could tell a lot about a man from his hands. Perhaps she had gotten in the habit long ago when she had climbed onto her grandfather's lap and traced the calluses and work lines in his hands. His were the hands of a hard-working man, but also hands that were gentle on the heads of his grandchildren and skillful when tending his garden. The sight of his hands folded in prayer had brought her such a feeling of peace.

She wondered what Captain Steiner's hands were accustomed to doing. Of course, one hand was held up higher than the other in its sling. But they were nicely formed hands with narrow knuckles and lightly spread with blond hair; the fingers looked supple and strong with short nails. On his left ring finger was the *SS* honor ring, its grinning silver skull gleaming.

Suddenly, he sat forward again. "*Fraulein*, take this down for me."

Hanne pulled out her steno pad and pencil as he began to rattle off measurements and then comments about changes in the design. She wrote continuously for a while, and when she paused to change pencils, he held up a hand.

"That's enough for now. This will give me something with which to start. Can you transfer it to type when we arrive?"

"Yes, if I can borrow a typewriter, sir."

"There will be an office for us to use while we are at the *Henschel and Son* factory. It is equipped with everything you need."

She should have known that German efficiency would have anticipated the tools they would need for this mission. "Very well, *Captain*. I will type it up as soon as we get there."

"And make three copies, please. Carbon will be fine."

Hanne nodded. "May I put away those papers for you?"

"Yes. Good idea."

Again, he laid the case in her lap and waited as she slid the papers in and clamped the lock tightly. This time, Hanne held her breath until he had leaned back away from her with the case securely cuffed to his left wrist. It was best to protect herself from the raw presence of the *Reich* in such close quarters.

But instead of drawing back completely, he turned toward her again. "So, tell me what you have done in the *SS* so far, *Fraulein*."

Hanne shrugged, letting the details slip out honestly. They were true, after all. "After my training, I worked in the *Reich Chancellery* for a while and was almost chosen as a secretary to the *Führer*. But. . . ." She lifted her palms in a resigned gesture.

He sighed. "Ah, yes, fate had other plans. I'm sure that was a grave disappointment." His eyes searched her face.

"Yes, *Captain*, it was." But not for the reasons he had in mind.

"Well, the work we are doing now may not have the glamor that one would enjoy at the *Führer*'s side, but it is nonetheless very important, an honor even."

"I do see it as such, *Herr Hauptsturmführer*." By Jove, it certainly was a coup for her.

"Then I am certain you will find it rewarding in its own way."

She met his eyes. "I'm sure I shall."

It was a mystery to Hanne why the captain was so chatty. Most officers she knew preferred to keep their own counsel, and speak to their assistants only to give orders or hand out rebukes. Of course, it was a fine morning if one discounted the bouncing from the ruts their driver seemed to find all too easily. The sun was shining and the fields beside them were filled with growing things. The flags on the front of the staff car were waving briskly in the breeze, announcing their official presence in every hamlet they approached. Every now and again, they would pass a platoon of *Hitler Youth* on a march or a German matron tending her flower bed. The pastoral beauty of the simple country life was numbing; Hanne felt more akin to these people than she should. Perhaps this was what her father missed when he spoke of his birth country. Or maybe she was just exhausted and her emotions were not quite dependable.

She hadn't slept much last night. Her dreams had been filled with tanks and *SS* captains whose metallic teeth glinted like the forked runes on their shirts. It was not comforting to be wearing those very emblems on her own jacket. The stiff white collar and thick woolen skirt of her uniform only intensified her identity with the people she had come to defeat, the nation whose ruin she had vowed to seek.

Hanne shifted in her seat and crossed her ankles. The Captain had fallen silent and was gazing out the window on his side of the car. They still had an hour to go according to her watch. Then the real work would begin, and there was more to it for her than *Hauptsturmführer* Steiner could possibly realize.

28

Kassel, Germany
Henschel and Son Werks

> *Those who deny freedom to others, deserve it not for themselves; and, under a just God, cannot long retain it.*
> Abraham Lincoln

The *Henschel Werks* was a beautiful target for a bombing raid.

That was Hanne's first thought as she entered the gates. Wouldn't that be a pretty sight; smoke rising from the rubble of a building complex that would never again turn out weapons? But alas, there were no bombers today, only her. It was her job to do the damage here; on her shoulders was the responsibility for whatever havoc could be managed. She'd start with a copy of those plans as soon as possible.

In the meantime, Hanne took in as many details as possible as she followed the captain into the belly of the beast. They were entering the office section now where a small room had been prepared for them. She was shown a desk with a typewriter and other secretarial paraphernalia. She sat down immediately to type out the captain's notes. He was engaged in conversation with another man in uniform; they stood a few feet from her desk but she could not make out their words since she had to be intent on the ones she was typing.

It was really a very good thing that she was an accomplished typist. Hitler actually would have been well served to have her on his personal staff. Well, he would have been until she'd managed to slip cyanide into his coffee or plant a bomb in his car. But, since she'd not been hired, he was safe for the time being. She would put her skills to work in this setting for now and maybe someday, another chance would come.

Hanne pulled the typed sheets out of the machine and put them inside a folder. She took the time to look through the drawers of the desk, noting the neat arrangement of supplies inside. She had just closed the last drawer when the captain stepped back toward her.

She stood as he approached. "Here are your notes, *Herr Captain*." She held the file and opened it so he could see them.

"*Danke*." He steadied the pages with his good hand and perused them quickly, his eyes darting over the words. "Excellent work, *Fraulein*."

He turned slightly and indicated a man standing in the doorway. "The *Sturmbannführer* is going to give us a personal tour of the works. I will need you to take notes for me as we walk through."

"Of course." Hanne removed her steno pad and pencil from her satchel and then placed the bag inside the lowest drawer of the desk.

The Captain stood back to let her pass in front of him and then followed her to where a stout looking man filled the doorway. "*Sturmbanfuhrer* Riefendahl, this is my assistant, *Fraulein* Lager."

Hanne extended her hand to the man who bent low and clicked his heels. "*Fraulein*, it is a pleasure."

"*Danke*, I'm glad to be of service."

"Now, if you and *Hauptsturmführer* Steiner will follow me, I will show you the wonderful workings of *Henschel and Son*." With a flourish of his hand, the man led the way out of the clicking machines and ringing phones of the office and into the hum and thrum of the war plant.

Eryk followed his female *SS* assistant into the factory, noting her smooth walk and graceful demeanor. In gray jacket and pleated skirt and crisp garrison cap, she was standard issue for the *SS Helferinnenkorps*. Still, she had a certain attitude that showed through and made her different from the other females he had encountered in military service. She had an independent streak that was unusual in a German woman, at least in those girls who had come through the days of the *League of German Girls*. He had spotted it from the first and supposed that it would make her difficult to work with, yet, despite his earlier misgivings, he believed she would prove a valuable assistant in this mission. She was bright and capable and even easy on the eyes, a point which might be distracting to the other men they would encounter. Perhaps her cool and assured attitude was her way of calming jittery nerves, though a woman who had been in the running for service to the *Führer* was probably not the nervous type. Still, maybe her distant approach to him would be a benefit; they would be working very closely, and he was already aware of her feminine charm.

Still, she had seemed untouched by his presence and that was something different in his experience. It was not uncommon for *SS* officers to be objects of great devotion by the young women of Germany. He himself had received numerous letters from *BDM* girls, written in the line of duty to the Fatherland, but laden with admiration. He had never lacked for female companionship when he desired it. If he had not been so intent on his other mission, perhaps he would have taken the time to cultivate a relationship with one of the girls from his hometown. As it was, his free time was limited and his interest often waned.

He noted that she was very interested in the workings of the plant, her eyes scanning the assembly lines and assessing the scale of the machines being built. It was quite unusual in his experience for a woman to be interested in engineering, still it was possible, he supposed. Or course, Propaganda Minister Goebbels would like all German women to be innocent of the violence of war and to be busy with hearth and children. But the sheer intensity and length of the war had made that impossible now. Women were being called upon to work alongside the men in order to preserve the *Reich*, and if women could work in the war plants, it wasn't too far-fetched to believe that they could be interested in the physics behind the designs.

Sturmbannführer Riefendahl was busily pointing out this and that, and Hanne was taking notes as she walked. When they stopped for a moment, Eryk took a couple extra steps to stand directly behind her and be closer to the work being done. They were looking at the tracks of the *Tiger Panzerkampwagon VI*. Eryk stepped forward to get a better look at the method being used to attach them to the hull. He was very interested in a redesign of the interlocking system since it wasn't hard for him to imagine these tracks oozing with mud and stuck in the deep trenches of the battlefield. If he had been able to get his *Panzer* out of the mud quicker, his crew might. . . bile rose in his throat, and made him take a deep breath and step backward. He had to hold himself together and focus on the design, on helping others to avoid the fate of his crew. He would honor them by making improvements.

He turned toward the *Sturmbannführer* and noticed his assistant looking at him with amused eyes. Was she laughing at him? Did she notice his discomfort and take joy in it? Beneath that pretty head must be a heart of stone. Eryk clenched his jaw and turned his back to her, facing their tour guide.

"*Sturmbannführer* Riefendahl, this is one of the areas where I am most interested in suggesting improvements. The tracking bogs too easily in the mud. Of course, that is partly from the weight of the machine, but I would like to look more closely at the schematic for the tracks to see if improvements can be made."

The other man was nodding as he listened, reminding Eryk of a tail-wagging puppy. "Of course, *Hauptsturmführer*. We will be glad to hear your suggestions."

Eryk turned to Hanne. "*Fraulein*, note the number of this station, *bitte*."

"Yes, *Captain*." She paused to write in her notebook. "Is there anything else you would like me to add to this section of notes?"

"No, I will dictate any further thoughts when we get back to the office."

She nodded as she started walking again. Behind her, Eryk noticed the wrench lying in the aisle just as her foot slipped on it. She stumbled slightly, and he reached out his good hand to steady her.

"*Danke, Captain.*"

"You're welcome, *Fraulein*. It is perhaps my fault you were distracted with taking notes. We can't have you ending up like me." He cocked his head to indicate his injured right arm.

The *Sturmbannführer* had turned around and noticed their slow progress. "Is something wrong?"

"*Fraulein* Lager almost fell, but there was no great harm done."

Out of his peripheral vision, Eryk noticed a hand reaching for the wrench. He glimpsed a striped sleeve as Riefendahl trod heavily back toward him. "It is the fault of our lazy workers that you were almost injured, *Fraulein*. I apologize for the inconvenience."

Reaching down, Riefendahl jerked on the collar of the man who was on hands and knees, retrieving the tool. "Stand up! *Achtung!*"

The man jerked upright, the wrench clasped in his hand, his stance rigid. Eryk was not surprised that the Kassel factory made extensive use of slave labor. Germany had seen the value of extracting needed manpower from those they subdued and imprisoned. He had never really cared about the fate of those deemed unwanted by the *Reich*. They were simply part of the equation. The man wore a striped uniform and flat expression and was quite thin.

Riefendahl's voice was tight with fury. "With your sloppiness, you have almost caused an accident to the *Fraulein*. We do not tolerate such inefficiency, such sabotage, in this factory."

The man kept his head down, utterly still.

Sturmbannführer Riefendahl called to a man standing nearby who wore a badge and held a riding crop in his hand. "This worker is lazy. Punish him."

"Yes, *Herr Sturmbannführer*." The burly man pointed with his stick toward the door. The prisoner immediately shuffled toward it, face still toward the floor.

Riefendahl watched them walk away and then turned back. "He will be punished, *Fraulein*. And again, I apologize for your discomfort."

Eryk thought he saw a hint of emotion pass through her eyes, but it was so quick he might have imagined it. "I am quite fine, *Herr Sturmbannführer*. Thank you for your concern." She didn't mention the prisoner.

Inwardly, Hanne was boiling mad. At herself and then at the despicable Germans who ran this horribly efficient factory. Why hadn't she been more careful? She could have prevented herself from stumbling and saved a man from a ruthless beating. For she was sure that was what was happening in the stone courtyard outside the walls of the plant. She had seen enough retribution on the part of the Nazis to know that they would exact their pound of flesh whenever given the chance. They would spare no effort in doing so.

She closed her eyes for a brief moment, mentally asking the man's forgiveness. What kind of terrors he now faced only God knew. But she knew that it would be heinous. Her days in Germany had given her many opportunities to observe these men of the master race in their dealings with the *untermenschen,* the ones they considered subhuman. The arrogance of their belief in racial purity and their disregard for traditional courtesies drove them onward to cruelty that often defied the imagination. Even she who had been trained in their ideologies and who had witnessed firsthand the atrocities of war was still mentally assaulted with images no person should ever have seen. The slave worker could be facing anything from an unmerciful beating to an execution-style shooting to a public hanging meant to discourage others from committing the same infraction of rules. There was no rhyme or reason to the Nazi code of punishment. It hinged solely on the mood of the officer in charge.

Silently, she willed the frail little man to have strength, mentally begging him to hang onto his dignity, to his life. Her father would have prayed for him to have strength to survive and comfort if he did not. But she was not her father. She wasn't sure God would hear her prayers. Besides, they were back in the office now and she needed to get on with the task at hand – arranging the destruction of the Nazis' new toy and with it the downfall of one *Haupsturmfuhrer* Eryk von Steiner. There would be cause for great celebration in that and perhaps the soul of the little man would be satisfied. It was the best a prodigal like her had to offer.

29

Kassel, Germany

> Once you've lived the inside-out world of espionage, you never shed it.
> It's a mentality, a double standard of existence.
> John Le Carre

They would be working at the factory for a few days. While in Kassel, the *SS* had provided accommodations for Eryk and his assistant at a local hostel. Their rooms were adjoining, but separate.

Hanne kicked off her shoes the minute the door to her room was closed. Her feet always suffered on these long days. *SOE* training had been insistent that a good operative cared for herself so that she could serve her country. Feet were especially important.

Sinking down onto the bed, she allowed herself to fall back against the coverlet, closing her eyes and reviewing the day. She could not write anything down, not here. Once she returned to Berlin, she might be able to record her thoughts and place them in her secret file. But for now, she had to rely on memory, and so it was imperative that she replay the events and scenes in her mind, cementing them into her recall. Tomorrow, she planned to use her camera-pen. Pictures would help the Allies know what kind of monstrous machine the Germans were now preparing. Then, somehow, she had to figure out a way to get the pictures and plans to her superiors. Maybe some of them thought she was dead. She had been out of contact for a very long time because she had been burrowing deep into the Nazi governmental labyrinth and trying to establish her cover as a dedicated and efficient German woman. But now, she really needed to make connections with her support system in London. She would do it too, as soon as she got the information she needed and figured out a way to manage the good Captain.

The architecture of the inn and the aroma of strudel filling the air took *Hauptsturmführer* Eryk Steiner back in time to a holiday outing his family had taken in the Bavarian mountains. There, they had slept in beds crisply made with eyelet eiderdowns and awakened each morning to a breakfast of cakes, pork sauerbraten inside flaky pastries, and coffee with rich cream. Beyond the window at the table stretched acres of lush green bordered on the right side with a sapphire-blue lake and on the left side by a massive wood with fir and hemlock, evergreen and spruce. It had been the best week of his life.

His little boy self had gazed out the window, his chin in his hands, longing to be a woodsman. His father had even allowed him to use the small hatchet and chop a few pieces of kindling for the fireplace. His sisters had flitted around like elfin princesses, making daisy chains and singing silly little rhymes. Even his mother had seemed improved by the beauty around them and the air of relaxation and quietness that was so refreshing. Eryk would have stayed there forever if he'd had the chance. He had been upset to return to the city with its busyness, its sirens, and its fast paced life.

But even as a child, Eryk had realized the ironclad grip of duty which held his father fast and beckoned to him even in tranquil moments, lurking like an ominous shadow at all their family outings. He knew its smothering grasp well for it now clutched at him with the same tenacity. Even in the moments when he was in the company of friends and the scenes of war were far removed, he felt rigidity in his soul that would never allow him to enjoy the bliss of civilian life. He was an officer, captive to his word, a bond slave to his own oath. In loyalty to that oath he had seen and experienced things that would forever sear his soul. There was no going back to the innocence of his boyhood, no hiding his eyes from the terror of the faces that he sometimes still saw in his worst nightmares. He could not run to his *Hauslehrerin* and be absolved of all guilt with the soothing caress of her hand on his head. No, he had blood on his hands. Like the man Cain of whom he had learned at her knee, he knew he was marked for life. Not in a way that others could see aside from the small *SS* tattoo on his left armpit, but definitely marked in a way that he could never erase, not even with the shedding of his skin. No, in order to be rid of the mark he carried, he would have to shed his very soul.

Dinner that evening was to be in the dining salon of the hostel where they were staying. Eryk had arranged for them to eat together since they would need to go over plans for the coming days. He now stood in front of his dressing mirror for a final inspection before going downstairs.

He flicked a piece of lint from his jacket and straightened his Iron Cross with his left hand. Curse the Russians and their shrapnel! He was anxious to be done with the cumbersome cast and sling that hampered his movements. He stiffened his back and clicked his heels, annoyed at his own impatience.

Hanne twirled the ribbons of her hat between her fingers as she waited for the Captain. On a whim she had dared to wear a different one tonight. Even an operative grew tired of regulation apparel and dressing up her appearance was a way to pick up her spirits after the horror of the afternoon. But, in spite of her festive look, her mind was not at rest.

Could there be a way to get the plans and sabotage the plant as well? If so, it would have to be carefully planned if she expected to save her own neck. Of course, the simplest way would be to detonate the bomb herself and be part of the sacrifice. But she could not hand over the plans if she were dead. Still, perhaps there was a way to send out the plans first and then plant the bomb. It would tip the Germans off to her erstwhile presence among them, but would the devastation be worth it? *HQ* might have other plans though. After all, she was the only *SOE* agent actually in Germany as far as she knew, and there probably wasn't time to get another one buried so far underground. There was so much that still needed to be done, and it was all on her shoulders.

She caught a glimpse of a uniform in the massive mirror in the dining room and realized that it was *Hauptsturmführer* Steiner. He was now entering the room where she stood, his eyes roving to where she waited. What could she glean from him tonight? The man was obviously loyal to his country, but it was up to her to find the cracks in his façade. She had to find a way to get into his brain. She had to find his weakness, his sentimentality, the connection to his heart that she could exploit. She must have no mercy, no space for consideration. Just as a lioness honing in on the weakness of her prey, she was on alert for Steiner's soft spot. Maybe the candlelit room and good food would put him off his guard. She heard soft music playing and felt gratitude for that. Now, she must discern how best to play her role. That was the crucial thing. She must help him let down his guard without him realizing it. It wouldn't take her very long to get the information she needed. But she needed a little luck.

30

Kassel, Germany
Hotel Führer Hof

> *All of us who are members of the Germanic peoples, can be happy and thankful that once in a thousand years fate has given us, from among the Germanic peoples, such a genius, a leader, our Fuehrer Adolf Hitler, and you should be happy to be allowed to work with us.*
> Heinrich Himmler, *Reichsfuhrer SS*

The dinner was excellent. Eryk was surprised at the good flavor, and especially pleased with the fresh vegetables served. The war was taking a toll on the fields and crops of Germany and many homes and even restaurants simply did without. He would have to inquire as to the abundance of produce in this area. Perhaps there was some local agricultural secret which was the reason for that bounty.

    He noticed that his assistant was enjoying her meal as well. It was the first really human sign he had seen from her. This afternoon she had seemed more like an automaton, taking notes, following him in the plant and then sitting down to type up all the information they had gathered. Even the incident with the factory worker hadn't upset her. He hadn't noticed a twinge of emotion whatsoever.

But that was common with these *SS* women. Whatever female gentleness had been in them was trained out of them. He had to admit it made him a little sorry. He hadn't been brought up to expect sternness and blankness from women, although his own mother had been so unbalanced that he might not have had any kind of standard by which to judge women had it not been for Zelda, and of course, her niece, Nadya. Where were they now? Alive? Or dead? Living in a Jewish ghetto or rotting in a mass grave like those he had seen in the Ukraine? He forced his thoughts back to the table and his plate and the words of *Fraulein* Lager. "I beg your pardon, what did you say, *Fraulein*?"

Hanne looked up and had the strangest feeling that she was about to find a way to connect with the man. So far he had been courteous and amiable but aloof. That was to be expected. But she had just glimpsed a faraway look in his eyes that gave her hope. It had something to do with the table and her presence. She decided to take a chance.

"The meal is delicious, *Herr Captain*. I appreciate you asking me to join you." She let her words float across the space between them, not smiling but coaching her face into soft, serious lines.

"You're welcome, *Fraulein*. I too am pleased. One never knows, in these times, which kitchens will be adequately stocked."

She allowed herself a slight smile in agreement. "The vegetables are especially good."

"Yes, a very welcome addition to the meal. I haven't eaten such good produce since before the war."

Hanne pounced on the opening with all the might of carefully silken words. So, tell me, *Captain*, did your family own vegetable gardens before the war?"

"Yes, they did. Wonderful plots of ground lush with beans and potatoes and herbs. I often sneaked a taste when I was playing." He lifted his eyebrows in mock consternation as he said it.

"I'm sure that was no great crime."

The captain forked a piece of beef. "Only if my mother caught me."

It was the way he said it that caught Hanne's attention. Here was a way into the treasures of his heart, but she would have to tread carefully. There was always danger when one got this close. One wrong word of vocal inflection or facial expression and she would put herself in suspicion. She had to choose her next comment carefully, yet she had to say something now because if too much time elapsed, the magical opening would close.

"She must have been a fastidious *hausfrau*, and I'm sure she wanted the best for you."

The minute she said it, Hanne knew she had misspoken. Emotions slid over his face that she couldn't even identify in the fleeting moment before he looked straight at her to reply.

"No, *Fraulein*, she was not a good *hausfrau*, but I can't see that as your concern."

Hanne was desperate to reclaim the ground she had gained. "Pardon me, *Herr Captain,* I meant no intrusion. *(although she did)* I am sure there were good reasons for her actions. I merely meant to compliment the woman who raised you."

Steiner laid his fork on his plate and put both hands on the table. She could see his SS ring glinting in the light from the chandelier, its skull laughing at her. "The woman who raised me was not my mother.

But both of them are now gone from my life, and I am a man left to my own way of doing things. Sneaking bites from the vegetable garden was a thing for boys, no? Now, I want to make a better *Panzer* that will protect its crew so that other mothers may still have their sons. That is what we should be talking about."

Hanne's legs felt wobbly under the damask tablecloth and her palms were clammy. She was glad she was seated and had the tableware to occupy her hands. She had pushed too far, too soon. The subject of his family was definitely closed. He resented her getting close to the information he held. She must get this interchange back under her control before she lost this chance entirely.

"Of course, *Herr Captain*. Again, forgive my rudeness. I meant no disrespect, and I do understand the urgency of your mission here. I am ready to help you in any way I can."

Steiner leaned back in his chair and crossed his arms. "Are you now? I'm glad to hear it. We do have work to do. Are you ready to take notes?"

Hanne took a sip from her water glass and then patted her lips with the cloth napkin. "Yes, of course. Let's begin."

Kassel, Germany
Arbeitslager

The long day was now over. As Zelda marched back with the others to the barracks, she sent up a silent prayer of thanks that she had made it through another day. These sweltering days of late summer were difficult, but not necessarily any more difficult than the freezing weeks of winter. Since she had been deported, Zelda had endured both seasons, and she couldn't decide which was more miserable, although it was less life-threatening to sweat than to shiver. But it was best just to be thankful, whatever season, for the grace to endure and survive. Not that the Father in heaven overlooked those who succumbed to the elements, for His love was open to all. But she was grateful for every day that her hearty German/Polish/Jewish constitution stood her in good stead. Her ancestry was of the warriors and survivors. Her people had settled savage lands and survived with little resources and endured, along the way, Egyptian slavery, Babylonian captivity, Roman oppression, unreasonable persecution, vicious pogroms, and rabid hatred. This latest round of misery was particularly barbaric, but God's people, her people, had not yet been eradicated from the earth. If she believed His Words, there was hope that they would come through even this.

As a child she had heard the words of Yahweh's ancient covenant with Abraham. The sound of the Yiddish rolling off the tongue of her father still rang in her ears. It was a story that grounded every Jewish heart, and since her family had been one of those few in Berlin who also accepted Christ as Messiah, the promises had held special meaning. Jesus had fulfilled the prophecies about His first coming; that meant that all the others would likewise come true. Zelda Goldman knew the promises about Israel being gathered together and given a land, Canaan, for their inheritance and dwelling place. She had not given up the faith that it would come true in her lifetime.

These were the thoughts that kept her company as she walked down the mucky streets of the German Lager. Five abreast, she and others like her quick-stepped toward the foreboding group of buildings where they passed the wretched night hours. The barracks were not comfortable and certainly not properly ventilated. The sanitary facilities were inadequate and filthy; stepping into the latrine area was always a messy proposition.

It was dark already; the laborers were driven to work long hours, from before dawn until after dusk. She left when it was dark and came back when it was dark. Besides glimpses of the outside from her work station, Zelda saw only darkness. Her world, once filled with color and texture and cadence, had been reduced to grays and browns and blacks, to scaly skin and protruding bone, to screams of pain, groans of despair and the maddening strains of march music which poured out of the bandstand at all hours of the day.

The German love of song had been twisted and perverted for the sadistic joy of the masters of the camps. It pleased them to provide serenade music for their victims, whether they were taking them to work or to death. So, every selection for transport and every departure of work detail was accompanied by the hilarious strains of polkas or the insulting fanfare of Wagner.

It was this fact that kept Zelda from declaring her usefulness as a musician. She had been prompted by others to let it be known that she once held a chair in the great *Berlin Philharmonic*. She would have been given better accommodations and clothing and a better chance at survival. But Zelda could not bring herself to offer her soul to the persecutors. Like her people of old, she had hung her harp on the willows. How could she play in a strange land? Her precious instrument was far away, hidden by her own hand before her deportation. She had had some sixth sense, some premonition that the trip she was taking would not lead to freedom and luxury. She had not been raised among the Germans and worked in Berlin for years for nothing; she could see through the glib promises and the glamorous phrases. There would be no family camps, no special status, no privileged work existence. One look at the train which came for her transport from Theresienstadt had proved it all horrifyingly true.

Beside the assurance that her Lord was with her, Zelda took consolation in the fact that her beloved violin was safe, waiting for loving hands to rescue it from its sleep one day. But there was another fact that awakened anxieties she could not lay to rest. It had been her constant torment from the day she stumbled into the transport train until now. She didn't know what had happened to Nadya. Perhaps, she was still in Theresienstadt, the "paradise" ghetto; perhaps, she had also been put on a transport to some wretched spot for backbreaking labor. But she was out there, vulnerable and alone. No, not really alone for the Father in heaven was watching. But Zelda ached to know the whereabouts of the child she had raised as her own, longed to do something to protect her. She wanted to ensure that she would live on, that the seed of her brother would not be strangled from the earth but rather bear testament, not only to the tribulation they had come through, but more importantly to the grace of God and power of life eternal.

So as the old woman turned to enter the smelly quarters that now held the only place of rest for her, she lifted her heart up in fervent prayer. This was how it was with her, day and night, remembering her two children, each of them lost to her in different ways, and interceding for them, doing her best to snatch them from the clutches of the one who has come to steal, kill and destroy.

Kassel, Germany
Hotel Führer Hof

Eryk stood by the window in his room and watched the light drizzle falling onto the street below. Though it was late summer, there was a chill in the air, and he was glad he had closed the window before going down to dinner. Now, the rain spattered against the glass and created smears of moonbeams on the pavement.

He was tired, and his arm was aching. It was probably time for a dose of the painkiller the surgeon had insisted he take with him at his last visit. They had told him that as the tendon healed, it would stretch and throb. They had been right. Perhaps he had jostled it more today than he'd realized. During the evening meal, it had begun to hurt quite a bit.

The thought of dinner made him think of his assistant, *Fraulein* Lager, and her questions. The woman was surely curious; he might even term her nosey, a bit too inclined to ask questions. That wasn't necessarily a good thing in a secretary. Yet, he had to admit that she had carried out her duties admirably today. He had no qualms about her typing; it was excellent, and she had shown an unusual aptness in catching on to his style of dictating notes. She had not complained about the long journey today or the laborious tour through the plant. As before, he felt there was something odd about her reaction or lack of it to the almost accident with the factory worker.

Actually, most of the SS women he knew would have uttered a few ugly words or given the man and the guard a tongue lashing. But she had done neither. That in itself was uncommon. Maybe she preferred to have as little contact as possible with the lower classes. That *was* typical enough behavior.

Eryk glanced back out the window, his eyes drawn to the pale orb of moon hovering above the city. In its glow he could see beyond the streets to the distant mountains shrouded in dark clouds. As always when there was a full moon, he remembered her words.

"Liebchen, when you grow up to be a man, wherever you are, look up at the moon at night and know that it is also shining down on me

somewhere and remember that I love you and my prayers go before you."

It was crazy to think that she might still be alive, and if she were that she remembered that promise. But *Hauptsturmführer* Eryk Steiner couldn't help the twinge of longing he felt inside; a tiny spark of hope that somewhere she was keeping her word. Yet the only way to reach out to her was to break his word, his oath that bound him to uphold the racial policies of the *Reich*. How could he do that? But what would happen if he did not?

Eryk turned his back on the moon and all it stood for. He needed to get some sleep. Tomorrow's tasks would be stressful.

31

Kassel, Germany
Arbeitslager

> *He laughed. He spoke of "doing away with useless mouths,"
> and that "sentimental slobber" about such people made him "puke."*
> Gitta Sereny, of interview with Franz Stangl, Commandant of Treblinka

The alarm for roll call sounded earlier than usual. Zelda could tell this even though she had no clock by which to judge the exact time. She could also tell that something was wrong. The *kapos* were always loud, but today their shouts reached a frenetic pitch as they screamed at the workers to get out of the bunks. Reaching up with cruel hands, they yanked on arms and shoulders and clothing and anything they could grasp to pull the weary women out of their bunks and hasten them outside to be counted.

The wooden planks creaked as hundreds of feet hit the floor. In the confusion, it was difficult to locate one's shoes and many lurched outside without them or with only one. This however was an offense that was usually punished, so the haste was not necessarily worth it. But the *kapos* had no sense of reason; they punished if one was slow and yet properly dressed, but they also punished if one were too fast and forgot something important. There was no pleasing them. All one could do was take whatever happened and try to protect oneself from the blows that were surely to follow.

Zelda managed to get her feet into her shoes and grab the piece of cloth that she generously thought of as her shawl. In reality, it was a piece of rough fabric from a supply bag that she had "organized" from the trash heap. But she protected it fiercely. That was a lesson she had learned on her first day in this surreal environment; what one did not protect, one lost.

She held onto the arm of a younger woman who had been sick in the night and helped her down the step onto the pavement outside. Together they hurried toward the roll call line. Already the prisoners were assembled, their flimsy striped dresses fluttering in the early morning breeze. Though it was chilly this morning, it was nothing compared to the scenes Zelda had seen in the winter when women had fallen and frozen while waiting to begin another day's work.

She helped the girl to her place and took up the spot beside her, planting her feet firmly as she trained her mind to settle in for another long siege. The women around her were doing the same. Most of them here were in reasonable health, at least the ones who were left. The weaker ones had died, their fragile condition worsened by the long hours of labor and almost nonexistent rest. Of course, only healthy prisoners were to be sent to a labor camp, but healthy was a word that had a different definition today. Those now marked "healthy" by the SS would have been hospitalized a few years ago. It was all a matter of who determined health. The SS were not known for compassion when it came to their workforce. Workers were expendable and replaceable, therefore, they worked the comparatively healthy ones until they died and then got others. The already sick ones were taken away; no one knew where. And roll call was often the proving grounds for who would make it and who wouldn't.

After a couple hours, the prisoners would begin to sway a bit from the tension of their upright position and continuously meager nourishment. Some would push through it; some would not. Those suffering from intestinal problems would groan with cramps and a need to dash for the latrine, though most of the time, they had to continue standing anyway and try to hide the evidence of their misfortune. The Germans were fanatical about the cleanliness of their prisoners. But they provided no means for washing bodies and clothing and even refused to excuse prisoners so they could care for bodily functions. When their victims were inevitably filthy and their clothing crusted with excrement and blood and mud, the members of the master race felt justified in cruel retribution. They were convinced that the point of Jewish inferiority was proven.

As she stood, Zelda focused her mind on the Scriptures, drawing comfort from the eternal words of God. This morning she mentally recited the ninety-first Psalm, her soul drinking up the reassurance of the inspired syllables.

"He that dwelleth in the secret place of the most High shall abide under the shadow of the Almighty."

She tried to dissect it and digest it, word by word. It was the best therapy she knew for her mind and spirit. Some of the other women mentally recited recipes or classic poems they had learned in elementary school or created letters to sweethearts and family. All of these methods were useful, but Zelda felt the power of the Word of God fed her spiritually as well as keeping her alert physically.

They usually lost several women in the morning. Those who had been hovering near the brink would collapse in a heap never to worry about another earthly roll call. Zelda often wondered what it would be like to leave this world at such a time and wake up in heaven to hear her name called out by the recording angel. That was one call she would gladly answer! But nevertheless, she had a tenacious clutch on the life she now lived, miserable though it was. She was determined to finish the task she felt was still hers to do – rescue Nadya and Eryk from their imminent deaths, one physical and one spiritual.

But this morning, only two or three women had collapsed when the call to attention was given again and the commandant began to speak.

"There has been an escape. We are looking for your fellow worker who has decided she does not like the accommodations here at the *Lager*. You will stand here until we find her. And when we do find her, you will wish that we had not."

Zelda slid her eyes to the woman at her side, willing her to stay strong, to stay upright. She was young and new to the camp system, both detriments. Zelda breathed a prayer for her, petitioning God for strength for her neighbor whose head scarf and thin dress and hungry belly were just like her own, and she kept praying, while the sun timidly peeked out on the horizon and then began its climb into the sky. Just when she thought her own legs would crumple under her, the bay of dogs announced the return of the searchers.

Zelda opened her eyes to view the tragic procession striding into the center of the camp. Between two guards was a pitiful scrap of a woman, her stick legs barely supporting her bloated stomach and awkward body. As she stumbled along, the SS were taking turns clubbing her on her back, her sides and her head. Blood was trickling down her limbs and cheeks. Finally, she tumbled down in front of the assembly, still trying to cover her head with her arms.

The commandant strode forward to where she lay and kicked her in the side until she turned over. Her mouth was open and her hands were stiffened in pain until they resembled claws. The officer towered over her, his face impassive, as if he dealt death blows every day, which indeed he did. In a voice that was smooth yet loud, he issued the verdict. "Prisoner 43877, you have shown ingratitude for your friends and your life here in this camp. After all we have done for you, you repay us with contempt." He paused and smiled sardonically. "Because you did not consider how this would make your friends feel, you will now have time to watch them suffer along with you. I have received an order for a selection of one hundred prisoners for a special assignment. You will be one of them, and so will ninety-nine of your fellow inmates."

With that, the commandant turned gracefully on his heel and walked away from the cowering woman in the dust. Zelda couldn't help but remember the story of another woman thrown to the ground in terror before a man in authority. But that man showed mercy and love. This one showed neither.

The guards dragged the inmate to a standing position, and then began randomly choosing other prisoners to fill the selection quote. Roughly, they pulled women out of the lines. Some protested and received a gun butt to the face in response; others simply ducked their faces in resignation to fate and stepped into the tragic queue.

When her number was called, Zelda was not surprised. She had always known the day would come when her usefulness would be transcended by the Nazi annihilation policy. Every inmate had but a few allotted days; she had survived longer than most. If the Lord was allowing her course to be finished, then it was time. Her one regret was that she had not been able to do more for her children, for Nadya and Eryk. But that was in His hands, not hers.

As she stepped out into line with the others selected, Zelda whipped off her "shawl" and balling it up in her fist, she handed it to the young woman who had been beside her all morning. Looking into the girl's haggard eyes, she whispered, "Hang on, dear, to life and to God."

Then Zelda Goldman, Jewess, governess, violinist extraordinaire, slave laborer and child of God, lifted her head and marched forward, bedraggled in appearance, but confident in the Keeper of her destiny.

32

Kassel, Germany
Henschel and Son Werks

> *I surrendered my moral conscience to the fact that I was a soldier, and therefore a cog in a relatively low position of a great machine.*
> Otto Ohlendorf

"*Herr Hauptsturmfuhrer*, I have been notified that all the details are ready for the test to begin." The young SS adjutant stood ramrod straight as he spoke the words.

Eryk looked at his assistant who was busily typing up a new recommendation he had figured out for improving the interlock system of the *Tiger's* wheel mechanism. "*Fraulein* Lager, I will need you to accompany me on this test and take notes."

Hanne's hands stilled on the keys and she nodded swiftly. "Of course, *Herr Captain*. Let me get my notebook and pen." She turned, opened a desk drawer and drew out the items, then reached for her cap.

"You might wish to take your purse as well, *Fraulein*. We will be going to another location."

Her eyes darted from him to the adjutant. "I see. Very well, here it is. I am ready."

Eryk stood up and smoothed down his jacket, then reached for his sling. While he worked inside, he could rest his arm on the desk. But when he had to walk or stand for very long, it was too difficult to keep the arm immobile without the sling. As he pulled the cumbersome thing over his head and slipped his arm into it, he thought how anxious he was to be done with it all. It seemed to be healing nicely, as far as the wound was concerned. But he knew it was the muscle damage inside that had really worried the surgeon. Until he was able to try using it, no one really knew if it would be fully functional or not.

The ride to the test site was not very long, but after they had gone a few minutes by road, they turned onto a field and proceeded to jostle over the uneven terrain for a bit longer. Sitting beside the Captain, Hanne tried to keep her steno pad and pen from falling onto the floor of the staff car. He had told her last night that there would be a test over the maneuverability of the present *Tiger*, and so she knew that it would have to take place out in the open and not in a contained environment. Steiner would be assessing the way the machine moved and turned and its ability to proceed to a target. He had said they would probably also test the tank's ability to neutralize impediments to its progress.

Since she had never seen a *Tiger* in action, Hanne was eager for this test. This was a chance to see the monster and what it could do on the battlefield. Her eyes and ears were on alert for any information she could gather that would help the Allies prepare to meet this metal nemesis. She hoped her eagerness wasn't showing through. Usually, when she was excited, her face would get that pinkish tinge that made the American boys call out "English Rose." Thinking of the Yanks brought a faint smile to her lips. They had been full of such derring-do, real sports. She missed the banter they had brought to the training grounds and barracks of England.

"I'm glad you're smiling, *Fraulein*. Not many women adapt so well to tasks which require tromping around in fields." Steiner was looking at her with amused eyes.

Hanne mentally jolted into the present. Enough of the daydreaming; it was too costly. "I'm glad I meet with your approval, *Hauptsturmführer*."

"*Jah, Fraulein* Lager. You have been a great help already. Now, I see we have arrived. Let me help you out of the car."

Hanne wanted to laugh. It was she who was supposed to be helping him. He was the invalid. Well, maybe that term was a bit too strong for a man as fit and ready as Steiner. He maneuvered himself out of the car very easily after the aide opened the door. Then he reached back a hand to assist her out as well.

She took it and climbed out as gracefully as possible, though as soon as her feet hit the ground they sank into the uneven silt of the field. She put one hand out to touch the car and steady herself then immediately wished she had one hand free to cover her nose. The stench that permeated the air was overpowering. She had never encountered a smell compared to it. It wasn't the aroma of farm-fresh manure or blood-soaked soil, but a stomach-churning mist of rottenness. She swallowed hard and tried to ignore it.

Steiner had already turned to discuss the details of the test with the officer who had appeared to meet them.

"Welcome, *Hauptsturmfuhrer*. We are all ready to begin. If you will follow me to the test area, we have chairs waiting for you." The man indicated that they should walk with him as he turned and skirted a small patch of woods which then opened up into another large field.

Here there was a small wooden platform with a few chairs arranged on it. The officer led the way to the chairs and waited while they were seated. Then he pulled out a sheaf of papers from his attaché case and handed them to Steiner.

"These are the statistics from the last test we made on this model. You may want to use these records for comparison with the notes taken today."

"Excellent." Steiner accepted the papers and glanced through them. "This will be helpful. Let's get to it. I'm ready when you are."

The officer turned back toward the woods and gave a signal. Hanne, watching with an almost giddy sense of anticipation, noticed columns of people walking out from the woods. As they emerged, she could see scarves on their heads and stripes on their clothing. Though they marched in an orderly fashion, she could see men shouting at them and clubbing some of them with sticks. She knew instantly who these people were. She had been around Germany long enough to understand the prominence of the camps and the state of the people who resided in them. But why in the world were inmates being brought in to witness a test for a tank? What possible purpose could they serve?

Then, suddenly, she understood. These people were the test. They were the impediments to be neutralized.

It must not happen. She had to stop this. Agent or no, she couldn't sit here while these people were murdered. And yet, if she tried to stop it, all the months of burrowing deeper into the *Reich* would be wasted. All the lies she had fought her conscience to tell would be pointless sins. All the files she had gathered would never reach HQ back in London. All she had come to do would not be done.

No, there was nothing she could do. She, Hanne Lager, daughter of a pastor, agent for the Allies, decent human being, would have to watch murder and say not a word.

Eryk was looking at the papers he had been handed when he became aware of movement to his right. His peripheral vision caught stripes and scarves, and he was suddenly very interested in what was happening.

They hadn't gone over the details of the obstacles to be put in the path of the tank. He had supposed they would use damaged aircraft or other hulks of unusable armaments. He hadn't counted on people.

What was the plant supervisor thinking anyway? It was no great feat for a tank to run over bodies. He had done it himself on the battlefield though he derived no great pleasure in it. After the initial jar of the impact, running over a human body was but a mere bump for the tank; the tracks would raise just a bit as they ground up and over. But he had come here today to see the *Tiger* encounter immovable objects, not the pitiful skeletons of inmates.

He gestured toward the prisoners. "Are these the obstacles for the test? I thought we were going to use machinery and buildings."

The officer beside him broke into a grin. "Yah, we are going to use some stronger objects than these for the final test. But, the commandant of the nearby labor camp thought you might enjoy seeing our *Tiger* make quick work of Jews as well. Besides, he had a punishment selection to make, and he was busy today. We are doing a fellow officer a favor. After they are dispatched, my crews will move the other obstacles into place."

Eryk was disgusted. This was unsavory, certainly not a seemly way to conduct a military test. What did it prove to run over a bunch of old women? Could the High Command in Berlin actually approve of such practices? Furthermore, he didn't relish the bloody scene that would enfold. It would be gruesome to watch, for the women were sure to scream and run as the *Tiger* came toward them. Then there would be cleanup afterward. Really, it seemed like too much trouble.

And what of his assistant? Would she have the guts to take it? He glanced over at her and noted that her hands were folded tightly in her lap and her eyes stared straight ahead.

Still, no matter how much he would like to rankle his assistant, Eryk couldn't go along with this ridiculous plan. Surely, they could find some other way to assist the camp commandant with his problem.

Then he saw her.

He was sure of it in an instant, though he had not laid eyes on her in years. The straight posture was gone; she wore no elegant clothing. She was older and stooped and clothed in a ragged dress. But he glimpsed a sad dignity in the way she moved and a rhythm to her steps that reminded him of the beautiful music she used to play.

It was Zelda.

He almost stood to call out to her.

All at once, she stumbled over the mushy ground, trying to hold onto the woman in front of her. But a hole in front of her made her jerk and then fall completely to the ground.

The guard screamed and whipped her with his stick, curses frothing out of his mouth. That's when Eryk found his legs.

Jumping off the dais, he covered the ground in long strides and reaching out his uninjured left arm, he yanked the whip out of the guard's hand and stood, feet apart, eyes grim, surveying the pitiful scene. He had no idea what he was going to do. He only knew he had to do something.

Looking up from the mud, Zelda Goldman heard a voice she would have recognized in her dreams. It was him. He was shouting at the man who had been whipping her. Her head had been struck several times. She was dizzy, and there was a ringing in her ears. She couldn't understand what Eryk was saying, but somehow, she knew he was in charge here, and she also knew, with deep conviction, that she would not die in the field today.

Just before she fainted, she squinted up in the bright sunlight and caught a glimpse of his face. There, beneath a cap with a skull, she saw blue eyes that begged her for mercy. Strange, she thought, when I am the one who is being pardoned. Then she slumped onto the dirt and wondered about it no more.

33

Kassel, Germany
Arbeitslager

Thou shalt not be a victim, thou shalt not be a perpetrator, but, above all, thou shalt not be a bystander.
Yehuda Bauer

Hanne watched in amazement as the *SS Hauptsturmführer* halted an execution. He had practically leaped from his seat to get onto the field. Now, she saw him talking in quick short bursts to the guard who accompanied the prisoners. She didn't know what to make of it. Why should Captain Steiner care about a bunch of filthy women inmates? It didn't add up, didn't match the profile of the Nazi aggressor every *SS* man was trained to be.

She couldn't hear what he was saying, but she saw him gesture toward the woman on the ground and then toward the others standing behind him. The woman suddenly slumped further down in the dirt, apparently having fainted. Steiner squatted down beside her and with his gloved hand, tipped up her chin to peer directly into her face. Nodding his head, he again spoke to the guard who suddenly shouted to another officer who had been part of the prisoner escort.

"Take this prisoner back to the camp to be held for interrogation. *Raus!*"

The guard hurried forward and helped his superior grab the woman under the arms. Together, they dragged her to the side, and then the younger man walked quickly back toward the woods, soon disappearing from sight.

Steiner walked back to the platform, dusting his gloved hands against each other, a disgusted look on his face. When he reached the chairs, he adjusted his cap and sat down. Hanne desperately wanted to know what he had said, but she made herself hold her tongue. She didn't have long to wait. Steiner seemed eager to spill his news.

"The woman there is someone I recognized as an important prisoner whom I must interrogate. She is being taken to a cell, and I will talk to her later."

So that was it. Somehow it still didn't add up to Hanne, although his words were spoken naturally enough and with the right amount of conviction. But she couldn't forget the look in his eyes when he had seen the woman. It hadn't been the look of satisfaction at having discovered a fugitive but rather one of terror, the expression one might have when seeing a favorite pet about to be mangled by an oncoming automobile. But she said none of this.

"A very good idea, *Herr Hauptsturmfuhrer*. Now, will we complete the test?"

Hanne wanted no part of this massacre but she couldn't very well say that. So, she reached down in her soul for the grit to bluff her way through. Maybe at the last minute she would think of some way to sabotage the plan.

But to her surprise, Steiner shook his head. "*Nein.* I have asked for the prisoners to be punished in some other way. I do not wish the wheel mechanism to be clogged with mutilated flesh. It sticks to the interlocking wheels you see, and could further delay the other tests we must run."

Hanne's blood pressure was already rising, though she knew, in her line of work, emotion was deadly. She must remain calm, as if they were discussing a load of fruit being crushed, not human beings. "A helpful observation, I am sure."

"Indeed." He smiled as if nothing had happened and gestured toward her notebook. "We will soon be starting the real tests. I understand they are bringing out several hulks of aircraft for this model to run against. You will need to be ready to take down my notes."

Then, he turned to the officer from the *Henschel Werks* seated beside him who was in charge of the test.

Inwardly fuming at his cool demeanor, Hanne looked back at the field and saw that the prisoners were being taken away. The young officer had returned with a hand cart pushed by two men in striped suits. They wore caps on their heads, but she saw no hair sticking out from beneath and their cheeks were sunken, their eyes hollowed. Stooping down, they picked up the old woman, one taking her arms, the other her feet. Then they transferred her to the cart and set off at a brisk pace through the woods.

Knowing the German obsession with cleanliness and the Nazi penchant for secrecy, Hanne was sure that the woods were used as a natural cover for the labor camp's entrance. While she hadn't been aware that one was this near to the factory, she was in no way surprised. The SS often used conscripted labor and many small camps for these workers had sprouted up all over Germany. Unlike the extermination camps which were mostly located in occupied Poland, away from the German people and in obscure locations befitting their heinous clandestine purpose, the labor camps were in the Fatherland itself.

Hanne wanted to see this camp, and she needed to document its location in case the Allied bombers would actually target the Henschel factory. Maybe Steiner would let her accompany him to the interrogation he planned to conduct. After all, he would need someone to take notes.

Zelda Goldman woke up, not in heaven as she anticipated a few hours earlier, but bumping along on a hand cart. She was lying face up on the cart and her first sight was branches hanging low, covering the daylight. It was cool here, and the air was fresh and pine-scented. She knew she was in the small patch of forest that skirted the camp, but she was unsure why. She didn't feel immediate pain in any part of her body; that was good. She craned her neck just a bit to see who was wheeling her stretcher, and glimpsed striped caps and a few steps back, a black cap with a skull. Inmates and a guard.

Where were they taking her? To a pit to shoot her? To the camp infirmary where she would no doubt die of infection or from some medical experiment? Was she going to be hanged on the camp gallows?

In spite of all she had so far endured, Zelda was tempted to panic. Was there no end to the terror the Nazis could inflict on helpless people? To think one was going to die only to be momentarily rescued and then to be carted off to another unknown destiny . . . it was unsettling, even to one who had seen so much that she figured there was little else to traumatize her. But the visceral quest for life was so deep that even she, who was at peace with her Lord, was unwilling to relinquish her grasp on it. There was fight left in her still.

She closed her eyes and admonished herself to wait, to see what fate had been decided for her by the Germans. No, wait! It had been

Eryk she had seen in the field, Eryk in the uniform of the Nazis with bars on his arm and a skull on his cap. What had he been doing in that field? Surely her boy was not supervising executions! Oh, gracious Father, surely not that! Better he had died in battle somewhere than to be part of this system that was strangling the life out of her people and many others. No, she didn't mean that either. Eryk wasn't ready to die. He did not believe in the Savior. Even if he was involved in killing, there was still a chance, as long as he was alive. Zelda stifled the sobs that wanted to erupt from her throat and tried to pray instead.

The little entourage was out of the woods now and headed back toward the camp. At least she wouldn't be shot and left for dead in the woods. And as they passed through the camp gates, the question about her destination was answered.

"Take her to the cellblock."

Zelda opened her eyes in tiny slits and squinted through them. The guard was gesturing toward the brick building where beatings and experiments took place. No! They were going to torture her because she had fainted?

Of course, that was not so far-fetched for Nazis, but still, she felt her resolve tremble just a little. She had heard horrible things about this building. Whatever was to come would likely not be pleasant.

Closing her eyes once again, she began a prayer in her mind. It was a chant, a lifeline to which she clung as they neared the entrance to the cellblock. "Father, give me strength just now. Father, give me strength just now. Father. . . . ."

34

Kassel, Germany
Arbeitslager Cellblock

> *One person of integrity can make a difference.*
> Elie Wiesel, Holocaust survivor and author

The smell inside the cell block was revolting.

Eryk had been in a great many places with a variety of horrible odors and this one ranked right up there with the worst. The mixture of dirt, vomit, excrement, blood and disease was a virtual mist that hung in the air, putrefying every breath one took. For all their obsession with cleanliness, the Germans cared little about the environment of their prisoners. In jackboots, gloves and overcoats, the guards kept as much barrier as possible between themselves and the prisoners. Whenever they came into direct contact with the pitiful creatures in their charge, they despised them even more for their hideous state.

Eryk refused to let himself be sickened by the smell and followed the guard down the dank hall. Though it was midday outside, it was dusky inside the building; the thick stone walls held out the sunshine as effectively as they did any shred of comfort or hope. There were few sounds coming from the cells and Eryk surmised it was because most of the wretches brought here were by now in no condition to make noise or had been threatened into silence.

The guard stopped at the last door on the left and unlocked it. He turned to Eryk. "Would you like the prisoner brought to the interrogation, *Herr Captain*?"

"That won't be necessary this time. I will let you know if I decide to do that later on." Eryk ducked his head to enter the small space.

"Very well. Knock when you are ready to leave. I will be listening." The guard locked the door behind him.

His eyes beginning to adjust to the dim light, Eryk turned toward the cot in the corner where a body was lying, legs extended over the side. He walked over and knelt down.

Her eyes were closed and her breathing labored. He touched her cheek hesitantly. "*Hauslehrerin*?"

She didn't stir.

He shook her shoulder gently. "*Lehrerin*?"

Her eyelids fluttered, drooped, then widened. "Eryk? *Liebchen*? Is it really you? Oh, thank God! Thank God!" Her hands reached toward him and she began laughing and crying all at once.

"Sh, sh! I am so sorry, but we must be very quiet. They mustn't hear what we are saying!"

She looked stricken. "Oh, of course. I wasn't thinking! But to finally see you again after all these years. . . Oh, *Liebchen*, I am so happy! But look at you! Your arm. What have you done?"

Eryk tapped his sling with his left hand. "A battle injury. It is healing."

"Ach, I am so sorry. I was always afraid when you were little and so enamored with war that you would grow up and be destroyed by it."

"But I'm going to be okay, *Hauslehrerin*. It's not a life-threatening wound."

"Eryk, *Liebchen*, there is more to be destroyed than your arm, precious though it is."

He refused to take the bait, to go to the theme she was suggesting. "You are the one who doesn't look so well, Zelda. How is your heart?"

She was struggling to sit up. Eryk helped her as she eased upright and then back against the wall for support. He swung her legs up on the cot so she could rest them, and he noticed that her ankles were thick with swelling. She met his eyes. "My heart is in God's hands. It always has been."

"Yes, but you always told me that my mother was in His hands too and look what happened to her."

"Oh, *Liebchen*, what did happen to your dear *mutter*?" Her voice caught on the words.

"She got worse and worse until they put her in a state center where she died of pneumonia, or so they say."

"I am so sorry, dear boy. But it is not God's fault that these bodies do not work right, *jah*? That came from the serpent. We are in His hands whether we are well or sick. Either way, the decision is His."

She hadn't changed. That was easy to see. Her faith was as undaunted as though this was a conversation in his boyhood when she was young and healthy, well-dressed and employed by a wealthy German family. While he was fascinated by the iron resolve that drove her, he did have to get to the real point of this conversation before the guard got curious or they were interrupted in some other way.

"Zelda, you must listen. I am here to help you."

She smiled at him knowingly. "I know that."

"No, I mean I have been searching for you, trying to find out what happened to you. I did not know that you had been deported."

"But you didn't know anything for years, Eryk. We had no contact with each other."

"I know that, and I feel so ashamed. Forgive me, please, I beg you." He couldn't keep the tremble out of his voice. As he said the words, the enormity of what he had turned from, of how he had avoided reality gushed upon his heart. He had chosen not to think of her. He had forced her from his mind and tried to expunge her from his memory. He was a traitor, and he felt blackened and monstrous.

The frail woman in the bed looked up at him with a shining light in her eyes and reached her hand toward him, her voice gentle. "Of course. You know you are forgiven. I have prayed for so long that I would see you again. What has happened in between doesn't matter."

"Thank you, *Hauslehrerin*. I am so glad to have the chance to tell you I am sorry and hear your voice again. But, it doesn't erase the wrong I have done to you, and that is also why I have come to talk to you now. I want to get you out of here."

"No, Eryk, you can't do that! How would you manage that? I am a prisoner, a slave laborer."

"Yes, I know. But today, you were selected for *special handling*. Perhaps with your number already in another file I can find a way to simply "lose" you in the paperwork, make it look as though you were killed today."

Zelda's eyes focused on him. "Is that what happened to the others, Eryk? Were they killed?"

He avoided her gaze. "Probably. I don't really know."

"Oh, *Liebchen*!" she put trembling hands to her mouth.

"But they weren't mauled by the tank, *Lehrerin*. I stopped that; I did all I could."

At those words, she sighed and reached out her fingers toward him. "Thank you, Eryk, for that."

"But, back to you, I have to find a way to get you out."

"Eryk, it's impossible."

"No, it's not. It can't be."

"But it is. Listen, *Liebchen*. Listen!" Her whisper was commanding.

"Yes?"

"Do you remember Nadya?"

Of course he did. Nadya, his playmate, his little friend with the black curls who didn't like to play war. "Yes, why?"

"She is still in *Theresienstadt*, Eryk. At least, I think she is. I haven't heard from her in so long. We were deported together from Berlin. Do you know where that is?"

"I've heard of it, but I've never been there."

"Oh, *Liebchen,* it is a terrible place. Not as bad as this camp, but still awful. There is no hope there for everyone knows the transports go out regularly and that the people never return. The dead lie in the streets and the children play with the carcasses of horses and smuggle in eggs through the wall. If they are caught, they are shot at the wall. Oh, Eryk, that is where Nadya is."

Eryk was eyeing the cell door and listening closely for any sound on the other side. The description she gave was wretched but then so were most of the detainment camps for Jews and Gypsies and other undesirables. Though he didn't like to think about little Nadya living in such a place. He leaned close to the old woman and whispered. "What do you want me to do?"

"Find her. Rescue her. Leave me and take care of her."

"No! You were my teacher, my friend, my. . .." He had almost said *mother*. "I cannot leave you here in this place."

She pushed back from the wall and leaned toward him, eyes blazing. "Eryk, every day I have prayed for two people – you and Nadya. I need you to find her because I cannot. That will make me happier than being free myself. I am an old woman. Nadya is young, and has so much left to live for. Please, do this for me." She fell back against the dirty cot, her momentary burst of strength expended.

Eryk raised his good hand to protest, but let it fall to his side. She was probably right. Even if he could get her out of the camp, it would be extremely difficult to get her well and find a place to keep her while he was carrying out his official duties. There were suspicious eyes and ears everywhere. But, his heart rebelled against the thought of leaving his Zelda in the hands of the guards here. He needed some time. "Let me think about this."

"No, Eryk. There is no time. Every day that you wait is another day that she slips even further away from me, from you. Please go to her."

Her voice was raised and she was almost crying. He had to get her quiet.

"Yes, of course, I will look for her, do what I can. But, after I find her, I am coming back for you."

"Thank you, Eryk. It will be well, I know it."

"I have to go now, *Lehrerin*. I may make it worse for you by staying too long."

"Yes, go. And remember, my prayers are always with you, *Liebchen*."

He knelt again by her, ignoring the filth on the floor that was staining his uniform. "*Lehrerin*, you saved my life so many times. I am sorry I can't do more to save yours." Tears he thought he had outgrown gathered in his eyes as he looked at the woman who had mothered him through his formative years and shaped the character that others saw in him now. How could he have turned his back on her for so long?

"Eryk, Jesus is the one who saves lives. I am praying He will save yours." She pulled his hand to her lips and kissed it. "Now, go, dear boy. Go, and God be with you."

Eryk nodded, not trusting himself to speak. He banged on the cell door, hoping to communicate irritation and disgust to the watchful guard.

He heard the key turn in the lock and then the door swung open. Eryk walked out, leaving behind the only human being who had ever really loved him sitting on a dirty cot, sick and alone. And he hated himself for it.

35

Kassel, Germany
Arbeitslager

> *This is a page of glory in our history which has never been written and is never to be written.*
> Heinrich Himmler, October 4, 1943

Waiting in the staff car, Hanne fidgeted and fussed, quietly of course. First of all, she was mad at Steiner for refusing to let her come along. What great information she might have gotten from being inside those walls! Second of all, she had the feeling that he was up to something more than a simple interrogation. Things just didn't add up. If he was going to conduct an interview, he would need her to write down the notes. He certainly couldn't do it with his right hand in a sling. What's more, his reaction to the woman on the field wasn't normal for an SS officer, despite his very casual attempt to cover it. It had been something more than a concern that skin and bones would gum up the wheels of the tank! Hanne almost shuddered at the flippant way that thought formed in her head. Was she becoming used to the killing after all? Did a pathetic group of prisoners mean nothing to her anymore? She needed to be vigilant, guard her soul against the hardening of emotion that accompanied this callous disposal of human life all around her.

But, be that as it may, she would still wager that the good Captain was hiding something, and this little interrogation ruse was part of it. He had been so fired up about the test and improving the precious *Tiger*, but after the prisoners had been driven off the field, he had seemed barely able to concentrate as the mighty machine mowed down all the other obstacles in its path. She had even had to prompt him for notes.

Eryk Steiner's thoughts were jumbled as he emerged from the cell, but he didn't have time to sort through them. He had to get back to the *Henschel Werks* and resume the work he was committed to. It was still important that he help produce a *Tiger* that wouldn't bog down so easily and would better protect the crew inside. He wanted to avenge the deaths of the men he still saw in his dreams, but other scenes from the past were now becoming stronger and confusing his focus.

He hadn't thought of Nadya in years, but as he walked toward the staff car, the memories came flooding back. When Zelda Goldman had left the service of his family, all of his ties to her niece had been severed as well. They had once been playmates. That was all. He recalled dark curls and eyes that he thought, as a boy, looked like brown velvet. The last time he had seen her, she had been a gangly adolescent who had come to help her aunt move some of her belongings out of the Steiner household. Her eyes that day hadn't been soft, but full of hatred. But the teenage boy that he was then hadn't cared at all, hadn't given a thought to what the future held for the two women. How he wished now that he had been less infatuated with the newfound sense of power he felt in being included in the Aryan world. How he wished he would have retained compassion for the woman who had taught him all the good and gentle things he knew about life. But he had not. Now, for her sake, he was going to go from being one kind of traitor to being another. That's what it boiled down to. He was now concocting a treasonous plan.

When they reached the entrance to the building, Eryk turned to the guard and barked, "I want to see the commandant at once."

"Yes, *Herr Captain*. I will take you to him."

The man motioned for him to follow and led him past several rows of barracks to a squat brick building. Opening the door, the lieutenant let him enter first and then followed, stopping at a desk just inside.

" *SS Hauptsturmfuhrer* Steiner to see the commandant." He spoke to the woman sitting at the desk. She wore the bars and the arrogance of the *SS Helferinnen*. Scanning Eryk's face and giving a saucy smile, she pressed the button on her intercom machine. "*Kommandant*, there is a *Hauptsturmführer* Steiner of the *SS* to see you."

The machine crackled as she released the button. Then a voice answered, "Enter."

The woman pointed toward the door to her left. "In there."

Eryk clicked his heels. "*Danke, Fraulein.*" He walked a few steps to the door and pushed it open.

The commandant of the *Arbeitslager* looked up from his writing as Eryk entered. "Yes, *Hauptsturmführer* Steiner... *Heil* Hitler."

Eryk raised his hand and returned the greeting.

"Now what can I do for you?" the commandant asked.

"Sir, you may have heard that I redirected an execution this morning that you had ordered."

"Yes, I am aware that you objected to the method."

"I did object on the grounds that it would have created problems with the machinery that I was using for military tests. I assure you, sir, that I am not in the habit of complicating orders."

The commandant grimaced as he spoke. "I am prepared to overlook it this time since it was not difficult to dispose of them. It doesn't take very long to shoot a hundred, you know, and we have plenty of pits for the job. Consider the matter closed. I understand your dilemma, though I had hoped to make an exhibition that would discourage other escape attempts. But, no matter . . . there will be another time, yah?"

Eryk swallowed. So the other prisoners were already dead. "Thank you, sir, for your understanding."

"Not at all. Can't have good machinery fouled up with Jew guts, can we?" He laughed.

"No, we can't, sir," and Eryk meant it totally differently.

"By the way, what about the prisoner you wanted to interrogate? Have you finished with her?"

"No, sir, I would like to have another opportunity to speak with her. I have some investigating to do first, but I would like to return and see what other information she can give me."

"Of course, that can be arranged. She's not going anywhere." The commandant quirked a smile. "Let me know when you want to see her again. But don't wait too long. These Jews have weak systems. They don't last very long." He winked.

Eryk felt bile rise in his throat, but he forced a smile. "I will come back very soon. Until then, *Heil* Hitler!" He saluted as best he could with his left hand, pivoted and walked out the door.

He felt angry as he walked back to the car. An adjutant opened the door as he reached it, and Eryk climbed in, raking off his cap as he sat. His assistant still sat in the seat, hands folded, gaze straight ahead, back stiff. She was mad. Too bad. No way was he going to let Miss Prim and Proper in on this secret. With her connections, she'd go right to Himmler and he wouldn't get the chance to rescue anyone because he'd be in a camp himself. But he made himself respond in a courteous tone. "Thank you for waiting."

"Did you get the information you needed?" There was heat in her voice.

"As a matter of fact, I did. It was a most helpful interview." He turned on his most charming smile. "I very much appreciate your patience."

She sniffed. "Of course, *Herr Captain*."

He sensed she wanted to say more but didn't. He had to admire that kind of restraint even if she wasn't exactly an ally, though suddenly, in a strange twist of feeling, he wished that she were on his side so that he could ask for her help in this matter. Somehow, he knew that she had the personal grit and daring to be an asset in this kind of venture. But maybe it was too risky, and anyway, he didn't even know how he himself was going to go about finding a little Jewish teenager in the caverns of the *Reich*. He needed more than an assistant; he needed providential guidance. Now that was another thought he hadn't considered in years.

Still, maybe it was a stroke of luck that *Fraulein* Lager had been sent to be his assistant. After all, she had worked in the *Reich Main Security Office*. Perhaps she could be a help to him. But he would have to be discreet. She was bright and easily suspicious. He would need to turn to the only thing a German officer had readily at hand – the charm of uniform and position. If he could loosen her up a little, perhaps she would help him without suspecting his traitorous intent. It was worth a try; there was no better time than the present to begin.

Summoning his courage but trying his best to be casually disarming, he said. "*Fraulein* Lager, I am serious when I say you have been most understanding and patient. I would like to thank you for it and for all the work you have been doing for me."

She turned to look at him, her expression one of puzzlement. "That's not necessary."

"But I say it is. I insist that I have an opportunity to properly express my appreciation. Would you let me take you to dinner again tonight?"

"We had dinner last night, *Captain*. You don't have to repeat it."

"Tonight, there will be no work involved, I promise. And it will be a nicer place than the hotel dining room."

She appeared to be thinking it over, but finally said. "*Danke*, I will accept."

"Good," Eryk said. "Now with that settled, we must get back to the office and prepare a report on today's tests." He leaned back against the seat cushions, his mind already plotting his next move in Operation Lager.

36

Kassel, Germany

May be you find out I could be useful getting people out of camps and prisons in Germany - just before they got shot. I should love to do it and I like to jump out of a plane even every day."
Christine Granville

The dining room where Hanne found herself that night was definitely an improvement over the one at the hotel. There were linen cloths on the table, gleaming goblets and heavy silverware. There was even a small bouquet of fresh flowers in a vase. She had to admit she was pleasantly surprised, but also a bit suspicious. She wasn't sure if the good Captain was working her over for his own interests or if he had been tipped off to her identity and was thus trying to trap her with his charm.

Captain Steiner did have considerable charm. The woman who couldn't admire the strong lines of his face, the military bearing and intelligent blue eyes hadn't the right to be female. But in her time in Germany, Hanne had seen many dazzling specimens of manhood in the officer corps – and every one of them, without fail, had been infected with Nazi poison. They could be charming and courteous and entertaining, but they were still prone to strut and preen and brag and then turn like vicious dogs on those they considered beneath them. In her mind these uniformed prototypes of the *Reich* had a very poor track record, and it was going to be difficult for Hauptsturmfuhrer Steiner to convince her differently. But that didn't mean she wouldn't take advantage of any softness he showed. After all, she had been trained to go for the jugular. She wouldn't hesitate if he showed vulnerability.

"You know, *Fraulein*, it interests me - your last name. Lager, meaning camp." Steiner was leaning toward her. "And now you are working with laborers from a German camp. Ironic, is it not?"

Hanne waved a hand. "I'm told my ancestry is of the silver mining camps in the Upper Harz region. The name Lager stuck to my great-grandfathers, I suppose."

"Ah, so your family was into silver." He took a drought on his cigarette and exhaled.

"Yes, for a great many years. However, my father was injured in an accident and could not carry on the tradition."

"How very sad. And your mother?"

"She was his nurse for many years. Now, they are both gone, before the war."

"I am sorry, *Fraulein*. It is difficult to make one's way in life without family for comfort and counsel. I understand this, you see. My parents are also both dead." Steiner took a drink from his beer mug and wiped his mouth with the heavy napkin.

Hanne did know his background, but he didn't know that, and she was a little surprised that he would volunteer such information. Though she had discovered in her time in Germany that many of the toughest men in the military were still very close to their families, it was unusual for a man who had come up through the *Hitler Jugend*

(Youth) to be so inclined. The *HJ* inducted boys as young as ten and became their family, replacing normal affection with loyalty to country and *Führer* and instilling military passion in place of sentimentality. She wasn't sure if there was emotion behind his revelation or if it was merely a statement of fact. But after what she had witnessed today, she wanted to know.

"I too am sorry for your loss, *Captain*. You must miss them."

"Yes, but it is harder for my two sisters than for me, I believe."

"You have sisters?" She knew that.

"Yes, younger sisters." He smiled briefly. "Annaliese and Frederica. Named for great-aunts. Neither of them are happy to be bearers of such names."

Hanne also smiled. "Yes, it is hard on the young to be burdened with the greatness of ancestry."

"True."

Hanne paused, watching him, wondering what he was really thinking. "What are they doing now, your sisters, on their own?" Hanne asked.

"Both are doing their year in the RAD. Annaliese is working in the Ukraine as a secretary and Frederica is a nurse at a *Lebensborn* birth center."

"They must be mature young women to handle such jobs. The East is certainly not a pleasant place, and crying babies can be a strain on the nerves."

Steiner smiled. "I take it you are not fond either of the east or of children, *Fraulein* Lager."

"No, I did not mean to say that, *Herr Captain*. But you have served in the East, have you not? Isn't that where you were wounded? You know how brutal it can be! And while I don't have children of my own, I do know that they require constant attention and that must be tiring."

Steiner held up his hands. "I am not offering judgment on you, *Fraulein* Lager. I do know about the East." His gaze darkened. "It is a cruel place, made that way by nature and by men." He was silent for a moment, his gaze unfocused. "As for children, I doubt that I would have the courage to take on such a job as my youngest sister."

Hanne took a bite of pumpernickel bread. It was one of the flavors she most disliked about Germany. She missed the honey-colored loaves from the kitchens of England. But it was a small sacrifice compared to the ones many others were making. She swallowed the bite. "From the way you speak, I can tell you think your sisters are courageous. Do you hear from them?"

"Yes, but not often." He grimaced. "They are too busy with work and dodging Allied bombs most of the time."

So, the Allies were even making the stalwart Nazis fearful with their bombing runs. Wouldn't the lads in London be delighted to hear that the carpet bombing of German cities was enough to make an *SS* officer frown! Hurrah for Sir Winston and his boys! Outwardly, Hanne made a tsk, tsk sound and shook her head, "How awful."

"Yes, it is. So many lives are being torn apart by these catastrophes. And now, *Fraulein*, with regard to young women in danger, I wonder if you might be able to help me." Steiner took another drink from his beer mug and leaned back in his chair.

"Certainly, *Captain*, I will try my best to assist you in any way I can." Now her mind was really reeling. What could he want? Did it have something to do with the woman inmate from this morning?

"I have been made aware of the plight of a young woman who was a friend of my family in Berlin. She has been erroneously charged and taken away to some camp in the greater German Protectorate. I was told she was in the ghetto at Terezin, and I need to locate her to see if I might help clear up the matter." He paused. "I understand that you worked in the *Reich Main Security* Records Office for a few months. I wonder if you might tell me how I could go about finding her files."

So that was it. There was somebody he wanted to get out of the Nazi clutches. But it couldn't be the woman they had seen this morning on the field. She was by no means young. It had to be someone else.

She took a deep breath. "We are a long way from Berlin, *Hauptsturmführer*."

"I know that, but perhaps there is a way to find out through one of your contacts, one of the other secretaries with whom you worked." He held her gaze, boring through her resistance.

She had to relent. "Yes, I can phone one of my friends there and ask."

He leaned forward, lowering his voice. "But it must be very quiet, *bitte*. There must be no fanfare about this request."

Aha! He did know something. But was it about her or someone else? She couldn't let him know that she suspected his reasons, so she raised her eyebrows as if in fear. "Is this going to make trouble for me, *Herr Captain*?"

"Not if you do as I instruct you. We will be careful."

"We?" Hanne asked. *By Jove, this did sound complicated.*

"Yes, we, if you will agree, *Fraulein*. You have proven yourself invaluable to me in this present assignment, and I need your help in this next one as well."

"So, it is official business for the *Reich*?" She almost laughed to herself as she said it. Surely, he didn't think she would believe him!

"We will consider it that, yes. And I promise, you will be under my protection."

Great lot of good that will do me, Herr Captain, *when I am facing a firing squad.* But Hanne had to admit Steiner looked up to the task. He was resplendent tonight in his pressed black uniform with his iron cross gleaming and his dress boots freshly shined. His blond hair was closely cropped in the popular *SS* style and his face was smoothly shaven. He fairly exuded manliness and power. But what good was the word of a Nazi? Was this some scheme to entrap her in an ill-fated rescue attempt? Maybe her cover had been blown. She had to be careful.

"Thank you, *Captain*. I will do what I can. When do we begin?"

"Right away. I can't allow my old friend to be held unjustly any longer than I can help it. We will make the call tomorrow."

Hanne nodded and folded her napkin beside her plate. "Thank you for the dinner, *Hauptsturmführer* Steiner. It was delicious."

"I'm glad you enjoyed it." Steiner stood and came around to pull back her chair. When she stood, he laid some money on the table and walked behind her to the front of the restaurant. The doorman opened the door for them and they walked onto the streets of Kassel.

The city was winding down, though it wasn't yet very late. It was a warm early autumn evening and the scent of green grass and trees melded with the aroma of freshly baked bread coming out of the bakery shops they passed. In the windows of merchants, there were still wares to buy, and passersby smiled at the handsome SS *captain* and the *fraulein* with him. Hanne wasn't sure if she wanted them to know the truth or not. Had she been anywhere besides a city in Germany, she should have been stoned to be seen in such vile company. But here, she almost wished that he weren't a beast and that the picture they represented wasn't so far from the truth.

But even with all those traitorous thoughts tumbling through her mind, it was a shock when Steiner suddenly bent his good arm and offered it to her. She almost missed a breath. He was certainly going all out for the charm effect. What's more, in spite of herself, it was working! This tumult in her stomach seemed more than the glee of an agent who had just softened a target. She quickly slipped her gloved hand into the crook of his arm, trying to act as calm as if she did it every day. This little cozying up would make her job easier anyway, to some degree. She couldn't help remembering what the old man at headquarters had said to her that long-ago day. Yes, feminine wiles were certainly useful at times. But in this instance, she hadn't had to use much. The man had come to her. Since she had to play the part, she might as well enjoy it, right? How very convenient that it would be pleasant for her in the process. The only thing she had to remember was that she might have to kill him in the end, and there must be no hesitation if it came to that.

Steiner acted as though they strolled this way down city streets all the time. Keeping her hand tucked in his arm made her walk much closer to him, and his presence was much more intimidating at that range. Yet, up close he seemed human and normal as well, and she wasn't sure she wanted to see that. He made small talk about the shops they passed and about how quickly dusk was turning to darkness. They had to be off the street soon since Kassel, as a manufacturing city, was a target for bombing raids and the curfew would begin very shortly. He reminded her to close her blackout curtain and promised to call for her in the morning for the ride to the *Henschel Werks*. In a very short amount of time, they were standing in the tiled hotel lobby. The breeze from the arms of the overhead fan stirred his hair when he removed his cap with his good hand and gave a short bow.

"It was an enjoyable evening, *Fraulein*. Thank you for accompanying me."

"I am honored, *Captain. Danke.*"

"Then I will bid you goodnight until tomorrow morning. Sleep well, *Fraulein* Lager." With that, Steiner turned on his heel and walked briskly away.

37

Kassel, Germany
Hotel Führer Hof

> *If the day should ever come when we [the Nazis] must go,*
> *if someday we are compelled to leave the scene of history,*
> *we will slam the door so hard that the universe will shake and*
> *mankind will stand back in stupefaction.*
> Joseph Goebbels, *Reich* Minister of Propaganda

He wasn't sure he had done the right thing. Perhaps trying to charm the woman had been too much too soon. She had been very calm about the whole thing, but she wasn't one of those girls with whom one could lightly flirt. She had a natural reserve that he respected, even if her obstinate manner often annoyed him. She reminded him of Zelda. That was it. Though much younger and in a very different station in life, Hanne Lager had the same bearing as his old governess.

No, what was he going to do about that situation? Had he made progress tonight with securing his assistant's help in the matter? Or would it become more of a liability because of the risk involved? He didn't know, but, at this point, he was already committed, so he would simply have to wait and see.

THE EAGLE AND THE STAR

Kassel, Germany

The next morning, Hanne made the call back to the building where she had worked in Berlin. Ilse, who answered the call, was her same old self.

"The office hasn't been the same without you, Hanne. My, there you are traveling around with a handsome officer and I am still stuck here looking at files. How I envy you! By the way, *Sturmbannführer* Beckmann is most anxious to see you. I'd wager he would be jealous if he knew whom you are accompanying."

Hanne rolled her eyes at the phone. "Oh, stop it, Ilse. Really! I am working out here, you know. It is not all glamor. I'm sure *Sturmbannführer* Beckmann will not lack for company."

She shook her head as Steiner looked at her inquisitively. "Now I need you to look up a file for me, please." She looked down at the paper in her hand. "The name is Nadya Goldman. Yes, that's right. It has to do with some official business. Yes."

Hanne covered the receiver with one hand and motioned to Steiner. "She has gone to look for the file."

The line was quiet for several minutes, and then Ilse returned, her voice sounding breathless. "Gracious, Hanne. I had to go all the way into the back rooms to find it. I'm not sure why this woman would need to be found. She was deported two years ago."

Hanne closed her eyes. "Yes, I know that. To Theresienstadt. The 'paradise' ghetto."

"That's right. So what do you need to know?"

"Where is she now? Was her number listed on a transport out of Terezin?"

"No. I see no further documentation. It appears she is still residing there."

"All right. Thank you, Ilse. You have been so helpful. I want you to know that I am sending you a little gift in appreciation." *And also to buy your silence.*

"For me? Oh, thank you, Hanne. I can't wait." She gave a little girlish squeal.

"Yes, you may expect it soon. *Danke*, and goodbye." Hanne put down the receiver and faced Steiner. "She's still in the Terezin ghetto."

He really should have guessed long ago that Nadya couldn't be living free. Jews in Berlin hadn't been completely safe in a long while and since the fall of 1941 had been disappearing from their communities and showing up on the registers of camps. Neither she nor her aunt had evaded the dismal fate of their race. True, Nadya was only half-Jewish, but that was still considered racially unworthy by the *Reich*.

Hanne gathered up some papers lying on her desk and then turned back toward him. "Do you want me to try to find out more?"

"No, I think I can do that. I can probably inquire without arousing suspicion since the *SS* are very involved in the running of that camp. Thank you, *Fraulein* Lager. You have been very helpful."

"You're welcome, *Captain*. Now should we get on with the dictation for today?"

For a moment, he was stunned. How could she go about business as usual when he had so much to plan? Then he remembered that her main task here was to help him refine the *Panzerkampwagon IV*. She knew nothing about his other plans, the ones centering on women who were enemies of the *Reich*. Or did she?

Sometimes he wondered about his assistant. She was keenly aware of things going on around her. In fact, her manner often reminded him of some training he had received. Of course, she was SS; he couldn't forget that. Yet, there was something more to her, something he couldn't lay his finger on that nagged at the back of his mind. He needed to think more about it and decide what to do.

But for now, ah yes, more notes and a new design for the commander's controls that he needed to go over with the Riefendahl. He went to his desk and sat down. "I am ready when you are, *Fraulein*."

38

Kassel, Germany
Henschel and Son Werks

> *It also gives us a very special, secret pleasure to see how unaware the people around us are of what is really happening to them.*
> Adolf Hitler

So, little Nadya was really in Theresienstadt, the "paradise" ghetto. He could well imagine the difficulty of her journey from the streets of Berlin to the hovels of the ghetto. In fact, it had only taken the name of the place to bring back glimpses of images he had long since stowed. With a "J" stamped on her papers, she had been condemned and deemed unfit to remain in free society. What had that been like for her? What trauma had her final days in school brought upon her? Had she been one of the children who endured the Nazi racial experts and their measuring instruments and hair and eye color samples? Had she guessed that her fate would not be amended because of her aunt's position in the *Philharmonic?* He tried to let his mind contemplate the horror of that, what it must have been like for a teenage girl the age of his sisters. But he couldn't. All he knew was the *SS* side of that equation, and it had always made perfect sense before. Now, it seemed like a crime.

It was as if someone had turned on the spigot of his memories and with them came the emotions he used to be able to feel. He couldn't explain the anxiety he felt as he wondered how she was doing and if he would actually be able to locate her. Then a new thought occurred to him. What if she wanted nothing to do with him? What if she wouldn't let him help? He was, after all, a Nazi. Probably she would take one look at his uniform and want to spit in his face. He would have to get help from Zelda. That was the only way. If their relationship was anything like it had been in the past, the girl would listen to what her aunt said. Whatever her feelings about a Nazi officer, she would obey the older woman.

It was time to pay another visit to his old governess. Eryk hoped she was still alive.

―――

Just about 4 hours away in a region of annexed Czechoslovakia, Nadya Goldman was fastening the latches on her violin case. "You played beautifully today, Ruth. It will be a wonderful addition to the recital tomorrow." She walked with her student toward the door.

The room in which she gave lessons was appallingly desolate. Wallpaper sagged where leaks above had weakened and loosened it. There were holes in the wooden floor that one had to sidestep in order to avoid injury. The one bulb in the middle of the ceiling gave off only a dim, yellow light and the smell of garbage and death would not be kept out by the majestic strains played in the room. It was, after all, a room for the dying, as was every room in this condemned village. They were prisoners who tried their best to avert the clutches of the grim reaper by engulfing themselves in music.

As Nadya glanced around the room, she thought of how different it was from the classrooms she remembered as a student in Berlin. There the walls had been swathed in swastikas and festooned with tributes to the Führer; there, posters urged the children to join the Hitler Youth and BDM. But back then, her eyes hardly saw the appalling display of National Socialism; she had trained them to skim over any such images. It was a game she and *Tante* had played – who could see less propaganda in a day. One had to report any images she remembered, and it had been terribly difficult to learn how "not to see." But after a few weeks, Nadya had become very good at it and could truthfully say that she no longer really saw the disgusting icons and inciting messages. It was a habit that stood her in good stead. She could not get away from the posters, but she didn't have to "see" them all the time.

The game of not seeing was only one of the many tidbits about life and teaching that she had tucked away in her soul, thanks to her *Tante*. As a teacher and as a person, there was none who could surpass her. Nadya missed her every day. She wondered how she was doing, and mostly she wondered if she was still alive.

Closing the last cabinet, Nadya walked to her desk, picked up her purse and satchel of books and folders and then started toward the door of the classroom. She stopped and gave one last glance around the pitiful room with its poor equipment for learning and couldn't help remembering the desks of her childhood filled with blonde children sporting rosy Prussian cheeks and blue eyes filled with hate. How she had struggled not to hate them back! She had tried to show them the mercy that her *Tante* had encouraged. She closed her eyes against the pain of the memories, recalling the sour taste of resentment that overtakes the senses. Even today, she had fought to reject it.

Still though, today, she better understood the terrible philosophy which had taken over the entire span of Germany and which nurtured in her former classmates their bitter loathing. It wasn't their fault that their parents had German blood any more that it was hers that she was a *Mischlinge*, a half-Jew, with a converted Lutheran Hebrew as a father and a despised Pole for a mother. As children, she and her schoolmates hadn't any say in what their parents were or did.

But, still she remembered how it hurt. How she had to listen to all those horrible lies the teacher had proclaimed about the regime that was even now killing her people, about how wonderful the *Führer* was and what a glorious future awaited the youth who remained loyal to him. She had kept her mouth shut and her head down because she wanted to stay alive. It took only a strong run-in with terror to discover that life was a powerful motivator. Nadya had learned it young.

Though those days were gone, the misery remained and was now an even stronger force in her life and those of her blood. Here in this "paradise" ghetto, she fought against hunger and disease every day in an effort to pass on to these forlorn little children a bit of the glory of music. She hoped that it might help sustain them in this place. She wanted to give them a little joy; soon enough they would face the realm of the dead. Perhaps through the gift of music, entrusted to her by *Tante* Zelda, and lovingly passed on to others through her heart and hands, she might deny death of his victims for one more hour or day or week. Perhaps she might claim a small victory in this mortal struggle, and perhaps somehow, the music would help keep *Tante* alive too, if only in her memory.

39

Kassel, Germany
Henschel and Son Werks

Resistance called for a lonely courage, for men and women who could fight on their own. But the solitude was an eternal strain.
Sonia Purnell,
A Woman of No Importance:
The Untold Story of the American Spy Who Helped Win World War II

"Who is *Sturmbannführer* Beckmann?"

Hanne looked up, startled, at the voice that sounded suddenly very close to her shoulder. Steiner stood behind her, having come from his own desk with a paper in his hand he was extending to her. She took it, and decided to answer his question; he would find out anyhow.

"A *Gestapo* officer I know in Berlin." It was true. Of course, there was more to the story.

"You are seeing him regularly?" Steiner moved around her desk and leaned one hip into it as he talked.

"No, *Hauptsturmführer* Steiner, I'm not seeing him regularly because I am here in Kassel on an assignment with you!"

The retort felt so good for some reason, but Hanne could have kicked herself a second later. All that work, all that softening of the target, was just now oozing down the drain.

He moved and stood upright. "I see. Pardon me for asking, *Fraulein*. I simply wanted to understand your situation, especially since I heard you mention him on the phone the other day and it seemed that the reference was a bit ominous."

Hanne sighed. "No, I should ask your pardon, *Herr Captain*. It was a perfectly honest question." She pushed back her chair and put a hand to her hair, smoothing the sides that were swept back into the regulation Führer bun at the nape of her neck. "We have been seeing quite a bit of each other when he is in Berlin on leave. I think he would marry me if I would agree."

That was pretty much the sum of their relationship in a few words. But what she didn't say was that she could tolerate the man only on the strength of her allegiance to her own country, and even that didn't make it palatable. The cultivation of Rolf Beckmann had been one of the most distasteful jobs of her whole career.

But Hanne didn't say all that. She lifted her hands in casual disregard as if the situation weren't all that serious from her point of view.

Steiner nodded his head slowly, looking at the floor for a few minutes before continuing. "And where is his present assignment?"

"When I saw him last, he was being assigned to a different unit. He did not tell me the location. I had the idea that he was going to work in a camp somewhere."

"Why would you think that?"

"It was just a hunch. I had nothing to go on." Hanne stopped for a moment, then blazed on. "I'm curious, *Captain*. Why do you want to know all this?"

"Jealousy can create many problems in a covert operation. I am just trying to stay ahead of anything that could complicate our task."

The way he said "our" sounded as though they were a true partnership, working for the good of mankind. "I have to be out this afternoon, *Fraulein*. After you finish up that dictation and file those drawings, you may leave." He turned back to his office and closed the door behind him.

Arbeitslager
Kassel, Germany

In the filthy hole that the Nazis called a cell, Zelda Goldman sat on her bunk and surveyed her hands in the dim light. They were terribly dirty, the skin scaly and rough and the fingernails broken and grimy. She wanted to clean them, but how did one accomplish that without any manicure tools? There wasn't even a stick or nail she could use. She shrugged. Did it matter anyway? Looking at her hands was painful enough without mourning the nails.

Once her fingers had been slender and supple, the joints able to move quickly. She remembered how it felt to grasp the sleek wood of the fingerboard on her *Gagliano* violin. Her bowing hand was now gnarled from grasping hand tools for hours on end while she worked in the factory. The harsh life of the camps spared no part of the body; limbs became twisted, hearts worked overtime, digestion was erratic and often violent, and minds often just went on a journey from which they never returned. Thankfully, she still had her mental faculties, or at least she believed she did. Surely, a person who could feel pain and regret so strongly was still holding onto some piece of sanity.

Though she did not have an instrument and doubted whether she could finger it if she did, the music was inside her. All she needed to do was close her eyes and see the page in her mind. That, the Nazis had not been able to wrest from her when they stripped away her clothing, cut her hair, tattooed her arm and reduced her to a number in their record books. She wondered what had happened to her beloved instrument, hidden away from Nazi hands. Perhaps when next it saw the light of day, it would be a world where performing good music didn't seem like casting pearls before swine – an apt image for those of Israel! And even in her present state, Zelda had to smile as she acknowledged the words of Jesus who knew exactly how to speak to the Jewish mind.

At any rate, she was glad she had hidden it away. Better her violin lay unused, its songs silent, than some haughty Nazi owning the piece of wood that had been her friend through sorrow and joy and concerts of beauty.

Of course, had she brought it, it might be lying in a warehouse or even have been split for kindling for *Wehrmacht* officers in some forest camp. She grimaced, closing her eyes against such an imaginary horror. Given that choice, it would be better to be in Nazi hands than in ashes. After all, anyone can be redeemed. That's what she believed.

It was the theme that symbolized her Christian faith and which separated her from others who shared her Jewish blood. Jewish tradition was built on devotion, passion and revenge. Rarely did the children of Abraham's line seek to forgive and restore those who had wronged them. Usually they sought their enemy's downfall and took pleasure in the outcome. "An eye for an eye" was the mantra of their forebears and it had become that of the present day Jew as well.

Of course, in the beginning, no one had believed that their fellow Germans were capable of such atrocities, and had been willing to forebear a little abuse. It had seemed like it would blow over; all such persecution in the past had. But when it became clear that the whole of the German people not only wished to be rid of them but would happily participate in their eradication, the attitude of her people began to change. The young Zionists were the most outspoken, calling down curses on the heads of their enemies and referring to their captors in evil epithets. Zelda suddenly remembered one such young man who had blistered her very ears with his language. Nadya had been present that night; oh, how she had regretted letting her sit at the table for the discussion. But even the gentle people, the merchants and bankers and doctors and artists among them had begun to feel a monstrous hatred for those with Aryan blood, and especially any who wore the Nazi uniform. The tidal wave of venom had surged against every restraint, and even she had to fight its onslaught.

Of course, most Jews considered her family traitors anyway. Her father had been the first to become a Lutheran, and it had continued in the family. But actually there were many Berliners who had adopted Gentile ways to some degree or another. Many of them, even if they hadn't converted to another faith, were barely religiously tied to Jewish Orthodoxy at all. Some of them had managed at least to keep the high holy days, but some didn't even do that. Up until the *Reich* had brought them all together under the Star, there was little unity in the Jews of Berlin. But now that everyone was in danger and deportation stalked them all, religion had become a high priority. It was hard to describe that as a blessing though it made Zelda wonder if things might not be different for them now if they had discovered this unity before the ascension of Adolf Hitler.

But though she anguished over her kinsmen and lamented the loss of her instrument and the destruction of her hands, she was tormented most over the fate of Nadya. If only she would hear something from Eryk. How astonished she had been when he turned up in that field! Though one would think that as much as she prayed she would have been expecting it. But for him to show up just when she thought it was her last minute to live had been completely out of the ordinary. Of course, God sometimes worked that way. It made her wonder what He was doing right now that she hadn't even begun to imagine.

40

Kassel, Germany
Henschel and Son Werks

> *He who serves our Führer, Adolf Hitler, serves Germany and he who serves Germany, serves God.*
> Baldur von Schirach, (speech to Hitler Youth, 25 July 1936)

When *Hauptsturmfuhrer* Steiner walked out of the office, Hanne knew her time had come. This was the moment she had been waiting for, the opportunity to find out more about the baffling officer for whom she was working. Sometimes she almost liked him, and at other times, her feelings were of pure loathing. Like most men of his position, he was complex and difficult to analyze. She blamed SS training for some of that. They were trained to laugh at death and stow away any emotion when faced with duty. She theorized to herself that this created a dual personality that made it easier for these men to commit criminal acts against other human beings without seeming to suffer any pangs of guilt.

When one couldn't get a good read on a person, it was always a good idea to rifle through his things to get a better understanding. Today was her chance to do that.

She waited until she saw the staff car pull out onto the road. He was headed toward the labor camp; she was sure of it. He was going to see that woman prisoner again. She had to find out why.

His door was not locked; she pushed it open. On the desk were a few papers and pens and a calendar for the year 1943. He had not left a briefcase or coat; those would have been her favorite places to look. But she would have to make do with the desk drawers.

They were locked, but that wasn't a problem. Slipping her picking tool out of her pocket, she had the first drawer unlocked in seconds. It slid open without a screech. At least, the Nazis kept things well-oiled, though it was probably a prisoner who got that job.

She went through the drawers systematically, being very careful not to change the position of the items and papers inside. But it wasn't until she came to the last drawer that the boredom of the search broke. She was beginning to think he had no secrets, that maybe she had misread the whole thing when she pushed back a thick kerchief in the bottom drawer and saw the glint of metal. Ah, here was something unusual looking.

Using a pencil, she uncovered the item even more until she could see it clearly.

She froze, her heart thumping loudly in her ears.

The thing she uncovered represented the very core of violence, hatred and prejudice that was being carried out in the name of the *Third Reich*. It symbolized the pain of abuse down through the millennia. It was a death sentence to the owner.

It was a Star of David.

41

Kassel, Germany
Arbeitslager Cellblock

> Do you know why most survivors of the Holocaust are vegan?
> It's because they know what it's like to be treated like an animal.
> Chuck Palahniuk, Lullaby

"*Lehrerin*, she will never believe that I want to help her. It will look like a trap."

Eryk stood once again in the squalid cell which held his old teacher and held out his hands, palms up, to illustrate his point. "I am *Waffen-SS*. We have a reputation. We are known for cruelty and death. That is what we are trained for."

Zelda held up a hand to stop his confession. "I know what you are, *Liebchen*."

The simple words were like hammer blows to his chest. He hung his head. Somehow it sounded so much worse coming from her. In the company of his fellow officers, the blood oath to the *Führer* and the consequences of loyalty to it seemed almost noble. But enclosed by dirty cement walls with a woman who had been broken by months of mistreatment, the words were a condemnation.

"But you forgive me?"

"I have already told you that I freely forgive you, Eryk. I know the little boy you once were and the man you were intended by God to be. Yes, I forgive you and love you. But it is the Father in heaven from whom you really need forgiveness. Only He can take that guilt that you feel and give you hope for your future."

The words called to him as if from the past, like a long ago strain of music that he recognized and that resonated in his soul. He wanted to embrace the comfort they offered, but something held him back. He wasn't ready, didn't know how to escape what it would mean in the present. So he let her message bounce off his consciousness to that other place where he stored things to ponder later.

"Yes, *Leherein,* I do intend to think more about that, but right now, I must develop a plan to bring your niece to safety."

"Oh my dear boy, you think that your plans and God's plans are separate, but you are wrong. They are one and the same. Do not try to do His will apart from His help." The woman coughed, her lungs continuing to rebel against the mold and dust and pollution of her residence. "But now, what is it you want me to do? How can I help you?"

Eryk reached into his case and pulled out a stenographer's pad and pencil and extended them toward Zelda.

"Write her a letter. Tell her I am coming to help. Ask her to trust me."

"Well, I will do my best, my son. But the trusting part will be her choice, no matter what I say."

Eryk realized that she was reminding him that there were consequences to the pathway of life one chose, and his had now become an obstacle.

Zelda reached for the items, doing her best to unfold her fingers from their gnarled position. For the first time, Eryk realized how crippled she had become. Those fingers had soothed his hair back from his little face, been laid tenderly on his forehead to check for fevers and coaxed magic from the strings of a violin. Now, they could barely hold a pen. He shook his head, willing away the agony of his remorse, and forcing himself to focus on what she was doing.

It took her a while to finish the job. She wrote slowly, stopping now and again as if thinking about the words she was putting on paper. When she was done, she held it up to the patchy light coming through the tiny window in the top of the cell and read it over to herself. He could see her lips moving. Then she held it out to him.

"I hope it will convince her, *Liebchen*. She has suffered so much and trusts so little. You will have a difficult task."

"Then maybe I shouldn't even try. If she is managing to fool the government and has a position, perhaps she is better off than if I try to move her and fail. Maybe she will even report me. How then can I help you or her?" His voice rose in spite of himself. He felt like a child again, waiting for advice and somehow it made him angry. Why was he, a trained officer, taking suggestions and criticism from a bedraggled old woman in a nasty camp?

She looked at him with a softness in her eyes that made him squirm. When he finally broke his gaze and looked away, she spoke. "Eryk, you are a grown man, able to make your own decisions. But you have asked to help me, your old teacher, and this is what I am giving you to do. If you do not want to try it, then say so and go your way. But if you do, you may be sure that I am praying for you every minute, every mile, every . . . .." Her voice wobbled and broke as she held back a sob, the tears making a muddy trail down her cheek. "Oh my boy, how I will pray for you and for her."

Eryk clenched his fists. He was a beast after all, a selfish person more interested in his own ideas than in the welfare of two women who had once been very precious to him. He dropped to his knees beside the mound of dirty straw that she used for a bed and picked up one of her pitiful hands. He held it to his cheek for a long moment, then looked into her dirt-streaked face.

"I will go, and I will find her and take her to a safe place. You have my word, *Hauslehrerin*. And I will depend on your prayers all the way.

42

Autobahn to Berlin

Monsters exist, but they are too few in number to be truly dangerous. More dangerous are the common men, the functionaries ready to believe and to act without asking questions."
Primo Levi, Holocaust survivor

The ride back to Berlin was silent and awkward, at least from Hanne's perspective. She sat in her corner of the staff car, and Steiner did the same in his. They didn't start a conversation. They had the documents they needed to deliver back to SS Headquarters. They had fulfilled their mission. There was nothing more to do on that account at the moment. She was trying to sort through a deluge of options as to her next move concerning the plans for the new *Panzerkampwagon*, of which she had made a covert copy, as well as what to do about the Captain and the star she had found in his drawer. She was sure it had to be connected to his reaction in the field and to his trips to the labor camp afterward. She had to decide now how to proceed. Should she let him know she had found it and see what response he would come up with? Or should she keep it in her mental file to use as security for a future untenable situation? She was quite certain that it was tied up in his dark mood this day; he seemed deep in uncomfortable thought.

Also, she was sure that he was anxious to get the wrappings off of his arm. He had been required to report to the hospital regularly while in Kassel to have it examined and the dressings changed. No doubt it was bothersome in this heat, and for a man accustomed to having two arms to get on in life, it had to be a trial. Still, she wondered if he might not be more of a risk to her when he was whole again.

Eryk was going over his plans in his mind. The direction he should take had come to him in the night, clearly. He couldn't account for such a direct leading; it was odd to be so certain when usually there were so many details that could go wrong. But he felt very sure of himself, and he was anxious to have the deed done. There would be risk, of course there would. But practically everything one did in Berlin these days involved risk, if not from the Nazis then from the Allied bombing runs. He was a man accustomed to risk. He handled it by managing his emotions, planning intricately and trusting no one. He would carry this out himself, quickly. He even knew the cover story he would use for the little trip into Poland.

Speaking of cover stories reminded him of his suspicions about his assistant. His gut response had never failed him, and he had sensed early on that there was something not quite right about her. He had to find out what it was. And soon.

Sturmbannführer Rolf Beckmann was not happy, but not on account of his new post. His temporary assignment as chief interrogation officer of the *Gestapo* force at the Small Fortress garrison at Terezin, was a feather in his cap. Just across the river from Theresienstadt, the Model Jewish Ghetto, the post had an important presence as an interrogation and intelligence site and the position suited his personality he believed. The rabble contained behind the walls of the ghetto were a difficult group to manage, greedy and arrogant and racially dangerous like all Jews. The many non-Jewish resistance members who passed through the area posed just as great a threat. There was a great need for a man with his capabilities to help keep things in line. That was not what made him unhappy.

The cause of his discontent at the moment was the absence of the woman he had been looking forward to seeing on his few days leave in Berlin. Hanne Lager was gone, temporarily out-of-town herself to assist an injured *Waffen-SS* officer on special assignment.

There were a lot of things wrong with that news besides the fact that he was eager for an admiring female audience. One of those reasons was that he had never trusted *Waffen-SS* officers. He had known many, and even worked with them now in the administration and government of the ghetto. But it was not a cordial relationship. He disliked their lofty approach to everyone; they believed in their powerful charisma and never backed away from a challenge. And Hanne was a lovely challenge for any man.

He was none too eager for her to be assisting a war hero either. The injury alone sometimes exuded a charm for women, a mixture of sympathy and admiration that could be intoxicating. He had worked too hard to get Hanne to let her slip out of his hands. He was accustomed to having what he wanted. He wasn't nice to be around when things went otherwise. If he ever caught up with that Steiner, he'd find a way to make him pay.

PART THREE
Terezin to Tegel

43

August, 1943
Train to Terezin

> *Some people like the Jews, and some do not.*
> *But no thoughtful man can deny the fact that they are, beyond*
> *any question, the most formidable and most remarkable race*
> *which has appeared in the world.*
> Winston S. Churchill

The plan was simple, but fraught with danger. In order to get the girl out of the ghetto, he would use the same ruse that had worked with her aunt – detain her on grounds of interrogation and then find some reason to transport her to another location and conveniently lose track of her on the way with the official statement being that she was shot trying to escape. If he were the only one to witness the actual "execution" there would be no reason for anyone to doubt him and the *Reich* would certainly not care that one more Jew died earlier than planned.

This was the skeleton plan he had constructed in his mind, but Eryk still had to flesh it out when he had learned a few more details about Nadya's situation. He had to find out exactly where she was in the ghetto, who knew her and might be a problem in the carrying out of the plan, find some reasonable crime with which to charge her and arrest her for interrogation, make sure she was taken to a place where she would not be traumatized further while he was setting things in motion, and then arrange all the details for her hiding place and "death." He could handle it all he knew, but he needed to get it done quickly. He had four days leave, and that wasn't much time to complete his rescue operation.

The biggest risk he was taking, of course, was the one to himself. If any of the officers on the staff at Terezin became suspicious, it would be a short walk to the wall for him. The *Führer* had one abiding motive for seeking vengeance: he could not tolerate treason; the sentence was always death. If a Jew was involved in the affair in any way, it would be even worse. He had to make this look really good, especially since the *Gestapo* had a significant presence in the running of the Small Fortress where he would have to take Nadya before transporting her.

Eryk had tried to find out all he could about the ghetto, the prison, the town and the Nazi staff which administered it, but there again, he had to be very casual lest someone get wary of his curiosity. These days in Germany, there was always someone who was wary. Though he had grown up in an era when one always checked his back, he sometimes wondered what it would be like not to do so. How did one live in an atmosphere where personal opinions were expressed without fear and where viewpoints that opposed the government were allowed? National Socialism was all he had ever known. He had no basis on which to judge any other type of community.

He was riding on the train to avoid using a staff car which would involve a driver. It was best not to involve anyone else. He had probably already gone too far by getting the help of his assistant. Maybe she would spend her leave squealing on him to the *Reichsfuhrer*. He wished he had gotten further in his attempts to gain her loyalty. But it was difficult for *SS* men to acquire the loyalty of any human being; even lovers and wives found it hard to get past the shell that duty and training had made of them. Though he knew many fellow officers who were married, he had heard enough stories to know that not all was roses and bliss in their homes. One could not drill a man to inflict pain on those who were weaker and then expect that he could have an intimate relationship with a woman who by nature was more delicate in being and manner. His father had been a soldier and he remembered the demons he had witnessed in him; many of them no doubt caused by the rigors of the military service he had seen. Now that he was grown, Eryk wondered if the cause of his mother's emotional and mental instability was, if not caused by, at least intensified by his father's inability to connect with the members of his family. While Eryk was sure that his father had cared for him and his sisters, he couldn't remember them being the objects of his affection and affirmation. His father had done his best to give them a stable home, an education and a future, but he had been ill-equipped to give them anything on the inside, which must have been why Zelda Goldman had been able to fill up Eryk's heart and create a place for herself that remained to this day. But still his father had been honorable. On that point, Eryk was firmly convinced. The words of *Major* Hunsdorf were still revolving in his mind. And it seemed all too probable that the elder Steiner had simply been too noble for the future intentions of the *Reich*. If what Hunsdorf intimated was true, his father had taken that walk to the wall that his son would likely take if his present actions were discovered.

The willingness to risk that end, Eryk was beginning to understand, was the dividing philosophy of the soldiers of his father's generation from the ones of his own. If it had not been for men like his father and *Major* Hunsdorf, he might not have seen the difference.

But since he had experienced them as a template since his childhood, he was realizing that the men now being turned out by the SS seemed to him like bullies, men who looked on maleness as a license for force, who admired health and strength and who despised softness and dependence. Perhaps this was the reason Eryk was trying to help two women in Nazi clutches. Deep in his heart, he knew that a man should protect womanhood, and in his mind, he hadn't seen any difference dictated by race that erased that code. He still hadn't sorted out his personal feelings for Jews now that he had experienced life beyond the cauldron of adolescence. All he knew at the moment was that he had a responsibility, and he had to do his best to fulfill it.

Theresienstadt Ghetto

In the corner of her attic room, Nadya stuffed her instrument case under the bed, as far back as possible so that the children who also occupied the space wouldn't be tempted to pull it out for a plaything. It had already happened once before in her previous quarters, and her heart had nearly stopped beating as the sight of a five-year-old holding her precious violin aloft in one hand and waving the bow crazily with the other. After that, she had trusted no one. There were some possessions that one would take to the death; for her, the instrument was that item. It was now much more than an identity or a source of joy; it was her one vital link to the life and love she had known, to the woman who had been her family and her foundation. She could no more let it go than she could drain Goldman blood from her body.

The evening meal was underway, such as it was. Meals were either anticipated or dreaded, depending on the family's resources of the day. When one was able to barter and gain something extra to add to the meager rations of potatoes or turnips or cabbage doled out by the council, it was a time of pure excitement. But these moments were rare. Usually, one ate with downcast eyes and at an intense pace – these were the traits of hunger and fear.

Nadya cradled her own small bowl of watery soup in her hands as she rose from securing her instrument. She dared not leave it unattended but could not eat while carrying her case. Now, she settled her back against the lowest bed frame, slipped off her shoes, and began to eat. The stuff was slimy and lukewarm, the slivers of cabbage trailing down her throat, making her gag, but she swallowed with determination. The only way to live was to eat whatever was available, as much as was available. She would not lie down and die. *Tante* would never forgive her for that. So she ate, trying not to remember the bountiful tables she had known in the past and wondering if somewhere her beloved aunt was eating anything at all.

44

Berlin
Reich Main Security Office

> *If you agree to work for us, half the time you won't know the purpose of your duties . . . and when we do explain, we might not be telling the truth. But that's the real world, folks . . ."*
> James Alan Gardner, *Trapped*

Hanne was desperate. She still didn't trust Steiner and she had to know what he was hiding. There was too much about him that rang hollow, and she was determined to discover the cause. Being back in Berlin while he made his little secret mission was ideal for her. She was hoping to make use of the vast resources of the *Third Reich* for her personal research.

Since the Captain's trip was unofficial, he hadn't announced it or gone through normal channels at the *RSHA*. He had merely taken a few days leave for "medical reasons." He had indeed, she knew, visited the surgeon who had finally removed the bandages and set him up with a therapy regimen to strengthen muscles that had been injured.

She knew this because she had accompanied him to the military hospital after they arrived in Berlin. The place was drab and austere, like every other Nazi building, but it was very much a place that bustled with activity, probably more so than some of the office buildings downtown. Casualties were one thing that Germans had in abundance. As she and the Captain walked the corridors of the mammoth place, she saw hundreds of young men in beds and wheelchairs and gurneys, in various states of illness and injury. Their youthful bodies didn't match their old eyes and the lack of vitality in their manner. Many of them were hardly more than boys, and she again felt a blaze of anger at the price Hitler was exacting for his cherished war against the Jews and indeed, against the entire world. Most people simply didn't know that last point yet. But that was precisely why she was here.

The surgeon who had put Steiner's arm back together was a short stub of a man with bristly graying hair, a coarse voice, and surprisingly gentle hands. She saw him turn the Captain's arm this way and that, running his fingers over the scarred skin, massaging the tendons deep inside.

"It's healed on the outside, *Herr Hauptsturmführer*. But the inside is what concerns me."

Hanne was sure Steiner was worried about his arm, but he had looked at the man impassively; not a flicker of an eyelash hinted at emotions of any kind. He sat stoically as the surgeon told him about the therapy and the exercises he could do on his own. He hadn't even said anything about it after they left the hospital, but had gone on to suggest some things she could work on in his absence that would help with their project at the plant in Kassel.

The man couldn't be that uncaring about the effect of his injury on his future. He was practically married to his mechanical machine if he was at all like the other *Panzer* captains with whom she had had contact. Some of them even slept in their armored vehicles on the nights before battle. She knew enough about Eryk Steiner to know that he was committed to returning to battle, or at least that is what she had believed until recently. Perhaps he was involved in a war of a different kind. At any rate, she had to find out; her life might depend on it.

So she was furtively digging through the charts and files of the *Waffen-SS*. Her assignment with Steiner had given her access to rooms and drawers and folders that not many would ever see. On the pretext of working on the *Panzerkampwagon* revision, she was in a dimly-lit office lined with cabinets containing the identifying information of the formidable fighting forces of the *Reich*. She stood in front of one of those cabinets, a middle drawer open, her fingers walking through the "St's."

There were a lot of them. But she had no trouble identifying the correct one; she could recognize the proud bearing and icy eyes immediately. She had to look quickly while no one was paying attention to her. If someone were to focus on the specific file she was looking at, she could be in big trouble.

Steiner, Eryk Wilhelm von
Division: Waffen-SS
Rank: *Hauptsturmfuhrer*
Division: Das Reich, *Panzer* **Commander**
Military Service: Wehrmacht 1939-1940;
                              SS Junkerschule Bad Tolz 1940-1941;
                              Waffen-SS 1941-1943
Marital Status: Single
Ancestry: Aryan; Subclass - Nordic
Parents: Helmut Steiner, Wehrmacht 1917-1938;
                              deceased – died in battle

	Magda (Zeiss) Steiner; deceased – pneumonia
Siblings:	Anastasia Steiner
	Frederica Steiner
Military Honors:	SS Dagger, SS Ring with Runes; Iron Cross with Oak Leaves

Convictions: none
Postings: Polish Campaign; Eastern Front

Hanne wasn't finding out anything helpful. The official record was sterile, though impressive. She needed to know his secrets. She had to find out what black marks might still be visible on the character of Eryk Steiner.

If only she could rendezvous with someone from the *SOE*. But there was no one from her old group who was actually living in Germany. Who else was there? She was so far underground that she had never tried to make contact with anyone in the resistance either. She had to make her own way and ferret out her own facts.

So, she decided she would begin with the person of Nadya Goldman. If her old instincts could still be trusted, there was a treasure trove of information hiding in that woman's identity.

45

Terezin, Czechoslovakia

Trauma laminates. It laminates the moment of trauma. Every sight, smell, and sound of it. It laminates the part of ourselves that cannot separate from the moment, that comes into being as a result of that moment. Encased, shielded, coated, unfading, cutting off access to the heart underneath, the flowing blood."
Levia Levinson

The train arrived at the *Bahnhofstrasse* railway branch in Terezin at 2:45 in the afternoon. It was a transport train in which Eryk was riding, bringing Jews from various places to the privileged ghetto of *Theresienstadt*.

Located in North Bohemia, along the Ohre River, the fortress of Terezin was less than 50 miles from the border of greater Germany. From the *Reich* perspective, it was the model Jewish settlement, boasting a Jewish council to run the affairs of the community which now numbered around 40,000 inhabitants as well as many cultural opportunities such as theater, symphony, art, lectures and recitals. There was a working Fire Department composed of Jewish workers, a hospital, and an improved water system. There were Jewish-run committees which helped new arrivals to acclimate and even social organizations for orphaned children and the elderly. There was also a large farm outside the borders of the ghetto, although the inmates who worked this ground could not eat the produce.

Into this "paradise" ghetto came transports of Jews from the Netherlands, Denmark, Bohemia and Moravia as well as *Altentransporte*, or transports of elderly Jews from Germany proper, and the so-called prisoners of "special merit" (Jews who either bore celebrity status or were decorated war veterans). It was likely that Nadya had been sent to Theresienstadt because of her aunt's status within the *Berlin Philharmonic* and possibly because she was only half-Jewish. Sometimes, that distinction made a difference in the immediate destination, but he doubted it would stay the final sentence.

Eryk had been riding in a car reserved for officers toward the front, but he had seen the prisoners loaded into the cars behind him before leaving Berlin. Unlike the transports of Jews to the camps in Poland, the ones from Berlin to Terezin were marked by calm and order. There were no shouting *Gestapo* and no screaming prisoners. Instead of cattle cars, these people rode in coach cars, taking their suitcases with them. After all, these people were the special class, and they were treated as such. But, in the *Reich*, *Sonderbehandlung* (special treatment) was not a label to be coveted. The language was a cloak.

There were children and families mixed in the group. Many of them dressed elegantly, the women in stylish hats and shoes, wanting no doubt, to make a good impression as they entered the new settlement for privileged persons. Children clutched toys or books, and the men carried attaché cases, instrument cases or medical bags. Many of these passengers were from the elite of Berlin society, contributing significantly to the educational, social and artistic cultures of the city.

But as he disembarked and walked toward the brick building that housed the railway offices, he tried not to look at the passengers. If he didn't focus on them perhaps he could ignore the fact that they were condemned to the same fate from which he was trying to save Nadya. Like her, they were victims of their birth, cataloged by their heritage, and snatched from their previous lives. These red brick walls would be the perimeters of their future, and he didn't want to bother now with thinking what that might include.

Still, as he walked down the street toward the *SS* headquarters, he couldn't help but notice the hopeful looks on the faces of an elderly couple who were lugging heavy suitcases and trudging toward the arched entrance of the ghetto. He could save them. He watched them look up at the entrance and hesitate as they surveyed the walled town they were about to enter. Yes, he could. His rank and office would permit him to divert them from entering this catacomb that might very well become their tomb. But what good would that do? He might find a way to alter their paperwork or help them disappear, but for how long? They were feeble, unable to make a fast escapes if necessary. They would, undoubtedly, be recaptured and then treated worse than if they remained here as part of this "privileged" transport. Let them believe that life was going to be bearable, that they might still be reunited with their grandchildren. Perhaps they would be some of the lucky ones who would simply die in their sleep or starve quickly or fall victim to one of the many plagues that hovered over the ghettos like a stagnant cloud. Hefting their luggage, they walked beneath the arch and disappeared around the corner. He let them go. He had the resources to save only one. He had to throw all his charisma and intelligence into that effort.

Though he had seen photos of the ancient fortress town of Terezin, he was still amazed at the sheer scope of the buildings which housed the masses of people ensconced here. They were huge brick affairs that had once been barracks for soldiers. He had heard the drafty quarters were now teeming with thousands dying daily of typhus and other diseases. Overcrowding was a threat to life. And so, on that pretext, transports were leaving on a regular schedule; most headed for Treblinka or Auschwitz. Not to slave labor, but to death. The Nazis would use impending illness as a reason to expedite death. It was a macabre use of German wit. The lists were continually being filled. Nadya's name could appear on them at any time.

Turning, he approached a guard standing on the corner of the street. "Good afternoon. Where can I find *Untersturmführer* Burger?"

The man saluted. "He has an office in the *SS* Headquarters, *Herr Hauptsturmführer*." He pointed down a street. "The brick building, you will see the flag."

Eryk nodded, already recognizing the earmarks of *SS* presence as his eyes swept the street and found the building the man indicated. It was gray, with large rectangular windows and a nondescript appearance, on a main street and with a good view of the town. The black *SS* flag with its twin runes was fluttering in the afternoon breeze. He returned the man's salute and hurried toward the building's entrance, flexing his fingers as he walked. His mind was racing as he contemplated his initial meeting with the commandant of the ghetto. He outranked the man so he had decided to go straight for the jugular and rely on sheer arrogance. But he would have only one chance to get it right. If the officer sensed his bluff, suspicion would be close behind and he would then be in a position to help no one.

Eryk identified himself at the main desk and then quick-stepped to the second floor as directed. He stopped in front of the commandant's door, squared his shoulders and adjusted the Iron Cross at this throat. Then smoothing the gloves on his hands, he rapped sharply.

"*Komm herein!*"

Eryk pulled himself to every inch of his height as he walked over the plush carpet and approached the desk. The man who faced him had a thin face and wiry mustache, dark hair and eyes. He looked up from his writing as Eryk came toward him. He was not smiling.

As the visitor, Eryk should have extended the expected *Heil* greeting, but he purposefully did not. Hoping his instincts had not led him astray, he led the attack. "*Kommandant*, I am here with a request."

The other officer eyed him with suspicion, which didn't surprise Eryk. "So, the Berlin office is paying an unofficial visit. And making demands."

Eryk was sure that his rank had already been noted and did not feel the need to point out the fact of his superior position. The man was in a sour mood as were most camp commandants of his acquaintance. It was, after all, a distasteful assignment to many, overseeing the detainment, distribution and decomposition of human beings rather than advancing the *Reich* on the field of glory. Perhaps that was why many commandants were plied with favors and niceties that others envied. Rudolf Hoess, commandant of Auschwitz, had an elegant villa for his family, Franz Stangl, commandant of Treblinka built and maintained a zoo for the enjoyment of his Ukrainian guards, and here at Terezin, there was rumored to be a swimming pool and cinema for the pleasure of the *SS* staff. But despite these little luxuries, the men who oversaw the mammoth concentration camps were usually a bit touchy on certain points. Being reminded that others were faring well in other deployments was probably one of them. So he simply nodded at the man's words.

"If you please."

Burger sighed and put down his pen. "What is it?"

"I need to interrogate an inmate in the ghetto and then arrange for a transport."

The commandant rolled his eyes. "You, of course, have authorization for this unusual procedure."

Eryk handed him the folder he had been carrying. Burger spread it open on his desk and leafed through the paperwork, his eyes roving the notations and various official stamps. Eryk stood at attention, ramrod straight, not even the flick of an eyelash betraying the clamoring storm within him. He had done his best to make sure the papers were in excellent order and very official looking. The fact that they were bogus was a minor detail. They looked very authentic and that mattered to a Nazi officer. Even the signature of *Sturmbannführer* Hunsdorf carried an extra flourish of appeal, though his office was not the one which would normally sign off on such an assignment. But Burger didn't know that. A *Sturmbannführer* who worked in the RSHA had clout by virtue of his office space.

After a few minutes, Burger clapped the papers down on the desk and pulled out a single sheet of letterhead. He scribbled a few sentences and his name and extended it toward Eryk.

"Here. Do what you came to do as quickly as possible. We don't need any additional clutter added to our hectic activities here. I am in the middle of planning the next transport to Auschwitz and my guards are all quite busy with keeping order in the ghetto. The Jews are an unruly bunch, you know. Even a sickly kike is dangerous." At this, Burger looked up with the faintest of smiles on his taut lips, as if he had made the best joke of the season.

"Yes, I understand there are ongoing problems in the camps with discipline and escape attempts."

At this, the commandant arched his eyebrows. "Here in Terezin, we deal swiftly with any unrest. We have our own cellblock and execution facilities. They are well used, I assure you." He paused. "Of course, there is also the *Gestapo* and their Little Fortress." He gestured out the window toward the bridge. "But generally, we handle our own affairs. They are too tied up with torture and interrogations to care about running the *Reich*." He tossed Eryk a dark look. "I don't owe you anything, Steiner, since your business here has no connection to me, but a word of advice anyway. Stay away from Beckmann. He's a nasty piece of work, even for *Gestapo,* a cur that stands out above the other mongrels. I'd sooner tangle with a Jew." Burger chortled gruffly as his own humor.

Eryk didn't flinch, didn't smile, didn't waver. "*Danke, Untersturmführer*. I'll remember your words. Now, I must get on with my task. *Heil*, Hitler!" He pivoted and walked briskly into the hall, eager to be out of the eyesight of the commandant.

The hunt was on, and he had to find his target before he became one himself.

46

Berlin
Reich Main Security Office

We place the instrument between the landscape and ourselves, so rather than our mind receiving the deep direct imprint of what lies before us, the film records the image.
Susan Sontag, on using a camera to record trauma

He was looking for a Jew.

He was trying to get a Jew out of Theresienstadt.

Hanne stared at the paper in front of her. After hours of diligent searching, she had found a deportation list with the name Nadya Goldman listed. A Mischlinge, half-Jew, whose aunt had been a member of the prestigious *Berlin Philharmonic*, Nadya was identified as aged 20 and a musician. She had been sent to the privileged ghetto in June 1942.

But that wasn't the end of the revelation.

Under the name of the woman was another name, another Goldman, Zelda, aged 52, violinist in the *Berlin Philharmonic*, a full Jew, deported to Theresienstadt in June 1942.

There were no pictures, but the profile was too compelling to dismiss. It was difficult to discern the ages of prisoners and she hadn't been close enough to get a good look at the woman on the field in Kassel, but Hanne had little doubt that she had just discovered her identity.

Sitting on the floor in the filing room, Hanne wondered about the backstory of those two. How did Steiner come to know them? Where had they been before the transport? What was the Captain's plan concerning them? Her agent mind began sifting through the likely scenarios.

It seemed evident that Steiner had known them previously. His visceral reaction to seeing the older woman on the field was more than a mere recognition. It had been an affirmation of a previous relationship. That would make his subsequent trips to the camp much easier to understand, as well as the fact that he didn't want Hanne to accompany him. Neither had he invited her on this present trip to Terezin. She realized that, ironically, this was a sign that her cover was still intact. He must not have suspicions about her true identity. She almost smiled at the thought that he was trying to work behind her back doing the sort of thing that brought her to Germany in the first place – resistance and espionage.

But, now she had a problem. Her gut told her that he was planning to spring the pair of women somehow, and while she didn't have any idea how he thought he would accomplish it, she had to admire his moxie. If it weren't so crazy, she might even suspect his motives. But an SS officer would have to be sheer crazy to attempt this kind of thing for anything other than true feeling for others.

Her problem was that she wanted to offer him help. She had valuable knowledge of resistance contacts who could aid him in smuggling these women out of the country. But, as much as he wanted to rescue his friends, he was still a Nazi officer. To reveal her sources without revealing her identity and mission would never work. If he found out that she had been working behind his back during this entire assignment, the consequences could be terrible.

What should she do? There seemed to be no way to navigate these waters. She thought about her old mentor. What would he say? Was this a case for wiles or for bravado? Was it time to cut and run? Take what information she had and disappear? But there was so much more to learn and what would happen to the women if she ran out on her assignment?

No, she was here for the long haul, to help the Allies win. If that meant keeping her silence about everything, she would. Even if it meant seeing those women recaptured and transported. Nothing must divert her aim from bringing down this rabid evil called the *Third Reich*.

Hanne slipped the file back into the drawer and closed it quietly. Once again, German efficiency had both blessed and cursed her. She needed answers, a way through.

Her father's words came rushing back, the torrent of thought spilling into her mind with all the force of convictions held long at bay. "God can make a way; sometimes only He can do that, Emma. Be smart enough to admit your limits."

Was it true? After all this time and silence on her part, would the God of her childhood really care about her fate? Was it possible that He would intervene on her behalf? She didn't think so. Why would He care about a foolish and rebellious girl who had turned her back on Him years ago?

Because it is His will to rescue and redeem.

The words again leapt into her consciousness, as though her father stood next to her in the room. She couldn't quite embrace that thought, but she admitted, as tears filled her eyes, that she needed wisdom beyond her own. Rarely did she feel despair. Usually she was confident that she could find a way out of the present predicament. But, now, she felt the first tinge of panic touch her throat. And like a child, she closed her eyes and raised a hand toward the ceiling, fingers uncurling and reaching up in the blank space.

"Okay, if You have any advice for me, I'm ready to listen. I really am."

47

Terezin, Czechoslovakia
The Little Fortress
Gestapo Office

> "Your work is a great work and a very useful and very necessary duty. . . . When one sees the bodies of the Jews, one understands the greatness of your work!"
> Professor Doctor Pfannenstiel,
> Professor of Hygiene at the University of Marburg-Lahn

Sturmbannführer Rolf Beckmann slammed his hands down on his desk, his face contorted in rage as he screamed at the man who was standing just a few feet away. "You will tell me the names of your contacts! You will tell me now."

The man did not speak, but stared, unflinching, into the gaze of the officer. Blood was dripping down from a gash on his cheek and onto the collar of his striped prison uniform. His hands were tied behind him and his bent posture indicated that he was having trouble remaining upright, but the loathing in his eyes was healthy and calm.

There would be no breaking this one. Beckmann had seen his kind before. Too stubborn to give in, loyal, committed to fanatical ideals even in the stench and horror of the Little Fortress. It would be the wall for this resistor, or worse.

He stood and walked around to stand in front of the prisoner, his face sliding into sarcastic planes. "I don't have time to waste on you, G. You filthy Czech traitors are all alike, sniveling boys playing hide-and-seek in the forests and gunning down our brave troops who are doing their duty for the *Reich*. You have been given a chance, but no more." He kicked the man's shin and took silent glee as he heard the crack of a bone. The man toppled with a painful grunt on the stone floor and tried to take hold of his leg, but Beckmann again kicked his hands away and spoke to the guard standing a few feet away.

"Get him out of my sight. Take him to the wall, if he can even stand; if he can't, throw him to the dogs."

Beckmann turned on his heel and walked back to his desk, glad to have that episode over. It was all so unpleasant, dealing with these underground fighters. Almost as bad as the Jews. But it was time now for a break in the monotony. He reached for his cap and then for his overcoat. The late September day had turned unseasonably chilly and he would need the warmth before his work was done. He buttoned the coat and then picked up his riding crop before calling his adjutant. "I am going to look around in the ghetto. Bring a notebook for any observations we might want to record."

"Yes, *Herr Sturmbannführer*." The man hurried to get the item and then followed Beckmann out of the Little Fortress and onto the street which led into the ghetto of Theresienstadt.

48

Terezin, Czechoslovakia,
Theresienstadt Ghetto

> *The Jews are like the lice of civilized mankind. Somehow they must be exterminated, or they will invariably resume their tormentive and molesting role."*
> Propaganda Minister Joseph Goebbels, after a trip to the Vilna Ghetto, November 1941

Eryk moved quickly to implement his plan and complete the mission. With his pass in hand, he retraced his steps out of the *SS* building and headed for the entrance to the ghetto. He had researched this place carefully, and knew that there was a Jewish Council in charge of the administration of the community. Well, at least the official wording was that they were in charge. He had read the reports of how these men selected people and then handed these transports lists over to the *SS* for deportation. He could not believe that they would turn on their own people in this way and so he suspected that Nazi deviance was at work in this plot. It was a ploy he had seen over and over in his travels around the *Reich*.

The *SS* command very often used the ethnic neighbors against one another or used Jews to guard or deport other Jews. Of course, there was implied disaster to one's own family if one did not come through with the needed information or action. When faced with the choice of harm to a stranger or a loved one, for most, the decision was a simple one. And in this evil way, the Nazis managed to further torment a people already doomed, to make even their last few days on this earth emotionally excruciating. There was no range of torture which the SS had not found a way to use to perfection – physical, psychological, emotional and spiritual. It was as if Satan himself were squeezing as many human lives from earth as possible.

As he passed under the arch and into the heart of the Jewish community, Eryk thought he could feel the desperation of the people who lived there. It was a living sensation that clung to everything in this dank and smelly place. He had been in many battle zones and had seen a great deal of suffering and much death, but he had never beheld a sight quite like that of Theresienstadt.

Everyone in this place seemed to be going somewhere and yet everyone seemed to be going nowhere. There was a feeling of intensity in the air and yet a sense of desperation. The buildings were massive three-story structures of a beige brick with red roofs, some of them covering an entire block. There were many windows and altogether the architecture was classic, even ornate. But the buildings were in stark contrast to the pitiful people who roamed the streets.

Although some were well-dressed and appeared healthy, others resembled scarecrows with tattered rags fluttering on their stick-like arms and legs. Some carried pots and pans; some carried bundles and boxes. There were even some carrying instrument cases and portfolios tucked under their arms, which he took to be collections of sheet music. But they weren't the only people on the streets of the ghetto. Some of them weren't walking, but lying, on the sidewalks and on the stoops that led into the buildings. These emaciated humans sprawled in awkward positions, their limbs splayed out so that often one was obliged to step over or around them. And that is exactly what the pedestrians were doing. No one stopped to bend over and see if the bodies were alive or dead. No one seemed even to notice that these obstacles in the path were actually people with skin and bones and not much else. The flies were the only living things that focused on the bodies, and this they did with a vengeance, attacking the staring eyes and cracked lips and the running sores that festered on many of the diseased forms.

A smell permeated the ghetto, a mixture of decaying flesh and open sewage and unwashed bodies. As he passed the gaping doorways on the street, he tried to look inside but saw very little; he could glimpse only shadowy outlines in the dark.

 On some street corners stood *SS* officers, observing the tired shuffle of humanity that was crammed into this walled "paradise." Occasionally, one of them pulled aside a person to talk to him or check his "merchandise" or even to arrest him. He saw a couple of teenagers dragged away after an inspection of their pockets revealed contraband – food packaged in such a way that the officer knew it was from the outside.

He noticed that the inhabitants of the ghetto avoided him, giving him a wide berth as he walked down the sidewalk, not meeting his eyes. They walked past him quickly with their heads down, intent on getting to wherever it was they were going. They all seemed to be going somewhere, but he couldn't, for the life of him, figure out where. The windows in the shops that he was passing were empty, so there couldn't be much need for shopping there, although he noticed a number of pushcarts loaded with various items. One of these carts was weighed down with ball gowns and top hats and all manner of hairpieces and lacy handkerchiefs; there wasn't much of a crowd at that one. Another cart held a few bedraggled vegetables with wilting leaves and dark spots, items his mother would have tossed to the family dog. But around this cart there was a vigorous auction being held, as people vied for the pitiful stalks as though for a treasure. Still another cart was being pulled through the street and it held hundreds of loaves of bread covered with a canvas cloth. As it moved slowly by him, Eryk breathed in the refreshing aroma of baked bread and then almost gagged. At the back of the cart, also protruding from the canvas cloth was a human foot, and he could see the shape of the body that was attached to it. He wondered if the men pulling the cart had any idea that not all of their cargo was fresh foodstuffs. Surely they hadn't put the body on the cart. Yet, there were others who were following the cart, Jews with long beards and robes, muttering unintelligible words. He knew enough about the Jewish tradition to recognize a funeral procession. So, the bread-bearers knew about the body; they were not only carrying life to the hungry inhabitants of the ghetto, but carrying out the dead as well. It was a gruesome irony. He averted his eyes and kept walking.

When he reached the building where he had been directed, it didn't take long to find the upstairs offices of the *Judenrat* responsible for the oversight of the ghetto. This was the beating heart of the community, the place where records were kept, official notices were prepared, regulations were enacted, and transport lists were created. This was the place where one could find the whereabouts of a person in Theresienstadt.

He entered the office without knocking and strode to the desk where a young woman sat clacking away at a rusty typewriter. She looked up as she heard his boots, and he couldn't miss the look of fear that crossed her eyes. But she held her composure ,and fixing her eyes on his chin, asked if she could help him, sir.

"Tell me where I can find Nadya Sara Goldman." He did not say please; he did not explain.

"I will have to go into the other room to get this information, *Herr Captain*. Please excuse me." She jumped up quickly and walked down a short hall and entered another room.

Eryk glanced around the office while he waited. It was dismal, its wooden floors scarred from years of use and it retained a musty smell, like an attic full of old books. He picked up a picture frame on the desk, turned it around and saw a photo of a young couple sitting on a river bank, arms around each other with a small child standing between them. The woman in the picture resembled the secretary who had just greeted him. He wondered idly about the man and child in the picture; surely, her husband and child. It crossed his mind that every Jew being deported and killed by the *Reich* had a personal history, just like this young woman. Every one of them was part of a family, a community; there were family portraits of them with parents and grandparents and siblings. Strange, that he had never really thought about the fact that the Jews were families and had connections to each other like other human beings. He was used to thinking of them as nonpersons. Well, he thought of all of them that way except for Zelda and her niece. He had no trouble visualizing them as people, and perhaps that was because he knew his old governess, and had been the recipient of her kindness and compassion and intellect. Was it possible that every one of these Jews, so despised by the *Reich* and the *Führer*, was as valuable as the frail old woman for whom he was now risking his life?

The girl returned, bringing with her not only a file, but also a man in a dark suit. He appeared to be in his sixties and wore a long beard and a Jewish *mulke* on his head. He bowed his head in deference to Eryk's uniform. "May I help you, sir?"

Eryk motioned to the file the girl held. "I believe the information I need is in that file. I have come to interrogate an inmate." He knew he had to be careful in everything he did here in case there was an investigation after he had gotten the girl out of the ghetto. He needed to cover his tracks as well as those who helped him. Though he was still unsure of his feelings toward the Jews as a whole, he saw no reason to bring more suffering on these poor creatures. The less they knew the better, and maintaining an impersonal, somewhat harsh, Nazi demeanor would arouse less suspicion.

Eryk could see that the man was troubled by his presence in the room and by his words. He could almost see the thoughts swirling in his head at the dilemma he was facing. Dare he question an *SS* officer further? Should he risk his life and his family's safety to help one ghetto girl? On the larger scale, what did it matter if one less Jew walked the streets of Theresienstadt? Surely, the man was tormented as he pondered the chasm between his loyalty and his safety. But, in the end, his words tumbled out quickly, as if he were anxious to be rid of them and face whatever consequence they brought.

"*Herr Captain,* has she done something wrong?"

Eryk knew that these words would have brought a terrible beating if spoken to other officers he knew. One of the inviolable rules of Nazi imprisonment was "no questions." This Jewish elder had dared to step over the line, and he had to admire the courage and devotion that took, even if it was foolhardy. But he could not let the man know that.

"That will be decided. I must find her and question her." He turned to the young secretary. "In which factory will I find her?"

The young woman was holding a sheet of paper from the file she had placed on the desk. She looked nervously at the elder beside her and then dropped her eyes to the lines on the paper and said softly, "She works in the Musical Arts Center; she teaches music."

The elder dropped his head as she read the words. Eryk knew he believed the secretary had just handed Nadya over to her death. He couldn't tell them differently. Instead, he nodded, walked briskly to the door and left the building. But as he shut the door behind him, he could hear the secretary beginning to weep.

49

Terezin, Czechoslovakia
Theresienstadt Ghetto

> *O God, thou hast cast us off, thou hast scattered us . . .*
> Psalm 60:1

So, Nadya was a teacher, a music teacher. How could he not have guessed that? She would of course, follow in Zelda's footsteps. He realized that life had become a mirror for them both. They had each grown up to emulate the person they most admired; he an officer like his father and she a teacher like her aunt.

Eryk wondered if Nadya found fulfillment in the work she did, then was aghast at his own stupidity. How could one find fulfillment in a place like Theresienstadt, no matter how one loved her profession? Of course, maybe she had held a teaching position before her deportation. Though, if that were true, it must only add to her pain now to be snatched from the life she had once known. Again, he had that odd feeling, for, in the past, he had wondered little about the personal and professional losses of the Jews. It had simply been something he hadn't considered. Or maybe hadn't let himself consider it. Whichever it was, never before had he been so aware of the great injustice that was being done to these people, who were losing everything – homes, status, wealth, friendships, relatives, health and their very lives. The knowledge spurred him on as he entered the musical arts building to find the girl he had known as a child.

Inside, the cacophony of sounds coming out of the rooms on his right and left reminded him of a university concert hall. Instruments of every kind were tuning and playing; mixed together, it made a boisterous carnival of sound. He came to a door that seemed more prominent than the rest and cracking it open, he could see children on a primitive stage, some in costume, with a director and pianist leading them in a rehearsal of some sort. He seemed to recall having heard something about a children's opera that was regularly performed here in the ghetto, an original work by a famous Jewish composer written especially for these interned children. It was heralded as a sort of masterpiece of music. Again, he wondered how these people could find it in themselves to compose and rehearse and perform. How could they lose themselves in music when the whistle of transport trains was the accompaniment to daily life?

Closing the door, he continued on, listening as he went, trying to discern where he might find his quarry. He wanted to disturb as little as possible. He didn't want these people to remember his face or his mission. A phantom escape was always the best.

Rounding a corner, his ears caught a familiar tune and he knew immediately he had found her. It was a little Polish waltz that Zelda used to play for him sometimes, light and happy, yet with a few melancholy chords here and there. His *Hauslehrerin* used to say that the tune symbolized life, mostly good but with a little bit of hard times to make one turn to God. It was amazing how much he remembered from her teaching. It seemed to be coming back in waves.

With his hand on the door, Eryk hesitated for a moment. He felt in his coat pocket to make sure he had the letter. He straightened his Iron Cross and smoothed his trousers and swiped the toes of his boots on his pants legs to shine them up. Taking a deep breath, he opened the door and walked in.

She was standing a few feet away, in front of five little children who also held violins. She was demonstrating a fingering position when she looked up and saw him. Her face blanched, and her bowing arm quickly dropped to her side. The children turned in one motion and looked at him too, their mouths falling open, but not making a sound. Nadya looked at him and then at the children. Seeming to make a decision, she said, "That is all for today, students. Please practice the scales we learned, and remember the finger positions. I will see you tomorrow."

The children got up from their seats, put their instruments in cases and left, a couple of the little girls looking backward at their teacher as she stood quietly, holding her violin and bow.

When the last child had closed the door, Eryk took a few more steps toward her, closing the gap between them. So this was how little Nadya had turned out, a slender, dark-haired scrap of womanhood, with delicate cheekbones and pink lips. As she lifted her face to look straight into his face, he saw the same velvety brown eyes he remembered as a child, though they seemed even more hauntingly sad. If she recognized him, she didn't show it. Her stance revealed her fear, but she stood her ground. He had to admire that.

All at once, he wanted to reassure her, let her know that he wasn't a threat. She didn't have to be afraid of him. He was going to help her. But, as the thoughts entered his head, he realized how ludicrous it was to try to persuade a Jew that an *SS* officer was her friend. The *Führer* had decreed that he was a member of the master race, and that she was *untermencshen*. It was foolish to believe he could even help her, let alone convince her that he wanted to. But, as he took another step toward the girl with whom he had spent so many playtime hours, he determined that he would try with every fiber of his being to make this attempt work.

50

Terezin, Czechoslovakia
Theresienstadt Ghetto

> *"After all, we do not want to look like frenzied sadists."*
> editor of the *SS* Newspaper, *Das Schmarze Korps*

His boots were highly polished. That was the first thing Nadya noticed. The trousers tucked into them covered muscular legs. He was lean; his stance firm. She lifted her eyes to glance at his face. It was shadowed, the brim of his cap masking his features. They were probably harsh as glinting steel. He was a Nazi, after all.

She put her violin and bow on the desk behind her, then turned to face him again, eyes lowered, hands clasped in front of her. "Can I help you, *Herr Hauptsturmführer?*"

"Are you Nadya Goldman?" The voice was pleasant and mid-ranged. He was probably a tenor. Nadya always noticed the timbre of voices, and even now, in a moment of escalating fear, she couldn't ignore her penchant for tonal comparisons. This man's tone was inquisitive, but not harsh, which was an oddity for an officer in the *SS*.

"Yes." She waited.

He reached into his pocket and pulled out a piece of paper. It was soiled, and she wondered what in the world it had to do with her. If it were something official surely it would be in better shape. He held it out to her. "Here, I have a letter from your aunt. Read it; it will explain."

If he had said she was free to leave the ghetto, Nadya could not have been more surprised. She had not heard from her *Tante* Zelda since she had left on a transport to the East, months ago. True, there were some who received letters from relatives on the trains, but they were oddly stilted communiqués, and she had always been suspicious of their origin. Now she wondered if this letter was also merely a ploy, though why they would use such ways she couldn't begin to understand. She was no one special. They could arrange for her transport as easily as they had her aunt's. Neither of them had any special status beyond her aunt's former position in the *Berlin Philharmonic*, and that had quickly faded anyway. If this truly was from her aunt, why on earth would she have used this man to make contact with her? *Tante* Zelda was probably not even alive anymore if some of the rumors she had heard were true. Perhaps this was a death notice, a cruel kind of Nazi joke. But, she had to be sure. After all, if he knew who she was and who her aunt was, there was nothing to hide anyway. In this game, the Nazis held all the cards. So Nadya reached for the paper, desperately wanting to know what was going on, but afraid of what she might read.

She unfolded it, trying to act confident and willing the officer not to notice her shaking hands. She looked at the words. The script was spidery and broken, and it slanted down the page, not at all like the beautiful handwriting she remembered as her *Tante's*.

> *My dear niece,*
> *If you are reading this, it means that our friend has found you. I have asked him to help get you to safety. My efforts to help you*

failed and I have been asking our Father to send someone to do what I cannot. You must trust him, my child; this is my wish. He is a man of integrity and will do his best for you because of the past we share. Maybe you remember him too. Do what he says and may our God guide and bless you in the days to come. Remember the Bach. I love you for always and into heaven, Tante.

It was from *Tante*. Had to be. No one else knew the code that existed between them – the reference to J.S. Bach. Nadya suddenly felt dizzy, overwhelmed with the proof in her hand that her aunt was indeed alive and well enough to communicate with her. It was more than she could have hoped.

But what about this officer? Obviously, he was someone from long ago that her aunt trusted. She sneaked a glance out of the corner of her eye. How would her aunt know an *SS* officer? Especially one who would want to help them?

She walked around behind the desk to put some distance between herself and the man and laid the letter down on the scratched surface. "Who are you? My aunt seems to think I should know."

He leaned forward, placing his hands on her desk. Nadya noticed the eagle insignia on his right hand. "So you should, Nadya." His voice was soft, compelling. "We played many hours together in my childhood home."

Taking a risk, she glanced up , and recognition flashed through her. The military bearing, the broad shoulders, and close-cropped hair – yes, of course, he looked just like his father. "No, it isn't possible! Eryk?"

He bowed in answer.

Her lips curled in contempt. "So, you became *SS*." The bonds of the past simply could not overcome the realization that this man was part of the *Reich*. There was no limit to the cruelty of the *SS*. She herself had seen sadism beyond belief carried out in this ghetto. How dare this person from her past pretend that everything was well just because he knew her poor, imprisoned, and probably dying aunt?

"Yes." It was a simple admission; nothing more.

Was that all? "You have nothing to say for yourself? You want me to overlook the fact that you are a Nazi? Perhaps Tante can, but I cannot. I haven't seen you since that day your father put my aunt out on the street, the day she was dismissed from her job in your home."

"Nadya, that was my father's doing. I was only a boy."

"Yes, but you didn't protest. I remember how you looked at us that last day, as if we were garbage."

"Yes, I remember that moment, and I have regretted it since. It was wrong of me."

She harrumphed. "Likely story. And now, you expect me to trust you with my life? It's unbelievable."

"Your aunt does."

"What does that mean?"

"It means I have seen her, talked with her, and promised her I would help you."

"Where? Where is she? How did you get this letter?"

"I can't tell you that. It would only endanger you more. You may be sure I will do all I can for her as well. But it was her wish that I see to you first. She insisted."

Nadya stood, holding the letter, fighting against the probability that her *Tante* had written these words in a place of suffering, not wanting to believe that she was being forced to trust a man who had once betrayed her. How could God allow this irony? There were no guarantees that she wouldn't be taken to a place just as bad. There was no assurance that he would actually do what he claimed.

"How could you have such a change of heart? We are still Jews, after all." She tossed her head as she said the words, a glint of pride in her voice.

"Nothing I could say would convince you, Nadya, or probably even sound rational to you, so I won't try. But believe me when I say that I am sincere."

"How can I be sure that you're not trying to trap both of us?"

"I don't suppose you can be sure right now. It comes down to simple trust, right? Like those stories your aunt used to tell me about faith in God. Isn't it possible that He might want to help you through me?"

What an abominable thought! Nadya felt nauseated at the suggestion. But she supposed it was possible. If God could use pagan kings like Pharaoh to save Joseph and a donkey to speak to Balaam and a great fish to swallow the prophet Jonah, then maybe He could use a despicable member of the *SS* to save one of His chosen people. But why did she have to be the one?

Nadya looked up and saw that his eyes were on her. She felt unnerved. This authoritative man was a far cry from the little towheaded boy she had known who played with his toy soldiers and ran through the gardens with her. Back then, they had been playmates, but now she was aware, more than ever, of the great gulf between them – a Nazi and a Jew. But she was also vaguely aware of another shift in their long-ago relationship – he was now a man, she a woman. In spite of herself, she was very much aware of the difference that made.

"How will you help me? What am I supposed to do?"

"I have arranged to take you with me, on a false interrogation charge."

"And where will you be? Waiting with the *Gestapo*?" As soon as she said it Nadya knew she was pushing too far. She'd better watch it or he would back out of whatever agreement he had made, and she couldn't take that chance.

"No, of course not! But it must look official, Nadya. I am risking my life here too, and it will do us both no good if my superiors find out what is going on. I will be shot and you will be taken to the East and never heard from again."

Stupid! She should have thought of that. But she had to admit to herself that she was a little fearful of facing this caper with him. Still, enemy uniform or not, he was the only source of help she had now, and to take it, she would have to follow this ridiculous plan.

He was pulling his gloves back on. "I will tell you the rest of the plan later. It is best if you don't know it right now. Go to your room; pack up everything you have and be ready. I will come for you soon." He locked his gaze on her. "Nadya, I know it has been a long time since you have seen me. We have both changed. There are many things about each of us that the other does not know. But I have made a promise to your aunt, my childhood governess, that I will do my very best to help you escape. You must believe that I mean it, on my honor. Still, it will not be easy or free of risk. You cannot say anything to anyone. No one must know that we knew each other before or that you have talked to me like this today. This must appear sudden and unexpected. And when I come to take you into custody, I will have to be harsh and indifferent. You must play along. Do you understand?"

She took a deep breath and nodded.

"Good. It will not be easy for me either, you know, to be rough with you, Nadya. Despite what you think now, you should try to remember the past. I always found you, didn't I?"

He stood silently before the door for a moment, then reached out a gloved hand to touch her arm. "Trust me, if you can." Then, he turned the knob and was gone, quickly, noiselessly, as fleeting as the shadows gathering in the room where she stood.

51

Terezin, Czechoslovakia
Theresienstadt Ghetto

Those Jews were and remained something mysteriously menacing and anonymous. They were not the sum of all Jewish individuals. . . . They were an evil power, something with the attributes of a spook. One could not see it, but it was there, an active force for evil.
Melita Maschmann

Nadya thought she understood. She thought she was prepared. But she found out that nothing can really prepare one for an *SS* arrest. When Eryk came to get her the next day, in full uniform, with another officer and with a hardened look on his face, her first thought was panic.

How could she have agreed to this? He had probably written the letter himself and told her a lot of nice things to get her to come along peaceably and now he was going to take her off to be executed for trying to escape. She should have been more skeptical, more careful. There was no way a Nazi officer was going to help a Jew escape, even if she were a childhood friend!

But Nadya willed herself to be calm. Everything was happening just as he had said it would. Maybe he would not harm her. There was nothing to do but play her part and leave the rest to him.

Yet Eryk's face gave no hint of softness or reassurance. He handled her roughly as he put the handcuffs on her wrists and pushed her in front of him out the door. Behind her, the students were horrified, not believing what was happening in front of their very eyes. Nadya felt sorry for them. But she couldn't have warned them. It would only endanger them to know details. So, she merely turned her face back toward them and looked at them as meaningfully as she could, hoping to instill in them somehow a defiance to death and a will to survive and a determination to carry their music someday to a Nazi-free world.

The walk to the *SS* headquarters was awkward and unpleasant. The other officer had no connection to Nadya; in his mind, she was just another filthy Jew. He had even tried to take her violin for himself, but Eryk had intervened, saying he needed to check it for evidence. Nadya was very aware that Eryk had no doubt built all of this on fake orders and her heart screamed in terror every time she chanced to think what would happen if his deception was discovered. So, she tried to focus on taking the next step and then another and another. Finally, they made it to the building where she was pushed up the stairs and into a little bare room with only two chairs. The door was slammed shut, and she was alone. But not for long. In a matter of minutes, Eryk was back, and he did not look happy.

With him was another man, a muscular, uniformed officer with curly black hair and an arrogant manner. He wore the insignia of the *Gestapo*.

Nadya's heart sank. How could they keep up this charade if the *Gestapo* got involved? Their specialty was interrogation, torture and death. She wished she could have a chance to talk with Eryk, but that was impossible. He was, at the moment, trying to convince the man that an additional interrogation was not needed, but it didn't sound as if it was going well.

"If this is important enough for Berlin to send an officer, it is important enough for the *Gestapo* to sign off on. My orders in this place are to oversee all prisoners suspected of illegal activities, and that includes this one." He stopped and looked over at Nadya, seeming to see her for the first time. "I will arrange for a session this afternoon."

He turned to go, but stopped in front of Nadya before he reached the door. "Be ready, Jewess."

Eryk wanted to punch the guy. For two reasons. And both were women. This was the *Sturmbannführer* Beckmann who had dibs on his assistant, Hanne. If that wasn't enough, he now wanted to trifle with his prisoner, Nadya. My, but the man was greedy. Not too unusual for the *Gestapo* who generally poked their noses into unwanted places and put their paws into every pot they could find, but still, he resented it, and more than that, feared it would be the end of the operation. And possibly the end of him, as well as Nadya.

Should he risk rushing her out of Terezin? Or try to talk the *Gestapo* man out of his interrogation? He could tell that Nadya was terrified, but she was trying to act as though she were not. She was shivering, though dressed in a woolen jacket and wearing scuffed boots. A small suitcase was at her feet. It seemed a pitiful amount of possessions for a young woman her age, but he reminded himself that most likely everything she owned in Berlin had been confiscated by the SS when they arrested her. He remembered the crisp linen dresses she used to wear when she came to his house to play. Always there had been a gigantic satin bow in her hair, pulled off to one side, holding back her silky dark hair. Surely, the little girl who dressed so beautifully had also owned attractive clothing for a young woman. Where were those things now? Did some young *fraulein* wear them now, a gift from her marauding Nazi boyfriend? Or had they been distributed to some *housefrau* resettled in the homeland and outfitted by the "goodwill of the German people?"

He would have to see to it that she had some better clothing when they were safely away from Terezin. If not pretty things, at least warmer. But, first he had to get her out of Terezin and not by way of the Little Fortress. How to elude Beckmann or evade him altogether was going to be the tricky part. Eryk suddenly hoped that Zelda was praying for him. If there really was a God, He would surely listen to her, and he really needed the help. It was going to take all his ingenuity and craft to get one little Jewish teacher out of the ghetto. If they survived that, the journey was only beginning.

52

Terezin, Czechoslovakia
SS Headquarters

> *A Jew is for me an object of disgust.*
> *I feel like vomiting when I see one.*
> *Christ could not possibly have been a Jew.*
> *It is not necessary to prove that scientifically — it is a fact.*
> Joseph Goebbels, in his attempt to win the eternal gratitude of Hitler

Nadya was terrified. She was trying to trust Eryk, at least she was trying to trust the old Eryk, what she thought he was. The man he was now unnerved her. In uniform, he was so commanding, so unapproachable. But her fear level had just escalated to horrifying heights. Eryk did at least talk to her with respect. The *Gestapo* agent she had just encountered was as close to a predator as she could imagine in a human. Compared to him, Eryk was an absolute angel.

As she waited now in the dismal little room in *SS* headquarters, she tried to hold down her panic. What if Eryk couldn't get her out? What if they discovered that he used to know her? What if they were using her to get to *Tante* Zelda? Oh, there were a multitude of reasons why things could go wrong. It made her remember some of the talks she and her aunt used to have before they were deported. They had talked of possible catastrophes on dark nights when *Gestapo* trucks were in the streets, hauling away people they saw everyday. They had tried to quell their fears by making plans, by formulating their responses to interrogation questions and by praying. Well, at least, *Tante* Zelda prayed. Nadya hadn't believed it would help much, but she did like to hear the words roll off her aunt's tongue and feel the comfort in the ancient words. Now she wished desperately that she could remember all those brave things they had said to one another. But she couldn't think of one! But maybe *Tante* Zelda was praying right now to the God of heaven. If so, that was more reassurance than any inner boldness she could muster.

Her legs ached from sitting in the same position and she shifted them slightly, wanting to stand up and walk around, but afraid to. There was a guard posted outside the door. She didn't want to give him any reason to be suspicious. Where was Eryk? Why didn't he hurry? There was no clock in the room, and she didn't know how long she had been there, but it felt like centuries. When was he going to return? What was he going to do about the other man?

Just when she thought she might become hysterical, she heard a lot of noise coming from the ghetto. It was very close and very loud. The building shook. But she had barely absorbed the sound when the door opened and Eryk stood in front of her, motioning for her to come with him. His feet were spread and he wore a long trench coat which somehow made him appear more sinister. But in that moment he had never looked more beautiful to her. Rising as quickly as she could, in spite of the stiffness in her legs, she hurried over to him.

He whispered in her ear. "Do exactly what I say, and ask no questions."

She nodded and then noticed that he was holding handcuffs. She turned around, put her arms behind her back and waited. She felt him snap them on, the steel cold and tight. Then, pushing her from behind, he walked her out into the hallway.

The guard had disappeared, and there was a lot of commotion in the offices. No one seemed to be paying much attention to the officer and his prisoner as they clattered down the stairs, into the main lobby and then out onto the street.

Out there, Nadya could see and smell smoke. It was billowing up into the air and seemed to be coming, not from the ghetto itself, but from a street occupied by the officers and their wives. But she had little time to wonder about this. Eryk was pushing her quickly down the street and around the corner, and she could sense his unspoken reminder to hurry. It was only after they had walked a couple of blocks that she finally saw a black car pulled to the curb. He steered her toward it.

Opening the back door, he pushed her onto the floor and threw a couple blankets over her. She pulled them up and huddled beneath, trying to make herself as flat as possible. A moment later, she felt the front seat sag with weight, heard the slam of a car door and then the rev of the engine. The car gave a lurch and started to roll forward. She was finally leaving Terezin.

53

Road between Terezin and Germany

> *You Einsatztruppen (task forces) are called upon to fulfill a repulsive duty. But you are soldiers who have to carry out every order unconditionally. You have a responsibility before God and Hitler for everything that is happening. I myself hate this bloody business and I have been moved to the depths of my soul. But I am obeying the highest law by doing my duty. Man must defend himself against bedbugs and rats – against vermin*
> Heinrich Himmler, in a speech to the SS guards

Nadya had no idea how Eryk intended to get her to a safe place. As she hunched in the back of the car, she trembled as he drove smoothly down the streets, making turns here and there. She could not follow the route in her mind. Since arriving, she had not been out of the ghetto part of Terezin, and so she had no knowledge of the layout of the fortress town. But as the car began to slow and finally rolled to a stop just a few minutes into the journey, she realized that they were at some kind of checkpoint, and panic clawed at her throat.

She heard a smooth male voice outside the car. "Papers, *bitte*, sir."

She heard rustling and assumed Eryk was handing over the fake orders. There was a pause while the guard must have been checking them. Then, "It seems to be in order; let me check with my superior to be sure."

But Nadya was startled to hear Eryk say in a firm, but arrogant voice. "That won't be necessary, *Unteroffizier*. I wouldn't want him also to know where you were last night. He can be very unpleasant when he hears something like that. I would like to get on my way as soon as possible, and you would like to stay in his favor. So, shall we just part ways now?"

How did Eryk know where the guard had been last night? Nadya mentally braced herself for what might come – the guard calling for backup, Eryk being forced out of the car, the back being searched, and she being arrested, taken back to the Little Fortress and possibly shot after enduring torture under that horrible *Gestapo* man.

But none of that happened. Instead, a moment later, the car began to move again. And Nadya dared to take a full breath.

The journey took hours; at least it seemed so. For a while, they traveled the back streets, she hunched in the back, covered with the blankets. Once they left the limits of the city, he lifted the covering and spoke softly. "You may come out now, but stay in the shadows."

Suddenly Nadya was profoundly aware that she was alone in a military vehicle with a Nazi officer. If she hadn't already endured so much, the shock of it might have overwhelmed her. Her head told her that this was Eryk, her childhood playmate and that he was rescuing her. But the deep fear in her heart which had long learned to distrust even those in the family told her not to be too sure. After all, it was quite ludicrous to think that he would take this effort to pluck one girl from the ghetto, based on a former acquaintance. The risk involved was enormous. Those who secreted the Jews were themselves deported or tortured and killed. She didn't know what the penalty would be for an officer who was found guilty of this treason, but it surely would be even more horrible. Why would he take that chance? Did her aunt really mean so much to him? Had he even seen *Tante* Zelda? A clever forger could have created the note and he could be part of a scheme that had been concocted to trap her as well as *Tante*. But for what? Both of them were already in Nazi custody; why would there be a need to trap them? Neither of them knew anything of real importance, no secrets or names or other information. Unless . . . no, that was impossible. *Tante* Zelda had been a world class musician, but to Nadya's knowledge, she had never had any secret activities. So, what was the reason? Even now, riding in the backseat of a car over the back roads, it was difficult for her to believe, as she stared at the back of his head under the starched cap, that he really wanted to help her. A trained dog doesn't forget how to fetch. Eryk had too long associated with the Nazis. She couldn't dare trust him completely. There was just too much she didn't know about him. There was too much at stake.

She stared out the window as best she could from her cramped position. The sun was getting lower in the sky. How long had it been since she had seen a sunset in freedom? The ghetto of Terezin had been her home for months. She had only expected to leave by transport – by one of the many departing trains or by means of the death cart that rattled through the streets and never seemed to stop. Thinking about it now suddenly seemed rather surreal to her. Perhaps this was one of the more insidious aspects of life in wartime – a hazy reality to everything one experienced.

The vehicle was noisy and smelled of fuel, and the country roads were pocked with great holes that caused her to bounce around on the back seat. After one particularly deep rut that sent her swaying against the car door, Eryk turned his head toward her so she could hear him say, "I'm sorry about the discomfort of the ride. It was the best I could do."

Again, Nadya couldn't imagine why he cared about her comfort. She was seized with a new terror that he didn't plan to rescue her at all. Maybe he would pull off into these dark woods and execute her like those stories that had been sifting back to the Jews in every German-occupied country. Perhaps she would even have to dig her own grave first. Would a bullet in the head kill her instantly? Her imagination, once given a bit of rein, galloped off, creating ever more horrible scenes. She put her hand to her eyes, trying to block the onslaught of fear. But, she caught his eyes in the rearview mirror and noticed that he was still turned slightly back toward her as if he was expecting an answer.

"I'm fine." She was furious at herself for feeling obligated to answer him at all.

He gave a slight nod and turned back to his driving. Now they were silent, bouncing with the ruts and straining their eyes for any unexpected presence.

After a few moments more, Eryk again caught her attention by raising his hand to the mirror. "We will soon cross the border back into Germany. I am going to stop in a few minutes and change clothing. You will get into the trunk and be quiet no matter what you hear. I hope to get away as quickly as possible. However, if I cannot dissuade them from making a search, I will gun the engine and try to get away. If that happens, just hang on." He looked directly into her eyes then. "If you are a praying woman like your aunt, now would be a good time to ask for help. We will need it."

54

Terezin, Czechoslovakia
SS Headquarters

> *The only thing we have to fear is fear itself.*
> President Franklin D. Roosevelt

Sturmbannführer Rolf Beckmann was furious. He was slamming things on his desk and screaming at his secretary. That wasn't the worst of it. When Beckmann was really mad, someone had to pay. Usually, more than one person. Heads were going to roll, a lot of them.

"Did no one try to stop him?" He was standing over his secretary's desk, gripping a folder in one hand and clenching the other into a fist. "The man comes in, takes the prisoner, escorts her out of the *Gestapo* headquarters while I am gone and no one even tries to see why? Am I surrounded by complete imbeciles? How could it have happened? How could you have let it happen?" He slammed his free hand on the desk, scattering papers everywhere. The girl jerked backward. She flipped her head and tried to stare back at him with haughty indignation.

"*Herr Sturmbannführer*, we were under the impression he was working with you. When he said he had come to escort the prisoner to another location for further interrogation and showed us the orders, we had no reason to question him."

"No reason? No reason? How long have you worked in this business, *Fraulein*? Do you not understand that the *Gestapo* deals with the craftiest of people, that it is our job to ferret out those who are deceitful, and who are trying to bring down the *Reich* through underhanded means? A *Gestapo* office worker always questions and never trusts what seems to be true."

The girl looked down. "I'm sorry, sir. He seemed so competent and authoritative and . . . . nice."

"Nice! I should have known. You were taken in by his prettiness just like all women." Beckmann leaned down to glare into her face. "You had better look to your ways, *Fraulein*. There are many other girls who are very well qualified to sit in this chair." He gave her a contemptuous look as he straightened. "Now, have you called the gate and asked them to detain all vehicles?"

"Yes."

"Then have my car brought to the front and rouse the men I usually take with me on these hunts." He walked into his office and then came back out, a sly smile on his face. "And ask them to bring the dogs."

Somewhere near the border between Czechoslovakia and Germany

About an hour later, Eryk slowed the car on a particularly deserted stretch of road and inched slowly over into the deep brush that was the beginning of a forest. The long branches of the undergrowth scratched the sides of the car as he pushed deeper into the shadowy cover. In spite of herself, Nadya felt panic claw at her throat and her earlier fears revived themselves. He had made it all up. The story about changing clothes was all a lie. He was going to shoot her right here. Would anyone ever know what had happened? Or would she simply disappear from the earth as had so many others? What was it like to be shot in the neck? She closed her eyes, not wanting to see his face when he came for her.

A blast of cold air startled her out of her macabre reverie, and she jerked open her eyes. Eryk was standing in the cold, holding wide the car door. She stared up at him for a moment, feeling stupid, trying to remember what they were doing, trying to see if he was holding his pistol. After a moment, he leaned down to peer into the car's interior.

"We have to hurry, Nadya. The *Gestapo* will be mounting a search. We must get past this checkpoint as quickly as possible." He reached out a gloved hand toward her.

After all her imaginations, she was afraid to believe his hand was offered in help and not malice. She chose to ignore it and got out quickly, avoiding his eyes. Let him think what he wanted. Her instincts were too abused to take risks. She walked to the back of the car. And he followed her, coming around and opening the trunk while she stood silently.

Inside the trunk were some blankets and a bundle. Eryk grabbed the bundle and handed the blankets to her.

"I'm afraid it is going to be a very uncomfortable ride from here on. Maybe these will help. And here is a flask of water. I hope you are able to sleep and that the fumes are not too terrible." He motioned to the woods. "I'm going in there to change. You can stand here and wait. There's no need to climb in there before it's necessary."

She nodded and turned her back to the forest as he disappeared into them. She wasn't sure if she was more afraid of her situation when he was with her or when he was gone. Either way, she felt alone.

Eryk yanked off his military tunic and dropped it onto the pine needles on the forest floor. There was no time to lose. If he was going to pull off this crazy scheme, he had to get into the mountains before that mad *Gestapo* agent found his trail. He knew Beckmann's type – rabid with power and thirsty for blood. The *Gestapo* were a special breed. They operated above the law, or at least they did as often as they could get away with it. They were fanatical about detail, especially in their "work" with those who resisted the Nazi regime. Many of them found great delight in bringing down established officers, often through the discovery of Jewish blood in the family tree or through some other little-known ancestor or long-forgotten misdeed. *Gestapo* officers loved their jobs and performed them with zest. For this reason, many of them had few friends. But, though, come to think of it, an *SS* officer didn't have an abundance of friends either. The public was often suspicious, and officer friends were often killed in combat.

He piled up his official clothing and shrugged quickly into the civilian outfit he had brought – rough pants, shirt, boots and a cap. As he looked down at himself, he was amazed at the transformation not only in his appearance but also in his feelings. He didn't sense the authority that came with the uniform, and right now, he really needed to exude power and confidence.

Gathering up the clothing he had discarded, Eryk crammed them into the bundle and slung it over his shoulder. It was good that he had a fresh uniform waiting for him in Berlin.

He walked quickly back to the car, where he had left Nadya. He didn't see her at first, and his pulse started to rise as he contemplated whether she had been captured or had run off on her own. But then he spotted her standing a little behind the car's open trunk. She was staring off into the distance, as if she was resigned to something. He wondered what she had been thinking. He knew so little about what she had been through. What was it really like in the privileged ghetto? What had she seen?

He called to her softly. "Nadya."

She turned and he noticed the grace with which she did it. Again, he was struck by how delicate she seemed and how her pretty face seemed out of place in the tug-of-war for life in which they were now involved.

"We have to leave. Come, let me help you in."

She walked toward him and stood for just a moment, eyeing the trunk. He suddenly remembered that she was afraid of small, enclosed spaces. Rushing back to him came the memory of a day when they had been playing and had shut themselves in the closet. She had been terrified, and he had tried his best to be the hero, finally jiggling the doorknob hard enough to free them from the space. But not before . . . yes, it seemed as if he had sneaked a quick kiss, though he had told himself it was to comfort her. He wondered if she remembered that. If so, this probably wasn't the time to bring it up. He had to reassure her. So, he ignored the fact that she was being aloof and reached out to clasp her hands. She looked up, surprised.

"Nadya, I'm sorry about this. It's the only thing I could think of. Please try not to be afraid. I promise that I will drive as carefully as possible, and that I will make sure you get to safety."

She looked at him then, full in the face and he saw that her soft eyes were wide, but there were no tears in them. "I'm ready."

She sat down on the edge of the trunk and then gracefully swung her legs around and over and into the small space. He handed her the blankets and helped wedge them around her. Then he shut the trunk carefully. Now it was time to make it really hard to open. Taking a hammer he had brought for that purpose, he slammed it against the lock on the trunk, doing as much damage to the mechanism as possible.

Next, he stuffed his uniform bundle together with his wallet and papers under the seat of the car and retrieved a small package in the glove box. From it he took horn-rimmed glasses, a fake mustache, and bushy eyebrows, and a set of papers identifying him as a traveling violin repairman. In the front seat beside him was a violin and a case of tools and some music he had handily discovered in the great warehouses of confiscated Jewish goods. He was depending on his limited knowledge of violins to get him through this. All those hours listening to Zelda play had surely left him with enough information to fool a couple checkpoint guards. At least, he hoped so.

But what if it wasn't enough? What if they searched the car, found Nadya and his uniform and papers? It would be over for both of them. What was he thinking anyway? How did he suppose he was going to get by with this very amateur scheme? He had lost his mind.

But, as Eryk started the car and pulled back onto the bumpy road, he remembered that Zelda was praying, and he knew that if any power anywhere could help them, it was the One to whom she prayed.

Berlin

Hanne sipped her coffee and wondered where Captain Steiner was at that very moment. Did he have his target in custody? Where was he taking her? Was he in danger? Of course, he was. But was he being followed?

She had tried to dig up everything she could about the two women and the so-called privileged ghetto of Theresienstadt. None of it was pretty, but it was helpful.

She had been able to find out that Steiner's father had employed a Jewess as a governess for his young son, a woman of education and talent and social standing - Zelda Goldman, violinist for the *Berlin Philharmonic* and a member of the upper-crust of Berlin society. She had been let go following the enactment of the Nuremberg Laws in 1938. The records further showed that she had been deported to Terezin, along with her niece, Nadya, in 1942 and that she was then sent to a labor camp near Kassel, Germany in the spring of 1943. Of course, there the official record ended. It was assumed that a Jew sent to the camps would die in one way or another and that would be the last entry in the log of humanity.

It hadn't been hard for Hanne to figure out that Steiner was going to get the younger Goldman woman. Everything pointed to it from an intelligence standpoint. But she did wonder where he was going to take her. Maybe he had contacts to get her out of the country. But she rather doubted it. Once in a while, one did run across a Nazi who looked the other way and did a small kindness for a Jew but it was usually with an eye toward future reprisals if Germany should lose the war. For an *SS* officer to be so well connected with the underground that he could get a fugitive safely all the way out of the *Third Reich* would be a true anomaly. She hadn't come across one of those in her time in this country. The Nazi education and propaganda machine was too well-oiled to allow for those types of squeaks arising in the population. Steiner had been bred into the Nazi movement from his days in the Hitler youty, so for him to have those kinds of friends was practically impossible. No, he would have to have help in getting these women out, and little did he know that probably his greatest asset was sitting right now in his office.

THE EAGLE AND THE STAR

German Border

Eryk rehearsed his plan.

Stop at the checkpoint. Show the false papers. Let the instruments be seen. Try to play off the German love of music. Hope that Zelda was praying.

As the border crossing came into view, he wished he didn't have anything in his stomach. His insides felt unstable. He bit the inside of his cheek and forced himself to play the deadly game he had begun.

The striped gate arm was down. The guard held up a hand. Eryk let the car roll to a slow stop. He waited for the man to motion before he rolled down the window. No point acting too eager.

"Papers, *bitte*."

It was always the same request, anywhere in Germany or in its neighboring countries these days. Eryk reached inside his jacket for the worn billfold in which he had tucked the paperwork, pulled them out and handed them to the man who stood unsmiling beside him. The guard opened the passbook and looked briefly at it and then back at him.

"You are Werner Zeishauf?"

"*Jah*."

"Musician?"

"Repair technician." He pointed to the tool case beside him. "I fix violins." He smiled broadly. "I travel to many places."

The guard eyed him. "Where have you been this time?"

Eryk was ready for him. "*Ach*, a string quartet in Warsaw, they have such troubles with their strings. Cannot keep them in tune, pegs coming loose. And a big concert was coming up for the *Meister*. So, they call Werner. I fix the problem."

"String quartet, you say? What did they play?"

Eryk reached for the music on the seat, willing it to be something suitable. "They gave me this copy as a remembrance." He handed it to the guard, his heart pounding. If this was something totally wrong, this game was up. He squinted up in the gathering dusk as he watched the man examine the cover.

The guard's face lit up. "Strauss! What wonderful music!"

It was something in the way he said it. Eryk trusted his gut and plunged. "Do you know Strauss, sir? Perhaps play an instrument yourself?"

The man leaned down and rested his arms on the window of the ancient car. "I played cello for my school's ensemble the year we held a Strauss festival. This was my favorite piece. I still remember how the cello line went, and it looks the same as I remember."

The sheet music must have been perfect for the lie he was telling. Eryk began to take full breaths again, and dared to hope he might ease by this checkpoint.

"Would you like to keep the music, sir?"

The man stepped back, puzzled, and Eryk was afraid he had gone too far. "But it was a gift from the musicians to you."

"Yes, but you see, I play only a little, and I would like for a true artist to get the good of it."

The guard nodded. "Of course, that is best and very generous of you. Thank you, Mr. Zeishauf." He turned away and opened the music again, starting to hum the tune. Eryk waited, not sure if he should make a break for it or take the risk of continuing to wait.

After a moment, the man turned back to him and waved a hand at him. "Go."

Eryk did, as slowly as he could make himself go. But inside he was racing away. The impossibility of what he had just witnessed was astounding.

55

Outside Berlin, Germany
Wilderness Road to the Harz Mountains

> *The Führer of the Third Reich has freed the German man from his external humiliation and from the inner weakness caused by Marxism and has returned him to the ancestral Germanic values of honor, loyalty and courage...."*
> Archbishop Gröber, from his *Handbuch*

Nadya must have fallen asleep because a sudden jolt awakened her, and she wondered why she couldn't see anything and why her space smelled so strongly of gasoline. Then, as she was jostled again, she remembered that she was in a trunk, and Eryk was driving. As the car bounced further still, she wondered if they were near their destination.

There had been a terrifying stop at the checkpoint. She hadn't been able to see anything that was going on between Eryk and the guards, so she listened to the muffled voices and huddled even tighter in the back, barely breathing, sure that in the next moment, the trunk would be pried open and she would be prodded out with the butt of a machine gun. Just when she thought she would suffocate from panic, the car had started to move again, at a normal speed. So Eryk had been able to convince them that all was well. They hadn't searched the trunk. She added it to the list of miracles that were occurring on this trip.

Now, the car jolted to a stop, and she hoped he would hurry to let her out. Her joints were screaming; the ache in them had long ago turned to burning, tingling misery, and she wondered if she would ever be able to walk normally again. Every muscle in her legs seemed asleep.

She heard him slamming the car door and then a crackling, popping sound with the heavier thud of footsteps as though he were walking on something. She felt the car dip down from a weight on the fender and then a horrible prying sound. Why didn't he use a key? The sound continued as he prodded and pulled at the lock and then finally, the lid of the trunk screeched open.

For a few seconds, all Nadya saw were shadows. Her eyes had grown accustomed to the darkness of the trunk and it was now dusk outside with just the faintest tinge of pink and orange staining the sky. She looked up and saw Eryk peering intently at her, his face inches from hers. She grimaced, stretching her stiff joints and trying to sit up.

He reached out a hand. "Here, let me help. You must be very sore from that ride."

She nodded, too weary and chilled to speak. She took his hand and intended to swing her legs up over the edge of the trunk and then try to hoist herself over and out. But as she rose from her crouched position, her feet got tangled in the cloth she had been using to keep warm and when she tried to stand up, she stumbled and lurched forward.

As she lunged toward the ground, Eryk took a step forward and caught her as easily as if she had been a sack of potatoes. Her hands flailing out in a mad attempt to stop her forward motion fell on the hardened muscle of his arm under the scratchy fabric of the coat he was wearing as a disguise. But, at that moment, his manliness was only a nasty little reminder that this wasn't really the Eryk for whom she had nursed a girlhood crush. This was a different Eryk, a Nazi, an SS officer. How many Jews had he beaten with those muscles? Nadya swallowed back the bile that rose in her throat and kicked her legs, trying to shake free of his grasp.

He chuckled. As if they hadn't just made a crazy escape, as if they were still kids playing together in the massive halls of his childhood home. He let her go, gently guiding her feet to the ground and letting her stand on her own. "Are you going to be alright?" The laughter was gone from his voice, and a serious note had entered it.

She nodded, though she wasn't sure he could see it in the dwindling light and wasn't sure she cared if he did anyway.

He must have seen her response or at least sensed that she was all right because he pointed to a small Alpine cabin, sheltered by great fir trees. In the dim light, she could see a crumbling stone fence behind it and a well. All around it, the lavender peaks of the mountains stood brooding in the dusk.

He started walking, leading the way to the door. Nadya followed, feeling unsettled and suddenly frightened again. What in the world was she doing anyway? Why had she let this man talk her into leaving the comparable security of the ghetto in Terezin and following him out here to this forsaken wilderness? What assurance did she have that he was really going to help her? The Nazis were notorious for deception. All of the fears she had been trying so hard to squelch came rushing back as she watched him set down her bag, pull a key from his pocket and unlock the door. It opened smoothly when he pushed it back. He turned back to her and motioned for her to enter, stepping back to let her precede him.

She hesitated. What kind of *dummkopf* was she?

Though Eryk had once been the boy she imagined marrying, things had changed. There was an impossible gap between them, and as an *SS* officer with a sworn oath to Hitler, Eryk was a man who could profit much from turning her in. As she forced herself to walk through the door, she resigned herself to whatever came next. But one thing was certain. He would not get from her any information about *Tante* Zelda. Death would come before she would betray her. Eryk followed behind her and shut the door.

If she thought being alone in the car with him was unsettling, it was nothing compared to the terror she felt as she realized she was alone with this man who had become a stranger, miles from anyone and dependent on him for everything. Possibly this was his plan all along – bring her to this place to kill her and then dispose of her body, telling her aunt that she was safely hidden. She took a backward step, trying to maintain an expression of calm. He was moving to a small table, lighting a lamp. She looked around the room for something with which to defend herself. There! The poker by the fireplace. She inched toward it.

He turned suddenly and she gave a small cry, in spite of herself.

Eryk looked surprised. "Are you feeling ill, Nadya?"

"No."

"Please don't be frightened. This is a hunting cabin that has been in my family for years. No one uses it anymore since my parents are both gone. You will be safe here." He pointed to a rocking chair. "Sit. You look exhausted."

But she was focused on something he had said. "Your parents . . . they're both dead?"

He walked closer and Nadya saw something indefinable in his eyes. "Yes. My father was killed in military action, and my mother died of pneumonia in a sanitarium."

She put her hands to her mouth. "Oh, Eryk, your poor mother. I'm so sorry. I remember that she cried a lot, and . . ." She hesitated. "I was a little frightened of her."

"So was I, Nadya, so was I." He came to her and knelt in front of the chair in which she was sitting, resting his hands on his bent legs and looking into her eyes. "You were so small and probably didn't realize everything that happened, but my mother suffered from mental illness. She was very unstable emotionally and often screamed in the night. I would be awakened by her cries. As a little boy, I was terrified that she would come into my bedroom and do something dreadful. That was why I took so quickly to your aunt. She was sane and strong and nurturing – everything my own mother was not. She took time for my boyish fancies and even for my fears. And then sometimes, she brought you along to the lessons." He quirked a grin at her. "How I did love to tease you!"

Nadya tossed her head, once again at ease with the boyish manner that reminded her so much of the Eryk she had once known. "You were just a pest! All you wanted to play was soldiers and war and then. . . ." She let her voice trail off as she realized that he had become the soldier he had once dreamed. "Now, you are a soldier, an officer."

He nodded, his lips flattening into a straight line. "Yes, I am. But before I was an officer, I was your friend. And, in spite of whatever you think of me, I am still your friend, and I am going to get you and your aunt to freedom. Please, if I am going to help you, you must try to trust me a little. You must realize that I have placed myself in jeopardy as well; that should tell you something."

She sighed, "Yes, I guess so."

He nodded. "Exactly. Now let's just lay this conversation to rest. Friends?"

"Friends."

He held out his hand to her.

But Nadya couldn't breathe. He was too close and too much like the old Eryk, the one she had thought was the most handsome boy in all of Berlin. With all she had come through, she was amazed that she felt her heart flutter with her hand in his once again.

56

Road to Berlin

Brave people are not the ones who aren't afraid. Those are reckless people who ignore the risk; they put themselves and others in danger. That's not the sort of person I want on my team. I need the ones who know the risk – whose legs shake, but carry on.
Antonio Iturbe, La bibliotecaria de Auschwitz

He was going to be back on schedule. Eryk was feeling reassured that this plan was going to work despite all the risks. In just an hour he would be in Berlin. He had left the cabin in the mountains after just a few hours' sleep so that he could arrive in his office ahead of his assistant.

It had been hard to leave Nadya there alone. He knew it was the only way and told himself that after all she had experienced, she was tough, a survivor. But she didn't look tough when he had bid her good night last evening. Her eyes held that terrified look that he remembered seeing one day long ago when they had watched the *SA* men goose-stepping down the streets of Berlin; then, as now, her gaze harbored a fear that tugged at his heart.

She understood, or at least he thought she did, that she was now being hunted, a fugitive. So was he. Except that the officials didn't know his identity. Yet. They would find out. He knew it was a matter of time. The day he had run out on the field to help Zelda had been the day he signed his own declaration of treachery. They would catch him sooner or later. He just had to make sure that Zelda and Nadya got out of Germany before that happened. So, for now, he had to reappear in his duties as if nothing had happened, and Nadya had to stay out of sight.

There was enough food and wood in the cabin for several days, a couple weeks at most. He had shown her the well, cautioned her against talking to anyone, took her into the cellar with the hiding cubby and left her with a gun and a promise to return as soon as he could. It was all he could do.

Now he was burning up the miles to Berlin. The old car he had scavenged for the escape had continued to run, and he was grateful. Zelda must be praying. Now all he had to do was dispose of the car and be in his office before his leave was up, and then think through the next phase of his plan while keeping his assistant clueless about his activities. None of that was going to be easy.

Berlin, Germany
Reich Main Security Office

Hanne was at her desk and waiting. If she was right, Captain Steiner would walk briskly into his office in a very few minutes. He was always prompt. Even if he had been away on a clandestine mission, she had no doubt that he would be here acting as if all was normal, and he had merely taken a couple days leave.

It was a beautiful late autumn day, getting closer all the time to Christmas. It would be her third Yuletide in the Fatherland. Funny that she had to come all the way here to find out how very much she really did love the traditions and festivities of her homeland. She let herself fall into a few minutes of reverie, remembering the garlands of green that hung in the village church and the melting candles in the windows of the little home that her mother always filled with the delicious aroma of shortbread and raspberry jam. Mum was of hearty Scottish stock and brought into the family all the stout love of heritage and the ancient recipes of her forebears. Every now and then she even reminisced about the heather hills she had romped as a girl and told her children of the stone cottages and great castles that dotted the land of the kilts. She was always ready with a laugh and a cheery "Good Morning, Lass" in her voice that still retained a bit of brogue.

Dad, on the other hand, was her opposite. He anchored the family in reality and stolid faith. He was a good man, respected in the hamlet where he was the rector and faithful to his wife and children. But he was rarely one for high spirits and preferred a quiet cup of tea beside his own hearth to large festive events. Ever since the war, he was often strangely silent even at home and never talked about his ancestry, though it was no secret that he was of German ancestry. The folks of the parish loyally closed ranks when the war started and refused to allow any seed of rumor to take root in regard to their beloved pastor. So, it was not on their end, but rather something in his own spirit that seemed to disquiet him.

Sitting now at her desk, Hanne wondered again if her father was squirreling away some secret that aroused all those strong feelings. Did he still love the country of his birth? Did he fear that he had relatives in the German forces who would be injured or even killed in this war? Was that the reason he had been so adamantly opposed to her joining the war effort? She had only thought that he considered military service beneath her station as a woman. But maybe there was more to it. If she ever returned to England, perhaps they could sort it out. Yet, with every passing day, Hanne's hopes for escape from Germany dwindled. For an agent, death was often the only sure escape route.

But enough of the macabre. There was much to do today. No matter what mess the Captain had gotten himself into, she still had a job to do. The plans were not yet safely into Allied hands. She would like to help Steiner with his humanitarian task. Rescuing helpless women from Hitler was noble. But the good men of the world were counting on her to do her part in removing evil and that had to come first. If sacrifices had to be made, so be it. No matter what, she was going to get those plans to the Allies.

57

Kassel, Germany
Arbeitslager Cellblock

> *These men are heading for utter destruction – their god is their own appetite, their pride is in what they should be ashamed of, and this world is the limit of their horizon.*
> Philippians 3:19 (Phillips)

Zelda Goldman could barely move her legs. Days of confinement in the damp cell had left them weak and unsteady. But it was the heart condition that had so long plagued her which was wreaking total havoc on her body now. She had long been without the medications she had used in Berlin. Now that she was confined to a small space, the swelling had become even worse. Her ankles were thick and bulging with fluid, and when she tried to stand on them, she wanted to scream with the pain. Of course, there wasn't really room to stand or walk in the small cell so sitting or lying were her only options, all day long.

The room was worse than chilly. It was miserably cold, so much so that she could see her breath whenever she raised her mouth from the smelly blanket under which she huddled. The temperature must be below freezing and though she didn't have a window in her cell, she was sure there was snow on the ground outside. Her fingers were throbbing as they always did when there was a snowfall. The arthritis which ran in her family was drawing them up, twisting the knuckles and robbing her of their use. She refused to think about how it would affect her ability to play her violin. Some things simply could not be thought about when one was in the camp.

So, she tried to get her mind off her own misery by praying for Eryk and for Nadya. She wondered how his rescue mission had ended. Had he succeeded in getting her out? Or had he been caught and even now was lying dead somewhere from an executioner's bullet? She prayed for strength to trust in the living God, to believe that His purpose would be accomplished in the lives of both of her "children."

Harz Mountains
Outside Berlin, Germany

In the tiny cabin tucked far back into the piney woods of the Harz mountains, Nadya stood behind the rough curtains and peeked out into the misty morning.

It had all seemed so simple and safe when Eryk had told her of the plan. She would stay in the deserted cabin, and he would return in a few days to check on her. But when she had awakened and realized he was gone, panic engulfed her. What if he didn't return? What if he did. . .with the *Gestapo?* What if a *Hitler Youth* troop on a camping outing stumbled onto her or saw signs of life in the cabin? What about hunters in the woods? What if she ran out of food and water? What if something happened to Eryk and he couldn't return? What if he changed his mind and left her there forever?

The rush of thoughts was terrifying. Nadya felt the familiar panic rising as her throat tightened and her heart started to beat faster. Clenching her hands, she willed away the fear and reminded herself that Tante trusted Eryk and sent him to help her. She shouldn't allow her imagination to make her doubt him. He would come back. Just like he had always found her when they played hide and seek as children. He would return.

In her mind, she saw his steady gaze and firm stance when he promised her that he would get her out of Terezin. He had done it. And he would keep his word this time too. She needed to wait and trust. And something else. She needed to do what Tante would do in times of fear. She needed to pray.

58

Berlin, Germany
Reich Main Security Office

> *We have only one task, to stand firm and carry on
> the racial struggle without mercy.*
> Heinrich Himmler

Steiner walked to the window and slammed his fist down on the sill. The woman was maddening. He remembered his feelings when he first laid eyes on his new assistant. He had been right. She was trouble. Despite her flirtatious moves and her very efficient ways in the office and on the field, she was a snake in the grass. And he was the one who was going to be hit with the poison bite.

He shouldn't have worried about beating her to the office this morning. She wasn't there anyway. All his hurrying and care to look especially official this morning had been for nothing. The emptiness of his office had mocked him.

But the note she left made him even more worried. She had "urgent business" with the *Reichsfuhrer*. She would return in the afternoon.

Eryk was furious. He didn't even have the advantage of a confrontation with her before she went and squealed on him. Oh no, she was going to go straight for his head. He should probably drive to a forest somewhere and put a bullet in his own brain before a firing squad could do it for him. If he was even granted the dignity of that. Probably he would be sent to prison, tortured, and then hung. Maybe with piano wire. Hitler and his henchmen had a special affinity for the sound effects that particular tool could evoke from their enemies. Of course, once his traitorous deeds became known, that's what he would be. An enemy of the *Reich*.

Helping not one, but two Jews was heinous. Family heritage, his mother's noble lineage and even his own military honors would never counterbalance the scale of Nazi justice. He was doomed. Eryk hit the sill again, the pain a small hint of what awaited him.

Hanne smiled as she climbed the stairs to the floor for Steiner's office. She would have loved to have seen his face when he read her note. Her agent's instinct told her that she had scored. She hoped so. She needed the momentum that such a shock would bring. If he only knew that the "urgent business" was no more than some benign files she had to deliver to the *Reichsfuhrer's* office. But he didn't need to know. He had left her out of his plans. Fine. Now she would use her own means of finding out what he was up to.

She stopped in front of the door to his office and took a moment to adjust her cap and square her shoulders. Then she opened it and marched in.

He was standing by the window, looking down on the street. When he heard the door, he pivoted around to face her. She had to admit he handled himself well under fire. There was no hint of fear in his face. In fact, he looked composed and business-like. But when he spoke, there was a hard edge of anger in his voice. "You are late, *Fraulein* Lager."

She smoothed the scarf at her neck and then answered. "I left you a note, *Herr* Hauptsturmführer., telling you where I was."

"Yes, I did see that, but I had no business for you to attend to at the office of the *Reichsfuhrer*. I do not like to come into my office and find my assistant missing. You work for me, not for the *Reichsfuhrer*."

Hanne could not believe the bravado of the man. He was really going out on a limb. If she didn't know that he was bluffing, she would think him very suave indeed to be thumbing his nose at a man who could have him killed at the snap of his fingers. Still, she needed to push him a little. If things didn't go well, maybe she could still duck out of the country.

"I beg your pardon, Hauptsturmführer Steiner, but the business was my own, not yours, and I was under the impression that the *Reichsfuhrer's* call trumped all others."

The veins in his neck bulged, and she heard him exhale deeply before he answered. She had to admire his attempt at control. "As you say, *Fraulein*. But as you are my personal assistant I must insist that I be informed of any meetings you have with my superiors."

He was frightened. Hanne was sure of it. But in a very Nazi-esque style, he was choosing to deal with it through anger. She had seen many agents do the same. It was more acceptable than shrinking. She had to admit she couldn't imagine Captain Steiner shrinking from anything. The man was not only a towering physical specimen, but also calm and self-assured and rarely ruffled. Even on the field out near Kassel, he hadn't shown much emotion. The fact that he was even letting her glimpse this much of his inner turmoil revealed that he must be truly fearful of what she knew and of what the consequences would be if she had told the administration. That, in turn, meant that there was something he was trying to hide.

She pursed her lips, turned toward him and folded her arms. "What would you like to know, *Herr Hauptsturmführer*?"

He advanced toward her and suddenly she was glad that they were in a building with others around. She didn't think he would physically harm her, but the man was positively intimidating at this close range. How much different from the night when she had held his arm while they walked the streets of Kassel, and she had flirted so obviously.

He stood merely a step in front of her and spoke softly but firmly. "I want to know what you told the *Reichsfuhrer*."

"I didn't tell him anything, *Captain*. I only delivered some of your paperwork to his secretary."

Steiner's face went slack in just the faintest of ways, but she caught it, and she knew that now was the time to strike.

"Why? Were you afraid I might show him this?" Reaching into her pocket, she closed her hand around the star and then thrust it forth in front of his eyes.

He grabbed her arm with such force that she knew there would be a bruise later. "Where did you get that?"

"In the bottom drawer of your desk as a matter of fact. Now it's my turn. Why was it there?"

"That, *Fraulein* Lager, is my business." His blue eyes were the hue of frozen steel. "You will now give it to me." He extended his other hand and put it in front of her at eye level.

"No, *Hauptsturmführer*, I don't think I will. Not without screaming for help. Of course, you could always tie me up and leave me behind your desk and then hope no one would find me. Or suspicion that you had done it."

For one long moment, she thought he was considering it. But then he sighed, released her arm and motioned for her to take a seat in front of his desk. Turning, he closed the door, locked it and sank down into his own chair.

"*Fraulein* Lager, I might as well be frank. And hope that you can understand."

"How frank, *Captain*? Are you going to tell me about the prisoner on the field and the long visits to the labor camp and this most recent trip out of the country?"

"What do you mean? I was away on leave."

"I don't believe that is all there is to it." She held his gaze. She knew she was treading on thin ice. He could throw her out of the office and accuse her of something that no one else would be able to dispute and then have her sent to prison or worse. But somehow, she felt that he wouldn't, that this was the time, that she had to take this risk.

He held up his hands in mock surrender. She noticed that he still favored the right one a little.

"As you wish." He took a deep breath. "*Fraulein*, I am about to reveal to you something for which I can be imprisoned and executed. But it seems I have no choice as you are already in possession of some facts that could incriminate me. Yes, I am trying to affect the escape of two Jewish women."

That was all. He just dropped the fact out in cold language and sat, looking at her, waiting for her response.

"Why?"

"The old one in the field was my childhood governess and tutor."

Ah, now the light began to dawn. "And the other one?"

"She is her niece." There was just the slightest bit of hesitation as he said the words and the way he averted his eyes from her gaze. She instantly knew that there was something special about the one she hadn't seen. She was able to read him pretty well by now. This Jewish niece had him hooked. In spite of her good judgment and patriotic resolutions, she felt a slump of sadness. But she would have to wait to sort it out. She held up the star. "And what does this have to do with this secret mission?"

"She once gave me one like it. It reminds me of her. I found it in a hut in Russia," he paused, "beside a dying woman."

"A Jew?"

"Yes."

"You killed her?"

"No."

"Have you killed any Jews yourself?"

"What would you have me say, *Fraulein*? You know the racial policies of the *Reich*. As a member of the *SS Aufseherinnen*, you have studied them yourself. Why do you care what I have done as long as it is in the name of the *Führer*?"

Now it was time for her to take the biggest risk of all. Why she felt certain she should, Hanne couldn't even say. In light of every bit of her training, it was stupid, utterly foolhardy. But she had learned long ago to trust her instincts. That habit had saved her life more than once. So, she extended the star to him as she spoke. "It is important because I may be able to help you."

He reached out for the star and brushed her fingers in the process. His were cold, and she knew that she didn't have to worry about him anyway.

He stared at her. "I didn't think I would ever see this again without first having a rope around my neck. But *Fraulein*, you can't possibly mean what you just said. How can you help me?"

"I may not be able to keep you safe, but I might be able to assist you in helping your friends."

59

Berlin, Germany
Reich Main Security Office

> *For the dead and the living, we must bear witness.*
> Elie Wiesel

If she had said she could give him wings to fly, Eryk would not have been more startled. He prided himself on being able to read human character, but he had badly misjudged his assistant. Who was this woman anyway? She no longer spoke with the deference of a junior officer. There was quiet authority in her voice and demeanor. He wanted to know just what was behind this remarkable change in her but hesitated to ask. Maybe he *didn't* want to know. Maybe it was too dangerous to be aware of how she could fulfill this promise. Then again, maybe she was with the *Gestapo*. Infiltrating was their specialty. It would be just like them to send a good-looking secretary to ensnare an officer they suspected. He would have to be very careful.

"How would you do that, *Fraulein*, if I were to believe this crazy suggestion?"

"I have my sources, *Captain,* although I must not divulge them, you understand, of course."

"Of course, perfectly." He couldn't keep the sarcasm from his tone. "No, I don't mean it like that. I only refer to the safety of all of us involved if we are able to pull this off."

"All of us? Just whom do you have in mind?"

"*Herr Hauptsturmführer.,* it is better for me not to say and for you not to know. But I have sufficient contacts to help you carry out this mission, if you choose to accept my assistance."

It was the way she referred to the escape as a "mission" that caught his attention. Was it possible. . . ..? He almost caught his breath at the absurdity and then at the audacity of such a stunt. Who was she really? He had to find out, and of course, if she could help him get the two women out of the country that would be good for his own health. The trick would be to get her help and disappear before she could turn him in or get too much information that would incriminate him.

"All right, *Fraulein*, I accept. Where do we start?"

60

Outside Berlin, Germany
Harz Mountains

> *They were nothing but numbers to the people who had started this war.*
> Ellen Marie Wiseman, The Plum Tree

The hours were dragging.

Nadya hadn't realized she could miss the noise and bustle of the ghetto. Though she was glad for a reprieve from the sight of corpses and the stench of refuse and decay, after being part of the throngs of people who had been crammed into Theresienstadt, she felt utterly and terrifyingly alone here. Of course, she had slept off and on for the first twenty-four hours, waking up to look around and determine where she was before falling back into exhausted sleep. But when she finally felt well enough to get out of bed and peek out from behind the heavy muslin window covering, she realized the location was very deserted. That was a good thing, she reminded herself. After all, she wouldn't feel safe in a house where she could see people walking by. In the ghetto, everyone walking by was a fellow sufferer, a Jew who struggled with the same fears and horrors and hunger pangs. But, out in the big world again, one never knew if the person would help you or turn you in. She was going to have to get used to thinking again about the possibility of capture at every turn. Maybe she had become naïve while she had been in captivity. Maybe she had forgotten how it felt to be the "hunted," the quarry, in this very real game of war.

She hoped it wouldn't be too long before Eryk returned. He had left her with enough food and blankets and wood for very small fires. But she missed human companionship. Well, truth be told, she missed his companionship After all these years, that was still the way it was with her. Despite his unchivalrous behavior as a teenage boy, despite his obvious affiliation with the Nazis, despite the years since they had been childhood playmates, she still felt her face grow warm when he looked at her, and she still felt safe when he was in charge of things.

Did he feel the same? Did he remember his little-boy proclamation of love? Or did he see her now, not as a woman he could love, but as a pitiful member of a hated race whom he was obligated to help because of childhood loyalties?

As she sat curled on the horsehair couch, bundled into quilts to ward off the chilly air which was only a little diminished by the miniscule fire, she finally let the hot tears come. She had held them off in the face of separation from her *Tante*. She had bullied herself into staving them off while she witnessed the savage life of the ghetto. She had prided herself on her refusal to release them in Eryk's presence. But now, here, she let her hand go slack on the release valve and wept into the uncaring silence.

Berlin, Germany

Eryk fingered the star, letting the sharp edges remind him that his objective had not yet been completed. In fact, it was barely begun. His assistant had requested the remainder of the day off so that she might make the needed contacts for their mission. He had agreed and made a bogus entry into the daily log that would satisfy any snooping eyes. Inwardly though, he was impatient and a bit resentful of her secrecy. He wasn't used to being left out of the details when something this big was being planned. It bothered him that she wasn't willing to tell him how she was going to help him. Yet, at the same time, he understood the need to keep sources confidential. There was only so much a man could take before he cracked. When the time came for him to be interrogated, Eryk didn't want there to be any chance he would risk another's life for this foolish thing he was doing.

He had no doubt that he would be interrogated. The *Gestapo* were very good at what they did, and there were plenty of greedy officers and even regular citizens who would be glad to tell them anything they wanted to know. The day of reckoning would come. But he had to hold it off until he got Zelda and Nadya into Switzerland or England or somewhere. At least he would die doing something noble. Surely there was redemption in that. Maybe deeply committing himself to this task would stop the nightmares.

61

Berlin, Germany

Courage is resistance to fear, mastery of fear, not absence of fear.
Mark Twain

Hanne shivered in the cool November dusk, as much from adrenalin as from the chilly air. She was walking briskly toward a place she hadn't dared go in the years she had been in Germany. The café where she was bound was the emergency contact. She had been warned never to go there on a whim. In fact, the only reason to attempt this contact was if lives were at stake. And not necessarily hers.

The old man had been adamant about preserving the anonymity of his sources. He had made her memorize the address and the coded sentence she was to use and then had thrown the paper into the fire. As she had watched the flames consume the information that long ago day, Hanne had realized that this thing she was doing was very serious, deadly serious. But she had not allowed herself to dwell on it. Indeed, she could not if she wanted to do her job well. It was better if she focused on the challenges and the audacity of her tasks, not on the risks. After all, she had volunteered for this job and trained to be an agent. She was pretty good at it. In fact, so good that no one had heard from her in over a year. Perhaps even the old man thought she was dead. Well, he was going to get a wakeup call very soon.

Of course, if she were honest, she would admit that she had debated long and hard over this commitment to help Steiner. After all, it was putting her mission into jeopardy and even delaying her focus on getting the intelligence she had into Allied hands. She didn't think she could do both at the same time. Even if she could manage to pass along what she had learned about the new *Tiger* tank, Steiner could find out, under the guise of helping the women, that she was also undermining the machine that he was helping to create. She didn't think that would sit very well with him. He might even be inclined to call off the whole thing or let everything go through until the women were safe and then rat on her. He was, after all, still a loyal Nazi. And, *SS*, of all things.

What about the women? She had been hoping to use a little female charm to get more information from him. But the captive niece obviously had a strong pull on him. That wouldn't help her chances to get close to him.

What was she like? If she had been held in Theresienstadt the chances were very high that she was Jewish. This was the biggest puzzle of all. Was it possible that a man of power and prestige as well as considerable physical presence could really have affectionate feelings for a Jewess? If so, it would be the first real relationship of this kind she had seen in her days in Germany. While there was no shortage of leering looks from the Nazi soldiers directed toward the Jewish women in their custody, she had never witnessed a Nazi officer who had genuine tender feelings for a member of the subhuman race that the Germans considered the Jews to be. The possibility of such a relationship leaned toward the absurd. That did make her suspicious.

THE EAGLE AND THE STAR

Kassel, Germany
Arbeitslager Cellblock

Zelda knew she was growing weaker. It had been only two weeks since she had been brought here after the rescue from the field, but in that time, she had felt her health slipping daily. She wasn't sure if it were better to be in this stinking, damp cell with the rats and roaches and foul-smelling straw or to be outside trudging through mud and fighting the ever-present threats of typhus-infected cell mates and the ferocity of the guards' violence.

At least, here, she didn't have much contact with the *kapos* or guards. But she did have the same threat of dysentery, starvation and most of all, pneumonia. The dank conditions were worsening the cough and her heart was fighting harder than ever. Her doctor back in Berlin had warned her against getting a respiratory infection. Her fragile heart would have a difficult time warding it off, he'd said. She wondered wryly what he would say now if he could see her.

Though, come to think of it, he was a Gentile and a Nazi. He might not care that her heart was failing. One less Jew to have to liquidate another way. In the old days in Berlin, it hadn't mattered to professional people that they might be serving people of another race. They were simply patients or clients or customers. But now, it mattered very much to many people. In the days before she and Nadya had been captured, there was hardly any place a Jew could go and receive any kind of public service. Gentiles wouldn't serve them; fellow Jews were out of business. It was an insane world.

Yet, hadn't Christ lived in an insane world? The Romans hated the Jews and oppressed them and took any and every opportunity to hurt or kill them. Even Christ's own people had disowned Him in the end. At least, that hadn't happened to her or most of the other Jews she had met in captivity. The former distinctions like religious or non, observant or not had fallen away. Now, in the trains and ghettos and camps, they were all simply Jews, bearing together the reproach that was their historic legacy and looking ahead to the deliverance they hoped would come.

Zelda was glad that she knew the real Deliverer, even if she died a prisoner in this wretched camp. She would then see the Messiah face to face. He had come to save her from eternal captivity, which was so much worse. He would help her endure this present suffering and then usher her into His presence. She was sure of it, and it gave her a sense of inner comfort as she shifted on the nasty straw bed and then drifted off to sleep.

62

Outside Berlin, Germany
Harz Mountains

The best remedy for those who are afraid, lonely or unhappy is to go outside, somewhere where they can be quite alone with the heavens, nature and God.
                    Anne Frank

Eryk found himself wanting to drive faster than the mountain roads would allow. Was Nadya all right? It had been a week since he left her in the hunting cabin, and he had no way of knowing if she was alive or dead. Had she been discovered? Did her food run out? What about the firewood? Had she remembered to make only very small fires and never to go out in the daylight? He simply didn't know, but he was worried.

More worried than he should have been about the niece of his childhood governess. After all, it wasn't like she was family or something. Well, yes, in a way Zelda was. She was almost more than family. But Nadya? How would he describe his relationship with her? Why should he have intense feelings for her safety and welfare? Was it because he knew she mattered so much to Zelda? He was sure that entered into it, but it was more than that. He didn't just want her to be healthy and safe when he showed up today. He wanted to see the sparkle in her big brown eyes and watch the firelight glisten on her satiny hair. He wanted to soothe away her fears and. . . .he stopped himself. Yes, he wanted to embrace her and promise her protection.

Maybe he really was crazy. All those days in battle and the recent losses and injury had damaged his ability to reason. Was he really having these kinds of thoughts for Nadya? A Jew he hadn't seen in ten years? Sure, he was basically a good hearted man. He had been well bred, though it was a fact that Zelda had done most of that. His mother hadn't been able to focus on anything other than her own miseries. His sisters were pitiful proof of her neglect, though the results of mental illness could hardly be fairly called neglect. And his father, a decorated war veteran and respected member of the military community, hadn't been able to understand the needs of small children. He had passed on the lessons he knew best – justice, determination and a sense of honor. But he would have been appalled at the idea of his son having tender feelings for a Jewish girl. Though he had been generally a fair-minded man, he had fully accepted the *Führer's* plan for expelling the Jews from Germany. Having lived through the hardship of the post-Great War era and seeing the wealth of many Jewish merchants in Berlin, the elder Steiner had no lack of love for the people. However, he would not have been in favor of their wholesale extermination. He might have wanted them out of the country and may have believed they were keeping other Germans from the wealth they deserved, but he was not a callous man, at least not that Eryk had ever seen. He couldn't imagine his father ever shooting Jewish women and children beside a ditch, and to Eryk's knowledge, he never had. But they had only briefly talked about the *Fuhrer's* new mandates before his father died. Suddenly, Eryk wondered if that was what Hunsdorf was trying to point out in their conversation about his father.

How had his father died after all? What kind of orders had he received before his death? Eryk tried to recall anything he might have overheard his father talking about. Had there been tension in his division? Of course, there had been problems with those in the old guard of the German army. Many of those men were not National Socialists at the core. But his father had accepted Nazism, at least for all Eryk knew, and his war record stated that he died in battle. But was that really true? Eryk now began to wonder even more. Maybe when this rescue operation was over, he could investigate quietly what had happened to his father. But then he almost laughed at himself. When this mission was over, he would likely either be dead or on the run.

63

Outside of Berlin, Germany
Harz Mountains

> *The spirit of resistance to government is so valuable on certain occasions that I wish it to be always kept alive.*
> Thomas Jefferson (in a letter to Abigail Adams, February 22, 1787)

There was no smoke curling out of the chimney.

That was the first thing Eryk noticed as he drove carefully up the last stretch of the terrible mountain road. Maybe she was just being careful. But he hadn't been gone that long. Surely she hadn't already run out of wood. His pulse quickened as he pulled up to the side of the cabin and stopped the motor of the nondescript car he had chosen for this trip. Glancing around quickly he got out, shoved the keys in his jacket pocket, and hurried to the door.

Stopping for a moment to catch his breath, he put his ear close to the plank door and listened. He simply didn't trust the *Gestapo*. It would be just like them to have already discovered her and to lay low, waiting for whomever was coming to get her.

He heard nothing. Like it or not, he was going to have to risk it.

Eryk thrust his key into the lock and turned it, his other hand on the *Luger* in his pocket. With his thigh, he pushed the door open and drew out his weapon as he took a step inside. He squinted in the dusky light, trying to see every corner and shadow. Nothing. Utter silence.

He turned around and shut the door, throwing the deadbolt. Then he began walking slowly from one room to the next, visually clearing them of threats and looking for the one person who was supposed to be here. Living room, kitchen, bedroom, storage room – there were no indoor facilities here. Maybe she was out in the privy. She had to feel very vulnerable leaving the safety of the house.

He would not call out. It was still possible that he was being led into a trap. He would not make it easy for the *Gestapo*.

There was only one other place she could be, if she was still here. He walked to the pantry and lifted the ring, opening the trapdoor to the cellar. He thought he saw a flicker of light.

He tried to listen, but could hear only the pounding of his own heart. Straightening his shoulders, he put one boot on the ladder, listening for anything other than the creak of the wood. Another step, then another. He descended slowly into the murky, damp space until he stood on the earthen floor. And then he saw her.

She was in a heap in a corner, a blanket under her and a candle beside her along with what was left of the food he had prepared for her. The candle was burning. That was the flicker of light. Why hadn't she stirred? Was she even alive?

Eryk took a step toward her. "Nadya."

She sat bolt upright, clutching a fire poker and looking wildly at him.

He raised both hands. "*Nein, bitte*, it's me. It's Eryk." He walked slowly toward her as she dropped the poker and started shaking. She wasn't actually crying, just trembling violently.

"I thought you were the *SS*."

He made a wry gesture with his mouth. "I guess I am."

"No, the other *SS*. You know."

He reached out and touched her hand. "Yes, I know. But it's just me. How are you, Nadya? Have you been down here the whole time?"

She raised guilty eyes to him and nodded. "I just couldn't stay up there. The windows felt like eyes. And the darkness just reached out . . . and. . . .."

He put his hands on her shoulders. "I'm so sorry. I should have thought of another way. I should never have left you alone here."

She took a deep breath and seemed to will away the hysteria. "No, it was something we had to do. I will be fine. Just please, help me out of here. I want to see the sun."

She stood up and gathered the few items around her. He grabbed the blanket and held onto her elbow as they walked toward the steps.

"Ladies, first." He pointed and grinned.

"Oh no, you don't! I remember the last time you walked behind me up some steps. You know how I hate that."

He did remember. As a child, Nadya had been afraid to have someone on the steps behind her, and he was sure she had even more reason to be afraid now. But maybe by playful teasing, he could shake her out of the shock she was close to.

"All I can say is you'd better get up those steps quickly if you don't want to hear me creaking up them behind you!"

She didn't need encouragement. She scampered up the steps as though her life depended on it. Following her, Eryk wondered if there had been times when it had.

64

Outside Berlin, Germany
Harz Mountains

There is a charm about the forbidden that makes it unspeakably desirable.
Mark Twain

The tramp through the woods had left Eryk's cheeks ruddy with the chill of the afternoon. His dark blue muffler and woolen cap stood out in contrast to the brown backdrop of the forest. Leaning against a stalwart pine, he seemed part of the landscape, a native of the noble Bavarian world. Not like a hideous Nazi at all. More like the boy Eryk grown up into a courageous warrior.

After he had coaxed her out of the cellar and given her a bowl of the soup he'd brought in a thermos, he had suggested they take a walk so she could get some fresh air. How wonderful! She had felt so cooped up in that cellar in the dark, thinking she might go crazy. Now, she felt stupid for not being able to handle staying upstairs while he was gone. What was wrong with her anyway? After all she had been through, why was she falling apart now? She had to be strong. *Tante* Zelda would have been in her place. She wondered what her aunt was doing right at that minute. Was she still alive?

"You look deep in thought." Eryk's voice snapped her back to the present.

She looked up at him. "I was thinking how silly it was to cower in the corner like I did."

"No, not silly." He looked into her eyes. "I might have done the same, Nadya."

"Truly?"

"Truly. You gave me quite a scare, you know. I was afraid something had happened to you."

It was the way he said it that made her wonder what was coming. His voice, which had always been kind to her, had gone almost . . . tender.

"That would have been bad for you, I guess." She tried to make a joke of it.

But he turned it around on her. "Yes, Nadya. I am realizing how very bad indeed."

His voice was soft, and as Nadya looked up at him in astonishment, she saw in his gaze a look that defied reason. Though long ago, as a schoolgirl, she had dreamed of Eryk falling in love with her, she wasn't sure she knew how to handle that possibility now. Feeling awkward and needing to do something with her hands, she began to brush the leaves from her coat. But she could feel his eyes on her.

She looked up and offered a nervous smile. He smiled back, and then leaned toward her to pluck a bit of branch from her shoulder. The distance between them now seemed infinitely less. He flung the twig away but did not step back. He was so close that she could inhale the spice of his shaving lotion. She risked a glance at his face and saw the blue steel of his eyes became soft and warm as he looked into hers.

Then he reached out and pulled her against him, holding her gaze as he closed the small distance between them.

I can't do this. This isn't what Tante Zelda *wanted!* Her blood was pounding as she tried to make up her mind. Yet, in spite of herself, she leaned forward, knowing what was going to happen.

The lips that touched hers were warm and strong. The hand that was still healing rested on her shoulder and with the other he lightly touched the back of her neck. He kissed her for a brief gentle moment before pulling away.

Above them the sun was settling down on a woodsy world that was altered irrevocably. Nadya felt changed too, and more confused than ever. She had done it. She had kissed an *SS* officer. A Nazi. Nadya waited for the revulsion to come, the urge to throw up on the Prussian boots in front of her. But the feeling didn't arrive. Instead, she felt relief. She had been right all along – he wasn't a monster. In fact, quite the opposite, if her renegade heart could be trusted. Maybe he really was different from the others. This was Eryk, after all. She had known him so long ago. Yet he was not a little boy playing war, but a grown man with duties in a very real one. Though they had once spent many hours together on the carpets of his big home in Berlin, the aura surrounding the man who had just kissed her was more than a little overwhelming.

She wasn't sure what she expected him to do next. His eyes were searching her face, as if he were looking for some kind of cue. "I'm sorry, Nadya. I did not intend to do that. I guess I was just carried away with the emotion of the day."

Nadya fought her wild thoughts. What should she do now? Slap him? Tell him never to try that again? Be insulted that he was making excuses? Or, let him know how her heart was somersaulting?

In the end, she did what girls have been doing for centuries when kissed – she blushed. But he had gone on talking, his arms still folded around her, and she wasn't sure he noticed her reaction.

"What I meant to say is that I have an obligation to your aunt. I intend to carry that out. Furthermore, I don't want you to think I'm ill-mannered and manipulative. I'm sure that's what you believe of all German officers, and now it seems I have given you proof."

Nadya could feel the sinew of the arms which still held her. She tried to clear her head. This was not the little boy Eryk she had once known. This was a man, a leader of others into battle, a Captain in the *Waffen-SS*, a man who had seen much, experienced much. Suddenly, she was afraid. Where did she think she was going with this little play-acting? They weren't Aryan lovers on a hillside in a free world. They were mortal enemies, thrown together in a bizarre way by a long-ago friendship and an old woman's request and a tangle of crazy chemistry. There was no way this could go anywhere. Why in the world was she letting him kiss her? He was a Nazi. She was crazy to imagine him as anything else.

He must have seen the change in her mood because abruptly he took a step back and looked directly into her eyes, his arms dropping to his side. "You must believe me when I say that I have never planned to take advantage of my role as guardian to you. I promised your aunt that I would get you to freedom, and I will."

Nadya wasn't sure what she wanted at this point. He was frightening to her when she remembered his official rank. But, he was thrilling to her when she recalled him as the boy she had adored as a young girl. Regardless of what his uniform symbolized, she wanted to believe in his integrity. "I have to admit that I am still trying to convince myself that I am safe with you."

"Really, Nadya, I don't think either of us is safe if we let this thing continue. This . . . complicates things, you know. I didn't plan on this happening, on having these feelings, this moment."

She wasn't totally surprised, but hearing the words said aloud shocked her all the same. She had caught him watching her at times, and they had a history that continued to pull them together. But still a small part of her was incredulous at his statement.

She had heard the official Nazi pronouncements about the inferiority of the Jews and even seen it demonstrated in the way her people were treated in daily life in Berlin. So, how could a Nazi officer, one who believed he was of the master race, even consider giving his heart to a woman whom he was taught was nothing better than vermin? She pulled back further and crossed her arms, trying in vain to protect her heart.

He looked away. "I don't blame you. It's rather impossible, isn't it? And why should you even believe me, after all?"

"No, it's not like that." She said quickly. "I want to believe you. I think . . . oh, I don't know what to think. Nothing is as it should be. Sometimes you seem like the boy I grew up with and then sometimes you seem like a total stranger. Which one are you?"

"I'm not even sure I know the answer to that, Nadya. Your aunt thinks I have at least a small degree of goodness left. She is trusting me to help you."

"She has no other choice."

"True, but she was more gracious than she would have had to be. It was humbling, Nadya, humbling and condemning. Seeing her in that condition was horrible. I have to get back to her soon." He straightened his shoulders and looked away. "I'm sorry I bothered you. It won't happen again."

Impulsively, Nadya reached out and caught his hand as he started to walk past her. "No, please don't say that. Maybe we can figure it out together."

He was silent.

"We have so much history together, and now you are risking your life to save mine and *Tante*'s. That has to mean a whole lot. But what could ever come of a relationship between us anyway? You could be executed for what you're speaking of." Tears formed in her eyes as she realized the horror of that possibility.

Eryk nodded and reached out to thumb away a tear on her cheek. "Are you worried for me, Nadya?" He smiled. "My, how things have changed since you used to tattle on me to your aunt when I wouldn't do things your way in the nursery."

She made a face at him, despite the serious moment. "Well, things were different then. You were. . . just being difficult to tease me."

He grinned. "I admit it. Teasing you was great fun." He ducked as she made a face at him. "But, I am not teasing now. I feel more than responsibility for you, Nadya. Being around you and wanting to protect you has awakened something very deep in me."

"You don't prefer blonde German girls?" She couldn't keep back the saucy retort.

He shook his head and winked. "I always did prefer black curls." He tugged a strand of hair that had blown across her shoulder.

Nadya blushed outright and ducked her head. She couldn't seem to breathe, and she knew he was going to kiss her again. Her heart began to beat erratically as he settled his back against a stone outcropping and pulled her into his arms. He was sure of himself this time; the hesitation in him was replaced by a soft intensity. She didn't even argue with herself for her surrender. He kissed her slowly, letting her sense his strength and tenderness, giving her a glimpse of his power and yet manfully protecting her with his restraint.

His closeness and the taut strength of his arms made Nadya shiver. The piney smell of the woods about them and the gentleness of his touch rushed against her senses, pulling her into the current of the embrace. She gave herself up to the delight of the moment.

She was a Jew; he was a Nazi officer. They were mortal enemies. But she dared to believe that this bliss wasn't a fable. Besides, she knew denial was folly; he held her very life in his hands, and now she had willingly given him her heart.

65

Outside Berlin, Germany
Harz Mountains

> *We are all fools in love.*
> Jane Austen

Eryk had kissed a good many girls in his time, but never before had he embraced a Jewish woman other than his childhood governess.

In spite of himself, he struggled for a moment. Words swirled in his mind. He imagined the sneer on the faces of his fellow officers and heard the laughter of his commanding officer. A Nazi officer gently kissing a Jew? They would call him despicable. Worse, they would imprison him. In fact, he could face execution for unlawful relations. He was risking the "purity" of his race. To profess tender feelings for this non-Aryan was a betrayal of every bit of his Nazi training.

Yet, he couldn't deny that he had feelings for her. He wasn't able to sort them out and label them in order; they were a bright jumble of protectiveness and delight for the little girl she once was and a surge of awe at the woman she had become. The adrenalin rush from kissing her was akin to the emotion of being in the commander's cupola, the excitement of traversing new territory. But Eryk was thinking right now that he much preferred holding Nadya to clutching the controls of a machine. The challenge of discovering the depth of her heart spurred him on.

She had matured into a lovely woman, with eyes that still mesmerized him with their velvet. It was a wonder that she was so alive and had the capacity to feel anything since she had been slowly starving in that ghetto. He held her softly against his coat and gently rubbed her back. She was so thin. What surprised him more than his own feelings was her acceptance of his caress. Was it actually possible that a Jewish girl who had seen her people brutally treated and murdered, whose beloved aunt had been sent to the camps, who shivered at the sound of military vehicles – was it possible that she could learn to love a Nazi?

Then again – was he truly a Nazi? According to Zelda, he was not. He was a faithful German patriot, a loyal officer, but not a Nazi. Eryk wondered if he believed his old teacher's assessment of him. Part of him hoped she was right. But, whatever his own feelings, he was definitely still under Nazi command, and that made this crystalline day in the woods much more complicated.

Eryk straightened his legs and stood up completely, drawing away from the stone he had leaned against. He reached out to adjust the scarf around her neck; it had twisted with his embrace.

"You know, you don't have to pretend for me, Nadya. If you reject my affection, I am not going to turn you in." He tipped her face back to look into her eyes, trying to emphasize his words. "You don't need to fear me. If you just say the word, I'll not bother you again."

She smiled shyly. "No, I'm just not sure this is really happening."

Eryk was delighted with the blush on her cheeks. She fascinated him now just as she had as a childhood playmate. Though he knew what it could mean if he were found out, it was up to him to find a way to protect this young woman.

He was on the verge of a great sin against the *Reich*. But he forced away the thoughts of soldiers and commands and laws and reached out to pull her close, delighted with the smallness of her in his arms. The time to worry about the law would come soon enough.

66

Berlin, Germany

> *The strength and power of despotism consists wholly in the fear of resistance.*
> Thomas Paine

The contact was made. Now that she had done it, Hanne was surprised at how easy it had been. The underground communities operating in Nazi territories were much more vibrant than many imagined. That she was part of such an organization still amazed her. How was it possible that she, raised in the rural English countryside, now hobnobbed with agents and operatives, that she was an integral part of this patriotic underworld intent on dethroning the monster Hitler?

Yet, when she remembered the risk involved, she knew it was no lark. This was a dangerous life and death business. Her contact had reminded her of that. His life was constantly on the edge, and he was putting it in further jeopardy by promising to assist her.

Of course, he was suspicious. Who wouldn't be of an *SS* officer talking about rescuing Jewish women? Hanne still hadn't quelled her own doubts of Steiner, but she had learned long ago to trust her gut and was willing to take this chance. Besides, there was the reward of having him defect to the Allies with his wealth of information about the inner workings of the *Reich* and the military machinery on which he was working. Surely even Prime Minister Churchill would be ecstatic about the possible intelligence gained!

So she walked briskly back to her apartment. She had to wait for Steiner to return and then they would make the trip together to the labor camp where the old woman was being held. There, the first phase of the plan would be put into place. While she waited, it was up to her to work out the remaining details of the rescue and to ensure that every precaution possible was taken. As she pulled the blackout curtains in her tiny room provided by the *SS*, Hanne prayed again for the second time in the past week. She wasn't sure if God was listening, but she hoped that the things she had believed in childhood were really true.

Outside of Berlin, Germany
Harz Mountains

Eryk threw another log on the fire and sat down on the stone floor, drawing his knees up and resting his arms on them. Nadya sat on the sofa, a quilt pulled up to her chin, watching him. They had eaten a simple stew after their walk in the woods before sitting down in front of the fire. She knew that there was something on his mind, and she tried to be patient, wondering what he needed to say. She was dazed from what had happened on their walk this afternoon. Since they had returned, he had stayed scrupulously away from her, not even touching her hand as he handed her the soup bowl. While she hadn't expected any of this to happen, she was confused now, trying to sort it out and figure out the real story.

Suddenly, he pivoted, facing her from his position on the floor. "Nadya, about what happened today...."

She looked at him, not giving him any cues.

He cleared his throat. "I wanted to kiss you. I wanted to be close to you. You know, if you think about it, that I have had special feelings toward you. But it's kind of crazy, isn't it? I mean, we haven't seen each other for years until last week. You don't really know me, don't know who I am or what I've become. It's almost like we're strangers as far as our knowledge of each other, beyond the fact that I'm a man and you're a woman and the feelings that come with that."

He reached out and lightly touched her hand. "I guess that's enough for me as a man to want to embrace you. You're pretty and womanly and remind me of the beautiful life I once had before the war. But, I don't want to take advantage of you, to use you to soothe my conscience or satisfy my longings. That wouldn't be fair to you. You deserve commitment, and a man who will honor and protect you always."

She pulled back. "What do you mean? What have you become? Are you really awful then? Are you saying that you don't honor me, that you see me as some wanton woman, ready to do anything for food and safety?"

He sighed and pressed his lips together. "I'm sorry. I dumped everything on you at once. Let me answer one question at a time. What have I become? I'm a Nazi, Nadya, a member of the *Waffen-SS*. You know that, right?"

She nodded. "Yes, What I know of them is horrible, but I thought you were different. I've tried to tell myself that you could never do the terrible things the others do." She stared at him. "Was I wrong? Have you?"

He didn't meet her eyes. "Nadya, I'm a soldier, an officer. I have done some things that would make you shudder, maybe even hate me."

"Have you ever killed a Jew?"

He looked up. "Not directly, no. But, Nadya, I'm part of a nation who has persecuted your people. I represent all the hatred and cruelty and evil that makes you afraid, that starved you in Terezin and that drove you to the cellar here. I'm not clean and noble. I'm tainted. You should hate me."

"I should, maybe, but I don't." Nadya shrugged her shoulders. "I'm not sure how to explain it. I can't see you as anything but Eryk, my old playmate and now my protector. Maybe *Tante* is praying." She lifted her hands eloquently.

"I have no doubt she is praying, Nadya. But is that enough to make you believe me? Can you really see me as your protector? After all the years I didn't care to find out about you? After I stood there while my father made you leave our house so long ago? There are many things you don't know."

She sighed. "Back when your father made us leave, I hated you already because you were a boy who had gotten too old to play with me, and because I could never make you like me or see me as something other than a little girl."

Eryk smirked. "You little sneak. So all those tarts you made me and the shirts you ironed for me weren't tokens of friendship but flirtations, huh?"

She blushed and looked away.

He reached up to touch her hand. "It worked, I guess. Not at that time, maybe, but I think I'm getting hooked now." He grinned.

"But you just said you only wanted to be affectionate to me because I'm a woman and I remind you of good things? I thought you didn't have tender feelings, just desire."

"That could be, Nadya. I don't trust myself anymore. Sometimes, I don't think I'm capable of tenderness and affection. But, I want to be. I know when I'm with you that I feel more tender emotion than I ever have for any other person, except maybe for your aunt. You two are the only people in my life who have any kind of emotional pull for me."

"But what about your sisters? Don't you love them?"

"Frederica and Annaliese are wrapped up in their own lives. We hardly see each other anymore. Besides, they are afflicted with the same malady as me. They don't know how to love. Our father didn't know how to give affection, and our mother wasn't emotionally capable of it. I was the blessed one. I had my *Hauslehrerin*, your aunt. Any positive emotion in me came from her, I think."

"So, what are you saying, Eryk?"

"I'm saying that I don't know how this thing will end. When I leave here, I am going to try to rescue Zelda from the camp, bring her here and then get both of you out of the country. It's a ridiculous, dangerous plan. I don't even know if I will live long enough to get the first part done, let alone all of it. They are looking for me right now, and you too. If I fail, or if we are caught, it will mean death for us all, and probably torture first. I can't stand the thought of bringing that on the two people I most care about. But, I have no choice. If I don't try, you both will most certainly be killed."

Nadya leaned toward him. "Is that really what happens, Eryk? Are all the people on those trains going to be killed?"

He nodded. "Yes, Nadya, it's true. The people on those trains don't go to a nice place to be resettled. They go to their deaths."

"No! Don't say that! I don't want to hear it!" She put her hands to her ears.

He tugged them down. "I'm sorry, *Liebchen*. I forget that you aren't aware of all the gruesome details. We don't have to talk about it."

Tears were beginning to trickle down her face. "How can they treat us so horribly? Back in Terezin, we guessed that things weren't right, but we didn't have proof. There were the postcards sent back to us from people who had been deported and the promises of the Jewish council. How could they have deceived us?"

Eryk held her hands and stared into the fire. "The council was probably trying to keep peace, to save those they could."

"But that doesn't excuse them. They sent my aunt away to her death."

"No, it doesn't excuse them, but I'm telling you that is what happened. The councils aren't given other options. They are forced to play along with the *Reich*, to choose the ones from their ranks who will be taken next to the slaughter. If they don't, someone else will choose and they will be taken as part of the deportation. They are not given reasonable options."

"But how will they feel after this is all over, when they think of all the people whose blood is on their heads?"

"Nadya, they won't have to worry about that."

"What do you mean?"

"They aren't going to be bothered with a guilty conscience, unless God lets them remember in the afterlife. They are going to be killed too. You don't think the Nazi leaders will let the most influential personalities and the greatest thinkers in the Jewish nation survive this war, do you? They don't want them to be able to testify against them if they should lose, and if the Nazis are victorious, they want a Jew-free world."

Nadya shivered, tears coursing down her cheeks. "It's awful, awful. I should never have left with you. I should have stayed with my people and suffered the end that is waiting for them. But I am a coward. I wanted to be free."

Eryk jerked her hand. "Don't say that, Nadya. I don't think that at all. Finding you and your aunt has helped me see this evil more clearly. I don't think I can ever go back to serving as I did in the *SS*."

"But what do these plans mean for us, for me and you? What will happen to you after we escape?"

"I don't know. That doesn't matter. All that is important is that I get you and Zelda to safety, and that I give what information I can to the Allies."

"So, you don't want to marry me?"

Eryk's eyes widened. "Marry you? You would want me to marry you? I'm a Gentile, a Nazi and an *SS* officer. Why would you want that?"

Nadya blinked her eyes and gave a half-smile. "Because you're Eryk. I've always loved you, I think."

67

Road to Kassel
Germany

To act is to be committed, and to be committed is to be in danger.
James A. Baldwin

The scheme was crazy, foolhardy. If she hadn't been part of such ridiculous plans before, Hanne wouldn't even dream of trying it. But she had set these wheels in motion and now she would have to see it through. The escape plan for the old woman that she and Steiner had decided on would put them both at great risk. It was likely that none of them would make it out alive.

As she bumped over the road, once again in the back seat next to the Captain, she watched the countryside gliding past and felt the incongruity of the pure whiteness of the snowy fields with the filth of the regime she had chosen to fight. The great evil heart of the *Third Reich* beat with the destruction of an entire race of people and its wheels were lubricated with the blood of millions of innocent victims.

Today, she was going to put a spoke in those wheels, she and Steiner. There was no way it would stop the whole machine, but perhaps it would save a couple lives and maybe even give her a chance to pass on the information she had secreted away. In spite of the recent turn of events, she had not forgotten that her assignment in this country was ultimately the gathering of intelligence to help the Allies. The notes she had coded and the diagrams she had copied might save a lot of England's brave fighting men, if only she could get them into the proper hands.

She realized that the risk associated with this present mission was great. If they failed, she might never get the chance to pass on her information. The old man would never forgive her for that. Hadn't he trained them all not to let sentiment get in the way of duty? How many times had he cautioned them against the greatest threat to an operative – emotion? Now, because she had a soft spot for this *SS* captain, she was willing to jeopardize all her hard work.

For a minute, she considered backing out, calling off the entire thing. But she knew she never could. Somehow she felt constrained to do this thing, as if God Himself were urging her forward. That in itself was strange, since she and God still weren't on the best of terms, though she had tried to pray several times lately. Did that count for something with the Almighty? Was He going to take her on a trial basis? Was the rescue of a couple Jewish women the way back into His favor?

Even as she thought it, Hanne knew that wasn't true. The Scripture she had learned as a child said that God's redemption was based not on works but on His character, on divine mercy that He extended because of love. But she couldn't help thinking that it would please Him for her to do her best to make this rescue happen. If she died in that attempt, maybe that sacrifice would prove that she had goals beyond herself.

Eryk sat ramrod straight in the seat beside his secretary, and doubted his own sanity. Perhaps his injuries at Kursk had been greater than he thought. Surely his ability to reason had been damaged. What he and Hanne were attempting was foolhardy. Worse, it was treachery. He could scarcely believe that it was he who was planning to spring not one, but two prisoners of the *Reich*. He, Eryk Wilhelm von Steiner who had been bred as a loyal son of the *Fatherland*, whose father had fought nobly in the Great War, who had been a faithful member of the Hitler Youth and who had an untarnished record as an officer in the *Waffen-SS*! The sunlight streaming through the window of the staff car glinted off the skull and crossbones on his ring. He remembered the date inscribed on the inside next to his finger, the date on which he had been awarded this honor from the *SS Reichsfuhrer,* Heinrich Himmler. The day he had scored his first *panzer* kill.

Himmler told every recipient that this ring represented a willingness to risk one's life for the benefit of all. Yet, the words were blocked out by the image of Nadya's white face, by the look of pain he recalled seeing in Zelda's eyes. In this personal war with love and hate, prejudice and past, there was no question who would win. He would give his best to see the Jewish women saved. Maybe his life too.

Kassel, Germany
Arbeitslager Cellblock

Zelda knew the end was near. She simply hadn't the strength left to live. In fact, she wondered if the plan all along had been to let her rot in this stinking hole of a cell. Since Eryk had left, she had not seen another person, only a hand reached in to remove the pail or to dump an almost inedible slop in her bowl. There had been no showers, no exercise, no chance to move about.

Her ankles were now so swollen that she could not rise from her cot with the dirty blankets. When she reached down to touch them, her finger made deep indentations in the fluid filling her legs. They looked like tree trunks rather than human limbs. So, she was reduced to crawling to the door to get her daily food ration. She tried to scoot the nasty pail close to the opening so that it could be emptied as often as the guards would come by. But sometimes she couldn't manage to move it, and the stench from the waste gathering in it was suffocating.

She was glad that it wasn't hot outside. The flies and bacteria would have been intolerable then. Of course, the chilly October weather was very uncomfortable too. The block walls of the cell trapped the cold and held it against her like a freezer. She shivered through the long, painful nights, wishing for death to come and relieve her of this suffering.

A glimmer of words from Scripture would come to her as she lay in the filth hour after hour. The Apostle Paul, who had also been a prisoner, surely knew the breakdown of the physical and the torment of being unable to change the conditions. He put hope in the Savior, who would change the "vile body, that it may be fashioned like unto his glorious body." Never had she been more aware of just how loathsome the human body can be when it is sick, aging and untended. She shuddered at the appalling condition of her own person.

She held on only because she was sure Eryk would return. She had never known him to lie. Though he was now *SS*, she dared to believe that this part of him had not changed. She was putting all of her hopes in the integrity she had tried so hard to instill in him. She was choosing to believe in the compassion and sense of fair play that she had seen so often in the little boy he once was. It was a long shot, she knew, but after all, faith was believing the impossible was possible with God. She was holding on until she saw him and knew that Nadya was safe. Then and only then would she surrender to the enemy gaining ground on her every minute.

The grim reaper was stalking her; she could sense his clammy breath all around her. But she also knew that she was held in the Father's loving hands and that He was the Giver and Taker of her life, not the Nazis or even Satan himself. Until He said the word, she was pressing on, willing her heart to beat, asking God to let her live just another day, another hour.

68

Kassel, Germany
Arbeitslager

> *I only ask to be free. The butterflies are free.*
> Charles Dickens

"We're here, *Fraulein*."

Steiner's words jolted her back to the present. Hanne had been lost in the thoughts of England, of her father's house, and her siblings beaming around the table. But at his statement, she recognized the iron gate of the camp which, like all German camps, had words painted above the entrance bearing the ubiquitous message *Arbeit macht Frei* (Work Makes you Free).

They were entering the lion's den. Only God could save them now.

Eryk instructed the driver to take them straight to the commandant's office. They jostled over the deep ruts in the sorry excuse for a roadway toward the solid-looking brick building midway from the entrance. A small sign announced that they had reached their destination. Nodding to Hanne, Eryk got out when the private on duty opened his door. He set his officer's cap securely on his head, tucked his riding crop under his arm, clutched his briefcase, and followed the youngster into the building.

The building and its occupants had changed little since his last visit to this dismal place. Funny that he should ever have regarded surroundings such as these as military installations. They now seemed to him as a forsaken barbaric outpost.

The commandant wore the same lofty expression when Eryk was escorted into his office. He looked up from the paperwork on his desk and didn't smile at the interruption though he promptly returned Eryk's salute. "Ah, Steiner. What brings you back?"

"Unfinished business, sir. I would like to interrogate the prisoner once more."

"The old woman you questioned last time?"

"Yes." Eryk made a show of rifling through his papers. "A Zelda Sarah Goldman, a Jew."

"What could that old crone possibly have to contribute to your investigation, Steiner?" The man leaned back in his chair. "By the way, just exactly what are you investigating?"

"Infiltration, *Herr Kommandant*. This woman was part of a network known to me in Berlin. I am tracking down a possible link between her and some sabotage activities which have taken place in the plant at Kassel."

Fortunately, Eryk had discovered that some acts of sabotage had actually taken place at the *Henschel Werks*. Though it hadn't caused significant damage, it was sufficient to warrant an investigation, and he had been all too glad to conduct the search. This had provided him with actual orders that he could show now to the commandant, giving him official cover for the moment. He extended the folder to the man at the desk.

The commandant opened the file and thumbed through the papers. Eryk forced himself to stand still, at attention, without fidgeting. He had to appear confident, brash, eager to find and dispatch his victim.

The man snapped shut the folder and slapped it on the desk. "This whole business wearies me, Steiner. Trapping and interrogating filthy Jews day after day, spending the war in this desolate stretch of land. Did you know that roses won't even grow here?"

"Sir?" Eryk was taken aback by his words.

"Roses, *Hauptsturmführer*, flowers. Surely you've heard of them!"

"*Jawohl*, sir. I just didn't follow your line of thought."

"Roses are a favorite of mine, a hobby, that makes me forget the mud and the whole boorish business here. But the soil here is unfit for growing anything, tainted as it is with the detestable remains of Jews."

"Yes, sir." Eryk was set to agree to anything the man said just as long as he made it out of there alive.

"Well, enough of that. Go, see the prisoner. She has taken up space long enough anyway. I would appreciate it, Steiner, if you could finish up whatever you need to do with her so we can move her along the line." He waved his hand at the window, a gesture indicating the assembly line of death that took place in this camp.

In his mind's eye, Eryk turned around and snapped the man's head back with a swift uppercut. But outwardly, he merely nodded and clicked his heels before turning to go. "Thank you, sir."

When Steiner got out of the car, Hanne leaned up to the driver and told him to take her to the *SS* office building in the camp. While the captain put the first phase of the plan into action, she had some tricks of her own to play. If they were to get the old woman out of the camp, they needed a vehicle, a different one from the staff car. It was her job to requisition one from the camp office under the guise of needing it for an assignment.

When the car pulled up to the austere brick building, Hanne adjusted the scarf at her throat, grabbed her case of papers and got out, waving the driver on. He had been ordered to return to the *Henschel Werks*. They were on their own now.

She struck a brisk walk as she went up to the building. Pulling the door open with flair, she entered, looking around with a bored, disdainful air. "Who is in charge of the motor pool?"

A laconic youth with a shock of reddish blond hair and a wolfish gaze pointed toward an office to her left. "You'll have to speak to the sergeant in there, *Fraulein*." He grinned.

Hanne turned on her heel, walking the short distance to the office, feeling the eyes of the silly boy following her.

The sergeant was no better. Hanne wanted to slap the leer off his face, but chose to offer cold disdain and keep the interaction as professional as possible.

"Why do you need a car, *Fraulein*?"

"*Hauptsturmführer* Steiner and I are from the *Henschel Werks* in Kassel. We are conducting an investigation into recent acts of sabotage and need transportation back to the plant after we are finished here."

"You would think the factory would send their own driver on such an important mission."

"So they did, Sergeant, but of course, we could not use a marked car for business of this nature."

The officer was intrigued. Of course, he was. The sensibilities of every German were now on high alert for anything that was out of the ordinary, that smacked of intrigue and secrets.

"Business of what nature, *Fraulein*?"

Hanne smiled serenely. "If I could tell you that, *Herr Unteroffizier*, I would be wearing more stripes on my uniform than I am presently." She softened her tone. "I only follow my orders; I do not know all the details."

He took the bait. "Ah, an admirable trait for a German woman. I commend you, *Fraulein*. Perhaps sometimes you and I can have a talk about this aspect of military life."

"Perhaps." Hanne let her lashes fall down on her cheeks as she extended the order signed by Steiner, requesting a vehicle. "For now, though, I must follow through with this duty." She made her tone of voice sound reluctant, regretful.

He took the paper, his hand brushing her fingers, examined it, signed it and put it on top of his files. Coming from around the desk, he opened the door and stepped back for her. "I will escort you there myself, *Fraulein*." He stiffened his posture and clicked his heels, eyes forward in respect.

Hanne followed, holding under her jacket the paper she had just swiped from the desk. The old man would have been proud. She and Steiner didn't need a paper trail.

Eryk felt his stomach lurch as he stepped inside the cell. No wonder the guard had buried his nose in his collar as he unlocked the door. The foul odor coming from the bucket just barely inside the door was about the worst thing he had ever encountered, and that was saying something.

As the door clanked behind him, Eryk wondered if he would be able to hold onto his breakfast long enough to do what he had come to do. Tightening his hold on his will, he searched the room with his eyes and finally saw the huddle of rags in the corner. It had to be Zelda.

Deciding to ignore whatever he stepped in, he moved to her side and squatted down beside her, his uniform protesting. "Zelda?"

At first, he thought she was dead. Even in the near darkness of the cell, he could see the pallid tint of her cheeks when he pulled back the dirty scarf on her head. But he couldn't detect breathing. Frantic, he fumbled with the buttons on the coat she was wearing and finally placed a hand on her chest and forced himself to hold his own breath as he waited. There. Faint, erratic. But she still had a heartbeat.

He chaffed her hands, rubbed her face. "*Hauslehrerin*? Can you hear me? It's Eryk." He tried not to say it too loudly. Compassion would be a dead giveaway.

Her eyelids fluttered. She gasped. "Eryk? *Liebchen*?"

He gripped her hand. "Yes, it's me. It's time to go now. Time to get you out of this hole."

She widened her eyes then and spoke haltingly. "But, what. . . of Nadya?"

Eryk smiled. "She's safe. She's out."

"*Gut. Danke*, my boy. *Gott segne dich.*"

"Of course. Now, it's your turn."

"Forget about me, Eryk. I am getting out too very soon."

"What? I can't do that. Besides, what are you talking about?"

She lifted a wan hand, pointing to the ceiling. "He is getting me out."

Eryk shook his head. "No, I think He has sent me to get you out this way. Now, please listen, *Hauslehrerin*. I am going to give you an injection. It will make you go to sleep. When you wake up, you will be free."

She tried to smile and reached for his hand. "You are so good to me, Eryk. Thank you for trying so hard, dear boy. I knew you would do it."

Eryk turned his head for a second, overwhelmed again with shame for the years he hadn't cared or thought about where his old teacher was. He shook it off. Time for remorse later. Now he had to act. He reached into his inner vest and pulled out the small packet containing the vial and syringe. Filling it as quickly as he could in the dim light, he bared her arm and sank the needle into the flesh, pushing the plunger to the hilt. Then he withdrew the needle, wrapped it all back up, and buried it again in the recesses of his inner vest.

The effect was immediate. Her head lolled to one side, and her eyes slipped shut. Eryk hoped the work of the drug wouldn't cause her weak heart to stop for good, but there was no other way. It was either this or leave her to rot in this rat-hole.

He stepped to the door of the cell and pounded on the door. "Unlock this door, *Soldat* I must come out."

Steps in the hallway and then the door creaked back, the young guard shielding his nose once again.

Eryk shouted at him. "How dare you turn your face from me?"

"I'm sorry, sir. It's just the smell is so bad. . ."

"*Soldat*, if you cannot endure this unpleasantness, maybe you need to spend some time on the front. There you will be exposed to smells so bad that nothing else will ever bother you again."

Eryk could see the raw fear in the man's eyes. Good. He locked his gaze on him. "Don't ever turn your face away from a superior officer again!"

"*Jawohl!*" The man stiffened and saluted and promptly wheeled around and vomited.

Eryk laughed. "What a pretty sight you are! Go outside and get your breath. I realize I must take charge of this. The woman in this cell is dead. The special unit must be called."

The guard swiped at his mouth and backed away, shrinking down the corridor as fast as he could.

Eryk walked to the outer office and faced the adjutant to the commandant. "Please call the *Sonderkommando*. The prisoner I wished to interrogate has died. I would like her body removed and examined."

"Of course, sir. And we must notify the commandant so he can start the necessary paperwork."

Eryk nodded. "Do so."

―――

Hanne bumped over the road, at the wheel of the car she had gotten from the motor pool. The dirt lane at the back of the camp was very uneven. She doubted official cars used it often. In fact, it was little more than a rut in places. The map the underground had provided proved it did lead out though. Now, she had to locate the squat block building that housed the crematorium. Steiner was supposed to meet her there in exactly fifteen minutes. The mission was underway. If he didn't show, she had to find her own way out of camp and back to the *Henschel Werks* with her emergency cover story.

She drove slowly, not wanting to call attention to the vehicle in an unusual place. Since it was dusk, she drove without lights, squinting to make out the outlines of buildings. As she rounded a corner and passed a stand of trees, she saw the building she was looking for. It had a smokestack. There was no doubt.

Hanne pulled as close to the back as she dared and turned off the motor. Then she slipped to the floorboard and waited.

THE EAGLE AND THE STAR

"The old wench finally croaked, yah? Well, good riddance, then. Did you get the information you needed before she died?" The commandant signed his name with a flourish, then looked up at Eryk.

"Yes, I did. She was almost gone, but I managed to have a few words with her."

The man smiled broadly. "Ah, German efficiency to the end, right, *Herr Hauptsturmführer*? Well, at least you're spared further trips to this cesspool. I'd certainly not come here if I had a choice." He held out the paperwork. "There you are. Give it to my adjutant. He'll make sure it's entered in the records."

Eryk took the file. "What can we say is the cause of death?"

"Pneumonia, *Captain*, pneumonia. Don't you know that all our prisoners here die from pneumonia or from gunshot wounds while trying to escape?"

"Ah, yes, I had forgotten." Eryk grinned. "I don't work with these terms every day, you know, so you must make allowances for me."

"Not at all, Steiner. I'm glad to help in your education." The man chortled.

"Thank you, *Kommandant. Heil Hitler!*" Eryk clicked his heels, saluted, spun and walked out of the room, his heartbeat coming in staccato bursts.

In the outer office, the adjutant took the file from Eryk's hands and casually turned to his typewriter. Eryk noticed the men in striped uniforms scurrying past him with a stretcher, their faces downcast, their feet silent on the tile. He pivoted and followed them.

The young guard hadn't returned to his post. Eryk silently pleaded for his bout of nausea to continue; he needed more time.

The men laid down the stretcher in the hall, and working in perfect rhythm, as if in a choreographed dance, they entered the cell, placed Zelda's hands on her chest, lifted her by feet and shoulders and swiftly laid her on the dirty sheet stretched between the carrying poles. Neither of them spoke. Nor did they look at him. They worked like shadows, wordless, silent. They reached down and easily picked up the stretcher. Eryk was surprised, considering the gaunt condition of the men, until he looked again at Zelda in the stark light from the bulb in the hallway and realized she was a piteous skeleton herself.

As he gazed at her, he thought he saw her chest rise with a shallow breath. This would not do. They had to get out of here. "Move, you stupid clods, get that garbage out of here!" Eryk didn't know he had such venom inside him.

The men though didn't even jump. They just started for the side door, at a slow run, jostling their load between them.

Hanne pushed back her sleeve so she could see the hands of her wristwatch. The lighted dial glowed up at her. Seven minutes remaining. *Hurry, Steiner. Every extra second is a death trap.*

Eryk followed the little ghosts of men as they snaked through the camp, keeping to the backs of the barracks, no doubt instructions from camp headquarters. When they finally approached the block building with the chimney, he spoke firmly from behind them. "Take that stretcher to the back of the building. *Schnell!*"

Again, the men didn't miss a step. They jogged around the block wall, tromping though mud, their wooden shoes making sucking sounds in the muck. Eryk grimaced as he followed.

The crematoria in the camps were nearly always built on the outside perimeter, away from the work centers and sleeping quarters. Even in this odd moment, Eryk felt grateful for the German disdain for uncleanliness that prompted this arrangement. Behind this particular crematorium was a grove of trees, also not uncommon. The Germans had a penchant for camouflaging their "special treatment" facilities. These two factors combined with the waning daylight gave them a better chance for success in this mission.

The men stopped and stood, silently, waiting for instructions.

"Put it down. Remove the body and return to your detail with the stretcher. Tell your *kapo* that this body was requisitioned for a medical experiment." Eryk pressed a small cake of bread into each man's hand and looked away.

The men tucked the bread into their waists, dropped the body and scurried away with the stretcher. As soon as they rounded the corner of the building, he saw them start tearing into the bread. It was a reward that would soon be lost to other starving prisoners if it was not consumed immediately. If their supervisor found out, they would be interrogated and perhaps condemned for stealing. He wondered if he had just sentenced them to torture and maybe himself to death.

But he had only a few minutes now and not enough time to spend on possibilities, however grim they might be. He walked quickly to the car and softly tapped the door. The door opened, and Hanne slid out. She went to the back of the car and opened the trunk, smoothing the quilt laying there.

Eryk slipped and slid precariously back to the spot where Zelda lay crumpled in the morass behind the crematorium. He bent down and picked her up, ignoring the stench and the mud. He moved as quickly as possible to the car, dumped her in and shut the trunk.

Hanne had started the car's engine. He walked to the front, trying to brush the grime from his uniform as he did. He slid in beside Hanne who had pulled her cap down over her eyes and sat ramrod straight in the driver's spot. "Go."

As though it were a common occurrence, Hanne pulled smoothly around the building and onto the main road. Eryk pulled his orders out of his case and smoothed his vest.

The ride through the camp would have been heart-wrenching if she hadn't been focusing on the mission at hand. Scarecrow people littered the fields, plucking limp vegetables from the soil and hefting rocks onto wheelbarrows. The weathered gray of the buildings in the twilight was eerie. As they made the final turn toward the gate, a whistle sounded. Work was over. Time for the evening meal.

The plan was working. Activity in the camp helped them arouse less suspicion.

She applied the brake and let the car roll to a stop at the gate.

"Papers, *bitte*."

She took the sheaf Steiner held out to her and passed them to the guard.

"*Danke, Fraulein.*"

The lieutenant looked them over, noting the signature and handed them back. He signaled the guard in front to lift the barrier.

Hanne lifted her foot from the brake and breathed a silent sigh. They were going to make it.

69

October, 1943
Kassel, Germany
Arbeitslager

> *This is not the end.*
> *It is not even the beginning of the end.*
> *But it is, perhaps, the end of the beginning.*
> Winston Churchill (November 10, 1942)

A black uniformed hand suddenly slapped the hood of the car.

Hanne stomped the pedal; the car jolted. She heard Steiner's quick intake of breath, and then an unwelcome but familiar voice.

"Ah, my Hanne, what a surprise to see you here!"

She turned, forcing a smile. "*Sturmbannführer* Beckmann! Indeed."

"I thought you were on assignment to the *Henschel Werks* with *Hauptsturmführer* Steiner."

"I am. We are returning there now." She looked up at him expectantly.

"You are impatient, Hanne, aren't you? About everything except our marriage, of course." Beckmann winked at her. "But humor me. Let me have a look at the papers before you go."

Hanne shrugged. "We have already passed the guard's inspection."

Beckmann leaned down even further, until he was eye level with Steiner beside her. "But I want to see them too. I am interested in this assignment. The *Gestapo* is interested in every assignment."

Steiner reached into his case and retrieved the papers, handing them again to her.

Beckmann took them greedily.

"They seem to be in order." He glanced up and then at the vehicle. "You have a car from the camp. I'm afraid I must ask to look in the trunk."

Hanne laughed. "But why, *Major*?"

His eyes were dark. "Because Hanne, everyday there are escape attempts from the camp. These dangerous prisoners are wily. I don't trust them, and neither should you. Isn't that right, *Hauptsturmführer* Steiner?"

"As you say." Steiner's tone was stiff. Hanne hoped Beckmann wouldn't notice.

"Ah, yes." Beckmann smiled. "So, the keys. . . Hanne?"

Hanne felt lightheaded. In all her work as an agent, she had never been in a situation like this. Even if she could save herself, her cover would be blown and the old woman and Steiner would most certainly be compromised. She pulled the keys from the ignition and dropped them into Beckmann's hand. The game was over.

Eryk tried to think of something he could do. He could feign ignorance. Maybe they would believe him; maybe not. But then he would have to denounce Hanne. After all his years of hiding from identifying with those on the side of the right, he could not bring himself to do it. It seemed there were no options.

He heard the key turn in the lock on the trunk and a roar from the *Gestapo* agent. Now, he remembered where he had last heard that primal tone. At Terezin. Beckmann had been the officer on duty when he rescued Nadya. This wasn't good. Things had gone from bad to deadly.

Beckmann strode to Eryk's side of the car. "There is a prisoner in your trunk, sir."

"What?" Eryk couldn't let Zelda go without trying something. "Come see for yourself. But be careful. You are being watched."

Eryk swung himself confidently out the car door and walked around to the trunk. There, still asleep, was Zelda, unaware that he had just gotten her into a worse situation than before. He feigned surprise.

"Filthy swine! Get this woman out of my car immediately!"

Beckmann appeared to be amused. "Oh, come, *Herr Hauptsturmführer.*, didn't you know she was hiding in your trunk?"

Eryk glared at him. "Sir, with respect, I resent your implication."

Beckmann stepped closer, his eyes boring into him, his breath sour between them. "You will resent me for much more than that before we are done." He turned to the guard. "It's a pity the Captain didn't notice that his friend here is unconscious and therefore unable to get herself into this trunk. She must have had help. Take him to the *Kommandant*."

He stretched out his hand to Eryk. "I'll take your gun now, *Hauptsturmführer* Steiner, and your case in the car." He turned to a junior officer. "Get it."

It was over. No more cards to play. No chance for him at all. He refused to look at Hanne; maybe she could find a way out. And Zelda . . . they were tugging her out of the trunk and heaving her onto a stretcher. The drug must still be working; she gave no sign of consciousness.

As he unstrapped his *Luger*, Eryk glanced around. Except for the two guards at the gate and Beckmann, no one was paying attention to them. It had all been a very quiet affair. Even the guard in the tower was looking the other way.

He took a chance.

He palmed the gun and started to raise his arm as if to surrender it. But instead of handing it to Beckmann, he flipped it quickly, torquing his index finger into the trigger guard and squeezing the trigger. He shot past Beckmann, once, twice, three times in a quick burst and started running, crouching low, keeping the *Luger* at his side. He wasn't sure about anything. He was going on instinct.

Around the car he went, then dashed toward the tower, aiming to get under it and out of range of the machine gun it held. He would hold onto freedom as long as possible; he had nothing to lose. Maybe it would help clear Hanne. Maybe with the attention on him, Zelda would be spared further cruelty.

But it was a foolhardy attempt at best. Only a desperate man would try to outrun the *Gestapo*. He knew that. It was a ridiculous thing he was attempting. But he ran on, zigzagging as he went, doing his best to make it difficult for the officers trying to bring him down. Bullets were zinging past him, and he heard the shrill crescendo of the camp's alarm. Next would come the dogs, yapping and trying to take a chunk out of him.

The ground was, not surprisingly, mud, the ignominious carpet of the camps. It pulled at his feet and slowed him down.

He plowed on, almost falling in the slop, then catching his balance at the last minute.

Eryk couldn't believe he had made it as far as he had. For a few seconds, he began to imagine that it was possible he'd make it. Though make it to what, he didn't know. There was nothing and no one outside the camp perimeter to help him.

There was shouting and running feet and the *rck, rck, rck* of the machine guns. How he was managing to dodge the hurricane force of the bullets he couldn't imagine.

Only a few more feet to the tower. He doubled his speed, sprinting as fast as he could.

Ten, nine, eight . . . the tower was so close.

Seven, six, five. . . the sun was just setting.

Four, three, two. . . a searing shock tore through his leg, and he felt himself spinning from the impact.

The fire of the pain was unbearable. Then he was falling, the sounds of the chase and the camp fading away.

He was hit. He realized that much. The spurts of blood were soaking his trouser leg. What happened now was beyond his control or involvement. He felt dizzy, and the ringing in his ears was much louder than the shriek of the alarm. As he lost consciousness, he thought of one thing. Nadya. No one would ever arrive in those mountains to rescue her.

70

Kassel, Germany
Arbeitslager

L'Chaim! (*to life!*)
(traditional Jewish toast)

Hanne watched the drama unfold like a woman in a box at the opera. It was a play, a charade. It couldn't be real. This was a failure of catastrophic proportions. They were going to kill Steiner in front of her very eyes. The old woman was as good as dead, and she didn't give very much for her own chances to escape the *Gestapo* torture chambers.

The various scenes playing out around her were like slow motion clips of a newsreel. In jerky cruelty, the SS guards were now dumping the old woman from the stretcher onto the cart for corpses. Even in the commotion, Hanne heard her body land on top of a few other stick-like shapes with a thud. She slid her eyes to the side and glimpsed the sickening sight, the old lady's swollen legs dangling awkwardly off the rough planks of the death cart. The guards were brushing their clothing, making obscene comments and gestures as they walked away. Hanne clamped down on her emotions. There was nothing, nothing she could do for the woman. But she also knew the next stop for that cart was the ovens. To have this woman for whom Steiner had risked his life and career end up being burned alive was almost too horrible for even the most macabre playwright to imagine. The only bit of comfort was that he wouldn't be alive to see it.

She could hear the shouting and shooting. He would never make it out of camp. She knew that. He knew that. He had simply decided to die trying than to be taken in health and sanity for the *Gestapo* to exploit. She had to admire his indomitable spirit.

But, she must think of her own situation. She was being held at gunpoint beside the car until Beckmann returned from the chase. Her options were few, but there was one remaining that was as old as time. If she had ever used her feminine wiles, she would demonstrate her skill now. The old man had no way of knowing that they would come in so handy. She had to convince Beckmann that she was an ignorant participant, only following orders from the Captain whom she was serving. She would do whatever was necessary. The Allies were depending on her. She knew too much. She must not be taken and tortured.

Hanne realized what this could mean for her personal virtue. It was something she had always known could happen. Thus far, she had fended off the innuendos and unspoken invitations, but never had so much been at stake. She thought of her father, of the light in his eyes when he called her his "sweet girl." He would never think that way of her again if she did this awful thing. The person's daughter would be soiled, shamed, sinful.

All of sudden, a terrible rage boiled up inside of her, so potent she clenched her fists against the almost physical onslaught. Hitler had done this! It was his fault that she was standing in a muddy cesspool watching a good man die and an old woman suffer and her own life ruined. Adolf Hitler was the madman behind all this insanity. At the moment, Hanne felt she could sink a knife in his uniformed chest if she could get to him.

But the *Führer* was not here, and she was.

A captive.

A woman.

An operative.

Trapped.

So, she smoothed out her skirt and patted a few stray hairs under her *SS* hat. She was going to knock the socks off *Sturmbannführer* Beckmann and give the grandest performance of her career. She would play the naïve, but desirable assistant role. She would get out of this mess, and then she would hate herself forever.

Hanne Lager softened her gaze and turned to meet the steely eyes of the man who held her captive.

71

Kassel, Germany
Arbeitslager Infirmary

> *The thought of the Jew is distinguished by a certain analytic or destructive character which, like his blood, derives from its chaotic or impure origins.*
> Professor Alfred Bottcher, "The Solution of the Jewish Problem, 1935

He was under something heavy. He couldn't get it off. Something was pressing down on him, keeping him from breathing, from coming to the top. Everything was fuzzy in his thinking. He felt hands on his body, on his leg. And his leg pulsed with a fiery, slippery pain.

Voices.

"We're going to lose him."

"No!" Even in his haze, Eryk knew this was a voice of one in command. It was the same roar. The beast who had tracked him down. "I want him alive. Do whatever it takes."

"Do you know what that means, *Herr Sturmbannführer*? He must have blood."

Eryk wanted to hear more, wanted to know. But the pressure on him became too heavy and he surrendered to its undertow.

Sturmbannführer Beckmann made a split decision.

He was good at those. This whole day had been startling in its developments. A man of decisive action was required. While it would be an odd form of revenge if *SS Captain* Steiner bled out entirely in the clinic of a labor camp, it would deprive the *Reich* the justice of prosecution. An officer who had sworn an oath of loyalty and then violated it must be forced to give account. The German people deserved it. So, he did the unthinkable.

"Give him blood."

"From whom, *Herr Sturmbannführer*?" The infirmary doctor was calm, if surprised.

"Him." Beckmann pointed to a young man in a lab coat, preparing instruments for the doctor.

"But, *Herr Major*, he is *Juden*."

"This officer has dishonored his own blood; let him live what life he has left on racially polluted blood. He won't notice the difference," Beckmann chortled.

The young man in the lab coat turned, the eyes in his gaunt face wide but saying nothing.

The doctor clasped his hands nervously then placed them on the table as he addressed Beckmann. "Sir, this man is my best assistant and he has not been well himself. You can see that. I ask you to choose another. . ."

"No! This officer must have blood now. He must not die. Proceed immediately."

The doctor turned to the young man and shrugged slightly, a pained expression on his face, and beckoned him. Other helpers scurried to place another table adjacent to the one on which Eryk lay.

The doctor walked to a locked cabinet, took keys from his waist and opened the door. From a shelf, he retrieved a case with the needed equipment for an inter-human blood transfusion. Every step he took echoed on the tile floor. Beckmann watched every move, his fury at this complication evident in his set jaw and unwavering stare.

A blood transfusion was risky business and a transfusion between two patients, riskier still, even though great progress had been made in recent years. Dr. Herschel had performed quite a few in his Berlin hospital work before the war. There, in sterile conditions, with his trusted nurses, he had been open to the challenge in the effort to save lives. But here in a camp infirmary where death was valued more than life, he found his hands trembling as he prepared the tubing and syringes and valves necessary for the process.

He had taken an oath in medical school to save life whenever possible. As a doctor, he had been trained to look past skin and race and crime and creed in the fight to preserve human life. He did it even here, as best he could, with the few resources he had at his disposal. He had not tended to a German officer until now. Being a Jew prevented him from being used to treat German *volk*. But, in this extreme event, the military command seemed to have chosen to overlook his race in their determination to keep the young officer alive.

An artery had been severed by a bullet. The staff had applied pressure and clamps to prevent further loss of blood but he would not last much longer without a transfusion. Dr. Herschel was involved in a mortal struggle.

"Hurry up, *schwein*!" The *Gestapo* major was afraid. The doctor could see it on his face. The man on the table was very important to him.

Dr. Herschel turned to Yacov, the young man he had shielded and trained and kept by his side in this hellish place of medical service.

How many times he had saved his life by claiming he was a valuable assistant. But this time it would not work. "On the table, my son."

The youth held his gaze for an eloquent second and then started to climb onto the metal slab.

At that minute, there was a commotion outside the room and the door burst open. Standing in the doorway was a young private, accompanied by two prisoners carrying a stretcher. A crumpled old woman lay on it.

Beckmann lost his temper with a roar. "What is the meaning of this?

"I'm sorry, sir, but this old woman is not dead. What can we do with her?"

"Dump her in the ash heap, you idiot! Bash her head in, throw her in the oven. I don't care." Beckmann stomped to the door, warming to his tongue-lashing, but stopped as he reached the pitiful entourage and turned around with a sudden, ghastly joy on his face. "No, bring her here. *Doktor,* you may keep your assistant for a while longer. I have found you another donor."

Doctor Herschel tried to forget. As he lay in his putrid bunk that night, he tried to block out the images of yet another travesty in which he had been forced to participate. He had not been given time to check blood types or to prepare the patients properly. The pitiful woman had been strapped to the table and drained of her blood without any precaution for her welfare. He could not have expected otherwise. Nothing a Jew owned was really his or her own, not even the blood in the veins. Everything was a potential sacrifice for Germany's Aryan people.

Doctor Herschel turned over and squeezed his eyes tight to force away the ashen face of the "donor." The transfusion had been too much for her weakened system to stand. He knew before he checked her wrist that she was gone, her life ebbed away for the despicable existence of an *SS* man. For as much as he tried to treat all who came to him, Doctor Herschel could not deny that helping a Nazi soldier recover to kill again was a test of his long-ago promise. Especially when it was done in such stark contrast as the event today, he struggled simply to maintain his composure.

The *Sturmbannführer* was impatient to get the wounded officer to Berlin. So against medical advice, he had the man bundled on a stretcher and put in the back of a truck with two armed guards. They sped away into the thick night while, out of the shadows, striped figures came to lug away the fragile body of the woman whose last ounce of life had been siphoned off so cavalierly.

Doctor Herschel hadn't been able to figure out all the connections in the pathetic vignette he'd witnessed that day. Truthfully, it was usually best not to care about such details. But as he buried his face in the foul straw on his bunk, tears came that he could not stop. At least he knew that there was still a little fragment of humanity somewhere within him.

72

Berlin, Germany
Tegel Military Prison

> *A god who let us prove his existence would be an idol.*
> Dietrich Bonhoeffer

Someone was praying.

That was the first thing Eryk noticed.

It was a prayer, he was sure. Not loud, but quiet and firm. A man's voice. Calming.

He struggled to open his eyes. The room had harsh overhead lights. He closed them again. Maybe he'd just lay there and try to remember. Where was he? How did he get here? What. . .

It came back in a torrent. The camp, the escape attempt, being shot, the blood. . . but it seemed there was something else, something that had gone terribly wrong. What was it?

Zelda. He had been trying to help Zelda. She had been. . . in the trunk. Oh, God, no, they had found her, dragged her out of the trunk, flopped her onto the hard ground. Where was she? Hurt? Dying? Alone? And no! Nadya. Alone in the mountains, frightened in the dark, expecting his return.

He had to get up. Eryk blinked his eyes open and forced his upper body into a sitting position. The room started spinning and hands pushed him back down.

"No, sir. You must not get up."

It was the same, calm voice that had been praying.

He used all his energy to focus on the face. A round face with lively eyes, thinning hair, and the hint of a smile in pale cheeks. "Please. I must get up. Where am I?"

The man sat back on his heels and drew a deep breath. Eryk noticed the white shirt open at the neck, the fine fabric of the trousers. "You're in Tegel Military Prison, friend. In Berlin."

Then, Eryk remembered the other part of the whole ordeal. He had been captured, found out. He was a prisoner. He couldn't help anyone. He put his hand down to his leg, barely daring to feel for it, trying to prepare himself for an empty space instead of a limb. But it was there, still attached. He hadn't lost it after all.

The man noticed his movement. "Yes, you were badly injured. We didn't think you would make it."

"Is that why you were praying?" Eryk didn't try to keep the cynicism from his voice.

"As a matter of fact, yes. I was praying for you. Praying that our Father would spare your life, help you to know His love."

"Love? You call this His love?"

"No, *Hauptsturmführer* Steiner, I call the death of His Son the proof of His love for every one of us. That, and that alone, makes even this place bearable." The man gestured to the rows of bunks in the block-walled room. "By the way, I'm Dietrich, and this is the prison infirmary. You've been here for three days."

"Three days. And at least one day on the road." Eryk tried to center himself. "What day is this?"

"Friday."

"Friday. That can't be! I must get up . . . . how do you know my name?"

The other man reached down and pulled up Eryk's identification tag. "This. Plus the nurses inform me of the new patients."

"Who are you anyway? A doctor?"

"No, I'm a chaplain of sorts. At least, that's what I call myself. The staff here has been so kind as to let me talk with and pray for the patients. They have agreed to do so as long as it doesn't agitate the inmates." He leaned closer conspiratorially. "They won't forbid anything that makes their jobs easier." He winked.

Eryk turned his face to the wall. He didn't like jailhouse humor. Never had. He had never been able to understand the few American prisoners with whom he had interacted and their penchant for finding levity in dire conditions. In the desolation he felt now, in this complete and total failure of everything he was supposed to be and do, he did not want to crack jokes. But, after a minute he turned back to face the man. He seemed to be the best source of information at the moment. "What are they going to do with me? Have you heard anything?"

The man looked down. A bad sign. Eryk was sure he knew more than he was willing to share. "Sir, you have been gravely ill, and they have been anxious for you to come around. And something was said about a trial, a court-martial."

"Yes, that would be about it. When?"

"I have no idea, but I had better let the nurse know that you are awake now. They don't have many staff here so she has been on the other side of the room, but they will want to know."

"Yes, I'm sure they will."

The man named Dietrich knelt down and clasped Eryk's hand.

"This is a terrible place, sir, but God is here too. If you will call on Him, He will not forsake you. No matter what has brought you here, He can give you a place in eternity. I promise that you will be in my prayers."

He started to rise, but Eryk gripped his hand with strength he thought he'd lost. "Just a moment. Don't waste your prayers on me. There are two women who were depending on me with their lives. I don't know where they are, what has happened to them. Pray for them, not me."

Dietrich smiled, a smile of courage and hope. "Of course, my friend. I will pray. God knows where they are." Giving Eryk a final handclasp, he rose and walked toward the nurse on the other side of the room.

Eryk wished he could die and be rid of whatever fate was going to be his very soon. But, in the next breath, he berated his cowardice. He had already let down Zelda. What about Nadya? They had both been foolish to trust him with their lives. They were all going to die. It had been for nothing. In spite of Zelda's faith and the optimism of this Dietrich, the life of Eryk von Steiner was about to be spilled out like rotten wine and there would be nothing noble about its memory.

73

Berlin, Germany

> *We are not retreating – we are advancing in another direction.*
> General Douglas MacArthur

Hanne had known the part she had to play was despicable. But it was only in retrospect that she realized how low she had sunk. *Gestapo Sturmbannführer* Rolf Beckmann was a monster, not only in his capacity for violence, but also in his treatment of women. His vile attention had been nauseating and only sheer force of duty kept her from vomiting at the remembrance of his embrace.

Even now as she sat at her desk at headquarters, Hanne felt covered in shame. Surely her stain must be noticeable to all. She felt it emblazoned on her much the same as Hawthorne's Hester Prynne.

But now she had to forget it, put it aside. She had such little time. For the second time in a month, she was going to try her emergency contact. There were very few options left but she was determined to try every one she could. What happened to her didn't matter any longer.

Sturmbannführer Rolf Beckmann leaned back in his desk chair and put his feet up on the desk. He hadn't felt such satisfaction in a very long time. The quarry had been found, and he was going to stand trial. Then Rolf himself would have the pleasure of kicking the bucket out from under Steiner's swinging feet. The reprobate would die as he deserved, in agony.

After that, he would tie up the other loose ends that still bothered him. Steiner's connection to the old woman in the labor camp might lead to something very interesting. He'd eventually have to do something about Hanne. For all her coyness, she was up to something. He could sense it, and he'd learned to trust his suspicions. He'd been gifted with the instincts of a bloodhound. He would use it fully. But he'd wait a while with Hanne. She was an asset at the present. He wasn't finished with her.

It was getting late. The office staff had left long ago. Here he was sitting in this darkened room like he had seen other older officers do, brooding over cases, imagining the thrill of the chase, the glory of the catch.

Beckmann stood up, straightened the stack of papers on the corner of his desk, gathered his greatcoat and cap from the rack and turned out the light. He shut the door and locked it. Before going to his apartment, he would go to the kennels and visit his dogs. They'd be glad to see him.

74

Berlin, Germany
Tegel Military Prison

> *When Christ calls a man, he bids him come and die.*
> Dietrich Bonhoeffer

The stone walls of his cell were damp. The air around him was frigid. Eryk wasn't sure what the temperature was outside, but it was near to freezing temperatures inside. He huddled under his blanket, sitting with legs drawn up on his cot. He wished for his *SS* greatcoat with the fur collar, for the warmth of his woolen underwear and heavy socks. But they were gone. In place of his uniform he wore striped prison garb, ill-fitting, smelly.

The infirmary where he first woke up hadn't been really clean, but he'd gladly exchange it for the crusty floors of this cell. The bucket in the corner was nauseating. He hadn't been able to eat while being in the same room with the stench. He was ashamed of his weakness. It must be due to his rundown condition. He'd always had a strong stomach, but now, his insides turned over at the slightest thing. His leg wound throbbed. He was worried that it was infected. It felt hot to the touch, and he thought he might have a fever.

His mind was tortured with thoughts of Zelda and Nadya, their faces appearing out of the dim light in the cell, reproaching him, begging him for help. It was worse than the physical pain. He knew interrogation and torture were coming. In a way, he welcomed it. Maybe it would drive the demons of memory and remorse away. Perhaps in the agony of broken bones and bleeding wounds, he would find solace from the guilt that burned in his soul. He would submit to it gladly if he could feel assured that it would atone for his sins against the only people who really cared about him.

The words of the man Dietrich came back to him. How could the man be so hopeful in a place like this? He had learned that he was also a prisoner, and if he was stuck in this place, it likely wasn't for a trifle. None of them had much hope for the days to come.

Eryk had always been a get-it-done sort of person. Maybe he got it from his father, the impeccable officer. He certainly didn't think it came from his mother. With her delicate mental and emotional state, she had braved few hardships outside of the inner torments that kept her in her bed. But since his boyhood, Eryk had forged ahead, even in difficult moments. Some of that, to be honest, was Zelda's influence. She had bolstered his flagging confidence many times, proclaiming her faith in his abilities and inner fortitude of character. She had encouraged him to find strength in her God.

Her God.

The oddity of it struck him now as he remembered that she had been a Jew, yet she had believed in the God that the Lutheran pastors had preached. In fact, he suddenly remembered, she went to a Lutheran church, a Protestant Christian church. Why had he never put that together? Her God-speak had just been part of who she was. That she hadn't been Orthodox in her religion hadn't registered with him as a child. As a Hitler Youth, he had been able to see only her race; nothing else counted.

But now she was gone. Had to be. He wondered about her last moments.

A rattling of keys on his cell door interrupted his thoughts. The small door swung inward and a guard stepped inside. "Get up."

Eryk slowly unfolded himself from the blanket and gingerly stood up, favoring his weak leg. He reached toward the wall beside the cot to steady himself, then hobbled forward, each step shooting fire up his leg.

The guard grabbed his arm and jerked him forward. Eryk let out a rough curse, then stumbled and fell onto the cement floor.

The guard shrieked at him to get up and he tried, but the energy just wasn't there. The man started kicking him in the abdomen, his jackbooted foot finding painful purchase in the tender flesh of Eryk's stomach.

This is it. He's going to finish me right here. The hangman won't get any pleasure out of me after all. Eryk closed his eyes and waited for unconsciousness, trying to protect his head and injured leg.

"Was ist das?"

Eryk knew the voice. It haunted his dreams. *Sturmbannführer* Rolf Beckmann was back.

"Get that man off the floor! Can't you see he's injured? You idiot! Put him back on the cot."

In his haze of renewed pain, on the brink of unconsciousness, Eryk wasn't sure if he had heard correctly. Beckmann was trying to help him? The beast had a kind side? The *Gestapo* had mercy?

Hands grabbed him under the arms and dragged him backward and dumped him onto the cot. "Ahhhh!" He couldn't stop the scream. His leg hurt unbelievably.

The guard threw the blanket at him and stomped out. When he didn't hear the door slam shut, Eryk looked up. Standing silhouetted in the doorway was Beckmann. Eryk grimaced and steeled himself for what was to come.

The man came nearer and loomed over him. "Steiner, I thought you were tougher than this. Thought for sure you could walk down the hall. But no, you made me come to you in this filth!"

Eryk looked up. He decided against saying anything. He just stared at the man.

"I'm going to have you taken back to the prison infirmary to keep you from losing that leg. I need you whole."

At that, Eryk almost chuckled. The man was unbelievable.

"And then, when we're sure you're going to recover, we'll continue this little talk at *Prinz-Albrecht-Strasse*."

So that's where he was headed. Eryk wasn't really surprised, but he almost shuddered anyway. Horror headquarters. There wasn't a German citizen who didn't fear the place. Not even the *SS* was safe from its reach. At least now he knew where his destiny lay. Eryk reached for his last shred of pride and tried to dust off the hubris of his former self.

"Fine, Beckmann, fine. Do what you must." He pulled up every ounce of strength and glared at the man, mentally daring him to lose his temper and hit an injured officer.

"You insolent Jew-lover! If I didn't want you to be well enough to hang, I'd finish you off myself right now."

Eryk glared at him. "You're a monster, Beckmann. Always have been."

The man leaned down then, putting his face inches away from Eryk, daggers in his eyes. "I'll do worse than kill you, Steiner. I'll tell you the truth." He let the words dangle between them, then slowly got back up, pulling up to his full height and leaning back with a smile. "Do you know what really happened to your little Jewish grandmother?"

Adrenaline rushed through his body. Eryk shuddered. He knew he shouldn't say anything. Admitting that he knew her would be sealing the already tight case against him. But he had denied Zelda for too long. He wouldn't do it any longer. "What . . . did you do to her?"

Beckmann laughed. "Me? I did nothing, Steiner. You did."

"What do you mean?"

"That's right, *Captain*. *You* killed her. Didn't know that, did you? Didn't realize that she breathed her last on that cold metal table in the labor camp after donating her blood to save your miserable life?" He smiled with glee as Eryk threw off the blanket and struggled to get to his feet. "You're pathetic. What do you think you can do to me? You can't even stand on your own feet, can't even protect one tottering old Jew on your own. If it wasn't for vile Jewish blood in your veins, you'd be dead right now. You're too weak to be *SS*. You're a wretched disgrace. I will watch your hanging with delight. Until then, remember that one more Jew was cleansed from this earth because of you." Beckmann turned and walked to the cell door, banging on it to let the guard know he was ready to leave.

As the key turned in the lock, he pivoted and extended his palm high in the air. "*Heil, Hitler!*" Then he clicked his heels and walked out, laughing.

75

Berlin, Germany
Tegel Military Prison
Prison Infirmary

*To endure the cross is not tragedy;
it is the suffering which is the fruit of an exclusive allegiance to Jesus Christ.*
Dietrich Bonhoeffer

Eryk didn't care if they took his leg off. It would be one less limb to dangle from a meathook in the *Gestapo* dungeon. For they were going to kill him slowly, he was sure, making the agony last as long as possible. The horrible truth was, he deserved it.

He had been the cause of Zelda's death. Eryk, the little boy she had loved and tended in the night hours when his mother's screams terrified him. Eryk, the student she had tutored in language and history and the arts. Eryk, the young man in whom she had instilled the traits of responsibility and chivalry and honesty. Eryk, the Nazi, the *SS* officer. He had turned on the one who had loved him most. She had trusted him and by his inept handling of the escape, he had brought her to a camp clinic to be drained of her blood for him. He wasn't worthy of it. Her Jewish blood was surely nobler than any Aryan type he naturally possessed.

For a wild moment, he wished he had a knife with which to slit his veins, to rid himself of the guilt of living off her blood. Buf he had no knife. He had nothing but misery and pain and shame, the moans of other men in the infirmary, and the torture of his own thoughts.

He was unbearably thirsty. That was a symptom of the dying. Maybe the infection would finish him off before Beckmann could haul him to *Gestapo* headquarters. He almost smiled at that. He reached to the table beside him for his glass. It was empty. He pulled his arm back to fling it to the floor, and looked up into the face of Dietrich.

"Good morning, *Herr Hauptsturmführer*. Do you need water? Let me get it for you." He held out his hand, and Eryk meekly put the glass in it.

Dietrich smiled and walked to the sink in the corner of the room, returning with a full glass. He set it on the table and leaned over Eryk, supporting his back as he sat up to drink. "There. That's better. Now, my friend, how are you feeling today?"

Eryk sighed. "It's no use, Dietrich. Spend your cheerfulness on someone who will appreciate it. You cannot help me."

"You are right. I can't. But God can. I have been praying for you. What is troubling you?"

"Look, why should I trust you? For all I know, you may be a *Gestapo* plant, trying to worm information out of helpless patients. Go away."

"No, *Hauptsturmführer* Steiner, I am not working for the German government. In fact, if you knew why I am here, you would understand that I am under suspicion of working against them." His words were very soft; his eyes were intent.

Eryk stared at him. "You worked against the government? A chaplain?"

"Only a fill-in chaplain here in this place. I am Pastor Dietrich Bonhoeffer, of Berlin."

"I've heard of you. You were part of that new church, the one the *Reich* refused to recognize."

Bonhoeffer nodded. "It was called the Confessing Church."

"Yes, you even had some sort of school or training ground that was shut down, didn't you?"

"It was a seminary of sorts. I spent some of the most enjoyable years of my adult life with those young students." He looked off, his eyes probing some distant vista. "My heart was so heavy when the *Gestapo* closed it down." He looked back at Eryk. "You would have enjoyed it too."

Eryk gave a disgusted chuckle. "No, you don't mean that. I'm the enemy. Not at all a suitable member for that sort of club."

"I see no enemy in you, *Hauptsturmführer* Steiner. I am really sorry for the pain, both in your physical body and in your soul. What can I do for you? Would you like to talk about it?"

Suddenly Eryk did. Maybe a confession to this man would release the anguish in his soul and allow him to die a better man. If he revealed the stain of his failure, perhaps God would, in return, allow Nadya to be rescued.

"I tried to save an old friend and failed. She died in a labor camp. I was supposed to go back for her young niece, but could not because of my capture. I'm sure she will die too if she hasn't already. I am the cause of both of their deaths. I have participated in crimes as a member of the *SS*. I know that God will not overlook them. Now, I am doomed to interrogation, torture and execution. I can do nothing for anyone. I've spent my life trying to figure out what was really true. And now, I know less than before. You see? I'm a waste of your time. Move on to someone else. Let God deal with me as I deserve."

Bonhoeffer bent down beside Eryk, his eyes alight with a strange fire. He grasped Eryk's hand in both of his, his voice fervent. "But don't you see, friend, that God does not deal with any of us as we deserve? He has offered His Son as the sacrifice, the atonement. Your wasted life is no match for His grace. Even in these last moments, He has wonderful mercy and peace for you."

Eryk pulled his hand from the man's clutch and hit the wall beside him in frustration. "No! You don't know the worst part. She prayed for me for years, loved me in spite of the way I had treated her. When I found her, I promised my old friend that she could trust me. I told her that when she woke up from the sedative she would be free. But she wasn't. She never woke up. I was shot in the action and was bleeding to death. They. . . .they used her blood to save me." Eryk turned wild eyes to Bonhoeffer and raised his arm. "There. In those veins is her blood. They used it to keep her killer alive. I'm worthless. I don't deserve to live off her sacrifice." A groan escaped his lips.

Bonhoeffer was still kneeling beside him, the strange glory-look illuminating his thin, pallid face. "Oh, *Hauptsturmführer* Steiner, you cannot see the truth, can you? Listen to me, please. She did wake up free, she did. She is freer than she has ever been, in the presence of our Lord. Just like our Savior, her blood became your source of life. He offers you His blood as a source of eternal life which will last much longer than this earthly one."

Eryk pulled his face away from the wall and stared deep into Bonhoeffer's eyes. The man continued. "I am sure that she does not begrudge you her blood. Nor does He." He almost whispered the next words. "They both did it for love. Love for you."

Eryk knew he had tears in his eyes. It had been so long since he had cried about anything. He didn't welcome this feeling of losing control. But he recognized that it meant the fountain of his soul was finally tumbling free. "I want to believe you, but it seems too good for me."

Bonhoeffer smiled. "It is. Too good for all of us. But that's why it is so wonderful. Receive Him, friend. Let Him walk into the *Gestapo* chambers with you."

Eryk swallowed his pride and admitted, for the first time in many years, that he was in need. "I'm not sure He wants to be in my company in that place, but I want His."

Bonhoeffer gripped his hand. "Thank God. You are about to be born again, my friend, into the greatest brotherhood of service known to man. You are now under loyalty to the One who died for you." He laid one hand on Eryk's head and began to pray softly and fervently.

Then, *Hauptsturmführer* Eryk Steiner, broken in body and bereft of earthly expectation, lifted a paltry petition to the Lord of whom Zelda had often witnessed and found that he was welcomed into a love that filled him up with unimaginable hope, even in the chilly infirmary of Tegel Military Prison.

PART FOUR
Tegel to Somewhere

76

Berlin, Germany
Tegel Military Prison

> *We shall not flag or fail. We shall go on to the end.*
> Winston Churchill

The day was as dismal as the outlook for his future.

Eryk could see gray skies through the bars on the window of his cell. It was the second week of December, and the weather was misty and very cold. He knew his time was running out. His leg was better. He still couldn't walk on it, but the infection was gone and he could stand with assistance. Not that he had any help. The last person who had really cared about his condition was Bonhoeffer, but Eryk hadn't seen him in a week. The man was an unbelievable force of good in the prison, praying, encouraging, smiling, cheering everyone with his contagious love of life and pointing all to the God of heaven.

Eryk still had moments when he was tempted to despair, when he thought about finding a way to end his existence before the *Gestapo* could slowly squeeze it out of him. But the new life that had begun to take root within him when he prayed with Dietrich would swell up within him like a mighty tide, and he knew he couldn't. He would face death with as much courage and resolve as his new Lord would lend.

It was almost ironic to have these thoughts as he heard a key turning in the lock on his cell door. He knew, with the gut knowledge of years in the military, that his time had come. He was being transported.

———

Eryk limped down the hallway, supported by two guards. His hands were cuffed, but it didn't matter; he couldn't have gotten away if they weren't. His wounded leg would never support his weight. The stairs were difficult to manage, and he fumbled as he tried to keep pace with the impatient young guards on either side. Every step brought him nearer the ground floor, the bottom level, the end of this interlude.

As they emerged into the courtyard where prisoners were loaded for transport, Eryk blinked at the bright assault of the sun. Because he had little mobility, he hadn't been allowed the weekly hour outside that others were granted. Not only was he hampered by the effects of his injury, but he was very out of condition from so little physical exercise. His legs gave way.

He stumbled, and fell, yelling as his weight plunged directly on his injured leg.

"Get up!" The guards jerked him upright and half-carried him to the back of the truck which was idling and releasing great puffs of smoke in the chilly air. As he tried to help swing himself up, Eryk noticed wryly that it was a *Henschel* two and a-half ton model. He couldn't get away from that plant even for his last trip.

The guards dumped him over the edge and walked away without a backward glance. The truck shifted into gear and lurched forward.

Eryk waited for his eyes to grow accustomed to the dark interior. After a few seconds, he glanced around. He was on the wooden floor of the lorry. There were no other prisoners. He wondered why he hadn't been taken in a car; after all, he had been a decorated officer. But just as swiftly came the thought that rank and past honor meant nothing now in the light of his present treason to the *Reich*. There were two guards riding in the back with him. Their guns were in their hands, and he could tell they had their eyes on him though he wasn't much of a threat in his condition. One of them moved to the rear and lowered the canvas so that he could no longer see out the back.

The truck meandered on, the exhaust fumes reminding him of other trips in military trucks, times when he had been part of the might of Nazi Germany, a respected officer. How different this trip was. He saw the ignominy as a small price to pay for the life which had been lovingly given him by one Jewish woman, not only physical life, but also spiritual life. She had been his rescuer his whole life long. He could bear this humiliation and pain for her.

The distance from Tegel to the office on *Prinz-Albrecht-Strasse* where the *Gestapo* had their infamous chambers was not a long drive; Eryk was familiar with the route. They should have arrived. But the truck was showing no signs of slowing; instead, it seemed to be picking up speed. Eryk tried to get more comfortable as he huddled in the cold and waited for his fate.

Sturmbannführer Rolf Beckmann stood in front of the mirror in his office and straightened his collar. He was looking forward to the day's events. Interrogation of *Waffen-SS Hauptsturmführer*. Eryk Wilhelm von Steiner was something he would enjoy. Even now the traitor was on his way from his cell to the SD.

The wheels of the *Reich* justice moved more slowly than he personally would have liked. It was a waste to spend the resources of the German people to keep alive a traitor like Steiner had turned out to be. Beckmann had long suspected that things were not as they should be. If nothing else, Hanne's loyalty to the man was irritating and raised his hackles whenever he thought about it.

The woman was as enigmatic as she was beautiful. In the beginning, his fascination with her had been solely based on her substantial feminine appeal. But as time passed and he observed her with greater focus, Beckmann had developed a growing curiosity about the confident, blond *SS Aufseherinnen*. She looked the ideal of German womanhood and had certainly never given any outward signs that anything was amiss with her, but Beckmann had always had a kind of diabolical sixth sense which honed in on those trying to get by with something. It was a little like the instincts of his German shepherd, Max, who could tell if a prisoner was edging toward an escape even before the man or woman made a move. He had seen the dog in action many times. And like Max, Beckmann was determined to keep his quarry in view. Hanne was lovely, and he would not hesitate to avail himself of all the related benefits, but still he would never forget that she was not above suspicion. In fact, no one was above suspicion when it came to the *Gestapo*. This was why so many presumed heroes in the *Reich* now sat in Tegel Prison and some, like Steiner, were even now entering the next and final phase of retribution.

Rolf Beckmann did not consider himself a sadist in principle; he defined his passion as extreme loyalty to *Führer* and *Fatherland*. So, he was determined to use every means at his disposal to extract the information from Captain Eryk Steiner. He had been digging in the files at the SD Headquarters and was becoming more suspicious.

The man had an impeccable record as a student at Bad Tolz and as an officer, but Beckmann had noticed some interesting details in his personal life. His family had employed a Jewish *Hauslehrerin* and tutor for Steiner and his two sisters. Though the woman had been dismissed in 1938, she had remained in Berlin and been a member of the elite *Berlin Philharmonic*. He had already investigated cases connected with that group. The principal conductor, Wilhelm Furtwangler, had an infuriating fondness for Jewish musicians. It was rumored that he helped shield them from deportation and had even helped a few escape to neutral countries. They had not yet been able to prove anything on the man who was considered by many in Berlin to be a national treasure, but the *Gestapo* never closed its eyes. They would get the details eventually. And when they did, the connection of Steiner's childhood governess with Furtwangler's orchestra was just too inviting a mystery to leave alone.

Beyond that, Steiner had a few untraceable leaves in his file record. It was not uncommon for an officer to be purposefully vague when going on leave; after all, no man really wanted his superior to know all his proclivities for leisure. But there was something about the absences that triggered the alarm in Beckmann's brain. The fact that Hanne had been absolutely uninterested in discussing Steiner's work habits had further intrigued him.

Also, a little detail about Steiner's mother had produced a nugget that might be very useful. By sifting through the meticulous records of the *Reich*, Beckmann had discovered that Mrs. Helga Steiner had suffered from a mental disorder and had been institutionalized a few years before, eventually becoming one of the participants in the *Reich's* T-4 program. This highly incriminating fact about Steiner's family genetics might even extend the investigation to other members of the family. Beckmann was most anxious to detain and interrogate anyone who could give information. He felt sure that Steiner had had help in the operation which put him at the labor camp with a prisoner in his trunk. He was going to track down the source of that aid, and crush whoever and whatever he found.

Steiner was being transported today. Beckmann had the rest of the afternoon to nose deeper into the files and decide on his tactic. The interrogation of the prisoner would begin tomorrow. He could hardly wait.

77

Germany
outskirts of Berlin

> *Never tell people how to do things.*
> *Tell them what to do, and they will surprise you with their ingenuity.*
> General George S. Patton, 1947

Eryk could not tell where he was but it didn't seem like the city any longer. The roads were uneven and every now and then, the truck jerked as the wheels bumped into a hole. His nose, which had become accustomed to the dank, putrid odors of the prison, detected a scent of fresher air once in a while, though the exhaust fumes were still quite strong. His leg was throbbing from the long walk to the truck and from being dumped over the side into it. He could do nothing about it though. His tied hands kept him from rubbing his leg or from wiping his nose which was still congested from the dampness of his cell and also, no doubt, from the multitudes of germs which continually lay in wait on the straw mattress.

The truck swerved suddenly to the left, throwing Eryk against the splintered wood of the wall. His head bumped painfully, and he grunted. The truck stopped, still idling. He heard the cab door open, and then a creaking of hinges. Then the cab door slammed and the truck inched forward. What little light filtered in through the canvas on the back was suddenly gone, and he heard the same creaking again and the sound of a bolt being latched. Then the truck motor stopped, and there was silence.

Eryk was confused. Was this the *Gestapo* headquarters at *Prinz-Albrecht-Strasse*? Wherever he was, he had little chance of getting away. The bolt had sounded massive.

"*Raus!*" The guards rose from the benches on the sides of the lorry and picked him up under the armpits, one on each side. The canvas was raised from the outside, and other hands reached to grab him.

They deposited him onto a wooden floor littered with straw but did not let go of him. His eyes, now adjusting to the darkness, scanned the room and noted that he was in a barn. There were no animals, but lots of straw and a small group of people. One of them stepped forward.

"Good morning, *Hauptsturmführer*. Steiner."

Eryk thought that surely he was hallucinating. Maybe his fever had returned. It was Hanne's voice!

Somehow he found his own, though it was barely more than a croak. "What is this, *Fraulein*? Are you a prisoner also?" Eryk looked at the men standing behind her, dressed in civilian clothing.

"I cannot answer all your questions, *Hauptsturmführer*. It would be best for you not to know all the details. These people are my friends, and now yours also. We are transporting you to another destination than the one planned."

His mind whirling, Eryk tried to follow her meaning. He had not been in *Gestapo* hands after all. He still had a chance for life.

One of the "guards" stepped over to him and produced a ring of keys. He indicated that Eryk should raise his wrists toward the light.

The man tried a couple different keys before he found one that fit. The tiny "click" as the cuffs opened was a glorious sound.

Eryk rubbed his wrists where the skin had begun to chafe and wriggled his fingers a bit to get the circulation going. He knew he was disheveled and dirty and his leg was still very sore, but it was amazing how just having his hands free and being in the open made him feel so much better.

Then the world started to spin around him as a small figure from the group stepped forward and came into the dim light where he stood. Dressed in rough peasant clothes, her hair pulled back under a cap, her eyes huge as she peered up at him, was Nadya.

She brought her hand to her mouth as she looked at the crooked figure that spoke with Eryk's voice. How could this be the robust man who had protected her from so much in the last few weeks? He was thin, his face pale and gaunt, and he leaned on others to support him when he walked, favoring a leg that was obviously injured. Nadya wanted to weep as she looked at the man who had been her childhood friend and then her rescuer, but she refused to give in. She would be strong for him; he had been for her.

She stepped into the small circle of light, and as his eyes turned toward her, she saw him stagger against the guards. His gaze widened in disbelief. She took the last couple steps toward him and put her hand on his dirty sleeve. "It's me. Really."

Tears formed in his eyes. "How?"

"Later." It was Hanne. Crisp. In charge. "We have no time for long stories. Both of you are getting out of here." She turned to the men behind her. "Get them into the vehicle."

The men came forward then and helped Eryk hobble forward toward the other truck he had seen. It was nondescript and not a military design. Eryk looked back over his shoulder at the "guards" and saw that they had taken off their caps and were clearing out the back of the lorry in which he had ridden. They had accomplished an amazing feat in his estimation. He wanted to know how they had done it. But even in his foggy state, he realized that the organization that had gotten him out of the heart of the *Reich* was vast and well-connected, and that it existed in a dangerous setting. He would not risk compromising the safety of his angels by poking his nose into the details of their business.

Nadya hopped into the back of the truck and started pawing at the piles of straw. Clearly she had been briefed on what came next. Eryk climbed slowly up onto the bed of the truck, gripping the wooden side and pulling his leg up behind him. Hanne motioned to the indention in the straw. He scooted himself into it. Then he grabbed his former assistant's arm and forced her to look into his eyes. "I won't ask you to tell me everything. I'm going to trust that you and your people know what you're doing. But what about you? Are you coming with us?"

She stared back at him as though trying to send him a coded message. "I'm staying in Berlin."

"What? Are you out of your mind, *Fraulein*? Do you know what the *Gestapo* is capable of? They will come after you once they find out I'm gone, you and anyone else who was close to me. You must not stay."

"They will not interrogate me, *Captain*. At least not now."

"Why?"

She didn't meet his gaze.

"Wait!" He lowered his voice. "Beckmann? Is that why?

Have you. . .No! That's too high a price. . . . "

She cut him off with a hard look. "Don't, *Captain*. You don't even know the full story. You don't realize my mission. I am doing what I must, not only for you, but for my country." She leaned down. "Please. Take this chance. Get this girl to safety and live with honor. Let me succeed in this part of my assignment."

"What do you mean?"

"Sir, you have valuable information about armaments. I have taken the liberty of assuring the Allies that you will assist them by sharing this. You can help end this war, *Hauptsturmführer* Steiner."

For a second, Eryk was stunned. She had committed him to treason. His training rose up before him. The *SS* motto beckoned to him. . . he shook it off. " *Fraulein* Lager . . . Hanne, I will not forget this. Thank you."

She smiled then, that stubborn streak showing. "I'm sure you won't, *Captain*. Especially when you're dining on London's finest. You'll be sure to remember." Then, she leaned close again and whispered. "Above all things, never let your blood group tattoo be seen, *Captain*. The *Waffen-SS* have a very bad name with the Allies. Though you are defecting and your safety has been assured, you must never let this be known."

"Yes. Very well. And *Fraulein*. . . *danke schoen*. God go with you."

She looked at him with a tinge of surprise, then smiled softly and gave a little salute. As she rose to leave, she put her hand next to his right one and opening his fingers, placed something in it, a cold object with sharp edges. She pressed a hand to Nadya's cheek, whispered something to her and then said to both of them. "Cup your hands over your face to create a breathing space, so the straw won't smother you."

Then she smiled and jumped off the truck. The men immediately began throwing straw over them. Holding tightly to the object she had given him, Eryk raised his hands to shelter his face and make a small niche to breathe. In a few moments, he couldn't see anything. He began to feel the emotional panic of being covered with the weight of the scratchy straw that was their sanctuary. He forced himself to breathe slowly, to focus on the muffled voices, the sound of the engine, anything but the fear of being smothered. He wondered desperately how Nadya was doing. She hated tight places.

He barely heard Hanne's voice give the soft command. "Go!" The engine revved, and the truck roared to life. He heard the creaking doors again, and then they bumped out into the open and hostile countryside.

He fingered the object in his hand in the dark and discovered the familiar points of a star. The Star of David.

78

Berlin, Germany
Gestapo Headquarters
Prinz-Albrecht-Straße

> *It was close; but that's the way it is in war.*
> *You win or lose, live or die – and the difference is just an eyelash.*
> General Douglas MacArthur, March 17, 1942
> (to General Richard Sutherland after their flight over Japanese held territory to reach Australia)

Sturmbannführer Beckmann was in a rage, and when he was, everyone knew it. He didn't scream or throw things. But his manner was completely taken over by a sinister spirit that emanated from him like an evil mist. It settled over the *Gestapo* office where he was lord and master, and the typists and assistants tiptoed past his door, their eyes darting to and fro, making sure to stay out of his way.

Behind his desk now, Beckmann snarled at the men in front of him. "How did this happen? Explain it. Now!"

"We do not know, *Herr Sturmbannführer*! But the truck with the prisoner left the prison and has been lost."

"Lost? Do you know what this means? He has been rescued, somehow, by the resistance. You should have checked the paperwork more thoroughly."

"But, *Herr Sturmbannführer,* all of the identification was in order! The seal was there, the proper signatures, all of it. . . ."

"Silence! I'm not interested in your excuses. Obviously, you overlooked something. And the *Gestapo* overlooks nothing! Nothing." His fist slammed onto the desk in front of him. "Not one detail is too small for inspection! Do you understand this?" His words were clipped, his tone gritty.

"Yes, *Herr Sturmbannführer.*"

"I don't think you do. Let me be very clear. I will have your heads for this. You will bear personal responsibility for this disastrous dereliction of duty, for the escape of this most important prisoner. Someone must pay," Beckmann smiled at them, "and you are the ones."

He pressed the button on his phone. "*Fraulein,* send in the guard. I have some detainees."

Eryk felt dizzy. He hadn't been eating well on prison rations anyway and with the unaccustomed activity of the last few hours and the depleted physical condition he was in because of his wound, he was quickly losing what little strength he had. He knew the escape they were attempting was extraordinarily dangerous. If they were discovered, certain death awaited them all. But first would come excruciating torture since the *Gestapo* would be eager to find out all they could about the resistance network that was operating so efficiently. He willed himself not to focus on all the risks being taken for his sake and for Nadya.

Nadya. She was here. Beside him, somewhere huddled in this straw. They were together again. His foggy brain could barely take it in. How in the world had Hanne put all the pieces together? It bordered on the impossible.

Then the words of Bonhoeffer came floating back to him. *Of course, my friend. I will pray. God knows where they are.* Was it possible that this God with whom he was just becoming acquainted would care that much for a Jewish woman in a mountain cabin? Would He go to such lengths to rescue one person?

Like a phonograph playing in his memory, he remembered other words, spoken by another person who had believed in God. *Our Father cares about His lambs, Eryk, each one of them. He knows your name, Liebchen, and where you are right now. He never loses sight of you, no matter where you are.*

Zelda had believed in a personal God, One who loved the individual. It was what had made her so different from the atmosphere of the nation in which he had come to manhood. Where people were human capital for the *Reich,* she maintained each person had great worth. Where children were commodities for the future of the Fatherland, she valued the gifts and dignity of each boy and girl. Where men were fodder for the war, she pitied every man in uniform. This God, her God, Bonhoeffer's God, must then have time and resources even to care about one person.

What did this mean for the larger group? Why didn't He rescue them *en masse?* Eryk didn't have the answer to that, but he was intrigued with the idea that there must surely be a Divine element to the events of the last several hours. For now, that was enough to make him hope that things in his life would turn out differently than they had begun.

He knew that now was not the time to talk to the woman lying just inches from him. They had to maintain silence; the fields and roads and villages had ears. But he needed to touch her, to reassure himself that she was real, to reassure her that he wasn't going to leave her again. Moving slowly, he squirmed his fingers through the layers of straw toward her. He felt fabric and then the skin of her arm and sensed her quiver at the unexpected touch. He trailed his fingers down to her hand and took it gently into his. He couldn't see her face, couldn't use his voice, but he tenderly squeezed her hand and felt her fingers relax into his. They were still in the very eye of darkness, but in his heart, there was light and warmth. Then he surrendered to the overwhelming fatigue and wooziness, and closed his eyes.

Nadya was terrified. The truck, the straw, the fear of the journey reminded her too much of past trips in the back of similar vehicles. It brought back memories of spectacles she had witnessed as she cowered in the ghetto. Grandmothers, clutching parcels of food and lacy shawls, were shoved onto greasy lorries; little children, in layers of clothing were handed up like so much baggage; and honest, laboring men were kicked and taunted as they tried to shield their families from the brutality. And always, the trucks opened up to swallow them all. Their faces clustered in her mind, haunted eyes peering down from the lorries, staring at a world that didn't want them and maybe never had.

Trucks were the servants of horror.

And the straw. Always prickly, smelly straw. It carpeted the floors of cattle cars, soaking up the body fluids and tears of the people crammed inside on their way to "resettlement." It lined the stained boards of the beds in the camps. It was the one luxury afforded to Jews. It was a constant reminder of the shame, the filth, of their lives.

Nadya closed her eyes against the tears which pushed at her eyelids. She would not be this close to freedom and give in to hysteria. What was a little more straw, another ride in the back of a truck? She must do this. Do it for *Tante* Zelda, for her parents, for her little students back in Terezin, for her people. God help her, she must!

When she first felt his hand fumbling for hers, she flinched, her mind not focusing on the fact that the man she had begun to love was in this predicament with her. Then, with a rush of relief, she felt his fingers close tightly around hers. It was Eryk. With her, in another dark and scary place. And though she knew that he had worn the uniform of the enemy, the little girl in her mind reached out to the little boy she remembered.. She began to wonder if, after all, he was a hero, a knight, wounded but unconquered in his strength of purpose. She was safe, as safe as possible for right now, and it made her smile just a little bit.

79

Berlin, Germany

> *Never give in – never, never, never, never, in nothing great or small, large or petty, never give in except to convictions of honour and good sense. Never yield to force; never yield to the apparently overwhelming might of the enemy.*
> Winston Churchill, October 19, 1941,
> speech given at Harrow School, Harrow, England

Hanne slipped into her silent apartment, going by feel to find her way into her bedroom. There had been no one waiting for her. Perhaps she had evaded the bloodhound once more. Maybe, incredibly, she would get by with this stunt.

Unexplainably, she felt bereft. She should feel elated that her part of the operation was done. Captain Steiner and the woman he had done so much to rescue were no longer her responsibility. They were in capable hands. The resistance was well equipped to carry out the rescue. All that could be done would be done. Why did she mind that she was here? She still had a mission to carry out. Only as she could continue to dupe the *Gestapo* would those on the run have a chance to survive. She had to play her bluff convincingly; many lives depended on her skills.

She wasn't sure she was up to it. Her normally indefatigable spirit felt wasted, drained. Tonight, she was missing warm lamplight and English tea, her mother's embrace and her father's voice. It had been so long. So long since she had truly been safe. It was surprising that she even missed that. Her adventurous nature had surely taken a terrible hit for her to feel so close to despondency.

But there was nothing she could do except carry on. *Keep calm and carry on.* The empire depended on her. The old man depended on her. Steiner and Nadya depended on her. The resistance network depended on her. Was there no end to the list of people who depended on her?

Who would help *her*? From what direction would she get support? She was deep behind enemy lines, on her own. All ties were severed now. She would not be contacting her people again. It was too dangerous. Until the end, hers or the war, whichever came first, she was completely separated from assistance. It had been her choice. Now there would be no help. She could look to no one.

Hanne Lager laid down on her bed and pulled a blanket up to her chin, wishing for the first time in a long time that she could be Emma Brighton once more. How good it would feel to run through the meadows of home, stop to smell a primrose, and then stand gazing at the blowing grasses on the distant hills.

I will lift up mine eyes unto the hills, from whence cometh my help. My help cometh from the Lord, which made heaven and earth.

The words formed in her mind, rising up from the years of sitting in the little chapel, listening to her father's sermons in the small country vicarage. They settled over her like a covering. Hanne repeated them over and over to herself, daring to hope they were true and knowing that, if she had a chance at all, it would come from the Lord, the Maker of heaven and earth and the Master over every tribe and nation, even Germany.

―――

Border between Germany and France

Eryk was awakened by bright lights. He could see them through the straw. The truck was stopped, its motor idling; there were voices.

"Papers, *bitte*. Why are you crossing the border?"

He tried to orient himself. A border crossing? The voice sounded German, but that wasn't unusual since Germany occupied the countries surrounding the mainland. He had no way of knowing in which direction they had been traveling. But a border, any border, was a possible disaster.

He wondered if Nadya was awake. He had no way to tell, no way to comfort her other than his hand holding hers. He held his breath and tried to listen to the muffled conversation. The driver must be handing over the paperwork. "I'm a farmer, visiting my brother to help him with some sick cows. I have brought extra straw for them."

Eryk heard the rustle of papers and could imagine the guard examining them closely and then peering intently into the cab of the truck, looking for anything out of place, any clue that something was amiss.

He must have been satisfied with his inspection of the cab and driver, but then Eryk heard him give the command to someone else he assumed must be standing by.

"*Achtung*! Search the back."

Eryk mentally groaned. They had little to no chance of evading a search of the straw. He gripped Nadya's hand and tried to think of what he would say, how he would respond when they were discovered.

He waited, afraid even to breathe, waiting for the uncovering of their hiding place or worse, the jab of a pitch fork through the straw. But it never came. Instead, the engine revved again, and the truck lurched forward.

He felt faint from relief. Was it possible that the prayers of Zelda and Bonhoeffer were shielding them even now?

They traveled on and on. He was sure it must be getting close to midnight. It was hard to keep track of time since they had been traveling for so long. What country were they now in? Where were these associates of his Nazi assistant taking them?

As the truck rocked and banged along the roads, Eryk dozed fitfully, his body screaming to change positions and his leg aching badly. His hand was still touching Nadya's, though he was uncertain how she was doing. Had the journey been too much for her? Maybe she had fainted. Would she cry out when she woke up and found herself buried in straw?

He didn't know how long it really was, but after what seemed several more hours, he sensed the truck slowing down, and then after a sharp turn and a few more feet, it stopped and the motor was silent.

He knew the situation was precarious. Wherever they were, the transfer from one hiding place to another was the riskiest point. He didn't have long to wonder about it. Hands reached into his burrow and tapped him on the leg in a kind of hurried code. Then a whisper "Slide out."

Eryk gave Nadya's hand a hard squeeze and started scooting down toward the end of the truck bed. Beside him, he felt her doing the same. It took just a couple movements until his feet were dangling in the open air. He felt hands guiding his legs to the ground and then helping to brush away some of the straw from his face and upper body. At last, he was standing, wobbly and weak, on firm ground. It was dark. They were behind some sort of building, in a lean-to. Nadya slid down next to him, and he grabbed her arm.

The figure who had helped him gave directions. In German. "Get down. Wait for my signal. We are walking to that door over there." The man pointed ever so slightly to his left. Eryk nodded. He and Nadya crouched in the shadows of the truck.

The man looked around, turning to assess every angle and then whispered "Now." And Eryk hobbled as quickly as he could, clutching Nadya's hand and half-leaning on her, half-supporting her. As they approached, the door swung open quickly and they went in. It was dark in the building, but Eryk could smell the tantalizing aroma of baked bread and surmised it was a kitchen. They were in a house.

There were no words from their guide. He motioned for them to follow a woman who stood in the faint glow of a single candle. Eryk nodded again, and pushed Nadya ahead of him. "*Fraulein, bitte.*" He whispered it as softly as he could.

The woman looked back at him with concern. "*Nein Frau?*"

"*Nein, ist Fraulein.*"

His new hostess shrugged, looked from Nadya to him, led them to a doorway and then started to descend the stairs. With no other choice, they followed. At the bottom, she walked to a closet door, opened it and pulled back a shelf to reveal another set of stairs. She pointed down, looking at them.

Nadya looked at him with wild comprehension in her eyes. A cellar. A hole in the ground. He shook his head at her and gripped her hand. They would do this together. He stepped forward with his good leg and started down, almost pulling Nadya down with him. The woman stooped to hand the candle to him and then waited until they reached the dirt floor at the bottom before lowering the door behind them. He heard the thump of the shelf being slid into place.

The place smelled of earth and vegetables and wood. He held the candle up to view their hiding place. Over in the corner was a pile of blankets; on a table there was a loaf of bread, some jam and a jug.

He put the candle down on the table and turned to Nadya who was shaking with silent sobs.

"It's going to be alright, *Liebchen*. We've made it so far already. Look at us! We are alive and together! You must tell me how this came to be." He pulled her into his arms and rubbed her back, soothing her as one would a hurting child. "You cannot know how I grieved for you; how I thought I would never see you again! It's amazing that you are actually here with me!"

He lifted her chin to look into her eyes, dark and soft as velvet, glistening with tears. "God spared you. I know He did." He brushed her lips with his mouth. "There. I promise not to kiss you until I can shave off these bristles and clean up a bit. I need to make an appointment for a manicure tomorrow too."

She giggled at this, and slapped playfully at his hand. "How do you know that I don't prefer bushy men?"

"Do you?" He captured her hands and held them to his cheeks. "Do you really prefer this prickle, Nadya?"

She sighed. "No, but I won't complain if you never shave again so long as we can get out of this."

"We will. I know it. God hasn't brought us this far to let us be captured now."

"Now you sound like *Tante*."

"I hope so. I am finally learning her secret to life."

"Then you have changed."

"Yes, in many ways. I want to tell you about it soon. For now, you'd better make a pallet for yourself and get some rest. I have a feeling we have some trying times still to come."

"But what about your leg? You need rest too."

"I'll make a place over here by the stairs." He winked at her. "Nothing will get you that way."

She tossed her head, showing her chutzpah, daring him, like in the old days. "You just do that, *Captain*."

But, in the end, she was the one who folded and arranged the blankets for him and then helped him lower himself onto it. "I'm so worried about your wound, Eryk. You need a doctor."

He put a finger to her lips. "Hush. Tomorrow, we'll talk of that. Now, go over there and get to sleep before this candle goes out."

80

Bedfordshire, England
Headquarters, Squadron 161

> *We shall not fail or falter; we shall not weaken or tire. Neither the sudden shock of battle, nor the long-drawn trials of vigilance and exertion will wear us down. Give us the tools and we will finish the job.*
> Winston Churchill, BBC Radio Broadcast, February 9, 1941

Flight Sergeant "Picky" Picard saluted his squadron leader and stood at attention.

"At ease, Pickard."

"Yes, sir."

"I have an assignment for you, Picky. We need to extract two people from France. It's a delicate job. You'll go on the first moonless night we have."

"Yes sir. I understand, sir."

"You've done good work since joining, Pickard. I'm glad to have you aboard."

"Thank you, sir."

The leader leaned back and skewered him with his gaze. "Be careful. I don't want to lose you."

Pickard clicked his heels "Yes, sir. You can depend on that, sir."

The commanding officer waved his hand toward the door. "That's all. Keep an ear to the ground for your orders."

"Thank you, sir. Good day, sir." Pickard pivoted, left the office and walked to the airfield. He'd better inspect his favorite girl carefully. She had a date very soon. A mission over France.

It all made perfect sense.

And it was perfectly insane.

The plan that had been laid out for them was daring and a bit foolish, but they had no other choice. Eryk was discovering that these people, these resistance folks, stared death in the face on a regular basis and chose to whistle about it, rather than dwell on it. Even now, as he followed the young son of the family to the washroom for a chance to clean up, he wondered at the bravado that seemed to anchor this entire household. Did they not understand what could happen to them if a suspicious neighbor gave their name to the *Gestapo*? Were they unaware that they would all die brutal, lingering deaths if their traitorous activities were discovered?

He shook his head in disbelief. The loyalty of this French family was remarkable. No wonder the Nazis had not yet been able to crush the underground! The movement was run by dedicated and well-prepared people, a network that ran efficiently. They had even produced a doctor who had cleaned his wound, redressed it and declared that it was slowly healing.

The boy stopped in front of the bathroom door and pointed. "Mama says that if you will please hand out your clothing, she will wash it for you. There is fresh clothing on the hook behind the door, *Monsieur*."

Eryk smiled and nodded. "*Merci.*" His French was limited, but he knew a few words.

He went inside, shut the door and quickly removed his clothing. Then, opening the door again, he handed out the soiled laundry to the boy waiting for it. In a hurry to be quick in his washing and unaccustomed to a clandestine life, Eryk didn't think about which arm was uncovered as he reached out the washroom door. It was only when he heard a sudden intake of breath that he realized his upper left arm was exposed, the one containing his blood group tattoo on the inside of his bicep.

Quickly, he pulled his arm back inside and mentally berated himself for his carelessness. He hurriedly washed and shaved and put on the fresh clothes. The pants were a little short and the socks were thin, but they were clean and no change of clothing had ever felt better.

He stepped out and limped down the stairs to the main floor, stopping in his tracks by the kitchen where he heard voices.

"He is *SS*, Mama. I saw his mark."

"Toulouse, are you sure?"

"Yes, mama, I am certain. Perhaps he is a spy, sent here to find out how we help people."

"I don't think so, son. He does not seem like a deceitful man to me."

"But mama, remember how the *SS* killed Aunt Celeste and Uncle Henri. They cannot be trusted. We must tell Jacque."

"No!" The woman's voice was firm. "We will deal with this ourselves. Go and help your Papa in the garden. I will talk to him."

Eryk knew he had to face this. He wondered if the woman would believe him. Clearing his throat, he stepped out when he could be seen. She looked at him, no fear, just determination. The boy darted from the table and out the door.

"Good morning, *Monsieur*. Did you enjoy your wash?"

"I did, *merci*."

"And the young woman with you, your sister, cousin?"

"She is my fiancée."

The woman smiled. "Ah, then you must both be ready to go home since your assignment here is done."

"Yes, we are. Most anxious to go home."

"And you speak German so well. Surely you must be important to the government."

"I hope I will be, *Madame*. We will see when we get there."

The woman stopped kneading the bread and brushed the flour from her hands in an emphatic gesture. "Come, *Monsieur*. We must stop fooling each other, no? You are German, not English. What is your business? Why are you being flown to England by the resistance?"

"Your son was right, *Madame*. I am *SS*."

She stopped all movement, her eyes narrowing. "So, now you arrest us?"

"No. I am former *SS*. I have with me my fiancée, a Jew. I am helping her escape. And I have promised information to the Allies."

"That, *Monsieur*, sounds impossible to me. A convenient story. Forgive me for not believing you." Her voice was icily skeptical.

"I don't blame you, *Madame*. Call the lady. She can tell you the truth."

"Very well, I will do that. Right now." The woman plopped the mass of dough into a bowl, wiped her hands and motioned to Eryk. "Let's see what she has to say."

Nadya leaned her head against Eryk's shoulder and finally started to breathe normally. When the woman of the house had burst down the stairs, demanding information about Eryk, she had thought the whole game was over. But her words which corroborated his story seemed to satisfy the woman. She returned to her kitchen, and left them again in the damp cellar.

With his good arm, Eryk pulled her against his shoulder. "Someday, *Liebchen*, we will write a book for our grandchildren about this journey and this place."

"About this cellar?"

"Why not? We can tell them that in the middle of the cabbages and onions, I asked you to marry me." He tightened his grip. "That will make for a great telling by the fireside, don't you think?"

"But I haven't given you an answer."

He took her other hand in his. "Well, don't keep me waiting. You know I'm an impatient man."

"Well, I think I had better do it, since *Tante* would never forgive you for kissing me if I don't."

He smiled, and there, beside pungent piles of root vegetables, Eryk kissed her very thoroughly. The whiskers were finally gone.

81

Somewhere in France

My times are in thy hand: deliver me from the hand of mine enemies . . .
Psalm 31:15

They crouched in the bushes, waiting. The field was in the countryside, several miles from town, and far from the closest battery of anti aircraft guns.

As Eryk sat on the ground beside Nadya, he listened intently for the sound of a plane. They were mere hours away from freedom. He couldn't believe how much he wanted that. He was surprised at how eager he was to leave his homeland.

Things would never be the same for him. He knew that. The safety being granted him by the Allies would surely involve secrecy about his past. He would need to forget his life here and learn to distance himself from anything military. Most likely, he would never again see his sisters or have any contact with his biological family. His life as a German was coming to an end.

True, in the exchange, he would get Nadya and a new chance at happiness. He looked over at her, trying to see the outline of her face on this moonless night. He could still scarcely believe that she was still alive. Against all the odds, in spite of every decree of the *Reich*, despite the death warrant for all Jews, Nadya was alive and well, and he was going to do everything in his power to complete this mission for her freedom.

In the last few days while they waited for the plans to come together, he had finally pieced together the story of her miraculous journey from the cabin in the mountains to the barn in the country outside Berlin. His assistant, Hanne, had been much more apprised of his activities than he had even guessed, and extremely well-connected, it turned out. He had to give her a mental salute for figuring out where Nadya was and putting together a team to get her out and whisk her away to the barn of a resistance member. He wondered how Hanne was doing, how she was warding off the questions and clue-hunting of the *Gestapo*. Beckmann was the worst kind of ferret, and he was no doubt gleefully pawing through every bit of paperwork and every report he could get into his possession.

Eryk feared for Hanne's life. She was playing a dangerous game. But he owed her so very much that he was having a tough time feeling any emotion other than deep gratitude. Someday, maybe he would get the chance to repay her. If she lived that long. If the Allies won. If he could find her when all this was over.

And it *would* all be over in the future. The military instinct he had inherited from his father and his own observation of what was going on told him so; Germany could not last much longer. Her reckless thirst for war, her cavalier use of her people, and her frenzied focus on death were weakening her, reducing her to a wretched nation of deceived and depraved folk. The men and women in the prime of life had already been crushed to powder by the gristmill of war; the young were now being thrown to the wolves, and the old were tottering off the scene, shamed and beaten. God would bring retribution.

If he remembered any of Zelda's teaching, it was that God was just. Surely He would call Germany to account for her terrible deeds, especially toward His chosen people.

But, since he had made his peace with Zelda's God, he no longer feared this judgment. He had a new confidence in the promise that life, the life the Almighty gives, could not be extinguished without His permission. Eryk was certain that He was working mightily to do something astounding for the Jewish people, just like the stories Zelda used to tell him of Jehovah's wonders in Egypt on behalf of the Hebrews. Life would win. No decree or camp or oven could change that fact. They would rise from the ruins of Nazism to the glory of the One who called them. To all who looked to Him as Savior, that life would never come to an end. He could now believe with all his heart that this had been so for Zelda.

In the distance, he detected a faint hum. The plane was coming. The men with them hurried to the field to light the signal fires. Eryk watched them, these men who daily danced on the border of life and death. They were heroic, and they would stay behind when he and Nadya found their wings. That was a kind of bravery that even a *Waffen-SS* officer had to respect.

The sound of the engine got closer. One of the men produced a flashlight and began to give the code for safe landing. The sky was dark and Eryk couldn't see much, but he could hear the engine getting louder and louder.

One of the men ran over to them. "On your feet. Hurry. You must be ready to board."

Eryk's leg was still weak, but he could stand on it much easier since he had been having better food and rest. He stood and pulled Nadya up beside him. "Ready?" He smiled despite the tense moment.

"Yes." In the faint flicker of the signal fires, he saw her head turn toward him. A lifetime of promise was in that word, a future of other places and other journeys and other joys.

The plane glided to a stop, motor idling. Their guide pushed them out into the open and together, Eryk and Nadya ran to the waiting *Westland Lysander*, their chariot to the heavens. Eryk tried to shield Nadya as they covered the distance that seemed far longer than it actually was. Away from the negligible shelter of the trees, they were in the unobstructed vision of anyone with a trigger. He prayed as they ran. Surely God, who had brought them to this moment, would see that they made it the rest of the way. Had not Zelda once told him that Christ was both the Author and Finisher?

Finally, they darted under the wing and reached the cold metal of the aircraft. Since they had to mount the side of the plane into the cockpit, there was a fixed ladder on the left side. The rush of wind from the front propeller added to the noise of the moment and pulled at the few strands of hair that escaped the cap Nadya wore. Normally, these aircraft carried only one passenger, but they had been told that this one could carry two, although it would be very cramped.

He helped Nadya get her foot on the first rung, then pushed her gently to speed her along. He was already starting up before she jumped over the side into the small space of the rear cockpit. Hoisting his bad leg up behind him, he pulled himself over the edge and dropped down beside her, tugging at the canopy as the pilot started taxiing over the uneven ground. The world dipped and swayed as he tried to fold his legs against the skin of the plane to give Nadya as much room as possible. In a few seconds, the aircraft leveled off and picked up speed.

Eryk looked out through the bubble canopy at the fading glow of fires on a deserted field in occupied France. He was leaving the reach of the *Reich*, alive, forgiven, loved.

He touched the pocket of his jacket where a pointed object reminded him that this was all very real. *We did it, Lehrerin. She's free. And I am too . . . because of you. Thank you.*

Then he put his arm around Nadya as the ground receded and the sky opened up to them. Life was ahead. There was so much more to come.

Endnotes

1. "Books Burn as Goebbels Speaks." *United States Holocaust Memorial Museum.* https://encyclopedia.ushmm.org/content/en/film/books-burn-as-goebbels-speaks. (accessed March 25, 2024), 36.

2. "Loyalty oath of Nazi SS troops, Feldherrnhalle, Munich, 1938." *Steam Community.* https://en.wikipedia.org/wiki/Hitler_Oath. (accessed March 25, 2024), 67.

3. "Nazi Songs." Academic Kids. https://en.wikipedia.org/wiki/Nazi_songs. (accessed March 25, 2024), 73.

4. Bytwerk, Randall. "Ceremonies for the War Dead of the NSDAP." Posted 2000. *German Propaganda Archive* https://research.calvin.edu/german-propaganda-archive/nstod1.htm. Accessed March 26, 2024, 152.

Author's Note

There is no official record of an SOE operative being embedded deep in Germany during World War II, but with the great volume of evidence recounting the risks and accomplishments of these brave men and women, it is not unlikely that such a feat was considered and even attempted. We may never know all the secret heroics of those who worked in the shadows to bring that terrible war to an end.

I have taken license in creating a labor camp near the tank factory in Kassel, Germany. It is a fact that nearly all munitions plants in the Reich used slave labor and photos of workers in striped uniforms at the Henschel and Son Werks *are on file*. There is also a verified network of thousands of camps and subcamps which operated in Germany proper in addition to the infamous extermination camps in Poland.

It is also important that the reader understand the dreadful menu of violence open to the perpetrators of the Holocaust. Almost no act of cruelty was beyond the imagination of those who blamed God's Chosen for the ills of civilization and thus wreaked their vengeance upon them without restraint.

Yet, it is also an established fact that there were many Berlin Jews who converted to Christianity before and during the Holocaust. Some of these conversions were, no doubt, initiated by the need to escape persecution. But, some were most certainly a genuine commitment to faith in Christ. German Jews thought they would be given consideration, especially those who were not full Jews. In fact, Jews who had lived in Berlin for years usually believed they were true "Berliners" and could not imagine that they would be targeted for deportation.

Glossary

Achtung – attention

Angst – fear

Arbeitslager – labor camp

Aufseherinnen – female overseer or attendant; women guards in the Nazi SS

auf verdersain – farewell; see you again

Bergenstrasse – a main street in Berlin in 1938

Bundt Deutscher Madel – the League of German Girls;

der Führer – the leader; Adolf Hitler's self-proclaimed title

dummkopf – fool; idiot

Einsatzgruppen – Schutzstaffel (SS) paramilitary mobile killing units

Frau – Mrs,; married woman

Fraulein – Miss; unmarried woman

Hakenkreuz – German for "hooked cross," the swastika – ancient symbol of good luck and associated with racial purity under the Nazi regime

Hauptmann - German equivalent of Captain

Hauptsturmführer – mid-level rank commander; SS equivalent to captain

Hauslehrerin – nanny

Hitler Jugend – Hitler Youth (for boys 14-18)

Hitler Jungvolk – Hitler Young Folk (for boys 10-14)

Jah; yah – yes

Juden – Jews

Judenrat – German word meaning "Jewish Council"; a term for the administrative agency within the ghettos, a puppet force actually controlled by the Nazis

Kapo – fellow prisoner who was an overseer in a Nazi camp

Lager – camp

Lebensborn – "Fount of Life;" an *SS* organization to increase the Aryan birth rate

Lebensraum – "living space," ideology purported by Adolf Hitler for additional land for the German people

Lehrerin – female teacher or tutor

Liebchen – a person who is very dear to another

Luftwaffe – Nazi aerial warfare branch during World War II

Mein – my

Mischlinge – a classification of the Nazi regime denoting a person with at least one Jewish grandparent

Nein – no

Obersturmfuhrer – rank equivalent of 1st lieutenant in the Nazi *SS*

Panzer – armor, term often used in German for tank

RAD – *Reichsarbeitsdienst;* Reich Labor Force; official state labor service in the Nazi regime, divided into sections for men and women who often helped in either jobs left open by men serving in the military or in "re-culturing" type jobs in the East for ethnic Germans

Raus – get up (like the English word rouse)

Rassenschande – racial shame or racial defilement, the Nazi term for intimate relations between Aryans and non-Aryans, punishable by law; it was broadly interpreted and included even mild interest

Reich (Third Reich) – German word for realm ro reign; a phrase coined by the author Arthur Moeller van den Bruck to denote two great German empires of the past and a possible third; used by the Nazis in their quest to claim the third thousand-year reign

Reichsfuhrer – special title and rank within the SS

Reichsadler – Imperial Eagle; used by the Ancient Romans and also by the Nazis as an icon of strength

SA – *Sturmabteilung* (German: "Assault Division"), byname Storm Troopers or Brownshirts

Soldat - enlisted man; rank of private

SOE – *Special Operations Executive*; British intelligence agency established in July 1940

SS – abbreviation of *Schutzstaffel* (German: "Protective Echelon") called Blackshirts for their black uniforms

Schnell – hurry; move quickly

Sonderbehandlung – *special treatment*; a Nazi euphemism for execution of individuals or groups and generally as part of genocide

Strudel – a pastry dessert like pie, often made with apples

Sturmbannführer – Nazi paramilitary rank equivalent to major; used in the *SA*, *SS*, and *NSFK*

Tante – aunt

Untermenschen – German word for subhuman

Unteroffizier – Nazi military rank equivalent to sergeant

Untersturmführer: paramilitary rank in the Nazi *SS*; equivalent to leutenant

Vernichtungslager – extermination camp

Waffen-SS – armed SS, elite fighting force of the *Schutzstaffel*

Wehrmacht – unified armed forces in Germany from 1935-1946